THE UMBRELLA MEN

THE UMBRELLA MEN

KEITH CARTER

NEEM TREE
PRESS

This is a work of fiction. Names, characters, businesses, places, events and incidents are either the products of the author's imagination or used in a fictitious manner. Any resemblance to actual persons, living or dead, or actual events is purely coincidental.

Published by Neem Tree Press Limited 2019

Neem Tree Press Limited, 1st Floor,
2 Woodberry Grove, London, N12 0DR, UK
info@neemtreepress.com

Copyright © Keith Carter, 2019

A catalogue record for this book is available from the British Library

ISBN 978-1-911107-05-7 (hardback)
ISBN 978-1-911107-10-1 (paperback)
ISBN 978-1-911107-11-8 (e-book)

Printed and bound in Great Britain
by Clays Ltd, Elcograf S.p.A.

"A banker is a fellow who lends you his umbrella when the sun is shining, but wants it back the minute it begins to rain."

Mark Twain (1835–1910)

"The experiences of many businesses across the country suggests that, at least within RBS, there are circumstances in which the banks are unnecessarily engineering a default to move the business out of local management and into their turnaround divisions, generating revenue through fees, increased margins and devalued assets."

The "Tomlinson Report" – Lawrence Tomlinson,
Entrepreneur in Residence at the Department for Business,
Innovation and Skills, 2013

CONTENTS

LIST OF CHARACTERS

LONDON – RARETERRE

Peter Mount	CEO
James Stead	Finance Director
Olivier Crochet	Director of Exploration and Mining
Carl Betts	Chief Mineralogist
Frits van Steen	Non-executive Chairman
Austin Roach	Senior Non-exec Director
Freddy Lee	Non-exec Director, Geologist

LONDON – PEOPLE

Ivy Mount	Married to Peter
Harry, Emma and Kirsty Mount	Peter and Ivy's children
Odile Callow	Friend of Ivy
Fulki Chopra	Friend of Ivy and Peter
Jerry Chimer	Ditto, married to Fulki
Kiara Molinari	Friend of Peter Mount
Max	Kiara's ex-boyfriend

LONDON – BANKERS

Julian Marian-Smythe	Director, NOMAD Securities
Stacey East	Equity Analyst, Hamlyn Securities
Montagu N. Montagu	Corporate Financier, Hamlyn Securities then Bloom & Beck (B&B)
Edward Bald	Relationship Banker, Royal Bank of Scotland (RBS)
Richard Videur	Director, RBS Corporate Restructuring Unit (CRU)
Sam Slight	RBS Banker, CRU
Fred Judd	RBS Banker, CRU

OREGON – RARETERRE

Rick Stone	Site Manager, Trillium Lake Mine
Friedrich Hegel	Consultant, Mine Geologist
Helen Fry	Senior Partner, Scythia Engineering Solutions

OREGON – PEOPLE

Amy Tate	Ex-employee of B&B, Environmental Campaigner
Hoxie Tomahas	Environmental Campaigner
Professor Palmer	Founder, Trail 26 Conservation Society (T26 CS)
Piet De Keersmaeker	Member of T26 CS, owner of Hungry Possum Diner
Jess	Member of T26 CS, friend of Helen Fry
Jolene	Waitress at Hungry Possum Diner

NEW YORK – BANKERS

Jay Andersen	Managing Director and Head of Principal Investments at B&B
Lori Taylor	Associate, Corporate Finance, B&B
Laurent Tavide	Senior Investment Banker, B&B
Dick Veroof	Founder, Veroof Capital
Dylan Hughes	Director, NOMAD Securities
Betsy	PA to Jay Andersen at B&B

PROLOGUE

LSE, LINCOLN'S INN FIELDS, LONDON, NOVEMBER 2008

"If these things were so large," she asked, gesturing with a gloved hand towards the poster with its colourful graphics showing the speculative causes of hundreds of billions of wayward dollars, "how did everyone miss them?"

Her Majesty the Queen asked the best question. Visiting the London School of Economics to open a new building in late 2008, she turned away from a poster presentation chattily entitled "Managing the Credit Crunch" and innocently put it to the assembled gaggle of economists, top men in their field, deferential despite themselves.

With this the Queen voiced what millions of her subjects, who would have to pay for the mess, had been wondering. The fawning cluster of economists shuffled uncomfortably; prizewinning schoolboys caught unprepared by the teacher. One of them was pushed to the front and offered a mumbled answer involving people relying on other people and thinking at every stage they were doing the right thing. When the Queen responded with a single word, "awful", no one was sure if she was passing judgement on the mumbled answer, the man who gave it, the others who stood around looking sheepishly at their shoes, economists in general, the financial crisis overall, or the bankers who had caused it. She was right, though. It was awful.

CHAPTER 1

"It's like being the ringmaster of a small circus," Peter muttered to himself as he ploughed through his email inbox at 11pm. "A small travelling circus with a single star act. A dancing elephant or something. Petunia the Performing Pachyderm."

Being chief executive officer of a big company, thought Peter Mount, who was CEO of a small one, must be like being the ringmaster of Cirque du Soleil: no animals, a great show with many stars, everyone a consummate professional, performance assured. But here he was, hoping Petunia would perform and distract attention from the toothless lion and the seal that keeps dropping the beach ball. The unfunny clowns. Was the CEO of Rio Tinto, he wondered, copied in on emails about some sort of perverse vandalism, involving bodily fluids, at one of his mines? Did the guy in charge at Newmont Mining have to check the arithmetic in the spreadsheets used by his finance team? Did he personally proofread legal documents, still finding typos in "final" versions? Squabble with advisors over their fees? He did not think so. Rather self-servingly, Peter thought bosses of smaller companies ought to be paid more than those of big ones, who are protected by extended teams of professionals and cosseted by supportive staff and advisors.

Rareterre plc, where Peter was in charge, was a small mining company, not a travelling circus. For Rareterre, the only star act – the dancing elephant – was the rare-earths mine at Trillium Lake near Mount Hood in Oregon, USA. The company was quoted on the London Stock Exchange, the Alternative Investment Market[1] part, one of a legion of small companies that had the nerve to behave like larger ones and, in exchange for exposing their every move to open scrutiny, could raise financing from the public. The shares in the business were therefore tradable daily on the market. One consequence of this public company status was that a good part of Peter's time was spent dealing with the demands of the stock market – supplying shareholder information, compliance with stock exchange rules, corporate governance, a perpetual nagging in an irritating contextual setting of implied mistrust.

Rareterre's business was hunting for and extracting obscure metals in far-flung parts of the world. It was fortunate that its biggest, most promising asset was the mine in benign Oregon. Peter had spent enough of his life in frozen deserts and flea-bitten regions of bewildering political instability and rampant corruption to appreciate a location where the greatest risks were black flies and boredom. "We have some of the most valuable empty holes in the ground in the world!" Frits van Steen, the Dutch-born chairman of the company, was fond of saying rather loudly, until someone diplomatically pointed out that it might make the wrong impression. Based upon geological surveys and confirmatory drilling, the company's shareholders were speculating that Rareterre would strike not gold but something more useful. As Peter and others in this growing business pointed out, the rare-earths Rareterre was hoping to extract might be rare but they were increasingly important, owing to their use in modern technology.

A plethora of gadgets vital to modern life all depend upon rare-earths: batteries, magnets in electric motors and hard drives; the special glass used in mobile phones and personal music devices. Even more in tune with the times, "green tech": those Toyota Priuses are laden with rare-earth metals; as are the turbines in wind farms, solar panels and the associated giga-batteries required by them. "The green tech revolution may be driven by the sun, wind and water," Peter liked to explain, "but it is harnessed and transmitted through rare-earth metals."

Ivy Mount had been married to Peter for 24 years, since she was 23, he 25. She was well-preserved and slim, despite her love for good food. Of average height and average weight, with average brown hair and average good looks, surprisingly, Ivy was a striking woman. She had the facial symmetry that is universally, unconsciously admired, blemish-free skin and attractively regular teeth. She was of above-average intelligence, had achieved a 2:1 in zoology from Cambridge without any great effort and had a naturally scientific mind. On leaving Cambridge and moving in with Peter, she had joined the Treasury as a statistician, where she stayed, perfectly content, bathed in an unreal world of numbers and job security until she became pregnant with Harry, the first of her three children. When the French side of her family – her mother's – expressed their surprise at her career choice, she would joke about the value of a degree in zoology when working in the British civil service.

The truth was, Ivy was not particularly ambitious, and Harry's arrival seemed to her the confirmation of something she always suspected: she was programmed to be a mother. Some of her friends from the Fabian Society were horrified by this treachery against years of militancy, against hard-earned equality, against the possibility   of workplace status on a par with those whose biology did not support gestation. Even more horrifyingly, Ivy's children had all gone on to progress through various fee-paying alternatives to state education, more expensive each term, boarding from their early teen years.

Physically, something about Ivy's assemblage of all those characteristics clustering around the median combined into a decidedly upper decile whole. She'd had plenty of opportunities for infidelity, including some surprising salacious approaches from men whom she had seen as friends of

Peter's. Nevertheless, despite his frequent long absences, she had remained faithful to Peter for all those 24 years. As she was a virgin when they met and fell in love, this made Ivy a rare example of a consistent, textbook Catholic girl, a one-man woman with little from the normally rich seam of sexual guilt to offer the priest at weekly confession. What she might have confessed to was a surprising materialism. Oddly, considering her soft left-wing views, Ivy was an enthusiastic, free-spending, brand-name snob – a fact that quickly became evident in most social situations. That she, an intelligent and generally socially aware person, did not notice this was the more surprising.

Ivy's wardrobe was a tribute to the power of the brand name and her home a monument to countless glossy interior decorating publications aimed at, well, people like Ivy. She liked to holiday in expensive resorts in distant locations. She enjoyed the theatre, the opera and the summer circuit of social events – sport, concerts, shows and the like, which kick off with the Chelsea Flower Show in May and wind up with Goodwood in August. She genuinely enjoyed the theatre; she disliked the opera but enjoyed its indisputable social cachet. For the rest, she mostly appreciated being there and being able to say she had been there. Her conversation was sprinkled with references to the completeness of her life; its value expressed in the currency of places she had recently been, what she had done there, and who she had seen. She even, most surprising of all, occasionally let slip the cost of some item of Beauchamp Place boutique clothing, a weekend in Paris at the Hôtel de Crillon, or a piece of jewellery. This is not to say she was not a nice person – everyone who knew her gladly agreed that she was – but it was despite the Gucci, Chanel, Moben and *Madam Butterfly*, not because of them.

The biggest difficulty posed by Ivy's "lifestyle" – as she actually called it – was that Peter's income from Rareterre was not sufficient to fund it. She had inherited a modest amount of money from her parents, but this was mostly reinvested in wasting assets in the shape of handbags, shoes, kitchen equipment, and in the particularly intangible asset of a chance encounter with some minor celebrity at The Ivy, which Ivy loved to frequent, for obvious reasons. "Not that it ever got me a discount," Peter grumbled. It was not that Peter was badly paid, it was just that Ivy really needed an investment banker as a husband, not the CEO of a small mining company, just to keep pace.

But there was the equity – Peter's shares in Rareterre plc. He had two and a half million of them, valued in the market at 120p each. £3 million! Ivy knew she was spending more than Peter's salary could support, but with three million in the bank, who cared? Peter reminded her of the warnings Maggie's government had rather patronisingly given to the public at the time of the first privatisations: "shares go down as well as up" – but neither of them believed for a moment that Rareterre's would do anything but rise as the American mine came on stream and so did the cash. In any case, it was impossible for Peter to sell any shares, even if he wanted to; he was CEO and no one likes an insider, *the* insider, to express such a lack of faith in the upwards trajectory of the share price.

It would have been good though to have been able to pay back his Dad, who had lent Peter £25,000 of his hard-earned savings, accumulated through years of diligent labour in his Glasgow hardware store. "Do you know, lad, how many tins of Dulux Satin I have to sell to earn this much?" Dad had asked as he handed over the cheque. Peter did not, but knew that his Dad would. And how many claw hammers, self-tapping screws, lengths of softwood floorboards. But Peter was sure of himself, certain that the deal was the chance of a lifetime.

That was ten years ago when, together with five other professionals, Peter had acquired Rareterre in what the accountant insisted on calling a "Management Buy-In", which sounded to Peter more like the objective of an off-site office junket. It had been a poor neglected thing; a shadow of a company unloved within AMB plc, a massive mining concern making all its money in better-established, high-volume minerals such as gold, silver, tin and copper. Rareterre and its business in the elements at the obscure end of the periodic table held no fascination for the mother company, whose management did not see any future for rare-earth metals and, in the words of AMB's smug company lawyer, were "too busy making money with real metals to invest in these weird things. Did you hear the names? Praseodymium? Sounds like a district court official of the Roman Empire!" He loved to sound educated, the smug lawyer, but because they had bothered to do their homework, Peter and his colleagues were better schooled about the mine at Trillium Lake.

The mine had ceased active production in 1999, owing to the low prevailing market prices for oxides and refined metals from its ores, and the parent company's "other corporate priorities". It was still shipping small quantities of oxides of a variety of rare-earth metals from a sizeable stockpile accumulated during the period of low prices. Separation and processing of the elements, found in varying small concentrations in the material extracted from the mine, was messy, difficult and costly, so below a certain market price for the resulting metals, it was unviable. However, that price had been exceeded for some time, so Rareterre had a small but useful income stream derived from the sweat of previous generations of miners.

What really excited the investors, though, was what remained as yet unmined in Oregon. The mine at Trillium Lake still contained one of the largest known workable deposits of rare-earth metals, in particular neodymium, but also some of the prized "heavy rare-earths": terbium, dysprosium, holmium, erbium, thulium, ytterbium. The appetite amongst technology manufacturers for the characteristics provided by rare-earth elements was such that Peter had few doubts that all these would find a ready market. All that was required was a detailed new feasibility study to confirm the rare-earth concentrations and the practicability of their economic extraction, as well as the construction of the required upgraded infrastructure to separate the value from the dross and to concentrate it.

As the new millennium came in, Peter and his five co-investors had become the owners of Rareterre – with a little support from friends and family, and some very helpful people at their respective banks. Peter had borrowed most of the £100,000 he invested, from his mortgage and from his dad. After seven years of hard work, a few false starts, a few dramas, an Initial Public Offering, a feasibility study and refurbishment programme massively over-budget and horrendously behind schedule but looking positive, Peter's £100k had become £3 million of locked-in value. Quite a lot of tins of Dulux and not bad, even if his mortgage had continued to increase in line with the demands of Ivy's "lifestyle".

Upper East Side, New York, June 2006

Amy hears his footfall out in the corridor. A curse; his key in the lock. A cold caress brushes her skin. She swallows a gasp. She can sense the inaudible sound of the key not turning. He swears again. The apartment's steel reinforced door is two inches thick, armed against New York City. He rattles the handle, smacks the door with an open palm.

"Changed the locks? Really? *Really?* Amy! You in there, Amy?"

She holds her breath.

"What's all my shit doing out here, Amy?" His still-reasonable voice.

She takes a swig from the bottle. It burns. She doesn't like liquor, he knew that. Another mouthful. She enjoys the unpleasant harshness in her throat. It is his bottle. It is all that is left of Shane in the apartment. She is drinking him. At the end of the bottle she will have finished him.

It is quiet. She imagines him trying to peer in through the spy-hole in the door. His boxed belongings line the corridor, glassware bong at one end, guitar at the other. Clothes. Surprisingly few books for a poet. The laptop she bought him: he wanted a Mac, *stupid.* The camera that should have been an SLR *if you knew shit about photography...*

"I know you're in there, Amy." He is controlling himself. "Look, about last night…"

She raises the bottle to her lips again. *She doesn't drink, the uptight bitch. Here, have some. You might start enjoying yourself for once.* She wipes her mouth with the back of her hand, just like he did, across his loose, sloppy wet lips. The bottle is nearly empty.

"You can't kick me out. Just because of…"

He is winding himself up. Breathe.

"My stupid friends don't mean any harm. They just want to have a good time." This is him, justifying. "If only you weren't so fucking *miserable* all the time!" He is losing it now. He kicks the door, and again, and again.

Silently, she sends her text message. Ten floors beneath them, Ronald, the doorman, nods to his brother – down as a favour from West 120th Street. He summons the elevator.

Shane kicks and yells, now pleading, now threatening. Then the usual, the insults – *fat, stupid, ugly, boring.*

She has positioned herself in front of the full-length hall mirror by the coats, to one side of the front door. The whiskey has infused her. She knows she is not stupid. She also knows his superiority, his edgy, skinny, artsy brilliance, is a sham. She looks at the mirror and sees her own defiance stare back, her big green eyes flashing hot from behind the round glasses. Her face is rounded, her padded features robbed of the angles that would have made her attractive. She should go on a diet; pay more attention to her hair. "But you're not ugly, Amy, no," she says, quietly.

A bell announces the arrival of the elevator.

Shane, in full spate, suspends his tirade. Ronald and he know one another. Shane's daily "hey-buddy" brotherhood-of-man act in the lobby always rang false.

"Hey, buddy," he says.

"I think we both know that we ain't real buddies, don't we?" says Ronald. "That's some pretty nasty stuff you telling Miss Tate right there. Well, she's kicking your ass out. And not a minute too soon, if you ask me."

Amy cannot hear the mumbled response. She can picture big Ronald with his bigger brother and skinny Shane in the narrow box-lined corridor.

"Well, that's some racist shit, I'd say, *buddy*," Ronald's voice, calm. "I didn't introduce you. This is my brother. He runs the boxing gym on 120th Street. He's come to help move your stuff. Nice, huh?"

One last suck on the bourbon and she holds the bottle to the light. Empty.

Shane was just part of it. Amy didn't exactly plan it that way, but she jettisoned all her hard-won New York baubles within a 24-hour period. Execution Day, she called it. It was exhilarating, and nobody was more surprised than her.

Unlike most people, including the Queen's crowd of economists, Amy Tate did sort of see it coming, the Great Bankers' Crisis of 2008. She had no more formal economics training than Her Majesty, but she did recognise unbridled naked greed when she saw it, and instinctively knew no good would come of it. So, in June 2006, she fled from New York and the rat race; she fled from Bloom & Beck, the bulge bracket investment bank that employed her, a menagerie of particularly sleek, sharp-toothed racing rodents. She fled her failed relationship. She retook control of her life and went west, to clean, green, honest Oregon.

Amy had been very well paid in New York and her savings, conservatively invested in a portfolio of low-risk income-generating stocks, meant she would be able to live the simple life she planned for herself without any formal employment – although she hoped to find something fulfilling to do, to supplement the dividends. Fulfilment had been absent from her job at Bloom & Beck. Money, however, had been ever-present. At B&B, money was all that mattered, literally all. Everyone's worth was judged entirely by reference to their share of the Pool. The bonus Pool.

By any normal standards it was a huge amount of money – hundreds of millions – to be shared unequally between a few thousand people. This vast accumulation of commissions, fees and gains on proprietary trading was announced monthly in departmental meetings to the obsessed employees, whose animal whoops of greed-fuelled pleasure sickened Amy. Pretty much everyone was entitled to participate in the Pool; management believed that this was the primary incentive to all staff to "go the extra mile". They thought of themselves as progressive for including the more lowly support staff, such as Amy, alongside the heavy-hitters of the hurly-burly bond trading floor and the courtly corporate finance department.

It was incomprehensible to those in charge at Bloom & Beck that anyone should look to anything other than dollars for their work satisfaction, and Amy was truly amazed by the sheer volume of money showered down on B&B staff. She was nearly sucked in; one year she felt genuine resentment when her bonus was both unchanged from the previous year and a smaller percentage of the total Pool. Her percentage was infinitesimal, but the Pool was just so huge that her share was five or six times the total annual pay of a skilled construction worker. She too was skilled, heading the Presentations Department, a team of 15 who supported the "customer-facing" officers of the bank with presentation services – PowerPoint slide shows spruced up, a corporate "look and feel" enforced, pitch books prepared and bound and returned to their authors overnight. Certainly Bloom & Beck's materials looked slick and professional and they seemed to do the trick, as evidenced by the bloated bonus Pool. But was she really worth twice the take-home pay of a family physician? And why was she unhappy at being so valued?

Amy had a liberal arts degree from Michigan State University and had majored in English and philosophy. Unsurprisingly she had found it impossible to get employment where her degree was of any relevance, and without rancour she had done a secretarial course and become a PA whilst looking around for something permanent. Soon it became clear that this was not going to be a stop-gap measure, so she trained in the advanced use of the Microsoft Office suite of products and quickly found work on Wall Street, which was booming and needed all the presentational skills it could get.

It was the mediocrity of the millionaires surrounding her that depressed her the most. When she heard the Head of Corporate Finance addressing the amassed department, with London, Frankfurt, Tokyo and Shanghai patched in by videoconference to the crowded New York meeting room, saying: "The Pool is awesome so far this year! I fully expect the whole bank to exceed my wildest expectations!" she could not disguise her disdain even as everyone else was punching the air, roaring. On the phone to her father at home in Michigan that night she tried to explain her feelings.

"He's in charge of a department of 300 people, Dad, all of them educated. He earns 20 million bucks a year! And he talks nonsense, complete nonsense! He said today that he *expected* his expectations to be exceeded! No one turned a hair!" She realised she sounded shrill.

"Well, he's just boosting morale, doing his job of keeping folks focussed and hard at work." Her father, a recently widowed, retired school-teacher who had never earned even one times the annual income of a skilled construction worker, was a big supporter of Amy, but also a fan of generous Bloom & Beck. He thought his daughter ought to be more grateful and less critical. "You know what your mother would have said."

She did. Something archaic about gift horses' mouths.

"Daaaad" – this in a drawn-out cautionary tone – "I saw four pitch books yesterday for the pharmaceuticals team and guess what? All the books were just the same, with the companies' names cut and pasted! Apparently DDG Inc. is a 'uniquely good fit' for all four to acquire!"

She could have gone on. The fresh-faced MBA graduates with no experience, aggressively pitching "eat or be eaten" opportunities to grizzled

CEOs with shareholders to satisfy and a payroll to meet. The mendacious analysis issued to investors as "objective" by B&B's "top-rated team of equity analysts" when, from her cross-departmental vantage point, she knew that corporate finance or B&B's own proprietary trading had a vested interest. The young men on the bond floor whose cocaine habit cost them more monthly than a nurse earned in a year. The junior trader she had overheard on the phone saying, "Three million bucks? For three million bucks I'd have all my teeth pulled out and give you a blow job!" She had looked at his Pool percentage, done a quick calculation and discovered that he had earned $1.3 million the preceding year. She wondered if he still had all his teeth.

Amy's problem was that she was unable to accept that the people she worked with were worth their pay, yet the whole ethos of her workplace continually reminded everyone that they were indeed worth it; that was exactly how their worth was measured, each differentially valued according to that Pool percentage.

So, oddly enough, Amy left Bloom & Beck because she did not care enough about money, yet cared too much that others cared for it so. Then what would keep her in New York? Like everyone else she claimed to love the buzz, the cultural superiority, the melting-pot diversity, but these sweet delusions were easily embittered by personal realities. Cramped, costly accommodation, stretched public services, intimidating multicultural encounters – but above all, Shane. And, like the rest of it, he was history now.

Only after Execution Day did Amy truly see the delusional forces that had bound her to Shane for so long. Too long. She was a steady, slightly nerdy girl from a rock-solid lower middle-class background; provincial, unexciting. She had curly chestnut hair and a pleasing, shy smile – but "homely" was the word most often attached to her. Since the age of 14 she had worn large, round spectacles. Academically she had always performed to the best of her ability, which was good but never brilliant. When it came to the crueller tests of adolescent social success, somehow – despite that smile and hair and the cuteness muffled within the puppy fat – she was always a B-grade performer. When this pattern continued through university she became resigned to a single life, or at best a utilitarian pairing off with an unexciting male equivalent.

Then Shane had paced moodily into her life, with no discernible equivalency at all. With his unfashionably long hair, he looked like Lennon in his early Yoko days, and said similar things, sometimes in Spanish. He took an unexpected interest in her. His erratic, unreliable back story was as exotic as hers was ploddingly dull: bohemian free-love parents who ended being "just totally uncool" but brought him up, their only child, in a peripatetic free-range trust-fund-fuelled whirlpool of cultural diversity. Mexico played a role, sometimes illicit Cuba. He shared his first spliff, aged nine, in a treehouse with his father; his first sexual experience was on the beach in Havana (or maybe Acapulco) on his 13th birthday. He played the guitar and sang Dylan. He was a poet – unpublished, and a screen-writer – freelance. He left university without graduating ("no, not like Bill Gates. Totally unlike Bill Gates"). He said he loved her. She fell for it – and him. He moved in. Introductions were made to friends and family (his friends, mostly, and her family; his mysterious, separated, geographically imprecise parents were forever elusive). She was 26, the breadwinner, and on a glide-path that increasingly relied on her sense of duty and the dual fears of embarrassment and failure.

Five years. It took five years of losing altitude until she saw the ground rushing towards her. The thing with Shane was founded on a shaky fascination on her part for a volatile, slightly unkempt, supposedly creative man clearly in need of a stability-providing woman – a need that developed without her noticing, until too late, into a disrespectful, loveless parasitism. He was abusive in only the most subtle, psychological ways; a live-in smiling assassin of self-respect. Amy fully recognised the years-long road she had travelled with Shane, from infatuation to fear, only when it approached its inverted end, when nothing was what it claimed to be. Kicking him out was not merely a retaking of control; it was an act of self-preservation.

With the proceeds from the sale of her 500-square-foot Manhattan apartment on East 86th Street, Amy bought a sprawling frontier-log-cabin-ranch-chalet-style home in the Mount Hood National Forest Park in northern Oregon. She had chosen Mount Hood by googling "wild" and "scenic" and "wilderness" and when she saw, on a realtor's website, a picture of her ranch located on the edge of the Salmon Huckleberry Wilderness, she felt a strange but immediate Eureka! Salmon. Huckleberry. Wilderness. It was all there: cold clear air, fishing with a rod in crystal waters, long lazy summers and snug woodsmoke winters, brown bears, trees, mountains, rivers. She made an offer before she made the plane reservations.

Trillium Lake Mine, Mount Hood, Oregon, June 2006

"The fat guy in the lumberjack shirt's been pissing in my cab again."

Rick pushed back his chair and inclined it to the position he liked for putting his feet up on the desk; he did not, however, put up his feet.

"Rick, I know it's not your fault an' all, but I can't be expected to work…"

"Yeah, I know, you have 'no alternative' but to inform your union representative." Rick made quotation marks in the air with his fat roust-about fingers. It was a standing joke between them, Sam being the only unionised employee. Sam was not amused.

"It's ever since those pussies, those Moore and Bruce guys…"

"Brice," Rick corrected, absently following Sam's gaze towards the Portakabin opposite, separated from theirs by a hundred feet of sun-hardened mud. "You gotta be kidding, Sam. Those guys don't look like they ever need to piss at all."

When Rick Stone, manager of Trillium Lake Mine, described his place of work he also made the quotation marks in the air around the word "mine" as he said it. Rick was one of those who remembered when they had mined here – really mined with dynamite and scrapers and sweat and lifting equipment. That was a long time in the past, but their hard labour had been such that, when the market went bad, they had accumulated a small mountain of extracted ore. It was a sufficiently high pile to keep today's crew busy concentrating and transferring it to Portland for processing, in 15-ton loads. And now word was that the market seemed once again to want the rare-earth elements the mine contained – something to do with demand for smart phones and renewable energy technologies, they said.

Having been through the good times and then the lean, Rick was sceptical about the renewed activity at Trillium Lake, even when geologists reappeared and started work on a new feasibility study after an absence of a decade or more. At the same time, CCTV equipment had made its appearance to survey the entrance to the Portakabins that constituted the "offices" of Rareterre, the mining company that was owner and operator of Trillium Lake Mine. Rick did not really understand what it was trying to protect – certainly not his ancient IBM desktop computer with its grimy cream plastic casing and green-on-black display, nor any of the battered office equipment or furniture; not even his electric desk light tastefully mounted on a deer antler. Somehow, Rick felt the pissing problem confirmed his gloomy view; the geologists might get excited about total rare-earth oxide to heavy rare-earth oxide ratios, but he was forced to inhabit a world of coaxing a truculent workforce using urine-soiled machinery into gradually nibbling through an unsightly mountain of old ore.

For the last few weeks, Rick's team of earth-moving equipment operators had been complaining, on apparently random mornings, of flat tyres, and local kids were thought to be the culprits. When the phenomenon continued and then in addition their vehicles had been soiled with urine, it was generally agreed amongst the team that it must be more than just some bored teenagers.

This disagreeable development had gone wholly unexplained; apparently an unprovoked act of occasional vandalism. The vehicles were huge, ageing, industrial-scale bulldozers and backhoes and diggers and dump-trucks built with scant regard for comfort, with hard-formed metal seats shaped to accommodate buttocks generally of a different size and profile from those of Rick's well-padded team, with unheated cabins, habitually exposed to the elements. The tyres were quickly inflated again and so not really a concern, and the urine problem could easily be rectified with a hose or a few buckets of water – but Rick had to concede that it was no way to start your day, washing piss off the seat in which you were about to spend several hours.

Then Rick had the idea of redirecting a security camera to cover the corner of the site where most of the large earth-moving vehicles were left to slumber overnight. The operation to do so was achieved quickly and bore fruit in the form of a fuzzy image captured at five o'clock one Sunday morning of a large man, in jeans and a lumberjack shirt, first deflating the tyres then clambering aboard one after another of Rareterre's monstrous rusting yellow beasts and peeing, liberally. Although it did nothing to solve the mystery, this evidence did at least exclude the consultant geologists from Moore and Brice, both of whom were skinny. At no time, it was noted, did the culprit expose his face, although he did of course expose another part of his anatomy, prompting some coarse comments from the team.

CHAPTER 2

Mount Hood, Oregon, June 2006

Hoxie Tomahas was named by his grandfather on his mother's side, the father having permanently absented himself as soon as the pregnancy was undeniable in the curvature of Hoxie's mother's belly. Grandpa took the first name from Hoxie Simmons, a much-photographed American Indian from the Rogue River tribe, an icon of the Wild West with magnificent feathered headdress, hide-tasselled sleeves and an indomitable look, a picture captured in 1870 by a nervous pioneer photographer. That look would, a 100 years later, make his photograph a popular fixture on dorm-room walls for a population of students newly made aware of the atrocities that their forebears had inflicted in the pursuit of the American Dream, in the tangible form of others' tribal lands. The romantic appeal of this distant Hoxie, the heroism of his pose and his position in the modern psyche – whether justified or not by nineteenth-century acts on horseback – were what recommended "Hoxie" as a first name to his grandfather.

As for Tomahas, the choice was made because Hoxie's mother furiously refused to reveal the name of the child's father. Her own father, a man of unbending if sentimental principle, forbade her to use his – and her – surname, and so something had to be found to fill the accusingly vacant space on the birth certificate where "name of father" should appear. Tomahas was the name of one of the martyrs, as Grandpa saw it, of the Whitman massacre. Hoxie Tomahas it was; this choice of name was perhaps unfortunate, exacerbating as it did the potential for a boy of Native American blood to harbour resentments, justifiable maybe, but unproductive, an erosive drumbeat that accompanied his growing up and moulded his adult mind.

Fatherless Hoxie Tomahas grew up on the reservation in the shadows of a photo-icon hero and a man unjustly put to death by interloping settlers as punishment for what today would be seen as a lamentable quid pro quo act in a bilaterally nasty guerrilla war. And so, Hoxie had every reason to be somewhat eccentric in his views of what it means to be an American and in his relationship to the lands now called Oregon.

Hoxie was a bright boy, a beneficiary of much well-meaning charity and, later, some helpful affirmative action. He did comparatively well in the schools he attended, well enough to be considered a suitable candidate for a programme designed as much to salve Ivy League consciences as to provide educational benefit to Native American and other minority students. Hoxie made the journey from the reservation to the reserve of the privileged and, mostly, the white – Yale.

There he majored in history, specialising whenever he could, which was often, in that of his own forebears – apparently no one saw anything obsessive in a boy called Hoxie Tomahas studying the Rogue River and Cayuse Wars, Lewis and Clark, Toussaint Charbonneau and all that. Surrounded as he was by what he saw as wealthy, WASPy, preppy, air-head fratboys and their Barbie-doll female equivalents, Hoxie was unlikely to emerge from the Yale experience a fully rounded human being, and he did not. He was, in the words of the old joke, shamefully repeated by one of his history tutors, well-balanced only because he had a big chip on both his shoulders.

Hoxie made the journey back to Oregon and, armed with a university education but no opportunity to deploy it beneficially, did very little indeed for five years. He worked half-heartedly in the reservation library and grew plump on liquor and fast-food items his namesake Simmons would have found impossible to identify, food won without the exertions of the hunt. The effects of idleness, a large degree of unfulfilled potential, a degree in the history of racial dominance and submission, combined with a resentment almost genetic in its roots, made of Hoxie a man deeply aware of his absence of purpose.

Amy's new extensive log cabin was built with more regard for the scenic views its position afforded than for the cost of keeping it warm in winter. Inside it was all high ceilings, exposed timber A-frame beams and extensive, geometrically interesting floor-to-ceiling windows. Its five acres of land was positioned on a small, unpaved road, a track, a few hundred metres off the Mount Hood Highway near the intriguingly named townships of Government Camp and Rhododendron. The main road was invisible from the house but closer than she would have liked, however the views of Mount Hood and the various surrounding wildernesses more than compensated for this, and anyway the traffic was not heavy. She had been into Government Camp several times, eaten at local hostelries of varying price and quality, was on nodding terms with several of her scattered neighbours, had joined the library and had a burgeoning, if superficial, conversational relationship with the librarians and a few shopkeepers.

Back in the city, Amy had wholeheartedly joined her fellow New Yorkers in overheating her apartment in winter, allowing her and Shane to walk around it in thin clothes better suited to the tropics, and cranking up the air conditioning to reduce the summer temperature to something closer to a brisk New England spring morning, with the result that she wore a sweater in her apartment far more often in the months of July and August than in January and February. As a New Yorker, she obviously had no car but made liberal use of taxis, with their five-litre engines and heavy-footed drivers, each mindless surge from the traffic lights a small but measurable addition to her considerable carbon footprint. And yet, despite her frequent airborne getaways that had been the norm back in New York, more lip-service was paid to the needs of the environment within two blocks of her Upper East Side apartment than within the boundaries of the whole state of Oregon.

Amy's turning point, the moment when she was transformed into a dedicated, environmental activist, can be identified to the minute: 07.36 on the morning of Tuesday 27 June 2006. She was sitting on her terrace sipping coffee from a large white mug bearing a cartoon picture of a moose wearing a knitted hat. This mug and a rusty collection of inexplicable garden tools were the only things left behind by the previous occupants of her house. The morning sun was shining through the trees on her land, casting long, cool shadows across her quiet lawn. That weekend she had seen a deer nervously nibbling at new vegetation at the edges of her property, and had been enchanted.

The preceding day, Monday, her morning had been less enchanting. At this same hour, her preferred time for her first cup of coffee, there had been no signs of wildlife. Instead, a noise began in the distance, gradually growing to an invasive whine of complaining machinery, followed by a crunched gear-change, followed in turn by the gradual increase in frequency and volume associated with a large vehicle gaining speed. Amy had not much noticed the sounds of traffic on the nearby road until then, mainly because the vehicles which most often passed were driven by powerful, modern engines that took the gradient and turns in their automatic-transmission stride.

What she heard for the second time at 07.36am on Tuesday 27 June was the sound of an old, tired and poorly maintained dump-truck from Trillium Lake Mine, laden with 15 tons of concentrate ore, a decade out of the ground, making its tortured way down the Mount Hood Highway towards the coast and the processing plant.

Up in his Portakabin at the mine, Rick had just introduced a new schedule of shipments – initially three a day, on a properly timed basis instead of the previous single daily truck which had left at whatever hour best suited its driver. "Hey, quit moaning," he had said to the inevitable complaints at the lost flexibility. "We should be glad to have the extra work. It's a good sign."

The new schedule had necessitated the recommissioning of retired machinery and men, all of which had seen better days and required some refurbishment of various kinds. Sam had muttered about changed conditions of work and Rick had considered responding with "yeah, as in, you have to do some," but thought better of it. Somehow Rick's self-restraint satisfied Sam's syndicalist needs and the new programme had been implemented relatively smoothly. Digging at the ore pile was increased, the underused and aged crushing, grinding, flotation and filtration plant was pressed into marginally greater service, and three concentrate-laden trucks left daily at 07.30, 13.00 and 18.30.

Amy was not aware of the minor operating efficiency revolution taking place at the mine a few kilometres up the road from her property; had she been, it would have made little difference. All she needed to know was that after a few short weeks of rural calm, wilderness bliss, she was for the second day in succession forced off her terrace, moose coffee mug in hand. Not out of physical discomfort – the noise from the road was nowhere near those levels – but rather out of irritation, a feeling of having been cheated out of something. Cheated not just of the communion with deer and other wild things, but cheated of something essential to her new life. In fact, the wildlife cared little about the noise from the highway, far less than Amy did, and had she been less consumed with her irritation she would that very morning have witnessed a delightful scene as a mother racoon led her fluffy brood across the unkempt lawn.

Her "friends" in distant New York were very unlikely ever to come and visit, despite the many assurances made during her final weeks in the city, weeks punctuated by last drinks and goodbye dinners. In fact, most of these friends' affection for Amy would have been insufficient to take them as far as New Jersey, let alone Oregon. Deep down she knew this, but in her mind Amy often rehearsed such a visit, imagining showing off her enormous new home, her trees and her little patch of wilderness, her view and... her peace and quiet.

The labouring sound of aged dump-trucks and the crashing of gears on neighbouring highways spoiled this reverie and undermined her imagined position of proud achiever: someone who had shown courage and taken the plunge, ditched an unworthy man and extricated herself from a loveless relationship, left the rat race. Someone who had empowered herself and was justly reaping the rewards paid in dividends of rural tranquillity to match her newly won internal peace. Rick's trucks demoted her, in her own fantasy, to apologising to her imaginary friends for the interrupted calm. Of course, the entirely hypothetical nature of this unsatisfactory scene somehow made the whole thing even worse. She realised that without the calm the noise would be less intrusive; after all, she had come to ignore completely the outrageous brute noise of New York's emergency services vehicles en route to a disaster at any hour of the day or night, bellowing like enraged beasts at junctions, and found it easy to do that against the background of the constant thrum of urban life. But here, in her property adjoining the Salmon Huckleberry Wilderness, the sound of Rick's patched-up diesels was intolerable in its contrast.

For the first time, she imagined the visitor from her past to be Shane, resentfully sizing up her new space. "Shame about the traffic noise," he would say with only a tiny, deniable hint of the pleasure it gave him. "It's great how you can dress just how the hell you like out here, though. Is that shirt *denim*?"

In subsequent days she found out where these trucks came from, a mine she had not known was there, extracting minerals she had not known existed, minerals useful for green technology like solar panels or wind turbines, she learned. It could have been consoling, that the loads in the trucks were somehow in the interests of the Environment. It was not; in the end, the capital E Environment did not matter when her own environment was being spoiled. She came to listen for the approaching vehicles, looking for trouble despite herself, willing, almost wanting, to savour her own anger.

Hoxie Tomahas *was* aware of Rick's increased activity up at the Trillium Lake mine; he'd seen the trucks. As a boy, Hoxie had swum and fished in Trillium Lake, mostly avoiding the teeming campsites and the ring-pull-scattered and burger-fat-smeared barbeque areas provided for the tourists, who came in increasing numbers each summer, with their improbable recreational vehicles and their equally improbable waistlines. Hoxie himself was in those days a lithe and swift youth, who, more and more, saw himself as a righteous, clean-living, healthy indigene and them – the tourists – as over-indulgent, soft, spoiled invaders living out some sort of replay of nineteenth-century colonisation. The mine was already there then, when Hoxie was growing up, and was fairly active. As an opencast wound covering several acres it was not a pretty sight, but it was remote and well-hidden behind an expanse of unremarkable and rarely visited forested land.

However, Hoxie was no more accepting of the mine than of the tourists; both were intrusions on what he had been taught was his ancestral ground. Despite the more profound despoiling of the land associated with the mine, the problem with the tourists was simply that they got everywhere. He could not then have said why the mine was no better or worse than the campsite. His feelings were strong but incoherent, and his youthful anger was mostly directed at the spoiled city kids up for a couple of weeks with their parents in a Winnebago. Still a teenager, he was not yet any sort of activist, although the effects of his name and heritage were already planting themselves firmly in his mind. The worst Hoxie did, as a boy, to express his tribal disapproval of the annual tourist influx was to let down all four tyres on a campervan parked on the periphery of the campsite.

The van belonged to a family from California: grey accountant father, equally grey schoolteacher mother and 17-year-old daughter, anything but grey. Golden, rather, in Hoxie's 16-year-old eyes, as he and his friend Gary spied on them from the undergrowth on the adjacent hillside. She seemed to be determined to return home as tanned as if she had never left, this pony-limbed Californian dressed mostly in bikini top and cheese-cloth beach-skirt, despite the field-sport environment in which guns and fishing rods and camouflage clothing were more in evidence than sun loungers and suntan lotion. The golden California girl stood out, an unobtainable object of sexual fantasy for Hoxie and Gary.

When Hoxie struck his first confused blow for his ancestral rights, stealthily approaching the camper after its occupants had left for the lake, he did so alone. Gary, an acne-ridden classmate of Hoxie's, was both too reasonable and too much of a coward to participate.

"You want rid of them, right, these tourists? You resent their presence here? So why make it more difficult for them to go by letting down their tyres?"

He had a point. Maybe it was something to do with the golden bikini girl who, if he was honest, Hoxie did not want to go at all. Ironically, had Hoxie's own preconceptions of the golden girl's prejudices and tastes not got in his way, his teenaged chiselled features, raven hair and bronze skin in combination with her coastal liberalism would have provided a smooth path to a holiday relationship. But they did get in the way, so he did not speak to her; he just let down the tyres of her dad's camper, and did not even stick around long enough to observe the reaction.

Because of his size, name, and Yale education, Hoxie was well known in the settlements neighbouring the reservation. He was well liked, despite his ill-repressed ethnic righteousness coupled with a careless disregard for socially acceptable behaviour, even that of permissive rural Oregon. To share a meal with Hoxie meant literally sharing a quantity of half-chewed processed carbohydrates; maybe that was what kept the women at bay, the first-date impression seldom being wholly positive. Nevertheless, Hoxie had a large circle of acquaintances, many of whom valued his opinions.

On certain subjects – such as those relating to the use of land, presentation of social history, even the aesthetics of town planning – to the average self-loathing Euro-American, Hoxie's indigenous views automatically qualified as more valid than their own. Some were in awe of his Yale degree – actually, any university degree – and respected his views on that basis. Whatever the reason, Hoxie was some sort of a pillar of the community, despite his sporadic employment status. It was thus that Professor Palmer, chairman of the Trail 26 Conservation Society, approached Hoxie to ask him if he would be interested in joining the society – indeed, in being a member of the Board of Trustees.

The Mounts' House, Chelsea, London, July 2006

By any standards, Ivy Mount was an excellent cook. Her Normandy-born mother taught her all she needed to know about French cuisine; knowledge then consolidated by a gap-year season spent catering for a chalet full of various skiing Sloaney clones and by a cordon-bleu course in Grenoble before she went up to Cambridge. She was also a popular hostess, exercising her skill in the kitchen in what had become an institution: her "New Friday" Thursday night dinner parties. These were the events Peter had come to refer to as Dinner Parties for the Chattering Classes, which Ivy had to admit was a pretty accurate characterisation. Of course, the food was always of the highest quality and the wines selected without regard to price but possibly by the prestige of the label, but people came because they enjoyed the conversation as much as for gastronomic satisfaction.

Ivy did the inviting – in fact Ivy did all the organisation – and most of Ivy's friends, who therefore predominated around the table, were politically on the left. Peter knowingly gave them an object of attack, exaggerating his own libertarian views for the benefit of a good heated discussion. Sometimes it backfired; occasionally the guests could not stomach Peter's trenchant, uncompromising positions and his unrestrained critical analysis of opinions he felt to be thoughtless clichés, criticism that could verge on the personal. In general though, Peter thought he and Ivy were an excellent double act, and their guests usually went home replete and content at having participated in a good debate – even if some wished for a cosier evening of shared prejudice, rather than having to defend long-held and cherished views against his sometimes harsh attacks.

Ivy preferred to avoid any sort of confrontation and often thought Peter went too far. She seldom said anything of this to Peter, however, as over the years she had learned that voicing her feelings would often result in a low-key but embittering disagreement. And so living with such unrelieved tensions had become the price of a quiet life. Such are the unspoken undercurrents that characterise many a British marriage. Ivy thought her French family had a better approach, where occasional emotional outbursts relieved tensions and kept the marital ship on an even keel, after the squall had passed. So it was that a group of six Chatterers converged on the Mounts' Chelsea kitchen one Thursday in July 2006, looking forward to an evening of good food – ox tongue in plum sauce had been promised – and stimulating chat. Ivy and Peter were in the kitchen, she at work on the rather gruesome task of peeling the rough, pimpled outer skin from what was all too evidently a large mammal's tongue, boiled after having been roughly ripped from its anchorage in the beast's mouth judging by the mess of flesh at the wider end. Peter was arranging cheese on the cheese board – bought from pricey Paxton & Whitfield, of course.

"It's amazing that something so grotesque tastes so good," he said, nodding at the mess on the chopping board in front of Ivy, whilst balancing a piece of Selles-sur-Cher goats' cheese from the Loire Valley via St James's on the top of a small connoisseur mound on the board. He picked the label off the cheese. "Doesn't 'cher' mean expensive?"

Ivy was focussed on her ox tongue. "You know it does, Peter. Expensive. But that little bit is not much and please don't go on about expense this evening – it only upsets people, you know, if they can't afford…" She flipped the tongue over with a squelching sound, "And besides, they all know you're loaded, with all those Rareterre shares."

Oh yes, the Rareterre shares, a daily barometer of how well he was doing – not just financially, but also as a businessman, a manager, a member of the peer groups to which he belonged, both consciously and not. At the beginning of the week another "mining minnow", as the press liked to call one of his corporate peer groups, had gone under. A small, risky uranium exploration company run by Steve Svensson, a man Peter knew slightly and certainly felt he had much in common with. Svensson, like Peter a real geologist and long-term mining man, had simply discovered that the mine's promising lode-bearing property actually bore very little indeed. The company had been liquidated with shareholders receiving almost nothing – their proportion of the residual cash, once the accountants, lawyers, tax man and other habitual bloodsuckers had taken their pound of flesh, amounted to a small fraction of the share price a few days earlier. It had been a sobering reminder to Peter of the precariousness of corporate life at the small end. Svensson had been found by his ten-year-old daughter, dead in the luxury of his leased Lexus, the engine still softly purring out invisible poisonous gases. Peter forced himself to focus on the evening ahead.

"Who's coming this evening?"

"Oh, Peter, I've told you twice already." Inadvertently, she sounded a little snappy. Ivy was used to his inattention and excused it by reminding herself of the stresses of his job – but she never found her own excuses very convincing. Often she seethed internally at the disrespect that his inattention implied, and sometimes she expressed her anger to a friend, always a female friend, normally to hear their own stories of husbandly faults putting Peter's in the shade, before it was agreed that all men were bastards, which, paradoxically, always seemed an argument for living with the status quo, disrespect and all. If the friend in question was husbandless Odile, however, she always happily confirmed Peter's shortcomings as a husband and as a human being, as seen from her privileged vantage point of frequent invitee to the Mount household.

There was an almost imperceptible pause before Peter responded. Did she sense an irritation? The inattention issue had been a point of contention quite exceptionally actually discussed between them. Ivy felt incoherent and petty raising the issue at all, somehow confirming its unimportance when she was forced to put into words Peter's apparent inability to see or acknowledge any problem or apologise for any implied relegation of her and her apparently unexciting world. Ivy knew herself to be an intelligent and eloquent woman, but increasingly she understood the frustrations that less educated people must feel when words proved inadequate in expressing why small things matter; frustrations she was sure led to the use of physical violence to make up for verbal inadequacy; to conflict, domestic cruelty, divorce or (worse) to indifference.

So here he was, irritated by her because she had the effrontery to inform him that she had already told him some minor facts, something which saddened her and she could not express without confirming the unimportance of the whole thing. And so, at this moment in July 2006, in this luxury Chelsea kitchen, a small measure of acid was poured into the vessel of the Mount marriage where it quickly mingled with the other fluids, the corrosive and the emollient, the intoxicating and the soporific, that had accumulated there over the preceding 24 years.

"Okay, let me guess. Odile, of course, and Margot. Phillip and Amanda. Fulki and Jerry."

She had to admit, this was a tension-diffusing answer and almost right – perhaps he listened more than she gave him credit for.

"Nearly!" She was not about to treat him like a clever schoolboy, surely? "Actually, not Phil and Mandy but Ernest and Rupert."

"Oh, great. Last time I saw Rupert and Odile in the same room together they pretty much ganged up on me, and Odile got all offended about something innocent I said, probably with my back to the wall."

"Well, if you're making excuses about ganging-up and backs to walls, maybe you said something less 'innocent'"– she stressed the word so as to emphasise its lack of credibility – "than you claim. Besides, you love to offend Odile."

"It's so easily done! Anyway, I'll be on good behaviour tonight."

Ivy's friend Odile Callow shared her Anglo-French background, whilst holding a more strident version of her political views. Odile's mother had been a minor aristocrat from Normandy who had married far below herself, to a British schoolteacher from Croydon, whom she had met on an exchange visit just after the war. The whole concept of "marrying below oneself" would have put Odile into a rage, Ivy knew. Peter had proven it. In any case, whether for reasons of social hierarchy or for others, Odile's mother had divorced the schoolteacher, declared herself a feminist and brought up Odile alone in a fairly unrelenting and righteous anti-male – rather than pro-female – environment. It was no surprise to anyone when Odile came out as a lesbian, it being the only intellectually consistent position for her to take. She observed the unwritten rules of political correctness to the letter, worked in some environmental advisory capacity for the Office of the Mayor of London and lived in Fulham with pretty, cultured Margot. Both were in their fifties and both looked ten years younger than that.

"I invited Rupert and Ernest to make it four boys and four girls, but is that right when two of the girls are..."

"Interesting question, Ivy, but doesn't Ernest bat for the other side too, so to speak?"

"No. I don't think so. He's just one of those bachelor types. Like Isaac Newton."

"Ernest is like Isaac Newton?" He made a snorting sound she recognised as one of the huge repertoire of noises he made whilst asleep. "You mean a great and innovative genius whose brilliance will outlive him by hundreds of years…"

The doorbell rang. She hoped he would not be in one of his sneery moods tonight. She waved her still-slimy hands at him and pulled a face that effectively communicated "you have to get it, I can't". He went to the door and let Ernest in.

"Ernest! We were just saying how like Isaac Newton you are, or rather Ivy was," she heard from the kitchen.

"I was not, Peter. Behave yourself. Ernest, you are unfashionably early. Did I say seven thirty or eight o'clock? Here, you can help Peter set the table." She gestured to a pile of cutlery and napkins on the three-inch thick "butcher's block" that the whimsical designer of Ivy's kitchen had placed in the middle of the room, adjoining a wholly unnecessary ceramic hob.

Apart from being single by choice and not apparently gay, Ernest Fellden had little in common with Sir Isaac. Being a serious and somewhat intense man of great integrity, he was well-named. Ivy agreed with Peter when he commented that although he was bright and reliable, Ernest was "not exactly a bundle of laughs". He was though, she thought, a good example of why a world populated exclusively by bundles of laughs would be a poorer place. Actually, when she considered it, it would be a hellish place. Ernest – a 42-year-old social worker from Islington – was who Ivy had had in mind when she asked Peter not to go on about expense; she was sure Ernest's monthly food budget, if not his entire monthly disposable income, would easily be exceeded by what she had spent on tonight's dinner.

"Have you come straight from the pit-head?" Peter asked, looking at Ernest's slightly soiled jeans and old corduroy jacket with elbow patches. "How are things in the worker's paradise of Islington, anyhow?" Ivy was accepting Ernest's somewhat inept air-kisses, cheek to cheek about three centimetres apart, and wondered whether to intervene to protect Ernest –

already, so early? Instead she shooed them out of the kitchen with their cutlery and napkins and a decanter of wine.

"Go, lay the table and stay in the dining room and make a start on the wine. Tell me what you think – I got it from Fortnum and…" She tailed off. Peter recalled the bottles he had just decanted – Chateau Angelus 2003. Must be £150 each.

"Excellent idea!" he agreed, and ushered Ernest out towards the dining room. "Guess who's coming tonight, Ernest. Fulki. Fulki and Jerry. Tom and Jerry, I call them. Laurel and Hardy. How those two got hooked up, God only knows!"

"Opposites attract, Peter."

Ivy's dining room – it was undoubtedly Ivy's, not Peter's – was furnished with a solid oak table and matching chairs, the extremities of both being artfully left rough, with bark still attached, highly varnished. There was a Welsh dresser, nearly filling one wall of the room, laden with framed pictures of the Mount children at various ages and occupations – skiing, all in matching one-piece suits, Kirsty smiling a gap-toothed eight-year-old smile on ponyback, Emma in a purple gymslip holding a medal at a sports day, Harry reading *Where The Wild Things Are* in a Tuscan garden – the sun apparently perpetually shining on them.

The furniture was not made by Viscount Linley nor even designed by him, to Ivy's regret. "At that price, I'd expect it to have been hand-carved by Prince Philip himself," Peter had said in the shop, loudly enough for the snooty shop assistant – a breed even nice Ivy despised – to hear. Ivy later wondered if she had bought the dresser, table and eight chairs to punish Peter for something. On the walls, which had been elegantly rag-rolled, were various paintings acquired at auction over the years – tasteful things which looked like the works of lesser-known impressionists, two quirky portraits of unknown people. It would have been better if they had been family, painted by semi-famous artist friends, prized for sentimental reasons, but sadly this was not the case. It was all bought. The Mounts were, in the snobbish words of some minor British government minister, "the sort of people who had to buy their own furniture".

Peter was becoming increasingly aware of the preposterousness of it all. All this… stuff, all this prosperity – it was a chimera, it was all appearances: it was an over-enthusiastic lending bank, an improbable increase in the value of Chelsea terraced houses, a victory of optimistic expectation against the proper conservatism more appropriate to the lending retail bank manager.

Not that the Mounts were in any way unusual – everyone was busy spending their unrealised wealth, and the bounty provided by a fractional reserve[2] retail banking system happily doling out multiples of what they really had. Earlier that day, Peter had had a call from someone at his bank cheerfully telling him that he had reached his pre-agreed mortgage limit of a million pounds – but not to worry, they would be happy to up the limit for so good a customer; after all, the house was worth much more than that, and his shares in Rareterre were held in security, pleasure doing business with you Mr Mount.

But Peter did worry. He was a small soapy sphere in a huge debt-filled bubble-bath. Worse still, although nearly half of what Rareterre paid to employ him went in taxes, and further tax was levied on every pound he and (mostly) Ivy spent for themselves, the government was also borrowing on a heroic scale. In some sort of delirious neo-Keynesian financial experiment it was spending far more money than it collected – despite the buoyant economy – thereby contributing ever more foam in the communal tub. Peter was not an economist, but deep down he felt that all this debt would end badly. He thought again of the mortgage; he thought of Svensson in his carbon-monoxide-filled garage. He really would have to rein Ivy in a bit.

From the kitchen Ivy could easily hear Peter getting going on one of his current favourite topics. *He's certainly not wasting any time tonight*, she thought.

"I wonder if Rupert will come in his Prius again this evening? All the way from Pimlico." He was distributing knives and forks around the table. Ernest followed with a handful of spoons, unconsciously straightening up Peter's efforts as he went.

"He's got a Prius? Good man!" Ernest said, slightly absently, as he started to transfer wine glasses from the sideboard to the table. "Environmentally friendly. They should just stop building the normal ones, really."

"Oh, you think we should all be forced to have hybrid cars then, Ernest? By government edict? Isn't that a bit dictatorial? A bit Stalinist?"

Ernest rolled his eyes and reached for a small pile of folded linen napkins. "Have you heard of Godwin's Law, Peter? It states that as an online discussion grows longer, the probability of someone making a comparison involving Adolf Hitler approaches 100 percent. Well, in this house the question is always 'how long will it be before Peter accuses someone of being a Bolshevik?' I think you've just broken your own record. But I won't be put off. Climate change is too great a threat. Yes, I think some things mean that we collectively submit to a loss of personal liberty. Like the liberty to pollute the planet and pump out CO_2 by driving gas-guzzling cars like your – what is it? Rover?"

"My Bristol is 30 years old. Built to last. Sure, its emissions aren't low, but have you ever thought about the carbon footprint embedded in every vehicle built? All the metal smelting and bending and forming and assembling. All those components, all that plastic. Heating the factories, transporting the workers to and from work. Shipping the cars from factory to market. In the case of hybrid cars, you have those huge batteries. Well, in my case, the build cost has been spread out over 30 years so far – fully amortised as the accountants would say.

"I bet if it was properly thought through, my Bristol is much more environmentally friendly than Rupert's Toyota. But people don't think it through; it's far easier to say: 'Look at selfish Peter with his gas-guzzling car, aren't I virtuous in my new hybrid shipped halfway across the world?'"

Peter had adopted a childish playground tone that didn't sound like Rupert at all.

"If Rupert was really interested in the environment he wouldn't come by car. Besides, have you seen how podgy he's getting? He could do with the exercise."

From the doorway came the sound of someone clearing his throat. Peter looked up guiltily; oddly, so did Ernest. There he was, sure enough – fat, inoffensive, rich Rupert. Solicitor, bon viveur, shallow Rupert. Chanel socialist, Peter called him, Louis Vuitton Labour.

Ivy could never understand why Peter found the views of wealthy left-wing people particularly unacceptable. In her mind, their embracing of a social conscience, their espousal of politics which could not benefit them materially, was all the more admirable for its lack of self-interest, for its inversion of self-interest, in fact. To Peter it was hypocrisy for people for whom money would never be a problem to, as he liked to say, "push the rest of us down a so-called progressive path which will, in all likelihood, cost the poorest their livelihoods in the long term, whilst the Gucci lefties are insulated from the effects of their economic and social self-indulgence". To Ivy, it was laudable that people with wealth should promote wealth-redistributive politics and she knew, and was tired of, Peter's argument that the really wealthy always had their loopholes; it was the rest of us who ended up paying the bill for all those nice, conscience-salving initiatives in the long run. Rupert's supposedly hypocritical hybrid car was just more evidence of all this.

"Good evening to you too, Peter," said Rupert, extending a fleshy hand. "As usual you got it all wrong, old boy. I got the Prius to avoid the Congestion Charge, that's all."

"I'll bet. Do you drive to work?"

Rupert nodded.

"And before? Before you bought that car?"

"The Tube." Rupert shuddered. "It was horrible."

Peter smiled triumphantly at Ernest, as if Rupert had proved a point he was making. "You see, Ernest? Unintended consequences."

"Well, I know how much you like those, Peter, but you hadn't mentioned any so far…"

"Rupert here buys a new car shipped from Japan, still considered 'green', despite a sizeable bundle of embedded greenhouse gases, and the consequences? Daily CO_2 emissions go up too, as he renounces public transport and drives to work. Brilliant. In addition, Rupert gets to show everybody how virtuous he is, whilst avoiding having to mix with the Great Unwashed on the Victoria Line."

"Hang on, Peter, I just said…" began Rupert.

"Yes, but CO_2 emissions *don't* go up, because it's a Prius."

"Nonsense, Ernest. Where d'you think the electricity comes from? The pixies make it from purest spring water mixed with distillate of moonshine? All Rupert's electric car does is shift the emissions somewhere else – probably to a great big coal-fired power station somewhere nearer where poor people live."

"Well, at least Rupert's trying," said Ernest sulkily.

"No, really I'm not. As I was saying…"

Ivy ushered Odile, Jerry and Fulki into the room. There was the habitual round of handshaking and air-kissing, inconsequential London complaints – Tube difficulties (Fulki), parking permit timings (Jerry), Congestion Charge anecdotes (Odile). Ivy noticed that Peter had not poured Ernest, Rupert or himself a glass of wine. Not like him.

"Well, Odile, if you've had Congestion Charge trouble you should do like Rupert, and buy a hybrid car," said Peter. "You know they're exempt? Besides, Comrade Ernest's First Five-Year Plan will force us all to drive hybrids, whether we like it or not."

Inconsistently, he said these words in an exaggerated Nazi voice. Ernest mimed chalking up a Roman numeral II. "Apparently, it's what will save the planet, arrest climate change, stop the sea levels rising, etcetera." Odile was regarding him with open dislike.

"Saving our planet is going to require more than a few snazzy high-tech cars," she said coldly. "Besides, I can't afford a Prius, Peter. You know that."

"Phew!" said Ernest, pulling a chair out for Odile to sit on. "Just as well, 'cause Peter says the unintended consequences would be dire. Driving a hybrid: you might as well go right out and set fire to the Brazilian rainforest."

"Unintended consequences like subsidised green energy making our economy even more energy intensive, you mean?" asked Jerry – unattractive, bearded, witty yet vulgar, Texan, self-made, undeserving married-to-Fulki Jerry. Like Peter, Jerry was a reveller in the paradoxes of political interference. "It's all a scam if you ask me. Just look at wind turbines: only work part of the time. Has there been a single fossil fuel power station closed down because of all these monstrosities? No! Ugly as hell, noisy, and did you know that each one consumes hundreds of litres of lubricating oil a year? I mean, it's gotta go somewhere. It's just vaporised and deposited on whoever is downwind."

"And they kill birds and bats. And – just like Priuses – think of all the emissions of greenhouse gases to build them, install them and maintain them. I wonder if anyone ever worked out what their time to carbon break-even is?" said Peter, failing to mention another environmental paradox, one closer to home: his daily efforts to advance Rareterre's participation in the green economy with its own messy rare-earth extraction and processing.

"Time to carbon break-even? Did you make that up?" asked Jerry, like an admiring MP asking an easy one in Prime Minister's Questions.

"And what about solar? Also intermittent," continued Jerry. "Don't get me started on photovoltaic solar panels! Do you know what nasty gases are emitted in making them? Hundreds of times more damaging than CO_2! And I was in Yorkshire the other day – *Yorkshire!* – as well known for its long days of uninterrupted sunshine as it is for the sunny disposition of its population. Solar panels everywhere!"

Peter laughed. "You'd only get that where taxpayers…"

"Just a minute!" Odile had raised her hand, like a traffic cop. She glanced to her left and right to ensure that, as well as representing the planet at large, she spoke for the right-thinking majority at the table: Fulki, Ivy, Ernest, Rupert and the still-absent Margot. "I hate to interrupt your little double act, Abbott and Costello, but this is no laughing matter. We're killing the planet and it is imperative that we reduce our emissions of greenhouse gases. I say they're all important, wind power and solar – as well as biofuels, hydro… everything working together, plus low-emissions vehicles – well done, Rupert! – and if that involves government subsidies and loss of some individual freedoms, so be it."

"But as I keep saying, or trying to…" began Rupert.

"Biofuels! Have you seen what happens to food prices when cultivation of biofuels displaces food harvests? It's all right for us," Jerry gestured at the plate Ivy had slid in front of him, slices of rich meat covered in a plum sauce, "but people at the margin *starve* when grain prices rise!"

"And producing ethanol produces its own pollution, uses masses of water and fertilisers, kills biodiversity, causes deforestation in underdeveloped countries…"

"Develop*ing* countries, Peter, are the very places most vulnerable to the effects of climate change. Bangladesh will practically disappear underwater if we don't act! Think of the millions of displaced people, it's one of the most densely populated places on earth."

Fulki said this with more emotion than she normally expressed. Peter looked at Jerry's wife regretfully, thinking: *Too bad, there goes the Jerry and Peter double act.* Fulki Chopra, front-line healthcare worker (actually a GP), a strikingly beautiful second-generation Briton whose parents, doctors both, immigrated from the subcontinent in the 1960s, unquestionably had identity politics pre-emption rights over him with respect to the Third World, and probably also with respect to anything to do with caring.

Fulki was a physician by vocation in a way that seemed to Peter to be increasingly rare. He never used the health service, but Ivy's squad of fashionably located private healthcare providers – Chelsea GP, Harley Street gynaecologist, dentist, hygienist also used by Robbie Williams – were obviously devoted mainly to the cause of their bank accounts, whereas Fulki was genuinely devoted to her patients' well-being.

"You're missing the point, Fulki. All I'm saying is that so-called alternative energy is not the answer. It seems to me that the problem is one of over-consumption of energy: how can the answer to that be new ways of producing more energy? Even if this new 'renewable' energy was perfectly clean, there's no way the alternatives can substitute more than a small percentage of consumption. And it's not clean. Not only that, the taxpayer-funded subsidies are misallocating resources and driving energy prices *down*. Jerry's right – not a single evil CO_2-emitting fossil fuel-devouring power station will close, and consumption keeps on going up. Feel free, Fulki, to congratulate yourself, like Rupert, on your virtuous support for environmental causes. But if you believe in anthropomorphic CO_2-generated climate change…"

There was a collective intake of breath. Had Peter said "if"? Odile was first to pounce on the miserable nonbeliever.

"*If*, Peter? The science is in! The science is in!" she barked. "Only a wilfully blind ignoramus – or someone with an agenda – would deny it! Surely you're not a climate change denier, Peter, as well as everything else?"

Surprising everyone, it was not Peter but soft-spoken, left-liberal metropolitan-elite Rupert who answered Odile.

"What on earth does that phrase mean, Odile, 'the science is in'? Does it mean 'there can be no more debate'? If so, that's the most profoundly anti-scientific thing I've ever heard. What about Newtonian physics, eh? That science was 'in' for centuries. Along comes Einstein. What did scientists say? 'What's all this *relativity* nonsense, Albert, old boy? You're very much mistaken, I'm afraid. The science is in, I think you'll find.' No! Scientific advance is precisely the reverse of the sentiment 'the science is in'. Science advances only by questioning accepted theories, by *trying to disprove them.* Not by shutting down debate." There was a moment's silence.

"But, Rupert... " ventured Ernest "... you drive a Prius."

"As I keep saying, and no one listens, I have that car entirely for the Congestion Charge benefits."

"What I meant by the 'science is in', is that 97 percent of scientists subscribe to the theory of anthropogenic global warming," said Odile huffily.

"Statistics!" said Rupert, feeling rather like an early Protestant questioning papal infallibility. "There's the root of the problem, right there. You can prove anything with statistics. Lies, damned lies and statistics. Ask Ivy, she spun numbers for the Treasury for years." Ivy was pulling a "don't-get-me-involved-in-this" face. "That 97 percent for example. Ninety-seven percent of what, Odile? I mean, did they poll all scientists? Including, ooh, I don't know, astrophysicists? Sociologists? Or did they just count so-called 'climate scientists' – defined how? Or maybe – as I suspect to be the case – they included only scientists who have identified themselves, in their published work, as having a view on the whole anthropogenic thing? Sample bias!" He prodded a piece of meat with his fork and transported it to his plump mouth. Odile, Ernest, Ivy, and Fulki looked at him, aghast. There was a brief silence; no one else chewed.

"I read an article about Al Gore's hockey stick projections," said Peter slightly nervously, but lent courage by Rupert's blatant apostasy. "You know, the graph based on tree ring data showing global temperatures over the last 600 years, where things really kick off in the twentieth century, correlating with the release of CO_2 associated with industrialisation and so on. It seems that was statistically dodgy too. Something to do with splicing the proxy data series with the data read off thermometers – which only counts for the data in the later years of course, the uptick part of the hockey stick."

"Well, I bet the article was in the *Telegraph* or some other Tory rag, aligned with industrial interests, big oil or whatever. Or you saw it on Fox

News. They're bought or unhinged, or both, a lot of these deniers," said Fulki hotly.

Peter thought better of drawing attention to the emotional loading of the word "denier", until recently reserved for hateful people who maintained that Auschwitz was a jolly work camp and not a place of mass extermination. It was, though, a bit much to be lumped in with these truly deranged, evil people – simply because you disagreed with the statistical handling of data relating to tree rings observed in bristlecone pines.

Surprisingly off-message Rupert spoke again: "Fulki, when I was a boy, my father told me that when someone indulges in insults or ad hominem attacks, you know their argument is weak. You suggest that scientists disagreeing with the consensus Odile just told us about are either corrupt or mad. But it seems to me that it takes greater courage to oppose a consensus view than to step in line. They are mostly academics, these scientists, only as good as their last grant application, many of them. Their career advancement is not exactly helped by disagreeing with their peers. It's not far from there to groupthink."

"But we have to have a consensus in order to take the action we must take. If you lose the consensus you lose the ability to enact the accords – look at what happened with the Kyoto Protocol."

"Here's what I think," said Rupert unhappily. "I think one can believe the whole man-made climate change, greenhouse gas, up to six degrees warmer and sea levels up by dozens of feet by the end of the century, cataclysm thing. But in that case the world needs to change radically. A few green gadgets, a bit of renewables just won't hack it. We all need to live in smaller houses, built quite differently; stop travelling long distances to work; especially stop travelling long distances to holiday; have fewer children; eat no meat; completely change our patterns of consumption generally – by which I mean reduce it, with fewer goods, less packaging, less transportation. As far as I am aware, no one voted for a package like that. If anyone even proposed one."

"And sure as hell no one here is putting it into personal practice. You holier-than-thou environmentalists are talking the talk but are not willing to walk the walk, as our American cousins are wont to say. At least deniers are not hypocritical," Peter finished.

"I'm actually kind of surprised Peter is a climate change denier," said Odile, emphasising "denier" and addressing the table, ignoring both Peter and Rupert. She was, in fact, much more surprised that normally reliable Rupert was a denier. "After all, Peter, aren't your mines busy digging up rare-earths or something, stuff that gets used in wind turbines and high-tech batteries and what-not? Surely all these efforts to live sustainably are good for business?"

"But that's my point,' said Rupert. "Where are the vested interests? Just as much on the renewables side as on the…"

"Odile, you don't know whether to damn me for being a denier or condemn me for being a profiteer! Either way, I'm a bad guy according to one or other of your dogmas." Peter flipped open the cover of his iPhone and began scrolling through his photos. After a couple of seconds he had found what he wanted. He held the phone landscape-wise in front of Odile and Ernest, who were seated next to one another.

On the screen is the image of a lone boy silhouetted on a spit of land forming a horizon about a quarter way down the frame. It is evening; the light is low and the sky coloured orange. The lower three quarters of the screen are occupied by an expanse of brown liquid, sickly reflecting the sky. On the brown surface skin, a disfiguring rash floats, pustule-like gas bubbles forming a discontinuous foam, a glutinous semi-permanent scum. Beside the boy, to the right, a large pipe angled upwards spews a torrent of frothing sludge; in the far distance, beneath the arc formed between this unremitting flow and the lake surface, an industrial skyline of flare-stacks, chimneys and cracking plant is just visible. It is hard to tell, but the boy appears to be wearing breathing apparatus. It is apocalyptic.

"Bautou, Inner Mongolia," said Peter. "Several square kilometres of opencast mining and toxic waste in a vast lake and tailings. Farm animals die, crops fail. There's a high incidence of cancer in the human population. Water table contaminated. This is the cost of cheaply produced rare-earths. This is the cost of our wind farms. We have exported pollution! This is the ultimate hypocrisy – real, actual, poisonous, direct environmental damage not requiring a single tree ring to be measured and squabbled over. I don't care who's right about global warming. We can do this so much better."

"What, your processes will not pollute, Peter? Pah!"

"No, Odile. They will pollute. Just much less so than at that mine at Baiyun-Obo. But at least you seem to have accepted that a large part of renewable energy is not really renewable. People like you, full of virtue" – he allowed his gaze to scan the entire table – "should take that into account." He was, if not shouting, speaking far more loudly than either the proximity of the rest of the group, or the acoustics of the room, merited.

"But…" began Rupert. Then: "Oh, what the hell."

Even if Ivy had possessed any notion of the issues on Peter's mind – oddly for this educated couple, Peter protected her from the sordid details of mortgages, credit card limits and such irritants – she would still have been shocked by his comportment that evening. There was no need for a nice dinner to be spoiled by this kind of confrontational, students' union, point-scoring type of conversation.

Later that evening, when the little group of Chatterers had dispersed and Ivy had finished loading the dishwasher, when they should have been feeling sleepy but content at a pleasant evening spent in the company of friends, both, in fact, felt a slight bitterness. Peter's clomping conduct had injected an acrid trace into the atmosphere, as though something plastic had recently burned in the house. An irritating and inescapable malaise bound them.

"I do wish you would be nicer to our friends, Peter. I know you like a good debate but, well, sometimes I think you could be, well, nicer..." she tailed off lamely, lacking the energy to focus.

"Our friends? Ha! They're all your friends really. And 'nice'? 'Nice'?" he minced, screwing up his face in a sneering, exaggerated nicey-nicey smile. "What, 'nice' like Ernest's 'nice'? Is that what you want? Eh? Me to be more like 'nice' Ernest?"

"Well, you could do worse. And maybe they are more my friends than yours, but you know all you have to do is invite someone. That's all. You're just incapable of staying in touch with your friends. That's why you haven't any." She was angry, she was tired, she was not herself; yes, she was intent on hurting him.

"Oh, you think it would be good for you if I were more like Ernest? How on earth, how on EARTH would you be able to live your life, d'you think, if you were married to Ernest. Do you have any idea about the money you spend? Any idea at all? You spoiled b—" He stopped himself before he said it. Bitch. He had nearly called her a bitch. The fact was that he really did not have any friends, not in the same way she had. But then he had no time, unlike her with her mumsy life and daily help and term time child-free leisure.

"I don't want to be married to Ernest. I just want YOU to be nicer. Sorry." She was in tears. "Sorry my vocabulary falls so far short of yours. Nicer, yes nicer. Not so rough, so bitter, so willing to personalise things..."

"I see. You want all the good stuff and none of the bad. A nice husband and one that earns enough to satisfy Ivy Mount Lifestyle Choices Inc. Well, wake up! He does not exist." Peter was angry, wounded at the "no friends" jibe, only partly aware of the nonsense he was talking, suggesting that nice people could not earn money, accepting that he was not "nice" himself, whatever that meant. Although he knew what it meant really, and he knew that too often he was not really it, not nice. Besides, he was concerned that he also lacked the financial musculature to continue supporting Ivy's tastes. What did that make him? Neither "nice" nor a good provider. A nasty Ernest.

Ivy was silently weeping. His instinct to take her in his arms and comfort her was no stronger than that to tell her to bloody well stop snivelling like the spoiled child she was. He stalked out.

Peter went back to the dining room filled with loving hatred, consumed by hateful love. Loving Ivy was the untold state of nature, their partnership following well-worn patterns requiring no expression. Life with Ivy had its own mute momentum. He simultaneously hated his anger and felt it justified. He wanted to hurt her to prove how he loved her. He wanted her to understand how he loved her, to realise how she loved him. He picked up the picture of Harry reading in an Italian garden, the same quizzical look on his six-year-old face as now when he read Carmen Laforet. The same thick shock of dirty blond hair fell over one eye, the same slightly pursed lips. He wished his children were not grown, he hankered for their holiday innocence, their unifying, moderating presence. He wished things would stay nice. That he could stay nice.

CHAPTER 3

The London Underground, August 2006

One heavy late-August morning, Peter was on the claustrophobic Piccadilly Line, half-crouched on the padded bolster attached at thigh-height beside the door – a sort of propping-up place which left the floor available for luggage. Probably in common with a significant proportion of his fellow passengers, he was just thinking "there has to be a better life than this" or something similarly self-pitying, when there was a sudden influx of young Italians. All insouciantly beautiful with sun-kissed faces, black shining hair and white flashing teeth and eyes, they appeared inexplicably keen to crowd around the doorway rather than obey the driver's tired request, "Move down the carriages, ladies and gentlemen, move right down."

This crowding, inevitable but not wholly necessary, forced a pretty Milanese 28-year-old so close to him that his head was wedged in intimate proximity to her well-formed upper body. Between Barons Court and Hammersmith, he was able to ascertain, at extremely close quarters and with great accuracy that, under her loose-fitting red-and-white striped cotton V-neck top, she was wearing a diaphanous black lace-trimmed bra and some quite expensive scent – Chanel No. 5 perhaps, or Miss Dior. Her breasts were smooth and firm and slightly shiny in the heat, the colour of acacia-blossom honey. When the train jolted to a brief, unexpected stop 100 yards from the station she instinctively reached out for the vertical steel handle slightly to his right, and for a delightful few seconds his face was physically in contact with her flesh, his nose nestling deliciously between her breasts. Miss Dior, most definitely.

Arriving in Hammersmith they struggled apart, making brief eye contact, him expressing a mix of apology and, he could not avoid it, pleasure; her, intriguingly, some sort of appreciation. She had lovely, uncomplicated dark brown eyes. *Probably she appreciates my not taking advantage of the situation, my British reserve and courtesy*, he thought, with no possible justification. They both got off, she with her voluble and excited group of students and him, that most lonely of creatures, a man alone in a London Underground crowd.

"So you're having lunch with your lesbo friend?" asked Emma. Ivy did not like stereotyping, particularly this crude, especially from her 15-year-old daughter. She frowned.

"Just use her name, Emma, dear, no need for her…"

"Sexual orientation?" asked Kirsty, the 13-year-old, helpfully.

"Is that what they teach you at school, Kirsty?" snapped Ivy, aware how old-fashioned and conservative she was sounding; but then sending the children away to board was not exactly in line with her centre-left orthodoxy either.

"Well, she doesn't like men, does she?" said Kirsty, smirking.

"She doesn't like Daddy at all!" agreed Emma. "Does she like you, Mummy? I mean…"

"Of course she likes me, and I'm sure she likes Daddy. Odile is an old friend. Full stop. The rest is really none of our business."

As their mother was out to lunch with Odile, all three children accompanied Peter when he went to buy the Honda, but only Harry had any interest in motorbikes – he was quite sure none of his Oxford friends had so cool a dad. The girls tagged along in the wake of masculine excitement and on the promise of lunch at McDonald's, where Ivy would never take them and whose food, therefore, had an additional forbidden attraction.

The showroom was located in a part of south London none of them had visited and involved a trip on the unfamiliar Northern Line, giving the whole outing an expeditionary feel. When they were not at one another's throats, the girls were a formidable team. Peter observed them, seated opposite him in the Underground carriage, one on either side of their elder brother, the better to torment him. They made an attractive trio, obviously siblings; the two girls animatedly speculating about Harry's love life now he was at university, Harry rising above their ribbing, the mature elder brother. Peter had an aversion to overtly proud parents – they brought out in him an ugly desire to point out the glaring failings in the objects of their myopic parental adoration. Once, waiting at the gates of the girls' prep school, he'd reduced a devoted mother to tears with a single derisive snort – true, the proud mummy had just outlined her darling offspring's overarching desire to be a ballerina, when the clumsy and hapless child tripped over her own feet and landed, bawling, on her spoiled little face. Ivy banned him from the school run when she heard of this incident. Nevertheless, as he sat watching his little brood joshing opposite him, Peter experienced a surge of paternal love and pride.

"She's from Madrid and is called Mathilde and she wears round glasses and reads to him in Spanish long into the evening," said Kirsty speculatively.

"That was last term. This term she's Chilean, a dark-haired beauty called Claudia who looks just like Penelope Cruz. He's all soppy about her, she's so *experienced*. *She* does *not* read to him long into the evening," Emma countered, poking the unresponsive Harry in the ribs.

The carriage filled at Clapham South and Harry stood to offer his place to a wizened lady in a sari, his tall athletic frame briefly sheltering her as she slipped into the seat. He was grateful to escape his sisters – by sheer chance Emma had hit quite close to the mark. Behind, a pinstriped young woman who definitely gave Harry a second glance, Peter sat quietly asking himself when his boy had become this poised and handsome man.

Despite his frequent statements to the contrary, it was therefore not quite true that Peter had never had a Tube ride he enjoyed; in fact here were two in quick succession. Both the pert, honey-coloured, Dior-fragranced Italian experience and this rare family outing were unusual and unlikely to reduce Peter's resolve to buy the motorbike.

They bought a Honda Fireblade. 1000cc of black and red shiny excess. James at work, the boring finance director, called it "Peter's dangerous toy" and Ivy described it as "a mid-life crisis on wheels", but from then on Peter travelled between his Chelsea home and the Hammersmith office on this overpowered superbike. His journey to work was a little over four miles on some of the most congested roads in the world. His bike could theoretically accelerate from zero to 60 in under three seconds, and had a maximum speed of over 200mph, but these were both wholly notional statistics for Peter.

Even when it was no longer a daily occurrence, he still occasionally had to use the Tube, suffering the slow, stuffy and complicated commute, requiring a change at Earls Court. It seemed to Peter so reliably unpleasant, with its hot fetid breath and insane shrieking noises – like travelling in the crowded throat of a pterodactyl. In the winter his fellow travellers all conspired to intermingle and share the prolific supply of microbes and viruses they had collectively brought aboard, and all means of ventilation were firmly closed, creating a steamy fug and a coating of condensed strep-tococcal bacteria on all the windows and hard surfaces. In summer it was unbearably hot, especially when the trains were full, which was always. On the Fireblade his commute was reduced to ten exhilarating danger-filled minutes, if one ignored the time spent donning and removing various items of protective clothing at each end of the journey.

Lonely Bear Bar, Mount Hood, Oregon, August 2006

Professor Palmer, Prof Pee, sometimes even Peepee when he was out of earshot, was the nearest thing Mount Hood had to an intellectual, although he was long retired and no one was quite sure at which university he had been a professor, nor indeed what had been his subject. It was generally assumed that he had taught something vaguely scientific at a minor West Coast establishment before retiring to the hills and hiking. A widower, he lived alone and spent his time on "community activities" and extensive nature walks. Although his age was unknown he was thought to be, and looked, ancient. A concomitant enlargement to his prostate offered his friends and neighbours a consistent explanation for the frequency and urgency of the visits to the toilet that underlay his nicknames.

The Trail 26 Conservation Society was Prof Palmer's idea. It was devoted not to conserving the road, of course, but to conserving the various wonders of nature in the countryside made accessible by the road: the wildernesses, lakes, hills, mountains and the things that grew, scampered, slithered and swam on and in them. The professor had originally called it "the Oregon Trail Conservation Society", under the incorrect assumption that the Oregon Trail of early settler legend followed the same route as the modern highway numbered 26 by unimaginative federal bureaucrats. It did not, and the professor could not recall who had drawn his attention to this embarrassing error. The name was quickly changed to the functional but less romantically appealing "Route 26 Conservation Society", later becoming "Trail 26" as a compromise. The professor did not know at the time but, had the Oregon Trail name survived, he would have had little chance of recruiting Hoxie Tomahas to his board, Hoxie being all too conscious of the history of that Oregon Trail, which brought settlers, soldiers, Whitman, Gilliam, and no end of trouble for his people.

Hoxie played a leading if unenergetic role at the Trail 26 Conservation Society, attending quarterly meetings and lending his name to posters and leaflets in public buildings, as well as giving periodic lectures. He gave his support to the conservation of threatened wonders of nature about which he cared little, other than in deference to his people's links to the land, and assumedly to its flora and fauna. Half-heartedly, he fought to protect the endangered trillium flower, an image of which, superimposed on a fine picture of snowy Mount Hood in winter, was the society's emblem. Hoxie was the one who pointed out the fact that the plant flowered in the summer and so the picture was a natural impossibility. Whatever.

The conservation society's meeting had been particularly boring, and Hoxie had gone down to the Lonely Bear bar for some deep-fried chicken wings and a beer or two.

It was early evening and the bar was almost empty. The sole other occupant was Friedrich, morose Friedrich whose girlfriend had just announced her ditching of him by the thoughtful means of a text message on his cellphone.

Friedrich was not, despite his name, German, but his parents back in Ohio liked to think of themselves as descending from this energetic and industrious people, although the family name of Hegel had never been traced to any real family back in Stuttgart. Friedrich was not a philosopher but a geologist, like his father. Neither had had, at any stage in their lives, occasion to research either their family tree or the great German philosophers – so it was by chance that he had been christened Friedrich, a wish by his parents to mark out their son from the crowd, not a desire to lay claim to some philosophical dynasty.

As Friedrich Hegel sat crying silently into his beer in the Lonely Bear bar on High Street, Government Camp, a well-padded Native American plumped himself down at the next bar stool.

"Hi." Hoxie proffered a meaty hand. "Hoxie."

"Hi. Friedrich." Friedrich did not abbreviate his name. What would it have been? Friedie? Rich? His dad had never approved of that; it defeated the whole exceptionalist objective of naming your son Friedrich in the first place.

"Friedrich? You German?"

"Well, my folks are. Originally. Hegel."

"Friedrich Hegel? You're kidding me!" Hoxie sprayed a mouthful of half-chewed peanuts on the bar, narrowly missing Friedrich. "Are your first two names," he racked his brains, "Georg Wilhelm by any chance?"

Friedrich recalled other people, smartasses generally, asking this question or something like it. The plump guy with the odd name in the lumberjack shirt seemed to think it all very amusing. Friedrich was not really in the mood to be amused.

"What if they are? What's it to you?" Friedrich looked forlornly at the witty sign attached at an angle on the wall behind the bar reading, "Leave me alone or I'll go and find someone who will."

"Georg Wilhelm Friedrich Hegel, 1776 to 1834, one of the greatest philosophers of all time, set down the ground work for Marxism…"

Yale guys have a justifiable right to show off. Hoxie had done a course in philosophy as part of his degree, and remembered a little of it. He had made up the years of Hegel's birth and death, but people seldom picked him up on such details, especially people in bars in Oregon. The words "dialectic" and "Marxist historical materialism" had lodged in Hoxie's brain; he had once written an essay entitled "The Colonisation of Western America – a Marxist Perspective" developing the case that the settlers were merely responding to an internal logic of capitalism, alienating them from their means of production or something. It hadn't mattered, it was a weak essay; Hoxie was keener on annoying his capitalist tutors and trust-fund fellow students than on learning. He remembered the earnest, bespectacled girl, the only communist in the class, asking him what she clearly thought a simple question in the tutorial, and his inability to summon up anything like an answer. He quite fancied the commie girl, earnest look and dungarees and all. The dungarees were paradoxically erotic, worn in summer without a bra, and permitting, from the right angle, the occasional glimpse of the curvature of an unencumbered breast. He wondered how far he might have got had he been able to give a high-quality dialectic-based response to her question. Well, he hadn't, and he hadn't gotten very far either. Racist bitch.

"Well, I'm pleased to meet you Georg Wilhelm Friedrich Hegel," said Hoxie. "Let me buy you another" – he nodded towards Friedrich's empty glass – "and we'll talk about… anything but fucking Marxism!" This was supposed to lighten the atmosphere as well as getting him off the hook of having to reveal, yet again, the surface-skimming shallowness of his Hegel knowledge. Hoxie was not an insensitive man, and even in the half-light of the bar he had noted Friedrich's sad mood.

"So, what brings you to Government Camp? Was it the lively night-life?" Another joke.

Friedrich sighed, accepted the beer placed in front of him by the barman, and made two decisions. One, that he would have to engage in conversation with this man, who seemed to be making an effort, and anyway there was no obvious alternative. He could hardly get up and mingle with the crowd. The other, that he would ask his advice about Kate, the girlfriend, the ex-girlfriend.

Although she had dumped him by text message, interpersonal communication was a thing for Kate. She had amused him for the duration of their relationship – fifteen months, eight and a half days, roughly – with some innovative ideas on communication. One of these had been never to ask advice on important matters from people who know you well. "They are biased, influenced by what they know about you already. They can't offer balanced advice. A complete stranger is far better."

It had seemed reasonable to Friedrich at the time, although as a result of this approach he had suffered Kate asking a man beside them in a line at Disney World, a lanky man in his mid-fifties, whether he thought she should give up college and accompany Friedrich across the USA in his career as a mine geologist. Once he was over his surprise, he had verified the question by repeating it back to her loudly, like a man giving a lecture fielding questions from the floor and trying to ensure those at the back of the auditorium had heard. The lanky man had looked Friedrich up and down and advised her against it. "You stay on at school, girl," he said. "Nothin' more important than education." He was right, of course, Friedrich saw that, but it did make for an awkward 20 minutes until they got to board the Big Thunder Mountain Railroad.

"I'm a geologist, a mine geologist. I work for Moore and Brice, mining consultants out of Portland. We're doing some work for the company that owns the mine up at Trillium Lake."

"Oh. I thought that place was pretty much shut down." Hoxie's mind was racing. His sporadic night-time activities up at the mine were beginning to feel both futile and irrational. Maybe this sad geologist could provide some substance.

"Well, yes and no. They have quite a lot of reserves, old stuff they mined years ago, but rare-earths are coming back big time. We're doing some work to confirm the reserves, the ones still in the ground, that is. I reckon it'll be worth bringing it back into production… " Friedrich was trying to think how he could possibly get around to Kate. Without her disarming spontaneity, her quick smile and pretty face, he could not bring himself to put into practice her unconventional ask-a-stranger technique. It was stupid, thought Friedrich, stupid that he needed her to help him understand how to manage without her.

Hoxie remembered that the mine was for odd-sounding metals. As a boy he had been disappointed that it was not a gold mine. In fact, the class had disbelieved it when Mr Jameson, their sixth-grade teacher, had explained that the earth up in the forest contained elements that were not visible to the untrained eye, not nuggets of shiny stuff. The output of the mine, once processed and refined, created materials with very useful and valuable characteristics, making them more costly than gold. Hoxie and his friends agreed that the mine was a gold mine, that they were being spun a yarn to make it sound boring and stop them going there to find loose nuggets of yellow metal amongst the spoil. As if in confirmation, Mr Jameson said he would try to arrange a field trip to the Trillium Lake mine, but it never happened.

When, a couple of years after, the mine had essentially closed, it confirmed to Hoxie that all he had been told was false. If these mysterious elements were so valuable, why was the mine closed? Of course, the closure did not support the gold mine theory either, but neither Hoxie nor his friends thought this through. They had long been in the habit of including the mine on their itinerary of apparently aimless walks. It was not a particularly dangerous place, the earth being scraped up from the surface rather than extracted from long, dark, ill-constructed tunnels deep into the hillside as they would have preferred. Of course, they never found anything resembling a grain of gold, and were chased off more than once by whatever staff remained at the site. Hoxie knew the Trillium Lake mine well. As a boy he had cared little, but it was an ugly opencast insult to the eye, something especially deplorable when viewed through Pocahontas-tinted lenses. Of course, Hoxie the Yale-educated adult was too sophisticated to be prone to such sentimentalism, but he still felt increasing anger at the shameless despoliation of what was once pristine, before the Europeans came.

"What do you mean, rare-earths? I always thought it was a gold mine." In saying this, Hoxie understood that in fact he had never thought it was a gold mine, he had never really disbelieved Mr Jameson despite what he said to his friends, yet here he was repeating his own convenient myths to a sad man whom he had just met in a bar. However, Hoxie was dissembling deliberately in order to extract more information. Trillium Lake was a local beauty spot, and the mine was only a few miles from it. Maybe he was a better trustee of the Trail 26 Conservation Society than he, or anyone else, had thought. He liked this idea; somehow it legitimised the anonymous acts of protest he had been making from time to time, under cover of darkness. Small, slightly demeaning acts which had been prompted by activities at the mine stepping back up, noticeable mainly in the form of increased heavy vehicle traffic down Route 26.

Friedrich kept thinking about Kate but what he kept talking about was the mine and his work, miserably divulging to a complete stranger professionally sensitive matters he would normally have known better than to reveal. He followed a bizarre derivative of Kate's "communication with strangers" strategy, travelling down a track of inappropriate communication of wholly the wrong kind.

Before Friedrich and Hoxie parted two full hours and several beers later, Friedrich had told Hoxie all about the rising need for rare-earth elements, explained the difference between heavy (HRE) and light rare-earth (LRE) elements, the lock the Chinese held on the market, the potential for environmental damage if things went wrong, and the potential for environmental damage even if things went right and the minerals were extracted and processed as planned, which Friederich had described as "the great big dirty secret of green tech". He also told him about the small British-based company that owned the mine and the rights to operate it, and the potential for massive fortunes to be made.

Hoxie never heard anything about Kate, his valued opinion as a stranger was never sought, which was probably just as well given Hoxie's own patchy record in developing and maintaining relationships with women. Hoxie never understood why this sad man with a long-dead German philosopher's name sat there, in the Lonely Bear bar, and gushed fact and surmise so informatively. But Hoxie Tomahas listened very carefully. He would definitely have to think of something more impressive than his "hiss and piss" campaign up at the mine.

Hungry Possum Diner, Mount Hood, August 2006

Jolene never had a chance with Brad. How could she? She never even expressed her feelings, never even got close to him except the time he cannoned into her in the corridor, rushing to some sports fixture or other. It had been she who apologised; he scarcely seemed to notice.

She had never been a smart girl. She was willing, she tried hard at school, but somehow things never quite gelled. Good-natured, even Jolene felt envious of her brighter classmates who lazily combined scholastic success with joshing inattention in class and homework sloppily completed on the bus home.

"You're a sweet girl, Jolene," her teachers said. "People do like you. And you have a lovely smile." She may not have been very bright, but even Jolene recognised faint praise when she heard it. What can a sweet girl with a lovely smile really expect from life, if that's the best people can think of to say?

Jolene even envied Brad, although she could not conceal her schoolgirl crush. Handsome, a year ahead in school, he played every sport available, apparently spending all his time on pleasure. Yet, it seemed, his taut pectorals and coiled-snake abs had their honed cerebral equivalents under his shining corn-coloured hair. After graduating from their high school he went off to major in finance, and had his pick from a coterie of eager cheerleaders. Crush or no, Jolene envied him. She started work waitressing at the Hungry Possum the day following her graduation. "No point in hanging around," her mother had said, leaving unspoken, "it's the best you're going to get."

Six years had not changed him much. There was no mistaking him, looking at the menu, fair-haired and tanned. Jolene's belly filled with little squirming eels, a nostalgic reminder of her silly unspoken feelings. Silly. She had heard he'd done well for himself, had his own house down in Portland. And wife. He had his own house and his own wife. She glanced out of the window and saw a flashy new SUV, the only car in the small parking lot she did not recognise. He was gesturing to her. Lifting her chin, she swallowed and walked over, order-pad in hand.

"Hi. Brad, isn't it? Brad Noah?" More words than she had ever addressed to him in nine years of shared schools. He looked up at her speculatively. Smiled.

"Well, hello!" He was determined to remember her name; "use of personal appellation" had been one of the things they were keenest on, and he had excelled in, during the bank's induction course converting finance graduates into sales professionals. "I thought you looked familiar!" Playing for time. Got it! "You worked here long, Julie?"

He took her in, from sneakers via apron to her uncovered head, hair held back in a ponytail with an elastic band. A Prospect. Never look at anyone, they had been taught, without seeing a Prospect. "How can you tell a Prospect?" Chad, the Direct Sales Techniques coach used to bellow, rhetorically. "It has a pulse!" the class roared back each time, the joke never palling. He smiled brightly. Jolene's silly little eels squirmed again.

"Jolene, actually, not Julie. Yes, five years, if you call that a long time. I like it. Can I bring you a drink?" He seemed not to hear her question.

"Five years, eh? Still living with your parents?" She caught her breath. Brad was showing an interest, of sorts. Probably just being polite.

"Yeah. I like it." Jolene did not notice how she kept saying she liked things, not exactly defensively, but things you wouldn't expect a 24-year-old woman to like very much. Clever Brad did notice though.

"There's some nice apartments for sale up at the library, near the elementary school. They look reasonably priced. You should get one. Cut the apron strings." Jolene looked down, doubtfully, at her apron. He hurried on. "I mean, you'd have lots more freedom. To do what you like." Jolene wondered what he meant. Did he know what she would like to do, had dreamed of doing for nearly ten years? She swallowed again.

"But I could never afford…"

"You'd be surprised, Jolene, what you can afford. With a little help."
He was smiling, looking her in the eye, using her name, ticking all
Chad's Direct Sales boxes. He reached into his shirt pocket and drew out
a business card.

Millennium Loans Inc.
Brad Noah
Senior Personal Mortgage Advisor

"Bricks and mortar, Jolene. Solid. Prices are rising at a steady 10 percent.
Y'know what matters with real estate, the three most important factors?
Location, location, location; nice places like yours will always sell at a
premium." It sounded like nonsense to Jolene, but Brad was so clever and
seemed to know what he was doing.

"I'm a bit worried about paying it all back, Brad. Piet only pays me $1,200
a month…" Brad had put his hand on her arm reassuringly, his face creased
into a sincere "trust me" frown as he looked her in her eye.

"Jolene, you worry too much. You get the tips on top, right? Let me
explain what I have arranged for you, Jolene." He was sounding a bit breathless and looked like he was expecting a drum-roll. "I've arranged," another
brief pause, "a 105 percent two-year interest-only capped rate mortgage
for you. You don't have to repay a penny for two years, Jolene, and your
interest rate is fixed at 2 percent too. And here's the best bit. You get to
borrow $157,500, 5 percent more than the cost of the property, Jolene."
He beamed at her. Now the drum rolls were over, a round of applause
was in order. Clever Brad had really pulled out all the stops for his former
classmate, as he put it, with questionable accuracy. "That covers the fees,
the first few months' interest, and leaves something for furniture, Jolene!"

He carried on beaming. He was quite surprised by her next question. So very few clients asked.

"What happens after the first two years?"

"Oh, don't worry about that, Jolene. What happens is… well, it depends. Normally the interest rate is reset and you start making repayments. But look, real estate prices are rising, they always do, so your place will be worth more by then. If there are any problems you can take out another loan – after all, your collateral will be worth over $180k in two years, Jolene. Worst case" – he looked at her with a "we-both-know-this-will-never-happen" look he reserved for moments like this. "Worst possible case, you sell the apartment and pocket the $30k profit! Not a bad worst case, right, Jolene?"

Jolene's loan went through without a hitch, just as Brad had said it would. She bought a two-bedroom apartment with a view for $150,000. It seemed a lot to her, but Brad had, after all, assured her it was an excellent investment.

Millennium Loans Inc. Weekly Conference Call, August 2006

Millennium's nationwide team of "originators" who signed up the new borrowers was organised in a pyramid of naked rivalry. Brad was part of the North-West Coast team. Great shame was heaped on the heads of those appearing near the bottom of the monthly performance table, who everyone knowingly exposed to cruelty and ridicule. For the high performers there was the possibility of acclaim, prizes, rosettes and visible rewards, on top of the automatic cash advantages of higher volume-related fees. It was not pretty, but it worked. Brad's regional manager, Thaddeus, embraced the system with gusto. He orchestrated weekly team meetings to keep the creative tensions high. The day after Jolene's loan went through, Brad dialled in.

"Hi Thad, it's Brad." He loved saying this. Brad was a high performer and liked to cosy up to the boss. His biggest rival in the region was a young Hispanic woman whose name, Immaculada, seemed ironic even to Thad.

"Hey Brad. Good, we're all on. I see you're over the half-million already this month, good goin' fella! Anything in particular to share with the team?" Thad did not believe Brad had any insights to share with the team, but wanted to offer him the chance to big up his achievements and make the rest hungrier.

"Well, I signed up a waitress earning $18,000 gross for a 2/28 of $160k. That's nearly a niner! Nine times her gross income! You wanna know how I did it? I got her to self-certify her tip income! She…" He could hear Immaculada make the short coughing sound which always preceded her speaking.

"Okay, Brad, fine. But she's hardly a NINJA, is she? I mean, she has an income, she has a job… maybe she has no assets, so she's just a 'NA'. Not like my unemployed Mexican janitor last week! Man, he was a real NINJA. He was a NINJAP! No Income, no Job, no Assets and no Prospects!" She laughed. "He was probably not even legally in the country and I got him signed up to a self-certified…"

"Yeah, we know, Immaculada, you got him a $250,000 mortgage to buy a hacienda-style property in Portland. But you played the race card, as usual. What do you call it? The Brotherhood of Hispanic Homeowners or something? Now, my waitress…"

"What would Chad say, Brad?" interrupted Thad, pleased to see the creative tensions still as raw as ever. Brad was crestfallen. He was just going to inform the team how he had played on Jolene's transparent infatuation with him to sign her up for a loan she would struggle to pay as soon as the two-year sucker period was over. A great example of "Easy-Peasey", Chad's Third Rule of sub-prime marketing, and he was going to have to cite it in support of Immaculada.

"Chad would say 'ECPC, Emotions Change Prospects into Customers', Thad," said Brad, through gritted teeth.

Brad and Thad, even Chad, saw only a tiny part of the picture, and only really cared about the bit concerning the share of the origination fee they personally kept from each loan. Brad did occasionally ask himself how it could make sense to sell doomed mortgages to people like Jolene, who had so little chance of being able to meet the payments, but hey, he was making out like a bandit on the fees, and Millennium seemed to thrive on this insane business.

Millennium Loans Inc had a very simple but most effective business model which, strictly for internal consumption only, was known as "V2-max". Maximise volume, maximise velocity. Write the business, skim off the fees, sell on the loans to Bear Stearns or someone else on Wall Street. Like tributary streams to a mighty river, all the loans originated by the nationwide army of Brads and Immaculadas flowed into the Wall Street reservoirs. Not that they stayed there for long either; Goldman Sachs and Morgan Stanley and the rest quickly blended them into pools to be diced and sliced and layered, then rated by the agencies, everyone taking their cut along the way. Then they were once more passed on like parcels in a children's party game. But, unlike in pass-the-parcel, these packages contained not a treat but something nasty, something denatured and synthetic. Something that sitting-duck investors ended up holding long term and that proved to be worthless when the music finally stopped. By then, any connection to Jolene, her apartment, her feelings for Brad, or indeed anything else real or human, had long been lost, washed up on the scummy banks of the mighty river.

Trillium Lake Mine, Mount Hood, Oregon, August 2006

Rick's third truck of the day noisily began the newly scheduled journey down the valley, the evening dispatch at 18.30, just when Amy liked to sit down with a vodka and tonic before dinner, on her veranda, amongst her nature. Three people took note. Amy, of course, primed and ready to be offended by any man-made sound. The second was Professor Palmer, who happened to be walking along Route 26 at the time the dump-truck took the curve, crashed its gears and roared its mechanical objection to the inexpertly slipped clutch – the driver needed more practice having been called back to the mine from a pleasant if financially stretched period of idleness.

Standing with his binoculars on a ridge overlooking the mine, the third person was Hoxie. He saw the trucks being loaded with anonymous-looking dirt. He saw Friedrich and several other hard-hatted men flitting around, in and out of a cluster of temporary office buildings and ageing industrial-type constructions. He watched as the truck left the mine in a cloud of black exhaust. Hoxie was back at Trillium Lake, evading the mine personnel like in the old days, but not at all like that – this time he had a real purpose, not related to finding imagined gold nuggets, but to finding real industrial intelligence.

Following his one-sided conversation with Friedrich, Hoxie had found himself unusually energised in a way that reminded him of his old self at various stages in his life – as a boy, when school sport had mattered to him and he had been a successful runner and swimmer; as a youth when, encouraged by Mr Jameson and others, he had known academic success unheard of in his school, success sufficient to win him a place at a prestigious university, and as an undergraduate, the only Native American in his year, awarded honour and praised. Positive experiences like these had been lacking in the years since Yale, and so had the energy and sense of direction they brought. Since the conversation with Friedrich, Hoxie was pleased to rediscover them.

Hoxie drove up Route 26 to Trillium Lake and parked his battered anonymous pickup in one of the tourist car parks, blending in with the other vehicles scattered around. He left on foot in the direction of the mine; it would be a long walk by his recent standards, but he wanted to go unnoticed. Hoxie enjoyed a little frisson of excitement at the thought that he was engaged in an act of espionage. Surveillance. Why were the words used in English to describe clandestine activities all French? Because the English wanted to distance themselves from such unsporting conduct probably, maintain their unjustified self-image.

The only Englishman Hoxie had ever met was Ambrose Cecil-Davies, a fellow student at Yale, also there on a scholarship. He was probably not a fair representative of his nation, but he had inspired a strong dislike of the English in Hoxie nonetheless. Because Ambrose was also majoring in history, they saw more of one another than either would otherwise have chosen to do. Ambrose was a brilliant student from Oxford, who had specifically targeted Yale for his third undergraduate year to benefit from the tutoring of a particular professor of international repute, and because he was brilliant, he got what he wanted – Yale was more than pleased to have him. Oddly, this put him and Hoxie in the same category – desirable, for different reasons, to have on Yale's student roll. In their contrasting ways they were both technically members of a minority group. However, there was no hint of sharing a common experience. Ambrose was from a bourgeois British family and had received the most expensive of private educations. He had a taste for fine wine, dressed in unfashionable tweeds, wore shoes specifically made for his foot by a bootmaker in London, who had also made footwear for his father and grandfather, as well as for Kaiser Wilhelm II of Prussia. His family lived in a large house in a country place in Wiltshire, but had a London house in Fulham and "somewhere in France". In the first days of their acquaintance Hoxie had been shown photographs of it all, including the horse-like younger sister, captured appropriately enough, astride a horse.

It would have been a touching story had these two very different students struck up a firm friendship, shared lodgings, visited one another's homes and astonished each other's families with their foreign ways; if they had laughed together at the unimportance of fate, fortune and cultures. But Hoxie was busy cultivating his chippy victimhood and Ambrose was a dreadful snob, arrogant and superior. As a result he came across to Hoxie as a racist, although in truth he was not. Ambrose was simply disdainful of anyone who was not lucky enough to be Ambrose Cecil-Davies.

Ambrose was a brilliant scholar whereas Hoxie was merely bright and hampered by his self-imposed over-specialisation. The ability gap between them was made all too apparent in tutorials shared and by grades achieved, and condemned their relationship quite predictably to founder. When Ambrose submitted a clever and provocative paper characterising the British Empire as a great civilising force for good, Hoxie was incensed. But his anger had worked against any chance he might have had of arguing in the discussion group against Ambrose's thesis, and he had appeared instead as splutteringly incoherent. Ambrose played to perfection the part of the patient and well-researched defender, with just the right amount of condescension. When the paper was published in the specialist review *History in the Making*, Hoxie's fury was complete.

By means of his personal exposure to this one Briton and the historical concurrence of the westward expansion of America with Great Britain's imperial zenith, Hoxie had come to associate the British in general with all that was wrong with, all that underlay, the past of America's First Nations. This was the colonial history by which he was busily defining himself. Of course, America was one colony that the British had lost long before Lewis and Clark clambered into their first canoe, but Hoxie reasoned that Lewis and Clark were of British extraction, most of the settlers were Brits, the language of the English prevailed… It was enough.

Friedrich had told him that the Trillium Lake mine was owned by a British company. He had told him that there was a strong probability

that the mine would be brought back into production. He had talked of
the great profits the owners were likely to make and of the consequences
of reopening the mine, which included a bigger scar on the surface of
the land. He had also outlined the sort of remediation that is normally
required of opencast mining operators.

Hoxie did not care to hear about remediation. What he heard was
about new colonial incursions, the rape of the land, the expropriation of
wealth, the destruction of peace. He determined that there would be no
remediation, because there would be nothing to remediate. Hoxie had
decided that he would stop this new intrusion. He didn't know how, but
this surveillance trip was the start of working it out. As he set off up a path
he had not walked since he was a lithe youth, a certain nostalgia, intermin-
gling with his new sense of purpose, coalesced into an uplifting, generalised
resolve to be active again, ambitious again; to take back control.

Hoxie, lacking any better ideas, stepped up his one-man tyre deflation
and urination campaign against the mine and its neo-colonialist owners.
As a history student he was of course fully aware of the Bolsheviks and the
landed peasants, *la Terreur* of the French Revolution, the Mau Mau, Pol
Pot and countless other examples of insurgency, violent protest, revolution
and counter-revolution. But Hoxie was not at all a violent man and liked
to think that the fearsome reputation of his ancestors was earned more in
reaction to invasion and land theft than to any genetic predisposition to
aggression. It was this that lead him to instigate his campaign of vandalism
in the first place, when he first noticed the renewed activity at the mine –
not, when he checked, new mining per se but heavy trucks, loaded with
ore from the stockpile, lumbering down the road.

In a resonance of the futile recreational-vehicle tyre deflation over
15 years earlier, it began with simple deflation of several huge-wheeled
and rusty vehicles, their tyres cracked and fissured like a puddle that
has dried. He had taken along his impressive hunting knife, intent on
slashing the tyres, but found their thick rubber walls wholly impervious

to his frenzied attempts, reducing him to using the valve, throwing the caps away.

His aim was to delay, obstruct and ultimately destroy the development of the mine, spoiling current and condemning future profitability. Hoxie could not think of anything else he might do which would be low risk to him, although he was keenly aware that his petty actions were unlikely to have the dramatic consequences he was hoping for.

Hoxie did not even leave any sort of explanation concerning his reasons for the night-time acts of vandalism at the Trillion Lake mine. Instead, he returned to the scene of his crime the following day, taking up his position in the undergrowth on a rise in the terrain which afforded him an excellent view of the mine and its main buildings, and found the vehicles all operating normally. A few days later, he watched as the working men re-pumped the tyres with a portable compressor, the job being done in a matter of minutes and with good humour. That was when he decided, with a feeling of depressed desperation, to add urine to the action. Hoxie could see it was a rather tremulous cry of protest, even after redoubling his efforts following Friederich Hegel's revelations. It would have to suffice until he plucked up the courage to do something more dramatic. Besides, it was not the immediately available representatives of Rareterre that he resented – actually, he felt quite neighbourly towards them – it was the distant board and shareholders of the company, resident in England, Perfidious Albion, that he wanted to punish.

CHAPTER 4

Jay Andersen was pleased with himself. Not just pleased with himself in general, which he generally was, but pleased with himself in particular. He was on the verge of doing what he liked best in all the world, better than sex, better than anything. He was about to close a deal which would make him a large amount of money, make his employer Bloom & Beck a very large amount of money, and therefore confirm to all his superiority as an investment banker, as a Master of the Universe, as a human being.

He glanced at lovely Lori Taylor, lustrous skin the colour of Java coffee beans, long black hair drawn back, nice full breasts perfectly presented in a starched white business shirt, very professional, except for one button too many undone.

Lori was undoubtedly the pick of the associates in the corporate finance department, the best of the 2006 intake of top-two-percentile, straight-A, Ivy League, Fulbright scholar, MBA graduate, gilded youth that annually clamoured to join B&B's overworked and overpaid junior workforce. Jay always got the pick of the bunch, always chosen uniquely from the female contingent – B&B was proud to be an equal opportunities employer on male-dominated Wall Street – and he always picked on the exclusive grounds of physical appearance. After all, Jay figured, they're all smart as hell, so why not go for the eye candy? With any luck, she will have low moral standards or – and this had happened more than once, such was Jay Andersen's superiority as a person – would genuinely fall for him, adding extra spice to long drafting meetings and gruelling business trips. He looked at Lori and winked. Out of habit he pressed the loudspeaker button on the star-shaped phone on the conference table to hear a dialling tone, double-checking he had indeed hung up.

"They'll sell, the stupid bastards! And they have no fucking idea what they've got. What I love about this" – he twisted his torso to look out of the 23rd-floor window, a movement he hoped showed his gym-honed pectorals to their full advantage beneath his Egyptian cotton shirt imported from Stephan Haroutunian of London – "is that they think they are getting one over on us! Stupid bastards!"

Lori had done all the research on the deal, had personally visited the mine in California, interviewed experts in the rare-earths field and reviewed all the literature. She had even employed a Chinese specialist to sift through the public and less public pronouncements of the Chinese authorities on the matter of export permits. She knew that the mine at White Crag was one of the biggest potential producers of lanthanides and actinides – rare-earth elements everyone from Toyota to Apple were desperate to secure for their high-tech products. She knew that the mine had been forced years before to shut down by a combination of economics and environmental and regulatory problems, and that the family that owned it was profoundly dysfunctional, rife with divorce and internecine strife.

Lori had provided Jay, the man who sat before her in the conference room with his Christian Lacroix tie and his $2,000 suit crowing about his anticipated triumph, with all the elements he had needed to pull off a spectacular deal. She knew this, and she knew his interest in her was neither wholly professional nor at all innocent, that she had not been picked out because she graduated top of her class at Stanford – but despite knowing all this she gave him her most brilliant smile and held up her hand for a high five.

"Yeah, we know the Environmental Protection guys and the Department of Defense are both on side and want the USA back to self-sufficiency ASAP, and the Hitchcocks think they're selling us a worthless great crater."

Jay, who could not think of a way of making the high five into a more intimate physical contact – there'd be time for that later – slapped her raised hand, managing to make good eye contact at least and, turning back to the phone, said, "Let's get Dick on the line and let him know."

B&B was the ultimate embodiment of free-market enterprise and dedicated to as unfettered a version of capitalism as was possible. Jay himself had expounded on the importance of "letting markets have their head" through an interview in *Barron's*, part of the "Young Turks and Wall Street" series that had included Goldman's 32-year-old head of proprietary trading, Bear Stearns' brilliant chemicals sector corporate financier and other youthful multi-millionaire participants in Wall Street's great transfer of wealth from its clients – both industrial and investment – to its own employees. They were just making things happen; nothing wrong with that.

Jay was 36, a managing director at B&B, and head of its massively successful Principal Investment Group. Adherence to free-market principles did not mean, in Jay's view, that the business people involved could not weight the odds in their favour, be it through contacts made at school or at the country club, or through the judicious pre-alignment of interests via the time-honoured brown envelope, or the more sophisticated trustee-held shareholding. Jay, to give him his due, was a diligent networker and always well prepared, thanks to the Loris of his world. For this White Crag deal, B&B had built a consortium with a like-minded hedge-fund manager, acting on his personal account, Dick Veroof, who would help with the finances and with various clandestine interests who could assist in other, more indirect ways.

Dick was the founder of Veroof Capital and had enjoyed great success, making double-digit returns for investors by the relatively uncomplicated means of leveraging his funds and buying and holding stocks in a rising market. Dick was not clever, but his self-belief, and an ability to spin a technical-sounding yarn referring to long/short strategies, stock lending, reverse arbitrage and riding the yield curve backwardation, plus the helpful market conditions, had brought him a positive reputation and a steady inflow of funds on which Dick charged a neat annual percentage plus a "performance fee" – "2 + 20".

Dick loved 2 + 20. He particularly loved being, with his confreres in the hedge-fund business, perpetually on the right side of a spectacular one-way bet – because 2 percent of a very large number is also a large number, payable annually. But, best of all, he got 20 percent of all the gains made above an undemanding annual threshold based on bank interest rates. Conveniently, he never paid out an equivalent amount if his performance resulted in a return inferior to this threshold. A one-way bet of massive proportions. Dick could not resist smiling to himself when he thought of this sweet arrangement. Can a man consider his clients to be suckers and yet serve them well? Dick certainly never asked himself this question, and even though he had amassed a fortune from the hedge-fund business, he still devoted time and his firm's resources to what he called his "PA business" – personal account deals too juicy to share with his sucker clients. Such a deal was the one he was hatching with Jay at Bloom & Beck.

Jay liked working with Dick Veroof. They understood one another and, more importantly, Dick was happy to make the side arrangements with the Little People, whose number included, in complete and assured anonymity, important but modestly paid functionaries in the Department of the Environment, responsible for many of the permits that govern and can therefore suffocate the operations of any business, as well as in the Department of Homeland Security, the most influential of all government departments in a terror-obsessed nation. In this way, Jay maintained what the CIA coined "plausible deniability". Although he liked to imply a connection with the security services to his younger, impressionable associates, he kept the plausible deniability doctrine to himself. Jay's self-preservation instincts were well developed, which was useful in the Principal Investment Group.

Within the nexus of greed that bound the firm together, participation in the deals of B&B's Principal Investment Group was the ultimate badge of success. Only Managing Directors qualified, and, functioning in the same way as the bonus Pool, the system was not in any way egalitarian. Such was the enriching potential of participation, that the partners jealously defended their rights; partner meetings when the newly promoted were initiated into this inner sanctum, or where retirees were bought out of their interests, were tense affairs, the air thick with pheromones and with alpha-male posturing. *Someone should film this for the Discovery Channel,* Jay thought to himself during one particularly confrontational meeting between his colleagues. *It even beats those buffalos with solid horn heads charging one another, and that's awesome.*

Lori knew about the membership of the Principal Investment Group. She knew she was years off qualifying, but she never questioned that she would, one day. In this belief she happily submitted to the 14-hour days, the lost weekends, the lost boyfriends, the unhealthy and intermittent diet, the whimsical demands for financial computer spreadsheets to be rerun overnight, Excel models to be built and rebuilt, the flirtatious, rich older men. She knew her efforts were enriching others, that her name was submerged on any work in the interests of others' glory – she knew all this and accepted it for her share in the avaricious dream that a future in investment banking represented. She wondered how much else she might be expected to accept. Wearily she dialled the direct line of Dick Veroof.

"Hey, wassup?"

"They're going to accept, man… and what's really sweet, they think they are robbing us!" Jay was boyishly buoyant.

"All the better. I look forward to seeing the look on that fat ass Fred Hitchcock's face when we start up production. Ha! One month's production of – what's that stuff called? Neodinnian…?"

"Neodymium," corrected Lori.

"Yeah, neodynniam, that stuff. Anyway, one month's cashflow at peak output will pay the whole acquisition price! It's sweet, baby! That fat ass…"

Dick liked making money. Better still, he liked getting the better of someone. This someone, the Hitchcock family who had owned the mine since the 1950s and were selling it after years of inactivity, had added the further spice, so far as Dick was concerned, by making a clumsy effort to hide some salient facts from Bloom & Beck, facts that should have depressed the value of the mine. The true reason for its closure had not been simple market economics, driven by Chinese over-production from the late 1980s onwards, of rare-earths. Everyone knew that the demand for rare-earth metals had massively increased, possibly stimulated by their low prices, but mainly because they were so damn useful for neat, modern high-tech consumer goods and environmental technology; everyone knew that the economics were about to come good again.

There had also been environmental and regulatory difficulties for the White Crag mine, potentially a far more intractable matter. The mine had ultimately been closed by the Environmental Protection Agency, not the Chinese. Most damning and most damaging of all was the "irreconcilable breakdown of relations with the authorities" that Lori had uncovered in the course of due diligence. Fred Hitchcock had been suppressing this information.

Hitchcock apparently did not understand the very human motivations of employees asked to choose between the interests of their past bosses and those of their future bosses. The fool – he thought he could outsmart the Truly Clever of Bloom & Beck! In a cool and wholly justified (to the minds of Jay and Dick, if no one else) double-double cross, Jay had dramatically "discovered" the withheld information he had long known, but only after he had resolved the problem for good via Dick's arrangements with the requisite officials. So, at the eleventh hour of the negotiations, a theatrically hurt Jay, an "I-thought-we-had-a-professional-relationship-and-this-is-how-you-treat-me" Jay had confronted Hitchcock, driven the price right down, but not quite so far as to risk losing the deal. Hitchcock still thought Jay was overpaying. Jay was getting a steal. Sweet.

"So, when do we close?"

"We've metaphorically shaken hands on the deal on the phone just now. We make a binding offer this afternoon subject only to credit committee[3] approval."

Jay signalled to Lori that she should get on with drafting the credit committee paper, bizarrely by writing with an imaginary pen in the air, rather like someone gesticulating in a restaurant that he wants his bill. Why the gestures? Was Jay trying to get her to leave the call? She recognised that this was, for Jay, one of the best moments, a chance to preen in front of a member of his peer-group. She knew better than to risk up-staging him in any way.

"Lori gets the lawyers to work immediately," he said with another gesture, more of a dismissive wave this time. "I get the Principal Investment Group together in a couple of days, you make the arrangements your end, we'll have it done by the end of the week, certainly before September's out." He watched with some regret as Lori's shapely form left the conference room. As she closed the door she heard Jay beginning to outline the potential deal risks. She knew them well – they were all set out in the credit committee memo, a draft of which she had placed on Jay's desk that morning.

Hungry Possum diner, Mount Hood, Oregon, October 2006

Amy had caught sight of the poster in the library, and there it was again in the entrance lobby of the Hungry Possum diner, dog-eared through people brushing past in their thick outdoor clothing, pinned-up between a public health notice about the evils of tobacco and, inexplicably, a tourist poster advertising the manifest baroque attractions of Bruges or Brugge. At the top was an artificial-looking picture of a large white flower shot against a snowy Mount Hood background, and the text "Trail 26 Conservation Society" in an old-fashioned font. The border was made to look like the edges of a walkers' map and in the middle, in smudged felt-tip:

PUBLIC MEETING 10/10/2006 7pm
Rhododendron Community Center
1. Proposed new camp site at Mirror Lake
2. Hiking Trail maintenance team
3. Clear Lake Spotted Frog population
4. Lobbying activities: Sen. Wyden
5. AOB
Coffee and soft drinks provided
All welcome

Amy took off her duffle coat and gloves and slid into the vinyl bench screwed to the floor rather too close to a worn plastic-topped table, set with ketchup in a tomato-shaped plastic bottle and mustard, each with an encrustation of hardened contents around the top. She asked her waitress about the Trail 26 Conservation Society. Amy knew this waitress from previous visits to the Hungry Possum, which she liked for the surprisingly good French fries.

"Jolene, what's this conservation society, the Trail 26 Conservation Society?" She had learned that communication with Jolene was most effective if she was given a conversational heads-up, a chance to prepare her answer.

"The poster in the entrance...?" she prompted again.

Jolene's expression passed from puzzled to relieved.

"Bruges! That's where Piet's dad came from. It's in Belgium. That's in Europe. That's why he has such a funny name…"

Amy sighed inaudibly and started again.

"Not that poster, Jolene, although I'm glad you explained it to me. No, the other poster in the entrance, the one about a public meeting on Tuesday. The Trail 26—"

"I, madam, would be delighted to enlighten you on the subject of the Trail 26 Conservation Society," said a voice from the next booth, "a matter on which I am something of an expert. If you will pardon the intrusion, I could not help but overhear your question."

Amy turned to see an elderly man dressed in thick twill trousers and, quite exceptionally for the Hungry Possum, a shirt and tie, and tweed jacket, all brown. Even his face was both the colour and the texture of a shelled walnut. He looked like he spent a lot of time outside being weathered by the sun and the wind, which he did. He also looked like he smoked a pipe, which he also did, his hide preserved by extended and frequent exposure to the smoke. His gravelly voice also betrayed the long-term effects of blends of Virginia and Burley tobaccos. He had half-risen to his feet, but had been arrested in his move by the difficulty of extracting a long, wiry and obviously somewhat inflexible frame from the vinyl bench too close to his own plastic table. Professor Palmer. Jolene introduced him.

"I am the founder and chairman of the Trail 26 Conservation Society, hence my apparently boastful preliminary comment, although I am not normally one given to self-aggrandisement. Indeed, the society itself is far from grand, a mere collection of like-minded souls who care for natural life, by which I mean the flora and, especially, fauna, in this particularly blessed corner of our fine country."

Amy enjoyed the English language and a well-turned phrase, but this was the most extravagant sentence she had heard since leaving New York, and a circle of off-Broadway artists and hangers-on, onto which Shane, and therefore she had occasionally hung. Even amongst these theatrical acquaintances such linguistic posing was tongue-in-cheek. She wondered if the long, wiry man now asking for permission to seat himself was kidding.

"If you have an interest" – he bowed slightly from the waist – "maybe I might join you at this table and offer any enlightenment you may require?"

"Please do!" She almost said, "Pray, make yourself comfortable, I beg you."

"Have you eaten?"

"I have indeed dined, madam, but would be delighted to partake of a cup of coffee and perhaps a dessert whilst you enjoy your meal." He apparently was not kidding, unless he held an unconventional view on how long to persist with a practical joke – quite possible given his Edwardian appearance. Whatever the case, Amy continued to be amused. She ordered a hamburger and fries, he a coffee and a slice of apple pie, which Jolene knew he would want without his asking, with custard rather than ice cream.

"This state is singularly well-endowed by Mother Nature, as you will have observed. Our county is home to some of the most beautiful and, in a Blakean sense of the word, fearful wildlife. The terrain is wild and rugged…"

"'What immortal hand or eye'…"

"'Could frame thy fearful symmetry?'"

"Ah, excellent, you know your Blake." Something lit up behind Professor Palmer's eyes. Amy was pleased to note that he was enjoying meeting her, a newcomer. Perhaps he seldom had the opportunity to discuss Romantic English poets of the early nineteenth century. Perhaps he was just lonely.

"Like most people, I know that particular poem. Or at least the first stanza."

"And the last."

"Yes! Probably that's why it is so well remembered."

"Well, that and the fact it is fine poetry. Although, of course, we have no tigers in Mount Hood, but we do have many bears of whom the same lines could be written."

"Well... 'Bear, Bear, burning bright / In the forest of the night'? Not quite the same. Far too much alliteration." They were both smiling. Her hamburger and fries arrived, and a stainless steel knife and fork tightly wrapped in a thin paper napkin. The professor took advantage of the interruption to make his excuses and headed off towards what he called "the lavatorium".

In truth, Prof Palmer was lonely. But so was Amy. Four months had passed since she had taken up residence in her chalet-style wilderness home; four months during which she had met many people – neighbours, shop assistants, librarians, waitresses. All people, she realised, who had not chosen to know her, but had been forced to by circumstance. Mostly people whom she paid, one way or another. Initially this had not bothered her; in fact, she rather liked the simplicity of these new associations. She congratulated herself on her independence, her adaptability, her distance from both past relationships and present ones, her splendid isolation. It was for something like this that she had come to Oregon. She could not however banish completely the thought that "success" was measured only in relations with, and to, other people: acceptance, popularity, esteem, respect, even fear. When she mentally enacted the imagined visit of an East Coast friend, for example, she knew that what she wanted to see between herself and the rest of the world were relationships of respect and trust. She wanted some sort of success that was not won by isolation, no matter how splendid.

Whilst he was away, Jolene placed a bowl of apple pie and custard on the table at the professor's place, caught Amy's eye and smiled. "Prof Pee," she said fondly, looking towards the bathroom. "Peepee. But never to his face." She wagged a finger. The bathroom door began to open. "He's my favourite customer, even if I only understand half of what he says." She smiled at him as he approached. "Aren't you, Professor? My favourite?"

"And you mine, dear girl, and you mine." The professor folded himself into the seat behind the bowl of pie. "Why, pray, were you expressing an interest in my little conservation society?" he asked Amy.

"Oh, well, I moved out here from New York to be closer to nature. If I'm honest, I was attracted by the name, 'Salmon Huckleberry Wilderness'…" Not for the first time recently she involuntarily conjured skinny Shane to mind. He was laughing cruelly, as he had so often, like the time she spilled Coke on her white jeans in front of a gang of his friends and, embarrassed, he had laughed with them, fuelling their mockery of his no-hope girl-friend. She swallowed. "I wanted to leave the big city. Didn't really research it much. Acted on impulse – quite unlike me. Anyway, I'm very happy with the change. Where I had a view of the apartment building opposite before, I now have a view of the forest and Mount Hood. I love to sit there, on my own, in the calm and…"

"Commune with nature?" Professor Palmer made a note that he would later, when they knew one another better, when it was less inappropriate to do so, gently sound out the subtexts in this rambling answer.

Amy went on: "Precisely! Commune with nature. The other morning, well, a few weeks ago actually, I was disturbed in my garden by a terrible noise from the road – I live fairly close to the highway – the noise of a really heavy truck, a dump-truck. I'd never heard anything like it before. Actually, I'd never noticed the road noise at all. Since then I've been disturbed daily, often more than once. I found out whose they are, these trucks, they come from a mine somewhere up towards Mount Hood, a "rare-earths" mine. It sounds silly, but they seem to be targeting the times I am sitting out on my veranda. Well, that seems to me like something a conservation society might want to do something about. I think peace is part of what we should be conserving in the region." Amy was surprised to find her eyes were full of tears. The professor was the first person with whom she had shared her problem. She hoped he had not noticed the tears; how could this stupid road noise matter so much to her?

Professor Palmer was sceptical, although he did not like to show it to his new friend. He had seen the tears, heard the passion in her voice. How could they do anything about road noise? Roads were public property, designed for use by motorised vehicles. Noise was an inevitable consequence. He had personal experience of the noisy old dump-trucks, in fact he had changed the route of his morning walk to avoid the possibility of encountering one. He knew that they were transporting concentrates from the mine at Trillium Lake. As a conservationist he was more concerned about the mine itself, in operation since before the world held strong opinions about the environment, even about opencast mining. But the road…

"Well, young lady, I suggest you come along to the meeting tomorrow and raise the issue of traffic noise under AOB. We would be delighted to count you amongst our number, and you will meet several people of like mind to yourself. We might even hope to prevail upon you to become a full member of the society."

Amy felt a small rush of gratitude, a warm feeling that someone else cared for her concerns, cared about her. And there was the prospect of meeting people with a shared interest, people she had not paid.

The professor went off to his lavatorium, innocently mumbling something about powdering his nose.

Community Center, Mount Hood, Oregon, October 2006

The Community Center in Rhododendron, as befitted the size of the community involved, was neither large nor plush. It was built with money bequeathed by a local innkeeper, but a dispute with his estranged but never divorced wife resulted in an unforeseen proportion of the funds being spent on legal fees, so an already small sum was considerably diminished when it came to erecting the building – and it showed. One large room furnished with cheap wood-effect folding tables, Formica corners chipped, which had been arranged by Professor Palmer and Hoxie into a square pattern to form an uneven pretend conference table with a rectangular space in the centre. Coloured plastic stackable chairs with grey tubular legs rested at unequal angles, owing to the effects of gravity combined with the bulk of some of the members of the community. Strip fluorescent lighting. One corner featured a small kitchen area equipped with an electric kettle and a steel sink, alongside a corrugated draining board stained with coffee and encrusted with hastily wiped cleaning products. It was a very communal place indeed, lacking the pride of anyone's ownership.

The pivotal meeting of the Trail 26 Conservation Society took place here on 10 October 2006. It was an event remarkable for the heavy rain and strong wind which buffeted them as they scuttled from their cars, but more so for the unusually extended discussion and its consequences.

Amy knew the public buildings of rural Oregon well enough to have gone to the Community Center with low expectations for the physical premises, but she could not suppress the optimistic mood engendered by her meeting the day before with the professor. Surely here she would find allies in her hoped-for battle to rid Route 26 of its noisiest traffic, to mount a successful campaign to have the larger, noisier trucks re-routed, banned, or perhaps replaced by smaller, quieter or more modern vehicles. She would be a leader in this minor yet important struggle, winning the respect of the other warriors, bonding with them. Judging by the chairman, the members of the conservation society were sure to be educated and cultured, the sort of people she would be glad to present to her New York cronies, if ever they came.

These hopes did not survive her quick survey of the room on entering, punctually at 7pm, jean-clad legs and pump-shod feet wet, unprotected from the driving rain and plentiful puddles. Although she knew she was no oil-painting – ("unless it was a Rubens!" Shane, her former boyfriend had liked to joke. "Y'know, you'd be quite cute if you lost a pound or 15" being the closest he got to a compliment) and genuinely had no expectation or even desire to meet any sort of potential partner, she had taken unusual pains over her dress, and even applied some make-up. Jeans, of course, are never particularly smart, especially not on a short, slightly dumpy woman in her early thirties, but Amy's were Giorgio Armani, a trophy from a week in Rome in her Bloom & Beck days. Under her duffle coat she wore a simple white cotton shirt, a silk Hermès foulard at the neck and a navy-blue cashmere cardigan. Smart casual, New York. A huge mistake.

She was surprised that the door opened directly into the meeting room of the community center, and that it opened outwards – the budget for the lobby having been spent on some lawyer's new golf buggy – and when she entered the wind caught it and threw it back against the exterior wall, simultaneously admitting a great wet gust into the room and announcing her arrival with a loud crash. Eight pairs of eyes immediately swivelled towards her. Six men, all except Professor Palmer dressed as lumberjacks as far as Amy could tell, and not in a good way. One of the men was Native American, a few points on the Body Mass Index score the wrong side of "overweight". One of the women was wearing what appeared to be a tracksuit made of an electric-blue synthetic material designed for maximum elasticity, two bands of white trimming up each leg and arm. The other woman could have been a cancer patient in chemotherapy, in which case Amy told herself she should be ashamed of her instinctive, uncharitable thoughts, or she might have been a butch, shaven-headed lesbian, which seemed far more likely given the facial piercings. Fleetingly, and quite unexpectedly, Amy imagined introducing Jay Andersen to any of this group, his accompanying her to this meeting; it was the first time Jay had served as her imaginary visiting friend – the most improbable yet – and it was not a successful image. She mumbled an apology, wrestled the door closed and removed her coat. It was the face-pierced Jess who spoke first.

"Oh my God, it's Jackie Kennedy returned from the dead to come to the Trail 26 Conservation Society meeting!"

Luckily, Professor Palmer was on his toes, metaphorically of course. "Oh, excellent, excellent, excellent. You made it, Amy!" He made it sound as if she had been frantically rearranging her diary to make space for the meeting, cancelling her tête-à-tête dinner with Hillary Clinton.

"Ladies and gentlemen, this is a newcomer to our community, a Mount Hood resident newly arrived from New York, and I permit myself to hope an addition to our little conservation society. Amy Tate. Please make her welcome."

There was a reluctant murmur of vaguely welcoming noises. Amy sat down on the nearest chair, which wobbled on its uneven legs. Clearly the meeting was just beginning. Palmer smiled encouragingly at her. The oversized Native American began to speak in a low monotone; it took a while before Amy realised he was reading the minutes of the previous meeting. It sounded like a hugely enjoyable affair where, amongst other things, the assembled group had considered what measures they should take to clear up the ground beneath ski lifts where skiers had dropped and lost items which were later revealed by the melting snows of spring, and constituted an eyesore for the summer-season hikers. They had decided to discuss the issue with the ski lift operating companies and seek their cooperation in sending out teams of local school children at weekends. Someone had suggested they might be asked to do it for free on condition they could keep the cool sunglasses they found. In Amy's mind, Jay briefly reappeared wearing a ski-suit and a pair of Ray-Bans, mouthing obsceni-ties at the oversized Native American, who, Amy noticed had an attractive, sculpted profile despite some excess flesh around the cheeks and neck.

For Amy, not without difficulty, playing the role of an interested observer, the meeting dragged on, more or less kept on schedule by Professor Palmer and the Native American, whose name Amy learned was Hoxie. He and the fearsome-looking Jess quickly surprised Amy by displaying an aptitude for logical debate and the possession of extensive vocabularies. She scolded herself for her prejudice. Furthermore, both seemed genuinely to care about the issues discussed and the fate of the Oregon Spotted Frog population of Clear Lake. The lumberjacks – none of whom were actually engaged in the timber trade, Amy gleaned (one was a teacher, two were local tradesmen and two more worked for the big hotel up at the mountain) – were also, it gradually emerged over the course of the meeting, thoughtful if ineloquent people. Hoxie was accustomed to couching his arguments carefully so as not to appear a single-issue extremist – someone at Yale had once accused him of being "a self-appointed American-Indian Robespierre" – but nevertheless Amy noticed the "protection of my ancestral lands" theme underlay many of his contributions.

Finally, the meeting having exhausted the topic of proposed amendments to the designation of protected areas in Mount Hood, a matter on which apparently the Trail 26 Conservation Society had been actively and successfully lobbying one of the State senators, Professor Palmer turned to Amy as he announced that unless there was any other business the meeting would close.

"Actually, Mr Chairman, I came here this evening to raise an issue which I think concerns us all, as residents of the valley and living close to Route 26." All eyes were on her – it was clearly quite unusual for there to be AOB, and far less so for it to be raised by an exotically dressed outsider. Amy wondered how long it had been since the Trail 26 Conservation Society had recruited a new member.

"It's noise, Mr Chairman, noise from the road. I am sure I am not the only one to have noticed that recently there has been an increase in heavy truck traffic, old heavy dump-trucks that make an intolerable amount of noise." Looking at their blank faces, Amy briefly wondered if she was making too much of it, if this was a petty matter, and she was getting it all out of proportion. Then she remembered the 45 minutes spent on whether the hiking trail maintenance team (three of the lumberjacks) should use gravel or woodchips to render muddy sections of the tracks less hazardous (conclusion: woodchips, they are natural and biodegradable). She soldiered on.

"I've lived up the road here for several months and at first it was idyllic, just what I had hoped for, really quiet and peaceful. I would sit out on my veranda and…"

"You bought the Franklyn place, right?" One of the lumberjacks, Jim the elementary school teacher, had spoken. Amy racked her brain, saw some of the junk mail she habitually returned to sender with the word "MOVED" angrily scrawled across the front in ballpoint pen, and realised it was mail addressed to Frank Franklyn. Frank had an unhealthy interest in war-themed computer games and hearing aids, judging from his correspondence.

"Yes, that's right. Well, it's quite close to the road at the point where it takes that sharp turn, and there's a steep slope just around the bend. I suppose the old trucks are underpowered compared to modern ones. Anyway, I had not heard anything like it until the end of July, but since then I hear it all the time." Amy considered this exaggeration justified, especially as her obsession with the disturbance of her peace was such that she literally did have it at the back of her mind all the time, particularly when outdoors on her veranda and in her yard.

"Two things. First off: can we really do anything about a road? It's public property and supposed to have trucks and things driving along it – we can hardly complain about that. Second off: now that fall has come, you won't be outside as much until spring and so surely the noise will bother you less?" Jess met her gaze. Amy noticed that she had lovely eyes – light blue and intelligent. Her face was pretty, well-proportioned with a nicely defined chin and jaw, a small nose. Amy wondered why she had shaved her head and had her nose, lower lip, eyebrow and ears (thrice on each side) pierced.

"Well, it's exactly that. They" – although she had ascertained that the trucks came from the mine some way to the east of her home, she did not know who "they" were, but felt unreasonably sure that malice played a role in their actions, malice and clever planning – "are probably hoping that no one will speak out until May, by which time it'll be nearly a year and they'll say 'tough, we've been doing this for a year now and no one has complained'."

Hoxie was observing Amy. It did not set him apart from his fellow frustrated man, or any fellow man, that he subconsciously checked her out for erotic potential even as he was mentally aligning his hatred of the mine at Trillium Lake with hers of its vehicular consequences. She was small and bookish, with her large eyes, slightly mistrusting, augmented by big round glasses. It was hard for him to judge her age. Sure, the jeans were a good fit and enhanced her shape, but there was a bit too much to enhance. The same went for the upper body, where the V of the cardigan produced a nice effect, but flattered curves which were part of too plump a whole for Hoxie's taste. She had agreeable smile lines and there was something oddly cute about her animated neediness when she complained about her lost peace and quiet – but she achieved only a middling score on his subconscious attractiveness scale.

He spoke up. "They can argue that they have been doing it for much longer than that. It's the mining company, the mine at Trillium Lake. It's their trucks. When I was a boy that mine sent ten or twenty trucks down to Portland a day. Worked at night as well." This too was an exaggeration, which had its desired effect of alarming Amy and, to a lesser extent, the others. He continued, "Although the road noise is very real, and I can see for Amy here, very intrusive, it is the manifestation of a bigger issue. Do we want the mine to start operations again? 'Cause that's what they're planning to do." Amy felt a rush of gratitude to this supportive, big man.

Hoxie had been wondering whether to bring the conservation society into his one-man crusade against the mine, and now seemed a good time to do so. Although it continued to give him something to get up for, a purpose in his life, he was not proud of his "hiss and piss" deflation and urination campaign, and certainly would not admit to anything so embarrassing and, above all, so ridiculously weak in comparison with its objectives. If only it had not been an opencast mine he could have collapsed the tunnels with judiciously placed explosives. Maybe Jess would have some ideas. Maybe this new Amy person might, although frankly he thought it very unlikely that someone wearing an Hermès scarf would be of much use manning the barricades. Hoxie really was no Robespierre, and although barricades had briefly occurred to him as a possible option – the mine was accessed from the highway only down a single track – but with all that earth-moving equipment on their side surely any effect on the mine would be very temporary indeed. Besides, although some form of revolutionary struggle was an attractive idea, Hoxie was not cut out to lead such a thing, having too high a regard for his physical well-being and his liberty.

Plus, the thought of the collective masses of the Trail 26 Conservation Society rising up in civil disobedience, under his leadership, or still more that of Peepee, was palpable nonsense on so many levels. Peepee was a grizzled old conservative, not a revolutionary. The combined masses of the conservation society certainly contained a majority of Republican voters, and anyway numbered a grand total of 32 full members, many neither young or vigorous, nor, as was his own case, in any physical shape for civil disobedience except perhaps in its sit-down protest form. Peepee was rumoured to be well connected in Salem and Portland; perhaps a subtle political campaign drawing on these connections would be effective? This new New Yorker, this Amy – she looked rich at least and had an admirable if slightly unbalanced determination about her. Perhaps she could pull some strings somewhere? Hoxie had been over his options so often and had always ended up right here: nowhere. He would see whether the combined brain power gathered in the Rhododendron Community Center tonight was able to help.

"The mine is opencast. That means they create great scars on the surface of the land, take what pleases them and ship it off to be processed – in your trucks, Amy. But not before they grind it down, douse it in acid, boil it up and drain out the concentrated stuff, leaving God knows what at the mine site. What we do know they leave behind is a denuded terrain, no trees, nothing growing there, no animals. A scar." The rain lashed the windows. There was silence. In his youth Hoxie would have added something like "my people knew about sustainable use of land. For countless generations we lived in harmony on these lands. These scars are like scars on the face of an old friend." No need to overdo things.

"I am assuming that such an enterprise is fully covered by appropriate licenses and permits. As Jess says about the road noise, it's difficult to envisage what our little group can achieve against perfectly legal activities," said the professor. "I have seen the mine. It is on the route of a walk I take past the lake and into Salmon River Meadows. It's certainly not attractive, but it is away from most things and well-concealed by the trees of the surrounding forest."

"Well, we're supposed to be 'working to conserve Oregon's flora and fauna as they are: beautiful'," said Piet De Keersmaeker, lumberjack proprietor of the Hungry Possum diner, quoting the motto of the Trail 26 Conservation Society. "This mine seems to be destroying it. The fact that it's being done in secret, behind the cover of the trees, seems to me relevant. Most criminals try to hide their crimes."

Even Hoxie felt that accusing the mine operator of a crime was pushing it a bit far, and as for secrecy – they were sending three very indiscrete 15-ton dump-trucks a day down Route 26, for Piet's sake! But of course, there were crimes against other things than the law. Against Humanity. Against Reason. Against the Environment.

"It's a British company, Rareterre Limited, the operator," said Hoxie quickly, wanting to maintain the tempo, build on Piet's points, and keen to share selected highlights of what he had learned from Friedrich Hegel. "Based in London, thousands of miles away. What do they care about Oregon and its environment? For them it's just a resource to be exploited! The metals they are extracting" – he made it sound like a painful piece of dentistry – "are widely available in China. We don't need to scrape up our rare-earths here in Mount Hood at all. It's all about money and damn the locals, like Amy here, like us. So what if they have permits, law on their side? In these circumstances the People need to take some direct action.

Fight for what's right." Hoxie was in fine rabble-rousing form. Wisely, he did not mention the proletariat, but he had definitely pronounced that "the People" with a capital "P". "Direct action", "the People" – you had to be careful how far you went in Oregon; the Trail 26 Conservation Society was hardly the Rote Armee Fraktion.

Nevertheless, to everyone's surprise, Clackamas County's answer to Andreas Baader, Professor Palmer, pitched in: "Well, of course, our nation was founded on a massive act of civil disobedience, the War of Independence, and it all started with a most excellent instance of direct action, the Boston Tea Party. We indubitably have powerful precedent on our side."

The discussion went on well beyond the conservation society's normal timetable. Everyone enjoyed the debate enormously – Amy had stimulated more passion than their little group had experienced since 1996, when Professor Palmer had mistakenly understood that the Outlook Hotel up the road, which had played a starring role in a memorable Jack Nicholson film, was to be changed into The Shining Theme Park, complete with Disney World style attractions including a log-flume ride down rivers of blood in the hotel corridors.

No one actually proposed a car-bombing campaign or suggested the taking up of arms against the colonialist–capitalist running-dog British despoilers of the environment. In fact, no one proposed anything in any way practical and Hoxie continued to keep quiet about the urination and deflation, but at least he had made a start.

For Amy, the evening went better than she could possibly have hoped. For the first time she felt she had allies against the trucks – even if they were motivated more by hostility to the mine than the vehicles. These people, so unprepossessing at first sight, were great – especially the big Native American with the noble profile and excellent vocabulary. Few in her previous life had been so supportive of things that mattered to her, not even those who should have been, not even Shane – especially not Shane. And as for Jay, she didn't care what he would say if ever her fantasy introduction between them took place, that snob, that money-obsessed snob.

That was when Amy had her idea.

Amy Tate's house, Mount Hood, Oregon, October 2006

Amy read about Bloom & Beck's acquisition of a North Californian rare-earths mine online in the *Wall Street Journal* – for some reason her B&B employee's subscription had not been cancelled when she left the firm. Although she had been employed at B&B for skills unrelated to finance, she had developed the habit of reading the financial press whilst working there and kept it up out of habit and in the hope of better managing her small fortune, the income from which now supported her. She knew Jay Andersen, widely and admiringly quoted in the article, from having worked for him on many occasions. Owing to her slightly nerdy home-liness, Amy never suffered Jay's sex-fuelled advances and maybe because she was not a potential professional threat, as were the other senior bankers, nor a potential rival, as were the junior males, nor potential conquest, as were the younger, slimmer females, Amy and Jay's relation-ship had been surprisingly good. The *Journal* article was a long and detailed one, of the sort prepared over weeks. It outlined the attractions and history of the rare-earth business, the dynamics of China on the supply side and the technology industries on the demand side. Amy began reading the article mainly because Bloom & Beck's name appeared in the strapline:

There's rare-earths in them thar hills!
Consortium buys into a modern-day gold rush
Interview with Bloom & Beck's star dealmaker Jay Andersen

The journalist had done a thorough job; she had played to Jay's narcissism – indeed the article was positive overall, Jay's reputation further burnished. As a good journalist, though, and as an attractive woman below 30 and not above a spot of flirtation in the interests of the story, she had managed to extract more detail than Jay would ideally have revealed, including information on the possible competition, and on the environmental challenges facing the mineral extraction business. What really caught Amy's attention was this:

```
... but the consortium will have to work for their
pay-day, and will not have the field to themselves. For
one thing, the White Crag mine has a chequered history
of waste water contamination and other pollution
infringements. B&B's Andersen described himself as
"intensely relaxed" with the mine's prospects for
future EPA (Environmental Protection Agency)compliant
operations but offered no detail. Certainly there will
be a costly refurbishment, the White Crag processing
plant has been idle for over a decade, and no one
wants a repeat of the arsenic and heavy metal leaching
that occurred in the early 1980s.
      Although it is probably the biggest deposit of
rare-earth elements outside China, in addition to the
Chinese, White Crag will face competition closer to
home. London-based Rareterre plc owns, operates and
plans to bring back into full production a smaller
but potentially higher-yield mine in Oregon, the
Trillium Lake property. Trillium Lake was mothballed
around the same time as White Crag, because the
prices for their oxides and the metals made from
them collapsed making this mine uneconomic too. But
```

Rareterre's mine never had the added EPA issues and
so can be faster to re-enter production. Add to this
domestic competition the large mines in Australia
and the smaller warlord-operated mines in parts of
Africa, and Bloom & Beck may be sitting pretty but
perhaps not quite as pretty as Jay Andersen would
have us believe.

Mount Hood, Oregon, November 2006

Amy's idea was evolving into "The Plan". She had a great feeling of support from the Trail 26 Conservation Society. The cold fall weather kept her off her veranda, yet Amy was no more at peace with the noisy mine vehicles on Route 26, which she observed had again increased in frequency.

Rick was sending five trucks a day down Route 26 now, as his ageing concentration plant was being brought gradually back into commission. There were plans for a full refurbishment of the plant and, since the summer, Rick had been host to a small crew of consultant engineers and metallurgists to accompany the geologists who had been busily surveying, drilling and assaying for over a year. All Rick had received by way of forewarning of the consultant engineering team's arrival was a two-line email from his distant boss Olivier, merely informing him that a nameless group of "six to eight metallurgists and engineers from Scythia Engineering Solutions (SES) will be spending a period of time looking at the concentration plant etc." and requiring him to "show them the requisite hospitality". Rick did not know whether this meant he should book them hotel rooms or arrange to take them to the pole-dancing club in Rhododendron. Luckily, he opted for the former.

Rick considered himself – quite wrongly – to be "a pretty broad-minded kinda guy" but he could not remember the last time there had been a woman on-site at Trillium Lake. Even his own wife had never been there, despite his 20-year tenure. Many of the "offices" were adorned with glossy images, detached from magazines, of photoshopped fantasy babes in poses of gynaecological rather than aesthetic interest. There were no dedicated ladies' toilet facilities. Yet one still August afternoon a ludicrously proportioned SUV containing six qualified engineers, all women, turned up outside Rick's Portakabin kingdom. Rick watched in disbelief as the massive car disgorged its occupants and, led by an impressive Amazon named Helen Fry, formed up in pairs, black laptop bags slung over their shoulders, and advanced up the rough wooden steps constructed as a temporary measure 15 years before. Sam, who happened to be passing and witnessed the alien invasion, stopped, mouth open, staring in a way that, had it been less childlike, could have been quite offensive. Someone on a backhoe wolf-whistled across the rocky yard. Helen Fry, with aplomb gained from much practice on innumerable male-dominated mining-related sites, flipped him the bird without even deigning to turn or slow down. Rick was admiring and fearful in equal measure.

They got themselves sorted out quickly, the geologists from Moore & Brice willingly making space for the exotic engineers from SES in the big, caravan-like temporary offices, which for the first time in years were nearing full capacity. Friedrich Hegel found himself sitting opposite Helen Fry, laptops back-to-back across the battered melamine table that served as a desk. It cheered him up no end.

CHAPTER 5

Mineral and Mining Conference, Hotel Georges V, Paris,
November 2006

Carl Betts, Rareterre's chief mineralogist, and Stacey East, Hamlyn Securities'
equity research analyst, bumped into one another in the lunch buffet queue
on the second day. As with most international congresses held in major
hotels and attended by thousands of spoiled international executives, service
providers and commentators, supplying food to everyone's satisfaction posed
such insurmountable challenges that even the French, even an establishment so reputable as the Georges V, really rather gave up on the task. In the
USA, the classiest of venues see nothing wrong in offering delegates "packed
lunches", with their tawdry components of white bread sandwiches filled with
mystery-meat, a pack of fluorescent corn chips and a nondescript pastry-type
dessert all too visible in flimsy transparent plastic boxes – yet still the overfed
attendees would hustle to secure one. But this was France, and eating had
to be taken more seriously than that. There was a buffet, with big steaming
silver serving counters manned by ill-mannered and ill-tempered hotel staff,
in vaguely ridiculous uniforms. Stacey wanted the boeuf bourguignon but
without *pommes vapeur*, and was met with an uncomprehending and hostile
stare when she asked for this in her Lancashire-accented English.

"Just the meat, please."

"Sorree, Mam'selle?"

"No potatoes for me, please. Seulement viande." Her schoolgirl French was mispronounced but comprehensible. He withheld the plate, just out of her reach, trying to appear puzzled but actually looking quite pleased. Stacey thought it all rather stupid, especially as she had just seen the same server, Jean-François from his lapel badge, refuse extra potatoes to a rather corpulent delegate from Montreal who certainly had no linguistic problems. Carl, who both fancied her and himself as a linguist, jumped in to help.

"*Ce que cette charmante jeune femme veut dire, c'est qu'elle voudrait que du boeuf, pas de pommes de terre, s'il vous plaît.*" He was quite fluent, admittedly, but Stacey had not understood the bit about "charmante jeune femme" at all, so that was wasted. Jean-François, a surly young man with a bow tie, white apron and big serving spoons, took in and correctly assessed the situation instantly. He was from La Rochelle, his father was a committed communist, he had been immersed in the politics of the class struggle since infancy. He hated Paris almost as much as he hated his smug George V customers. He was not about to let this self-satisfied, smart-suited, grey-haired capitalist *rosbif* get his way, now or later, if he could possibly help it.

"Sorree, Sir. I don' unnerstan'." Jean-François knew that there was nothing more annoying to *un anglais* who speaks French fairly well, than a response in the English language which indicates a near total ignorance of it. It says: "You obviously think you have just spoken to me in rhyming couplets or something. I shall imply that my lamentable English is still better than your French, you show-off." He shrugged his shoulders and pulled a face, which said, "I'd like to help you out but, because of your poor communication skills, we have no means of progressing. Now stop trying to impress the girl and just take the stew and potatoes, like everyone else."

Up to this point Stacey had not been in the least bit impressed. She was standing in a queue of rather badly dressed mining executives – admittedly, Carl was an exception there; he had expensive, budget-stretching tastes including a liking for Savile Row suits – in a frankly over-the-top Louis XIV gilt-and-stucco, out-proportioned dining room. It looked like

Marie Antoinette's wedding cake. She had just sat through a morning of excruciating presentations on the radioactive challenges of co-extraction of rare-earth elements with uranium, the virtues of on-site ore separation and concentration, and one by Carl on the importance of accuracy in reserves estimation (Rareterre being in this regard a paragon of virtue, the audience was informed). She did not particularly like boeuf bourguignon, but the other choices on offer were even worse. She was hungry but on a diet in preparation for her wedding. The room was too hot. The young man serving the food was a stroppy git who had just performed a textbook Gallic shrug. This Carl, whom she knew slightly, was at least trying to be helpful. Resignedly, she took Jean-François' proffered plate, potatoes included. Little victories like this over the bourgeoisie made Jean-François' day.

The corpulent Canadian, whom Carl knew well, was making his way to an empty table.

"Hey, Michel! You wanted more *pommes vapeur*? Here!" Carl took Stacey's plate and deftly transferred the potatoes, making sure that Jean-François witnessed this. They were, all three of them, highly paid, highly educated senior professionals in their selected disciplines; all three were unbecomingly pleased with this petty dénouement. This little double victory over the surly staff of the George V was the flimsy basis upon which Carl managed to entice Stacey into his room, and his bed, that afternoon. That and the programme of presentations scheduled, the highlight of which appeared to be a discussion of developments concerning the US Federal Mine Safety and Health Act of 1977, as amended by the Mine Improvement and New Emergency Response Act of 2006.

Western Australia, November 2006

Whilst Stacey was engaged with Carl in excessively energetic and, for her, painfully unpleasurable carnal gymnastics, Dan Groundcherry, the man to whom she was engaged to be married, was in Australia. Dan and Stacey were colleagues at Hamlyn Securities, both equity analysts in the mining and mineral group, of which he was European Team Leader. The long hours demanded by their shared profession, hours often spent in one another's company, limited their access to a normal or healthy social life. Neither was naturally very gregarious anyway, geology and mineralogy being disciplines which attract the differently sociable. In the sexual attractiveness ratings game, she easily out-ranked him, being a 6 (Bo Derek, famously, being a 10) to his 4. But he was richer, wittier and a little bit exotic, being of some indefinable Middle Eastern extraction – that surname was his grandfather's choice on applying for British citizenship; he had seen it on a fruit stall and thought it sounded both reliable and friendly. Dan was good at his job and Stacey admired his work – well-researched and nicely written booklets on little-known companies, analysis which was supposed to help clients make smart investment decisions. Their relationship developed almost out of necessity, her biological clock ticking away. For each of them the sheer convenience of the thing seemed to offer compelling enough a rationale to compensate for the lack of the emotional pull to which others, particularly with healthier work–life balances, responded.

Dan and Stacey, and their many colleagues analysing companies for investors in the "sell-side equity analysis" game, made good money by a most indirect means. Their work, if it was good, was used by their firm's equity sales team to persuade clients to invest in shares and trade them through the stockbroking part of their integrated investment bank. The trading gave rise to dealing commissions, small percentages on the value of the shares traded, but small percentages of big numbers add up very fruit-fully – all those little gold snippings hoovered up, melted down, quickly becoming ingots. It was not just the quality of the research that caused an institutional investor to favour one broker over the others – the personal relationships with the equity sales teams, diligently nurtured through many blood-spattered grouse moors, Michelin-starred nosh-shops and sleazy lap-dancing bawdyhouses, were equally if not more important.

The little shards of gold left in the slipstream of the institutional trades are, of course, taken from the pockets of the pension-plan member whose paltry savings, agglomerated with those of thousands of their workhorse kind, the institution is managing. No one should worry unduly about that though, so long as the lap dancers have nice tits.

Apart from the Chinese companies, obscure, state-owned yet mysteriously listed in Shanghai, and several minor companies trading on regional Canadian exchanges, which Hamlyn did not regularly "cover" by publishing analysis, the universe of public rare-earth companies was small. Rareterre plc, with its promising heavy rare-earths mine in Oregon, was conveniently based in London and well covered by Hamlyn and its competitors. REM – Rare-Earth Metals AS – a larger Norwegian company quoted on the Oslo exchange with more diverse and well-established interests, mainly in the less valuable light rare-earths, was covered only by specialists like Hamlyn and a couple of others in London, and some local Scandinavian banks. Finally, C. Brown Pty., whose large Western Australia site housed a rich deposit of both LRE and HRE, was covered by the same London analysts and some in Australia and the USA. Only Hamlyn, as the leading sector specialist, covered them all and Stacey's work was considered influential and respected as being well-researched and well-informed.

The good analyst is really worth his weight in gold snippings, however, when his skills are deployed in support of his colleagues in the corporate finance and Mergers and Acquisitions – M&A – departments, for here the gold comes already stacked up as shining, hallmarked kilobars. The in-depth knowledge of the industry brought by the specialist analyst, coupled with a combination of an aggressive and bonus-hungry investment banker and an ambitious or desperate corporate client gagging to do a deal, is a high-octane fee-generating mix. It was on such an assignment that poor, overworked, high-income, cuckolded Dan was standing in the middle of a huge building site in Western Australia, red earth swirling around him in the wind. He was accompanying his investment-banking colleague Montagu Montagu (whose parents, Dan reflected, must have had a strange sense of humour) on an initial relationship-building trip to C. Brown's huge rare-earths mine and its new concentration plant construction site.

The concentration plant was going to be the biggest in the world, several orders of magnitude greater than Rareterre's modest and ageing plant at Trillium Lake. It was also budgeted to cost an equally impressive multiple of the sum that had been pencilled in for Rareterre by its board, even after they had been forced to revise it upwards twice. Montagu, or "MNM" as his friends and colleagues called him – his middle name was Nicodemus – was hoping to win C. Brown as a generous fee-paying client. The financing of the concentration plant was going to require some $100 million more than C. Brown's existing resources. The money would be raised through a London listing of their shares, perhaps, alongside their less prestigious but timezone-complementary Australian Stock Exchange quote. C. Brown would also require M&A advice – the Chinese were rumoured to be interested in building a stake, meaning the company might be ready for some highly priced bid-defence advice. MNM was determined to propose to the CEO of C. Brown whatever he could bloody well think of so long as there was a deal and a fee in it.

MNM, like all his colleagues in investment banking at Hamlyn, was paid what he considered a modest salary of £120,000 but got to multiply this, subject to his bringing in deals and the associated fees. "One eats what one kills," he told his horrified father, a Classics professor who specialised in the philosophy of Plato; "One is only as good as one's last deal." Professor Montagu, who lived in rooms and dined in hall at his Cambridge college, and therefore had little contact with or use for the stuff, had always considered money to be a necessary evil and really rather vulgar, yet here was Montagu, his only son, telling him proudly of his annual earnings, and in such terms as made him picture a blood-smeared

Neanderthal hunter-gatherer, not a highly qualified professional. If only young Montagu, who had read both Latin and ancient Greek since the age of 11, had continued with the medieval history he had studied so diligently. His work on Thomas Aquinas and the *philosophia perennis* had shown such promise.

"We could fucking beat any team from Bloom & Beck, fucking show them who has the biggest *cojones*," MNM, the Thomistic philosopher, was saying to Bruce Shaw, no-nonsense CEO of C. Brown, as a huge low-loader bearing reinforced steel girders rumbled past dusting them all with fine red earth. Prim and scholarly at home, Montagu liked the Aussies, he loved their earthy ways, their foul mouths. He quickly adapted his own style to fit in with theirs. "No one bloody well knows more about the rare-earth sector than our specialists at Hamlyn. Like Dan here." Dan had noticed that MNM's mouth when he voiced the word "fucking", which seemed to be pretty much all the time in this hemisphere, was strikingly similar to the mouth of the round cartoon-character candy on the front of a pack of M&Ms. This thought so amused him that he was not listening to what MNM was saying, just watching the mouth and hoping for another obscenity. He got the "like Dan here" bit, and hurriedly tried to recall what had gone before.

"Dan, I was just telling Bruce about those wankers at B&B," prompted Montagu.

"Oh, have they been pitching for the M&A role? The financing?" asked Dan.

"You bet your sweet arse they have," said Bruce, who loved to wind up bankers of every kind and nationality. Bastards deserved it, stuck-up gits the lot of them. This Montagu character seemed okay though. Salt of the bloody earth, despite the poncey name.

"Well, that really is quite wrong of them, quite inappropriate. I hope you didn't give them any confidential information. I hear they are major investors in the consortium they put together to acquire the mine at White

Crag in California, not just advisors. They'd be conflicted, big time." Bruce was impressed.

"Wow, I didn't know that. That's serious. Hey, you're good."

"We're better than good, Bruce, we're fucking awesome!" said Montagu Nicodemus Montagu, with British reserve.

Oregon and New York, November 2006

It took her several weeks to summon up the courage, and it surprised Amy that she even remembered the phone number. Although she had left Bloom & Beck less than six months ago, it felt like a lifetime. She visualised the huge, high-rise downtown New York office building, all smoked glass and brushed-aluminium effect outside, inside either brutal minimalist utilitarian or plush mahogany and deep-pile genteel, depending on where inside you found yourself – trading and back office or advisory and client hospitality. It seemed like another world. She was pleased to note that she did not regret the urban/rustic trade after all, despite the associated social/isolated trade.

She dialled Jay's number and, as she knew would happen, got Betsy, Jay's long-suffering PA. For image reasons as well as practical ones, Jay never answered his own phone; even the official one of his two cellphones sat on Betsy's desk whilst she was in the office. Thus Jay was protected from nuisance calls from clients he no longer considered worthy of his personal attention, jilted females who had been stupid enough to take him at his word and, once, an abusive and threatening husband. Betsy had calmly informed the latter, when he had stopped ranting, that she had taped the whole thing and the recording would be given to the police, in the unlikely case he was not all bluster. Jay had heard no more of it, and Betsy had received an extra-high bonus that year. Luckily, Amy and Betsy were long-standing allies in the ranks of B&B support staff, confronting and sharing the same daily outrages of excess and entitlement, both – until Amy had made her escape – prisoners of their bloated remuneration, impossible to match outside Wall Street.

"Hey, Betsy, guess who?"

"Amy! You're kidding me! Amy Tate? She of the Great Escape from the Presentations Department?"

Although they had enjoyed a good relationship in the office, Amy and Betsy had not been very close socially. Betsy was older – Jay had tried younger PAs, it never worked for anyone – had a nice but boring accountant husband and lived with her two kids out of the city in a commuter town – Scarsdale or Bridgeport, or somewhere. Amy, childless, was living in the Upper East side of Manhattan, trying to have someone's – she sometimes asked herself whose – idea of a full and culturally rich metropolitan life. Shane and Amy had been invited to Betsy's dormitory house for lunch one Saturday, and the sheer ordinariness of it had sparked in Shane, who liked to think of himself as a liberal broad-minded type, the sort of sneering condescension that some liberal broad-minded types reserve for the ordinary. It had shown, with countless little barbs – "Oh! A den with a huge flat-screen TV. How quaint!" – to which Betsy was too polite to react. When Amy went to her office to apologise the following Monday, mild-mannered Betsy had said, "You don't have to put up with him, you know, Amy," which seemed odd to her at the time.

At work, however, they were foot-soldiers in the same army, she and Betsy.

"The very same. How's things at the battlefront?"

"Oh, same old same old. How are you doing? How's single life? How's Montana?"

"Oregon. Oh, it's great. I've got a big house with a big yard and a big view. At night I can see the stars! It's very quiet. You and Fred should try to get out here some time!" Amy's imaginary visiting New York friends had never included Betsy, still less her monochrome husband. They chatted on for some time, Amy deftly avoiding discussion of her new single status or its projected duration. Finally, Amy could tell from her tone that Betsy was no longer at liberty to talk.

"Betsy, I was wondering whether I could have a quick talk with Jay – I saw his interview in the *Journal* about the rare-earths mine and think I might be able to help him with something." She had rehearsed this as, although Betsy would definitely do her a favour if she could, even Betsy's powers of access to Jay could not be assured. "Tell him I live near to Trillium Lake. He'll want to talk to me."

"He's right here at my desk." Jay had been standing there fidgeting for about 15 seconds, sighing and looking at his watch. He liked his minions instantly available.

Out on her Salmon Huckleberry Wilderness range, Amy felt a clear, satisfying sensation down the line of ranks closing. Betsy would do her best. She heard a muffled and brief conversation taking place on the 23rd floor – one of the plush floors – thousands of miles away. Jay came on the line. She could just see him, taking the call at Betsy's desk, it being not important enough to return to his office for, not sensitive enough to need a closed door. He would be leaning against the screen dividing Betsy from the other PAs, looking out of the window in the horizon-scanning way people do when on the phone standing up.

"Hey, Amy, this is quite a surprise!" (*"This better be good"* was the unspoken but clear subtext. *"I don't know why I agreed to talk with the plump little dweeb."*) "What's up? Betsy here says you live in Oregon."

"I'm fine, thanks, Jay," she said, realising too late that he had not asked how she was. Oh well, serve him right for being rude, if he noticed at all, which he wouldn't.

"Great! Great!" (*"Like I care."*) "Soooo… Oregon?" (*"Can we please get to the point?"*)

"Yes, you probably remember, I left to have a complete change – not just from B&B but also from the city. I live beside a place called the Salmon Huckleberry Wilderness. It's lovely. Mount Hood is just up the road."

"Wow! There's some skiing up that way, isn't there? That's great. Quite a change from Manhattan… Anyway, Betsy mentioned Trillium Lake?" *("Jeez, Salmon Huckleberry Wilderness, one dumb name, and who the hell cares? I sure hope that this is not just about her new life or some lake…")*

"Yes, Jay, a lovely lake set in a forest, overlooked by Mount Hood. But it's not the lake itself that I want to talk to you about. It's the mine that takes its name from it. You know it, I think."

"I certainly know *of* it, Amy." *("This is more like it.")*

"I read your interview in the *Journal*. Congratulations on the White Crag transaction. A Principal Investment Group deal?" she asked. She knew Jay's role at the bank and that for good deals B&B would quietly co-invest; a spark of the old B&B covetousness glinted briefly. She really didn't care.

"Thanks! It was one of the better ones, sure." *("Mind your own business.")*

"Well, where I live is just down the highway from the Trillium Lake mine that, if I understand right, produces the same rare-earth elements that yours in California is going to extract once it's back up and running. Only Rareterre is ahead of you. I can tell you that right up, because the trucks loaded with ore pass my place on their way to the processing plant."

"Yeah, well, it's a big market and Trillium Lake has never had any permit issue, no, well, regulatory reason not to carry on operating. They stopped though, years back, because of the pricing." *("Why am I bothering to tell you all this? So you know that Rareterre is ramping up production already. Big deal. We knew they would. British bastards.")*

"Word here is that their heavy rare-earth content is particularly high." This had been one of the Hegel-facts Hoxie had told the conservation society. Without fully understanding it, Amy knew that it was a good thing, and a good thing for Trillium Lake Mine, and Rareterre was, she knew, going to be seen by Jay as a very bad thing. Jay was a greedy man. Jay loved to make money, but it went beyond that. There was going to be enough demand to float everyone's boats, but Jay hated to share. The idea that his juicy rare-earth revenues were going to be shared with a single competitor company made him angry, stomach-pit greedy-angry. Those Brit bastards would not only reduce his volumes but also the prices he achieved, supplying the market with their superior ores. Getting there before him. Bastards. Amy had the satisfying feeling of playing this arrogant man in his distant location like a sports fish on a line. She should have remembered that if the marine simile was true at all, Jay was a sharp-toothed shark.

"Yeah, like I say, it's a big market. Anyway, Amy, apart from to give me some intel, for which I am grateful, why did you call?" *("Get to the point, dweebette.")*

"Well, Jay, I am a member of a local group, the Trail 26 Conservation Society, you know, locals who take care of environmental protection, flora and fauna and all that." She was not yet a member, but little matter. "It's a small group and mainly worried about stopping campsite development, preserving the endangered lake frogs and so on."

Jay was not a patient man and his appetite for information on the habitat of the lesser-spotted tree newt was strictly limited. His competitive greed-blood was up about Rareterre, and it looked like she was, after all, just going on about a lake. "Well done, Amy. Good stuff. Community environmental tree-hugging club member. Attagirl! Sounds like you're fitting in just fine out there in the Salmon Twain Wilderness." *("Call over, you loser! No wonder you couldn't hack it in New York City.")*

"Huckleberry. Well, Jay, I was going to make a suggestion to you about how I can help with your little Trillium Lake problem. But you might like to take the call in your office. In fact you might like to call me back on your cellphone." B&B, as an SEC[4] registered financial services company, almost certainly recorded its telephone lines. "You see, Jay, I think that Rareterre may have more permit issues than they realise." Recorded call or not, she had to say enough to make him want to know more, to call her back. This was another line she had rehearsed: nice and passive, apparently relating to past not future issues. She had him.

He called back a few minutes later. Amy, used to the daily humiliations of a support worker by people like Jay, the daily reminders of her lack of importance, was enjoying herself.

"So, Amy, just how do you think you can help us?"

"Well, the Trail 26 Conservation Society has a member, a Paiute Indian, who is pretty angry about the mine coming back into production. Angry enough to take some direct action, I think." She felt an unexpected upwelling of sentiment for supportive Hoxie.

Jay was alone in his office, door closed, inevitably standing at the window staring at the horizon, or rather at the Hudson River visible between two buildings. This scrap of a view was another much-coveted signal of his success. Lori and her peers worked in a windowless "bull-pen" ten floors down, 200 of them in one massive partitioned office, awash with paper piled high on desks and floors, the odour of stale pizza in the air. Angry Indians? Direct Action? She was insane.

"What has this angry Native American got to do with Rareterre's permits, or anything that matters, Amy?" *("Are you wasting my time, you crazy bitch?")* He used the more PC "Native American" knowingly. She had not, and if such things mattered to her, and he suspected they did, it would be a small point to his advantage, an irritating little nick in her flesh, the start of his re-establishing control in this relationship.

"Your mine, you know, White Crag, it stopped production because of environmental violations and the EPA or someone withdrew its permits, right? Waste water management issues, contamination of the ground, that sort of thing? Anyway, big problems with the authorities and no permits to operate for years. But now, miraculously, it's back in business now that B&B owns, what d'you call it, 'the asset'?" She had done quite a lot of research, digging around in cyberspace, exploratory mining of her own. Her conclusions were superficial, a guesswork structure built upon the shaky footings of the internet, reinforced by the more solid buttress of an intimate knowledge of how B&B, and Jay in particular, operated.

"Well, Amy, you sound as if you know the official line is that the market prices for rare-earth minerals did not support the continued cost of keeping the mine operational and compliant. Now the economics are different, full stop, *basta*. I'll stick with that line, if you don't mind." *("Shit, how many people have joined these dots? Good guesswork, dweeby is quite the little surprise. I don't suppose many people have either the time or the interest to bother with this. Let's hope so. Let's hope Dick Veroof did his job discretely.")*

"That's fine, Jay. You stick with your official line."

("Fuck. Is she going to blackmail me?")

"I don't expect anything else. My question is: how would it be if something similar happened to Rareterre's 'asset' at Trillium Lake? Would that be a good thing or a bad thing, Jay?" She was mimicking him now. One of Jay's irritating ways of asserting his intellectual superiority was by telling people, "That's a bad thing. It's not a good thing, it's a bad thing," like they were kids or something.

"Are you suggesting..." Jay was not often lost for words. Angry Indian – Direct Action – problems with authorities – no permits for years. He pulled himself together. "That would be a good thing, Amy." *("A very, very good thing. Very good indeed.")*

Long Island Sound, New York, December 2006

On the Sunday after their first conversation Jay had called Amy again, this time from the confidential cellphone number he had given her at the end of the previous call. She wondered if even put-upon, trusted Betsy knew this number existed. He was all business, no niceties.

"I've checked with my experts and we think we have the perfect answer. The authorities are most concerned about threats to the ground-water, because of course the politicians are worried about what voters most fear, and that's water contamination. It's sort of fundamental, clean water, human rights stuff." Jay stretched out his legs on the leather sofa, not bothering to remove his loafers. He was dressed in standard international investment banker and hedge-fund manager weekend attire: Gucci loafers, chinos, polo shirt, cashmere sweater draped over his shoulders. He looked out at a windy, lead-coloured Long Island Sound. He could hear Lori preparing lunch in the kitchen a floor below. She had turned out to be quite a surprise, that Lori.

"Listen, Aims, I haven't much time. I feel this can work out really well. We're thinking a toxic blend of cyanide, arsenic, a few metals including thorium and uranium. They should show some radioactivity, enough to get them worried. Cyanide and arsenic are both associated with mine tailings, but of course they also have a brilliant profile in the public psyche."

Amy hated being called Aims. Shane had called her that, possessively, even when he was making her feel anything but wanted. She decided it was not worthwhile correcting Jay. Besides, she was rather more troubled by his voicing of the fact that, in the world they were entering, she and Jay, "toxic" and "brilliant" were synonyms.

"But this 'blend', how much will it be, I mean how many pints, and how will I get it? How dangerous will it be? I mean, when we handle it. And can they actually be harmful? I mean, the idea is to shut down the mine, not to kill the waterways of Mount Hood really, for real. And why does the public psyche come into it? Surely it's the authorities we're trying to impress? I mean…"

In his Long Island house Jay felt a complex mix of emotions. He was in a hurry to end the call because Lori would have finished whatever she was doing in the kitchen pretty soon, and he did not want her asking any questions. He was already impatient with his new associate, Amy, and her babbled stream of concerns, yet he was keen for her to carry out her plan that involved minimal cost and risk for him. He was worried that when it came to it she would screw up, lack the guts to go through with it, choose her accomplices badly. He would have to be double sure that nothing could be traced back to him. Jay was just not used to dealing with amateurs, he did not like the unpredictability, the risk he could not quantify and therefore could not control. He interrupted her.

"Aims, Aims, Aims. Calm down. It's not dangerous. Not to you, not to your precious lake, not to anyone. Not really. They said they'd make the toxic blend concentrated so it'll only be around a gallon, but you'll have to dilute it. We'll let you know how and where to get the materials. You just do the rest, as we discussed, and everyone's happy. Except Rareterre, of course." He allowed himself a wry smile. Then he saw Lori standing at the top of the mahogany spiral stairs, barefoot, wearing nothing but one of his business shirts, half-buttoned, collar turned up, the chocolate satin of her skin contrasting perfectly with the starched white cotton. He hung up without speaking further into the phone.

"I didn't hear you coming." He sat up.

"I thought not." A curious look, fleeting, left her face. Nervously he tried to recall what he had said, what she might have overheard. Lori was a trusted insider but still knew no more than she needed to about the high-level arrangements already skilfully made by Dick Veroof and his friends; this ground-level Trillium plan was an order of sensitivity worse even than that. Had he said "cyanide"? "Radioactive"? Hell, how long had she been there? "Toxic blend", definitely; she had definitely heard toxic blend. Despite his worry he noticed that her nipples were clearly visible under his shirt. It was really for summer use, this house, and chilly despite the heating at full blast.

"Just helping a friend with her swimming pool problems. Terrible algae." It was weak, but maybe it would do.

Lori was there, off season at Jay's underheated beachfront property, for career rather than romantic reasons. She was realistic and amoral, arguably perfect for Jay, arguably the reverse. She came from a broken Chicago home, had a difficult relationship with her mother, who had raised her alone from the age of 12. The alimony had ceased two years later when her father disappeared leaving a sizeable mortgage but no explanation. They had been forced to move out of their large, colonial-style suburban house. She was by this time beginning to realise the power she might have over men, as her body rapidly transformed, with perfection, in response to the adolescent wash of hormones. Lori never discussed it with her, but was acutely conscious of her mother's fear of tumbling from one American stereotype – the one linking hard work with achievement regardless of race – to another, that of the black single mother barely keeping her head above water.

Always bright at school, Lori soon combined her unquestionable attractiveness with academic effort to further her ambitions that, by the time she was 18 and applying for university, could easily be defined in material terms. She wanted $10 million by the time she was 30. Simple. The best way she could see of achieving this result was a career in investment banking. She was not overly given to self-analysis, but had she been she would have found ample excuse for her presence here, almost naked, in Jay's panoramic North Shore living room.

Despite her success at interview – securing Ivy League scholarship, plum internships, her job at B&B – being at least in part due to skilled professional flirting, Lori considered herself a feminist. Who is the greater enemy to the sisterhood, the man who abuses his workplace position to procure sexual favours from female subordinates, or the woman who grants those favours and wins unmerited professional progression? She had no hesitation in answering that one. He is; all she does is use his masculine weakness to redress the gender imbalance a bit.

Lori had overheard the last part of the conversation with Amy and was in no way convinced by the hurried swimming pool story. She had heard him mention the name Rareterre and knew the little British company well from all her due diligence for the White Crag deal. Then he had terminated the conversation without saying goodbye as soon as he saw her. She was a clever young woman and she knew instinctively that she had learned something that might be of value to her, but something she could do nothing with immediately. She went over to the sofa and, lifting the shirt slightly, sat astride his legs facing him. She bent her head and spoke softly in his ear, affording him an excellent view of her unfettered breasts.

"We have half an hour until the quiche is baked. What could we possibly do to pass the time?"

Amy's house, Mount Hood, Oregon, December 2006

"It's really practically risk-free."

Amy was beginning to ask herself if she had made a mistake with Hoxie. She looked at him across her kitchen table: physically very large, size enhanced by the bright check lumberjack's shirt, thick unkempt head of black hair. His big-featured Paiute Native American face – severe down-turned mouth, long straight nose, high cheekbones, arched eyebrows, verging on handsome – could so easily have been noble, courageous, fearsome. Yet something hard to identify undermined the effect; surplus flesh around the jowls, a heaviness in the chin, a slight evasiveness in the eyes; no, Hoxie's appearance was not deceptive. He looked as he was – a big, timid man, a man willing to theorise on perceived wrongs and their causes, but loathe to commit himself to action that might address them. Maybe he was just sensible. Amy sighed.

"We're talking about moving just a few flasks around, basically. Diluting and distributing the contents. The most dangerous bit will be the handling, y'know, whilst we dilute. But we'll wear protective clothing, gloves, goggles, whatever you want."

"But – arsenic, Amy? Cyanide! That's dangerous shit!" Amy sighed again. It was precisely because these substances had this emotive capacity, were commonly known primarily for their poisonous qualities, that they had been selected.

"And what if we're caught? Have you thought about that? I mean, this stuff must be against the law big time! It's probably a federal offence. We'd end up in jail. And then there's my position in the community to consider…"

"What about the things we said, you said, at the meeting of the conservation society? Surely you're not just going to sit by whilst that land-grabbing British company continues to despoil your ancestors' lands?" With these words she had broken an unspoken taboo between them; she had from the start, since that first meeting in Rhododendron, recognised the tribal grievance aspect of Hoxie's approach to everything, but she had also noted his careful avoidance of voicing the Native American argument, the trump everyone knew he had up his sleeve. Neither of them had ever identified it explicitly like this.

They had met up again twice since the Trail 26 event, both at her arrangement. The first meeting, at the Hungry Possum, was purportedly for her to complete the membership formalities of the conservation society, which she could as easily have done with Professor Palmer. But Amy had an unconscious desire to be better acquainted with Hoxie, quite separate from the conscious thought that he would be a good ally to help her execute The Plan, a role for which the professor would be ill-suited. Besides, the nature of The Plan demanded strict limitations on the number of people involved, and clearly disqualified the conservative professor as one of them.

She had bought them both a cup of coffee and a Belgian waffle, served with whipped cream and melted chocolate, quite a lot of which ended up on her parka, which was in Hoxie's direct line of fire. She achieved her objective of getting to know him better, and was again impressed by his ability to express himself; for the first time she noticed his darkly reflective eyes – slightly vulnerable, defensive. They had discussed the mine, and the environmental angle of its newly increased activities and probable full recommissioning. She invited him to visit her home and hear for himself the "noise pollution", as she had taken to calling it.

"I know no one thinks of it as important, and really in comparison to the other pollution and contamination risks I agree, but it's here and now and happening, and I'd appreciate your experiencing it for yourself." Her intention was to reveal The Plan to him at that time, in the private environment of her kitchen, not the public space of the popular Hungry Possum.

Then she'd had her second and truncated conversation with Jay, and begun to understand what she had unleashed with her idea, had been confronted with the highly active role she would have in the affair and the nature of the substances she would be handling. Jay suddenly hanging up almost mid-sentence further emphasised to Amy the danger and shadiness of The Plan. In the event, she had hesitated to outline The Plan to Hoxie, so he had merely heard the noise of Rick's 3pm shipment as it took the bend on the highway and confirmed to her that it was intolerable, even though she knew he was humouring her. The unspoken something else about her invitation was mirrored in his quick acceptance of it: an awkward joint contrivance for the testing of feelings in the hope of finding them to be mutually held. Immature, embarrassing, adolescent. That, too, remained unsaid. They had consumed more coffee.

He was leaving when she blurted out, "I have a Plan, something to stop the mine. Stop it for years, if not for good."

He had his coat on, was halfway to the door, knitted Inca-style hat in his hand. Since the Trail 26 Conservation Society meeting when the mine had been discussed, dominating the proceedings in the end, he had stopped his infrequent trips up to the mine. Urination and deflation: it was ineffective, demeaning. It was aimed at the wrong target, honest mining workers merely looking to feed their families, not the foreign capitalist owners of the mine. Furthermore, the honest workers looked brawny; he had seen the CCTV had been moved and was careful not to show his face, but still the risks were increasing. He had varied his timing, but had still more than once been forced to turn back when he spotted a lookout posted at the mine. Now the mornings were dark and cold, and his fervour was also dimming and cooling. The meeting of the conservation society had been good, a meeting of minds on the threats that the mine posed – but it had still been inconclusive, no one offering any sort of plan, not even one as pathetic as his "hiss and piss" campaign. Now here was Amy, whom he did not find uncute. But was she cute? Here she was, not cute but not uncute, noise-pollution obsessed Amy, claiming to have a Plan, a capital "P" Plan. He removed his coat.

It was then that Amy finally outlined the whole Plan to him and he had reacted not as she was hoping, with admiring enthusiasm, but with nervous apprehension. With her invocation of his ancestral lands, she feared she had overplayed her hand, making explicit what he always implied but never expressed, somehow exposing him. But she had not failed. The reference to the "land-grabbing British" chimed in an unconscious corner of Hoxie's mind, resonating with a resentment retained from Yale. Ambrose Cecil-Davies, in his paper "The British Empire and its Subjects: a Reappraisal", had an entire section subtitled "Land-grabbing Can be Good", explaining how only the civilising British had brought productivity and plenty to the agriculture of Zimbabwe or somewhere. Hoxie felt the rage still – no longer a specific anger but a more diffuse, generalised need to right some wrongs.

"Okay, supposing we go ahead with this. Where do we get the chemicals? How do we know where to put them? And even if we do all this, how can we be sure that the right folks at the EPA will pay attention? We can hardly call 'em up and say 'Hi, guys, Hoxie Tomahas here, ever thought of taking a look at the land around the Trillium Lake mine? It looks reeeal contaminated to me.'" He spoke these words in a hick Southerner accent, which he did rather well. Amy had not mentioned Jay, or Bloom & Beck.

"I'll take care of the materials. They should be available soon, or at least I'll know where to get them. If you could survey the site, see where best we can place the materials, that would be good." Amy was going carefully now, she preferred the word "materials" to "chemicals" and certainly to "toxic blend". She was coaxing him, judging that anything hinting at an imperative from her might push him back over the line he seemed to be crossing. "As I understand it, the water – y'know, the groundwater, springs and streams, ultimately the lake itself – that's what they go for. I guess it stands to reason – contaminated land is inert, but once stuff gets into the water it's dynamic, spreading out. Plus aquatic life seems delicate, I suppose it's because they breathe the same thing as they drink." She paused, hoping to have found a good equilibrium between reassuring him on a plan well thought through, which frankly it was not, and appearing to covet a leadership role, which she certainly did not; she feared that Hoxie was one of those men who had trouble being led by a female.

She did not have much to go on, Jay having hung up before going into any detail on the issue of materials placement. She assumed that his "experts" would have a suggestion. The objective was simple enough – provide sufficient evidence to instil a general concern in the minds of the authorities – the environmental and mining supervision groups in whose hands lay the granting and rescinding of the multiplicity of permits required to operate a mine. Anyway, Jay had mentioned water and she had repeated it to Hoxie. She did not even know if the verbs "breathe" and "drink" applied to fish; she suspected not.

"Okay, but we are not actually going to poison the water, are we? That would be…"

"Oh, of course not! All we'll be doing is leaving traces of the materials in places where their surveys will pick them up. They'll assume that the traces are evidence of a bigger problem, and close down the mine, remove their permits. There'll be a lengthy investigation, the Brits will have to do their own work, propose a remediation plan, negotiate with them. It'll stop the bastards for years." She could see then that she had him.

"I'm still not sure how we get the attention we need from the authorities, though. Who would it be, anyway? Someone federal, or is it done at a state level?"

"Don't worry, Hoxie, we can be sure that the appropriate bodies will be involved. Trust me on that one." She was in turn trusting Jay on that one, he was good at that sort of thing, but Hoxie did not need to know. "And once they have conducted their tests or whatever, we, the Trail 26 Conservation Society, can ensure that it gets the local attention and publicity it deserves. I have a feeling Professor Palmer will enjoy that."

Quite without noticing it, Amy had already bought into her own scheme, creating a new reality, as she really felt the righteousness of her cause to protect her beloved home state's environment. In a way Hoxie was the more grounded of the two. He was about to say "the attention it would deserve if it had been for real, you mean", but thought better of it. She wanted to believe her own lies, fine; in his view the end justified the means, and he was beginning to like the means.

Until she told Hoxie about The Plan and he had, however reluctantly, signed up, Amy had endured a feeling of culpable impotence. She had started something, put herself forward as a protagonist in a dangerous scheme of her own invention which was gaining momentum, forces beyond her control were acting upon it. Her plan was a raft on a fast-moving river and alone she could not steer it clear of the rocks. But now that she had Hoxie on board Amy felt suddenly safer and more confident in The Plan and its outcome. She even felt more comfortable at the questionable morality of what she was proposing to do. As she stood watching Hoxie's substantial form make its way down her drive to his car she felt a warm stirring of gratitude, a notion of affection that pleasantly surprised her, as had the unnecessarily tight bear hug he had given her on leaving.

Mount Hood, Oregon, December 2006

Hoxie had volunteered unprompted that The Plan was best kept between them – Amy and himself. She had been pleased, agreeing that the fewer people that were informed the better; the two of them could easily manage the task. She would not have admitted it to herself, but the sharing of a secret with this big, complex man, their complicity, was becoming a pleasure to her – she had begun to look forward to their meetings for reasons beyond the execution of their Plan. Now that she was a member of the Trail 26 Conservation Society, she and Hoxie meeting frequently seemed to raise no eyebrows in their small if scattered community. Amy saw to it that they both also met with other active members, especially Professor Palmer and Jess, both of whom Amy was growing to like. They in turn seemed delighted that the arrival of this New York newcomer had galvanised their somnolent organisation. Their discussions were not only about the Trillium Lake mine, but it was still the major subject. Amy and Hoxie had agreed that they would get the group aligned and ready to respond when the mine site was found to be a source of contamination, to ensure that the permits were revoked as planned.

"We've gotta know when any inspection takes place and be ready to act. I wouldn't put it past those perfidious British bastards to bribe the inspectors and have the whole thing brushed under the carpet," Hoxie said. Amy, delighted as she was that he had embraced The Plan so whole-heartedly, did not pause to reflect that, in the balance of things, they were hardly in a position to be too judgemental.

Ten days passed before Jay made contact again and the subgroup, the "Trail 26 Activists" as Amy mentally labelled them, had met three times, favouring the Hungry Possum as their venue. Hoxie particularly liked the French fries, and occasionally the Belgian proprietor, Piet, also a member of the conservation society, found time to join them. The ideas they discussed – not The Plan, of course, but the support Amy and Hoxie were constructing to complement it – were mostly on how to gather intelligence about the mine, the company that owned it, the permits that enabled it to operate, the suppliers of energy, chemicals and the individuals involved.

"Maybe we'll find out that they are missing some vital piece of paper," Amy had said. "Or perhaps we can slow them down by appealing to a sympathetic employee. Maybe we can get at them through the parent company somehow." All of them experienced a little shudder of excitement when she used the expression "get at them", but this was not a group minded to take direct action. There was no appetite for personal confrontation; even the hardcore of Hoxie and Amy were counting on maintaining an indirectness, a disconnection was central to The Plan. There were still plenty of ideas about bona fide activities for the other activists whilst she and Hoxie got on with the main business, and everyone was entering into the spirit of the thing. Professor Palmer revealed that he had "certain connections within the structure, elected and unelected, of the administrative bureaucracy of our good state", which they all agreed sounded quite useful, although no one was altogether sure what exactly he meant. Jess revealed that not only had she been up to the mine and "checked it out" over the weekend – "it sure ain't pretty!" – but she had also befriended an engineer working at the mine, whom she had met by chance at the supermarket.

Helen Fry had seen Jess in the cereal section, trying to decide between the multitude of mendaciously presented flakes, clusters and briquettes, each loudly claiming to be a healthy breakfast option, in stark contradiction of the sugar content packed into the colourful boxes. Noticeable for her shaven head, body piercings and eccentric dress sense, Jess looked like a fairly butch version of Melissa Etheridge and this, it seemed, was what brought Helen over to engage her in conversation.

"Her opening gambit was 'Nice studs'," a laughing Jess reported to the Trail 26 sub-group. "I sure hope she was talking about these babies," she gestured to her eyebrows and nose. "But I got the impression she was interested in more than just facial adornment, if you know what I mean." Professor Palmer clearly did not know what she meant, but she chose not to offer any further explanation. "Anyway, she helped me find the sultana bran flakes and we got talking. She told me that she was an engineer, a specialist in mineral extraction and concentration plants, working up at the mine as a consultant. You'll never guess – all the metallurgists and engineers are women, the consultancy company only employs women. Isn't there a law against that? Anyway, she's a real-life Amazon, and when I heard about where she works I thought I'd encourage her. The things I do for the cause." She rolled her eyes and brought her left hand to her forehead, palm outwards, a silent-movie melodrama victim. The professor looked bemused.

An esprit de corps was building in their newly purposeful environmental congregation, their group of believers, amongst whom Hoxie and Amy were a radicalised jihadist cell.

Amy was beginning to think that Jay had changed his mind. Nearly two weeks had elapsed since their abruptly truncated call, without any sign from him. It had allowed her the time to build what she was coming to see as her "team", the activists, but she knew that Hoxie was keen to proceed without delay. Reasonably, he pointed out that winter would soon come, and the next few months would be cold and outdoor work uncomfortable. Amy, who had not told him her expected source of the materials and was therefore unable to explain the delay satisfactorily, felt like saying, "Oh dear, it'd be awful for you to get cold toes whilst you are out poisoning groundwater and sabotaging mines! Maybe we'd better call it off until spring." Neither even thought of the risks snow cover could represent for them in their clandestine operations – not risks of discomfort or injury, but risk of discovery.

Amy was standing in her oversized pine-clad living room with its huge triangular windows up to the roof, looking out over the veranda at her view, when the phone woke her from a reverie. She had been wondering how best to use Professor Palmer's "certain connections" within the state legislature. He had a track record of successful lobbying with one of Oregon's senators, and now that she knew him better Amy felt sure he could be highly effective, despite his age, or maybe because of it. His academic mind was still fully functioning, and she had discovered that his discipline had been biochemistry, which although not directly applicable to the better understanding of water discharge permits and so on, could be helpful.

They had agreed over coffee and waffles with Piet – special regulars' rates were being applied at the Hungry Possum for members of the Trail 26 Conservation Society – that the professor would focus on permits and approvals; Hoxie and Jess would concentrate on people, as both already knew mine staff and contractors, Friedrich Hegel and Helen Fry in particular, and Amy and Piet would look at suppliers and the parent company – a less focussed task as no one was quite sure where this route might lead. Piet was anyway too busy to devote much time to the project, and Amy had The Plan to occupy her. She had just decided to encourage the professor to spend some time in Portland exploring the permits situation fully, when the phone rang. It was not Jay.

"Hello, is this Amy Tate?" A man's voice, deep and harsh, indistinguishable accent.

"Yes, this is she," said Amy, feeling intuitively defensive.

"I am calling at the behest of mutual friends in New York, who told me you would be expecting this call. Please pay attention as I will not repeat this." Nervously Amy looked at the display on the cordless telephone. "Number withheld." She felt goose-flesh rise on the back of her neck.

"A delivery has been made to your home. It consists of a single one-gallon plastic flask. The contents are highly concentrated and will require dilution ten to one before use. Agitate the container well before dilution." It sounded as if he was reading from an instruction manual. "After dilution it will still be dangerous to handle; wear protective clothing. You are to distribute half the materials on and around the final 50 yards of the waste water piping located to the north-west of the site, before it terminates at the evaporation ponds. Introduce the remaining materials into the substrate via the exploratory drills numbered 70 and 71. Do it soon. We'll take care of the rest, completing over the summer."

"Over the summer? Why so long?" But there was a click and the anonymous caller was gone.

Amy's head span. She scrabbled for a pen and scribbled "NW, 50 yds, 70 + 71, 50/50" on the back of a copy of *Time* magazine on the desk beside the phone. She sat down on the sofa. She stood up again, returned to the desk and added "10:1". She picked up the phone and took it back to the sofa. She started dialling Hoxie's number, then thought better of it. "Shit, what have I started?" What had the man said, what tense had he used? The delivery has been made? When, who? She felt suddenly vulnerable. People unknown to her calling, knowing her phone number, her address, coming here, to her home. People who don't even give their names. And that bastard Jay, he's quickly out of the picture, getting his henchmen to do the dirty work. The man on the phone probably did not even know him.

Then it struck her. "If I've just been talking to Jay's henchman, what does that make me? A henchwoman? I'm just as much his lackey, but I volunteered for the job – worse, I created the job." With bitterness she realised that she would probably never speak to Jay again. He was getting what he wanted, *basta*, as he would have said. She threw open the French window onto the balcony, stepped into the chill December air and inhaled deeply. A laden truck from the Trillium Lake mine was just struggling around the bend on the highway, its mechanical protest plaintive through the trees.

Behind a wooden lounger, cushionless on the right-hand extremity of the veranda, the edge furthest from the drive, she saw a blue plastic container with a black top held in place by yellow metal clips. It looked like roughly a gallon.

Hoxie and Amy were standing in her garage, a neon-lit double-sized subterranean cave beneath her house with a smooth concrete floor, automatic doors and a full-width workbench at the rear. Amy had never used the workbench, which was empty apart from, dead centre, the blue plastic container with its black lid and yellow clips. It looked new, was not marked in any way. They stood close together in silence, side by side, five feet from the workbench, like an ill-matched couple in an historic church gazing at the altar. Hoxie, wearing Amy's gardening gloves, had carried the container down from the veranda.

The first thing Amy had done after calling Hoxie, once she had calmed down, was to don the blue overalls she had for gardening, painting and other dirty jobs, but she did not approach the blue container. When Hoxie's dirty pickup had made its way up her drive she had put on her blue quilted ski jacket, which in combination with the overalls and her round glasses gave her the appearance of a diminutive Michelin Man. Wordlessly she had led him to the veranda.

"The materials?"

"The materials."

"Well, we'd better not leave them there." Hoxie looked around as if expecting to see a spy hurriedly pop his head back behind one of the trees surrounding her land. She pulled her gloves out of the overalls' pocket and handed them to him. With a struggle he put them on and, cautiously holding the container out in front of him like a brimful Ming vase, followed her down the steps to the garage.

He broke the silence. "So, you were saying, we've gotta dilute this stuff?"

"Ten to one. Yes."

"With water?"

"Yes."

"Here?"

"I guess so."

Silence fell again. He began to remove the gloves, edging them off finger by finger. Outside, a gentle snow began to fall, the first of the winter, settling damply on the grass but not on the path or the drive. It was Hoxie that pulled them both from their shared unhappiness, an ill-defined gloom brought by the gradual realisation that The Plan was inexorably sliding towards action, with its risks and implications for their consciences. He threw the gloves onto the workbench and smacked his hands together, holding them there as if in prayer.

"It's the right thing to do, Amy. We'll stop them doing a bad thing, a big bad thing, by doing this…" He didn't say "little bad thing" but it hung in the air.

"We've got to do it." Amy straightened her back, squaring her shoulders. "We'll be needing face masks, you know, like the Japanese wear on the subway whenever there's a pandemic scare, a big, 12-gallon barrel with a spigot on the bottom, that way we can keep handling to a minimum and only do one big dilution. Rubber gloves that actually fit you, a funnel, some more one-gallon or maybe half-gallon containers. Do you have any overalls?"

He did not, but didn't like to admit it.

"I can get most of what we need at the garden centre. I'll go tomorrow," Hoxie volunteered.

They tramped back up the internal stairs to her kitchen. She put on the coffee, wondering when The Plan was going to feel exciting again; there were so many uncertainties, it was hard not to focus on them.

"In your explorations of the mine, have you ever seen any drills? Holes the geologists have made to take samples, check the concentrations of the minerals, their depth and so on. About 6 inches in diameter?" she asked. Hoxie knew what an exploratory drill was, but was embarrassed that he had not been up to the mine for some time, certainly not since she asked him to survey for good places to drop their little toxic bombs when she had first outlined The Plan to him. Amy continued, "It's just that I've been advised that if we find drills 70 and 71, they would be a good site to place some of the materials."

Hoxie had never expressed any curiosity about the source of the materials, and did not know about the source of Amy's "advice". He had grown to know Amy well, his initial dismissal of her as anything but an acquaintance had evolved, via a grudging respect for her determination, to a pleasure in her company that he rightly judged to be mutual. Like her, he had come to enjoy the intimacy of their joint Plan, their shared secret. He looked at her, focussed on spooning coffee grounds into the perco- lator, and wondered why the English language had no word for women like Amy: not cute, but attractive. He had noted her consistent use of the passive voice regarding the materials – "I have been advised", "the appropriate bodies will be involved", "the materials will be made available soon". She did not want to go into detail, clearly, and he was touched that she sought to protect him in this way. Besides, a little internal voice of self-preservation, one that frequently spoke to him, agreed it was probably better not to know.

CHAPTER 6

Stacey completed the Hamlyn Securities annual rare-earths note. Perhaps in an effort to prove that the authors are not complete nerds and do not take themselves too seriously, many analysts' notes include a pun in the title. Last year, when Hamlyn's theme had been the emergence of C. Brown and Rareterre as well-advanced non-Chinese possible sources of rare-earths for the green tech economy, the title had been "Yuan for the Money, Two for the Road: the end of Chinese dominance?". This year's edition was titled "Medium Rare or Half-baked?", and the theme was the difficulty of converting a promising geological phenomenon into a producing mine. Rareterre's difficulties in completing its bankable feasibility study on time were dealt with at some length. When Frits read it he immediately called Peter.

"I'm going to sue those guys!" Peter braced himself for one of Frits's charging-horse medieval-joust tirades. "Did you see what Stacey wrote? 'Rareterre is likely to disappoint yet again—' Yet Again! '—as the all-important feasibility study and the environmental impact assessment that goes with it are falling well behind schedule. We have pencilled in 2010 for production to commence, pushed back from 2008, and adjusted our valuation model and target share price accordingly'. I mean, she's exaggerating! And, how does she know? And did you see her treatment of C. Brown? Man, they don't even have the cash to build their concentration plant, ours is already there! Yet she says, 'Of the leading players in the race to develop environmentally sensitive, i.e. non-Chinese sources of rare-earths, C. Brown appears to be pulling away from the competition.' It's completely unbalanced. Even REM gets fairer treatment than us!" Frits had a particular dislike for REM, a Nordic competitor prone to underhand marketing tactics. He had said all this without drawing breath, and the last three words were croaked out as the final contents of his lungs were squeezed past his vocal cords, barely producing the required vibration.

Peter seized his chance. "I have read it and agree it's very annoying, Frits. She does seem to have an uncanny ability to touch on the raw nerve. And you are right, it is not at all balanced. The problem is that Hamlyn's team is very well respected, people will take note." He had heard the huge inhalation and wanted to get a point in before Frits got back in the saddle of his charger. "But the fact is, she's right. And she has not woken up yet to the financial side, the extra cost Olivier's consultants are telling us we need to budget for."

But Stacey had woken up to that side. She was simply biding her time; another note just before Rareterre's annual investor road-show[5] would be most effective. The Rareterre share price had softened nicely, she thought, but she was confident she could do better.

Bloom & Beck's Offices, Wall Street, New York, January 2007

Jay was on to his next deal and his next chick.

Lori was great, one of the better ones, but life moves on and B&B had recently hired a spectacularly beautiful and, unlike Lori, spicily exotic Tunisian girl as an equity analyst, covering oil and gas. Jay had already begun to discover a new fascination for hydrocarbons.

White Crag was a great deal, one of the better ones, about to be improved further by the felicitous intervention of Amy, and what he correctly imagined to be an unlikely band of angry and powerless locals. But Jay, like a shark which must continue to swim or die for lack of oxygen, moved from deal to deal leaving to others the mundane task of managing the businesses once his and Bloom & Beck's ownership were appropriately, indelibly, established. Jay was now working on the acquisition of an over-leveraged supermarket business which, its once-enthusiastic bankers had told him over a cocktail in the Beekman bar, was close to breaching its loan covenants[6] and whose family owners, the suckers, were desperate to protect the continued employment of their loyal staff. Jay loved it: he would appear as a saviour to the poor owners, sympathise with them that their equity was worth so very little. Then he'd merge the chain with Cheapsave Inc, already a B&B company, sack half the combined management, close neighbouring stores, slash costs and make a fortune. The bankers did not yet know it, but they too would be made to take a share of the pain by writing off a nice proportion of the debt. Jay really loved it.

He had made his practical arrangements regarding Trillium Lake with Amy indirectly, of course, through Dick Veroof's men – not his hedge-fund thugs-in-suits but his real, bone-fide thugs without the pretence. It was not the sort of thing he normally got involved with himself; far better for it to be twice-delegated whilst he swam restively on. The materials, the toxic blend supplied to Amy, had been quite unusual and so would be the subsequent monitoring of their use, but dealing with the required officials was mainstream activity, little more than a variety of lobbying really. Veroof's men could do that in their sleep.

Portland Public Library, Oregon, January 2007

Professor Palmer was thoroughly enjoying himself. He had always relished a research task and had been a modestly successful biochemist as a result of this and a fertile, questioning mind. He was in Portland's public library, surrounded with big, dry books containing state records of mines and mining claims and permits covering decades, but seated at a computer terminal. He realised that he could do internet research at home, but this felt more like real background research, as he had known it in his youth – only now it was in pursuance of a very modern cause, his newly energised conservation society's environmental battle with a polluting mine. He would shortly have to leave for his lunch appointment with Alexander Spink, an acquaintance of his from the Portland bridge club he and his wife had frequented before her death and his moving up-valley. Alexander was nearing retirement but worked in a fairly senior capacity at the Oregon State Assay and Mining Authority. He had been a public servant all his working life and, although he was considered rather old-fashioned and perhaps not as dynamic as he might be, was generally respected as a man of unimpeachable moral standards, in addition to being an expert on the regulation of the mining industry in Oregon. What a bore. *Perfect for my purposes, however*, Palmer thought.

Mount Hood, Oregon, January 2007

Amy and Piet were having a sub-subgroup meeting, just the two of them, as they had been asked to research Rareterre, who owned the mine. Both had guiltily spent half an hour or so on the company's website immediately before their rendezvous. It was the first time Amy had done anything to learn more about the organisation and people, thousands of miles away, whom she had come to view as "the enemy". Part of her regretted it, as she saw the mugshots of the directors and action shots of what she assumed were Rareterre staff going about their daily business. She regretted the unexpected introduction of a human element; the enemy was a small company manned by a bunch of pleasant enough looking people, and she learned from viewing the site that the Trillium Lake mine was the company's key asset. Rareterre plc, until now an evil, faceless, multi-national mega-corporation, suddenly took on an all too human aspect. It was Piet who had looked through a company presentation and seen the drilling report.

"They have put it all on the website, Amy! It's amazing. There's a cross-section diagram showing the layers of different minerals, and a hyperlink to the detailed report!" This had been Olivier's idea, intended to prove to the world that Rareterre, unlike so many miners before them, was not prone to unsupported hype. In Piet's overheated opinion, held with all the authority of a proprietor of a small-town greasy-spoon, albeit one with superior Belgian fries and waffles and melted chocolate, the diagram and report revealed the company's intention of adding a deep-shaft mine to the existing opencast operation. "Think of the machinery, the spoil, the" – he waved his hands vaguely – "noise. Think of the noise, Amy." Amy was thinking about the precise location of exploratory drills 70 and 71.

Hoxie had bought the equipment they needed at the garden centre: a small water butt with a capacity of about 20 gallons; a couple of funnels, large and small; three pairs of protective gloves, two XL and one S; a pack of ten white fibre face masks; a pair of overalls, XXL. He added a roll of protective polythene sheeting to cover the workbench and a plastic broom-handle to act as a stirrer. He was in line to pay when an excited Amy called his cellphone.

"Do you think you can get a GPS, you know, a hand-held device like hunters and hikers use?"

"Sure, Amy, this is Mount Hood, home of trekking, huntin', shootin' and fishin'." He unconsciously imitated Ambrose, who had been a devotee of these pursuits and seemed to think them a distinguishing badge of class. Back home on the reservation they were anything but. "Why, though?"

"I know the precise coordinates of drills 70 and 71, Hoxie."

After the garden centre, he went a couple of miles up the road to Neil's Outdoor Pursuits Emporium and bought an entry level Garmin GPS.

Consulting his notes, Professor Palmer gave a wordy report to the activist subgroup concerning his preliminary findings on the subject of permits.

"Numerous governmental permits and approvals are required in order for Rareterre to proceed with its modernisation and expansion efforts. These may include Conditional Use Permits and a reclamation plan approval, air permits, water usage permits, an agreement and permit to alter any streambeds affected by any new plant site, building permits as appropriate and permits related to the use and storage of radioactive or hazardous materials."

"That sounds very promising, Professor," said Amy. *Hazardous and radioactive materials such as those sitting on my garage workbench, for example*, she thought. "Were you able to find out where they actually stand with all these permits?"

The professor had been a little disappointed by his lunch with Alexander Spink; as soon as he had tried to talk in specific terms about the mine at Trillium Lake, Alexander had raised a cautionary hand and warned him that he could not, of course, discuss any actual companies or operations, as it would be a breach of his professional trust, he was sure the good professor understood. The good professor did understand, but had still been able to extract a small amount of additional information.

"I was able to ascertain that, because they never completely ceased operating the mine, and their milling, flotation, concentration etcetera machinery has been in uninterrupted use of sorts, many of their permits are what is, somewhat condescendingly to one who has himself achieved the exalted status of grandparent, described as 'grandfathered', by which I take it they mean to say 'too old to be messed with', a sentiment with which I am normally fully in accord, but not in this instance."

Amy and Hoxie exchanged knowing glances. Beneath the table their legs were touching; neither moved in response. They were not as deflated as the others; no amount of grandfathering would protect the mine's permits from what they had planned.

Trillium Lake Mine, Mount Hood, Oregon, January & February 2007

When Hoxie and Amy found drills 70 and 71 two days later, they laughed at their own over-preparation. Clad in hiking boots, they arrived at the tourist car park separately, early, to allow time for what they both felt sure would be the first of several frustrating searches for abandoned holes in the forest floor. Although the futility of looking for two six-inch holes in the middle of a wilderness seemed guaranteed, Amy had confidence. Firstly, the accuracy of the Garmin device Hoxie had bought was supposedly astonishing: this little thing, no larger than the average pocket calculator, would locate itself, the packaging claimed, to within three metres on the ground by correlating its position in relation to seven or eight satellites orbiting 12,000 miles overhead.

The other reason for Amy's confidence was her source for the choice of drills 70 and 71. Anonymous and intangibly threatening the henchman may have been, when she had studied Rareterre's surveys and diagrams she could not help admiring their professionalism, if a henchman can be professional. Had any contamination come from a leak in the waste pipe, it would have soaked into the ground above the area of exploratory drilling, which in turn was on the plane of the slope to the creek that fed the lake. Drills 70 and 71 were the best placed drills at which to find contamination consistent with this story.

Following the GPS, plus with a large-scale map in hand, they had walked south towards the mine for about 90 minutes through trees and across rough terrain, mainly uphill, until Hoxie, consulting the GPS, announced, "We should be there any time now." Simultaneously, through the trees, Amy saw a red pole protruding vertically from the ground. As they approached it an extensive area of land opened up where the trees had been roughly cut down, laying scattered more or less where they fell, bare earth and rock churned by heavy vehicles, roots inelegantly disinterred and facing upwards. There was a track leading towards one of the old forestry roads. Apparently randomly placed across this extensive site were 20 or 30 of these vertical red six-foot poles, each about six inches in diameter. About the width of a drill hole.

Hoxie grimaced. "Well, here is a little forest of exploratory drill-hole markers, I'm guessing. Not as nice to look at as the real forest they replaced. But they sure made it easy for us."

Amy was making her way across the muddy ground to the nearest pole. "Very easy. They're labelled with their numbers! This one" – she kicked the pole nearest her – "is number 70!"

Quite uncharacteristically, she did a little victory dance. Hoxie had to look away, the comical sight of this miniature Michelin Man boogying in a muddy man-made forest clearing was enough to make him have to stifle a laugh. He reached for her, scooped her off her feet with ease and, Amy's legs swinging, they briefly pirouetted amongst the tree stumps and drill-hole markers. When Hoxie lowered her back to the ground they were both breathless and elated.

It was not the dilution, nor any reluctance on their part that had made them take so long before implementing the next, active phase of The Plan. It was the weather.

The dilution was completed one Thursday afternoon. Kitted out with masks, overalls, gloves and, as an afterthought, ski-balaclavas pulled down over their heads, they transferred the contents of the blue plastic container with the black lid to Hoxie's water butt and measured in ten gallons of water using a gallon plastic milk carton. Had someone observed them during this process they would, not completely without accuracy, have surmised that they had come across some sort of insurgents' bomb-making factory. Amy and Hoxie had placed the water butt on the workbench, spigot protruding over the edge for ease of transfer into the empty milk containers, five of which were neatly lined up beside the butt. The plan was to transfer the materials into gallon milk cartons and carry them up to the mine three at a time in four trips, Hoxie carrying two in his rucksack, Amy one. They would then do their work distributing the toxic liquids and return with the empty milk containers.

Once they finished their task, Amy felt that some sort of celebration to mark their progress might be in order, but Hoxie had planned to have a beer with Friedrich Hegel, Helen Fry and Jess at the Lonely Bear. When they learned that Helen and Friedrich had become friends, Hoxie and Jess had joined forces in their campaign of getting to know the mine staff.

Hoxie stripped off his protective clothing and, kissing Amy on the cheek – neither recalled when this affectionate little habit had started – walked quickly through the snow to his pickup. She watched him going down her footpath, leaving dark footprints in the new snow. She called after him.

"Hoxie! We can't do it. We can't…" although her house was isolated she thought it best not to shout their toxic Plan out loud across her yard, so she hurried down the slippery path to him. "Look. Look at our footprints. We can't go trekking up to the mine, especially not the evaporation ponds, which aren't far from the mine buildings. We're going to leave tracks like these behind us, like Pooh and Piglet and the Woozles in the Hundred Acre Wood!" The cultural reference was lost on Hoxie, but he saw her point.

"We'll just have to watch the weather forecast closely. It's supposed to be an El Nino year this year, so perhaps we'll have thaws, even up at the mine. Otherwise we can do it when we know to expect a new snowfall or a big wind, something to cover our tracks."

During a brief thaw mid-January, in a pre-dawn trek that neither enjoyed, they managed to deposit three gallons of their materials near the last 50m of the waste water pipe as instructed. Another two gallons were poured onto the ground beneath the pipe at the end of the month. It was not until late February that they agreed the weather forecast, a snowstorm due late afternoon, was favourable to their making the final trip to the drills. They took all the remaining six gallons with them.

It was already beginning to snow, hours earlier than forecast, low leaden clouds sprinkling scattered flakes across the contused landscape. Gradually the surrounding hills and distant mountain faded into a milky obscurity. Like religious fanatics they both felt it right, cleansing, that they should suffer some physical pain in their devotions, but they did not welcome the snow. The bitter cold was discomfort enough, gnawing at their gloved hands and exposed faces.

Amy held the funnel to the drill hole in the hard ground. Hoxie hefted the first flask from his backpack and began carefully to pour the toxic blend deep into the frozen earth. Within ten minutes, Hoxie and Amy, environmental guerrillas, had completed the execution of their part in The Plan. It seemed so right to both of them when Hoxie leaned over Amy and, taking her in his arms, kissed her properly.

When Hoxie and Amy first kissed, properly kissed, standing in a snowy forest clearing despoiled with mining drill-holes, both had initially put it down to the euphoria of having completed their difficult and possibly dangerous shared project, The Plan. Despite its spontaneity, the kiss was not a wild, abandoned act of transporting sensuousness, an urgent expression of deep physical needs. They were not adolescents, they were far from innocent. This embrace, shared over a poisoned patch of Oregon forest – doubly poisoned, first by the mining activities that left the area scarred, then by this pair of environmental activists with their toxic materials – was not pure. Even as it happened, neither of them was swept along unquestioning in a wash of sentiment; each was thinking their own thoughts.

We're doing this out of a feeling of release, that's all.

It's the tension, the risks.

She's not my type.

I only like skinny guys. Don't I?

She's short. And serious. But kinda cute. And we do have fun.

He's acting on an impulse. It won't last. I hope it does; just a bit longer.

I'm acting on an impulse. Nice though.

I wonder if…

I wonder…

And so it went between them. This surprising but equivocal start was, undeniably, a start. Even beauteous perfectly matched Hollywood couplings are contaminated with rationalisations and calculations; for this odd couple, Hoxie and Amy, contamination initiated their relationship, pervaded it, almost defined it. But to both their surprise, it was a relationship. Something much deeper than simply their collaboration against Peter Mount's mine. Secrets to share in addition to The Plan.

Sushi Restaurant, St James's, London, February 2007

It had been laughably easy for Stacey. Lunch with Carl at a St James's sushi restaurant – anonymous, midway between his Hammersmith offices and hers in the City – only the smallest amount of flirting, a hint of possible future pleasures. It was still incredible to her that their relationship had continued. Incredible that he, even though he was a geologist and unlikely to be interested in her work, should still be willing to have revelatory chats like this. How could he be so unbelievably arrogant? She'd obviously been insufficiently clear in Paris that it had not been a mutually enjoyable experience and was definitely not one to be repeated, but she had been beset with disgust at herself and an overwhelming desire to escape. Still, how could he be so delusional as to believe so readily that he was in any way attractive to her? Fucking sleaze bag.

They talked about REM, whose share price had suffered following an unpromising survey on one of their Greenland assets. They shared the gossip about C. Brown's CEO abandoning a marriage of 25 years for a sociable interior designer of similar vintage. They discussed how the Chinese might react to the development of so much non-Chinese rare-earth mining capacity – Carl thought they would temporarily flood the market with stockpiled ores, forcing prices down.

"They've kinda done it before, that's how we ended up with them being pretty much a monopoly today. What's to stop them doing it again? They bide their time, wait until the rest of us have started big investments in finding and proving our deposits and building the processing plants we all need, then they strike! Wham. Investment case collapses overnight along with the price of the elements we aim to produce, projects get moth-balled, shareholders get disappointed, the good times are over before they start properly. I know Peter's worried about it."

Stacey had not heard Carl's theories about the Chinese and their proclivity to fix markets before, but it all seemed rather far-fetched and her mind was wandering. She was holding a prawn nigiri sushi between her chopsticks, a squashed cylinder of rice topped with a flattened raw prawn held in place by a band of seaweed, and wondering whether to put the whole thing in her mouth, tail and all and rather too much for one mouthful, or try to bite a bit off, a challenge of dental dexterity in which she knew from experience she was unlikely to succeed. No wonder so few Japanese were fat. Then Carl mentioned Peter's worries.

"Oh, why's that? Surely conspiracy theories about market fixing are, you know, a bit looney... is it all being masterminded by Elvis from his residence on the moon?" She was rotating her hands either side of her head, minstrel-style, and had widened her eyes but Carl was bristling. *Good God, he takes it seriously*, she thought. Stacey did not want to lose sight of her objective, and so she amended her derisory tone, straightening her face. "Besides, have the Chinese got stockpiles? Anyway, Rareterre will not be affected any more than anyone else, will they?" She was digging for Rareterre specifics. Carl was still annoyed at her mocking.

"Well, you might laugh." He reached into his trouser pocket and pulled out a pound coin. "Here, I'll bet you a pound that my Chinese conspiracy theory is proven right sometime in the next five years." He slapped the coin down on the counter in front of her.

"Done." She said, putting a coin of her own beside his. "Now, why would Rareterre be affected worse if ever prices were to fall?"

"The concern is that as one of the smaller companies we are more exposed, less able to stay the course. Like most small companies, we end up financing ourselves in bite-sized chunks. Plus, at Trillium Lake we mine the heavy rare-earths, but they are less concentrated, harder and more expensive to extract, so more sensitive to price variation." Stacey made a mental note. *A good point, cheers, Carl*, one to keep in mind for later perhaps, but not enough. Stacey's needs were more immediate.

They were sitting on bar stools, side by side, facing a conveyor belt charged with colour-coded mini-meals under plastic domes. Stacey had chosen this place precisely for its seating layout, enforcing a certain distance, rendering physical contact between them of any sort contrived at best. He did contrive and she avoided him with ease. It was when she brought the conversation around to feasibility studies, adjacent to Carl's area of responsibility, that Stacey's little mining operation hit pay dirt.

"So, we should be hearing the results of the final BFS and EIA for the scale-up at Trillium Lake soon." She was referring to the late stage feasibility and environmental studies required before the processing plant refurbishment and mine reopening could be fully planned. The costs and timings would give the markets an idea of future profitability on the Trillium Lake mine, and hence of Rareterre as a whole.

"Not as soon as all that. That idiot Olivier hired the wrong people to do the job, they wasted a load of time on repeating work done years ago, and now…" He hesitated. Carl did have a conscience, an organ devoted only to professional not personal matters, and it was quietly reminding him to whom he was talking. Stacey, sensing the hesitancy, shifted on her stool and faced him, looked into his eyes and gave him a better view of her cleavage.

"Is Olivier that good-looking Nazi in charge of Mining and Exploration? I didn't ever think of him as an idiot," she prompted. She knew perfectly well who Olivier was, and that Carl and he had a "difficult" relationship.

"Good-looking? I thought you had better taste than that, Stacey. Yes, he's a complete idiot, and he tries to do everything from London instead of being on-site. He's trying to get the studies done by remote control and obviously he can't. Trillium's about nine months behind schedule, if not more, and it's sure to go over-budget. It's a disaster!"

Bingo! She had her killer point for the next analyst's note on Rareterre.

Rareterre Plc Offices, Hammersmith, London, February 2007

Peter Mount preferred not to describe Rareterre as a "small mining company". It was a "specialised rare-earths exploration and extraction company". The Trillium Lake mine was not just an "established rare-earths mine" but "an exceptional concentration of proven and probable heavy rare-earth elements primed for renewed extraction". The Rareterre management was not an assortment of typical mining industry misfits but "a dynamic, highly qualified leadership team".

Peter looked around the table at his colleagues in the brightly lit conference room and the travelling circus analogy, despite his best efforts, kept popping into his mind. Probably it was because they were preparing for a road-show. He saw his reflection in the window – a full head of light-brown hair, allowed to grow long and just the right side of unkempt, greying in places, a look he hoped achieved an air of slightly maverick maturity. Gazing despairingly back was a reluctant showman, trapped in the room with his elephant trainer, his bean counter and a couple of the unfunny clowns, planning the next show. He turned back to the pages on the table in front of him. Two hours into the meeting and finally they had reached slide 15. The one with the "Complicated Truth" contained amongst the bullet points. He loosened his tie.

"I am trying to imagine the scene. We are sitting in a room with one of our shareholders. Our loyal shareholders. Owners of our company. Our employers. Last year we told them 'Rareterre is now funded through to profitability'. More specifically, *I* told them – based on your plans, Olivier, and your financial projections, James." There was no need to rub it in again, he thought, seeing his director of mining exchange glances with his finance director. They'd been over this enough already, but still Peter felt he had the right to be angry, given his role as the buck's inescapable stopping point. "We only see them twice a year. It's our big chance to remind them what a good idea it was to invest in Rareterre. And here we are after only 12 months, our latest numbers showing a further financing need of $35 million. Can we really hope to get away with mentioning it, or rather failing to, in these two bullet points? 'Bankable feasibility studies (ongoing)' and 'finalise concentration plant and staff training (ongoing)'. They all know these steps were supposed to be complete by now."

James shuffled uncomfortably. "It's the de Tocqueville conundrum. I mean, the truth is simply too complicated to explain. We have the extra financing needs, yes, but we know we have a great solution to the problem. The RBS loan. Only we can't tell the market about that until it's signed."

Now Olivier was looking uncomfortable. He did not like finance and nor did he have more than a vague notion of who de Tocqueville was. As a geologist he was not much interested in political theory. James saw his quizzical look.

"Sorry, Olivier, Alexis de Tocqueville, you know, the *Democracy in America* chappie, although what a Frenchman's doing lecturing the Yanks on democracy is a mystery to me, especially as he was writing just after the July Revolution, y'know, not the French Revolution as such, although it was *a* French revolution, of course, just not *The* French Revolution…" He glanced at Olivier whose Teutonic features were increasingly confused.

"What James is referring to, Olivier," Peter interjected quickly, "is something de Tocqueville said that we both rather like, and frustratingly often seems to apply to us. He said, 'It is easier for the world to accept a simple lie than a complex truth', or something along those lines. We have a complicated situation and 60 minutes, max, with each shareholder. All they will care about is that we might have to raise new money."

"But what's so complicated?" asked Olivier. "We *do* have to raise new money."

"Well, yes, but the shareholders will be afraid that they will be asked to provide it by buying more shares. They don't like that, they either cough up or it dilutes them. But we have a way to avoid having to issue more shares, to avoid diluting the current shareholders – by borrowing the money instead." He looked across at Olivier. Still confused. "Dilution's[7] bad," said Peter, desperately distilling things.

"For Olivier, money's money, Peter." James was still trying to help. "He doesn't care if it's borrowed or new equity, so long as it pays for plant refurbs and feasibility studies. Am I right or am I right, Olivier?" Olivier briefly looked like she might answer James, but instead he turned to Peter.

"What is this dilution?" he asked, simply, not sure he cared what the answer was.

"When a company sells more shares, the existing investors have to buy some to avoid their percentage share being reduced. That's dilution. If you hold three million shares today, you have about 3 percent of Rareterre. If we issued, say, another 35 million shares and you didn't buy any, you'd be down, *diluted* down, to 2 percent. Same numerator, bigger denominator. You've been diluted by a third."

"And the new shares are always issued at a discount to the market price, diluting the dilution. Or rather, adding dilution to the dilution," added James encouragingly. Both Peter and Olivier frowned.

"There is the Complicated Truth: we have an unforeseen cash need, which looks bad, but we have a good solution in the shape of RBS. Unfortunately, we can't tell the shareholders on the road-show about the solution, because it's not in the bag as yet – so we have to downplay the problem. The Simple Lie would be that an equity round, a dilutive round, is inevitable," Peter concluded, unsure whether Olivier had got it.

"So, if debt is better, why will the shareholders assume we will expect them to buy new shares instead?" Olivier asked. Good question, thought James, for a Franco-German mineralogist. He sucked his teeth, concaving his cheeks thoughtfully.

"Debt is only better when everything goes according to plan. No dilution, as Peter says. But debt is riskier. If things go badly, then wham! The bank is really in the driving seat. Then they can do what they like, shareholders don't get a look in. Then dilution is the least of anyone's worries. Shareholders are at the bottom of the pile. The back of the queue. No place at the table."

"Besides," Peter interjected, "not many companies like ours, with our financial profile, can borrow much. RBS is proposing something quite innovative. It will be unexpected. Quite frankly, I can hardly believe they are suggesting it myself."

"So better not tell anyone about it until we're sure? Am I right or am I right?" A quicker learner than they gave him credit for, that Olivier.

This road-show promised to be somewhat less than an unalloyed pleasure, as James would put it. Peter never quite knew whether James did it on purpose, but he had a personal speaking style guaranteed to confuse the verbally less agile – foreigners and mining engineers, for example. Peter himself frequently had to act as interpreter, on one occasion leaping in with, "He means 'yes'," just in time, when James assured a suspicious Leeds-based investor near the end of his patience that he "didn't necessarily disagree" with him. James's double negatives and convoluted syntax did have the positive advantage of confusing and infuriating Olivier, whose German mother's Teutonic genes must have been dominant, easily subjugating the father's feeble French DNA, at least so far as physical appearance was concerned. It was always amusing annoying Olivier, because he had no sense of humour and was vain, being handsome in an exaggeratedly Aryan way. He looked like an extra from a film about the unpleasantness between the years of 1939 and 1945. Jug-eared James, who was slight, dark-haired and several inches shorter, once told Peter he was "not unconcerned that Olivier might fail to see the funny side once too often and summon his friends in jackboots". Typical English, James.

Peter was neither English nor German; he was Scottish. Not a radical Scot, no Tartan Taliban, but a proud Scot nonetheless. He hated it when people, not exclusively Americans, referred to him as being English when they meant British. Like so many of his countrymen, he could be quite sentimental on the subject of Scotland. His tendency to romanticise the country of his birth indicated an emotional side to his character, one not always best suited to the position of CEO.

Central London, February 2007

Peter, Olivier and James were nervously about to embark on their week-long road-show of investor presentations whilst harbouring their humdinger

Complicated Truths – that the feasibility study and environmental plan at Trillium Lake were massively over-budget and horribly behind schedule, not to mention the plant refurbishment programme, and the deeply unwelcome connected fact that Rareterre was going to need more money.

To avoid asking shareholders to buy new shares, with the associated dreaded dilution, behind the scenes Peter and James were hard at work arranging loan financing. There was the fact that the new funding requirement was not foreseen, which reflected badly on them. Then there was the share price. Hamlyn Securities' note annoyingly entitled "Medium Rare or Half-Baked?", which had seemed both strangely well-informed and – to Peter and his colleagues – unbalanced in its emphasis, had stridently emphasised the risks of slippage in the company's programme to develop the mine at Trillium Lake. The effect of the note – whatever the source of the information – had been to weaken the share price to the 100p range, a level at which the board would not be happy to issue additional shares any more than the shareholders would be happy if expected to purchase them.

James had contacted Edward Bald, Rareterre's "relationship banker" at Royal Bank of Scotland, RBS. Edward was relatively new to the Rareterre account and relatively new to RBS. He was unlike most of his commercial banking colleagues, having stayed on at university to do an LL.B. law degree after a first degree in English. Having thus commenced a trajectory from artistic to material, from pure to worldly, Edward's washing up on the shores of the commercial banking industry surprised nobody including himself. Edward stood out. He was bright and ambitious in a crowd of timeserving career bankers, and was quickly promoted from the branch network to the London epicentre of what had become the world's biggest bank by many measures. Being biggest mattered to the kind of men who run such organisations, long before the delights of being "too big to fail" became clear to all. Edward was fast-tracked for promotion, and Rareterre somehow found itself on Edward's route in this overtaking lane. James liked Edward; he was young, fresh, and spoke English like an

English graduate, unlike his costermonger colleagues. James liked people to be educated.

Shortly before the road-show, James had visited RBS at their airy Bishopsgate offices just at the time the bank announced a mega-acquisition in the Netherlands, in a deal that confirmed RBS to be the biggest, the smartest, the ballsiest bank on the planet. Even Edward, normally a reflective sort, was swept along in the swirling waters of corporate vanity and hubristic pride.

James had explained why he wanted to meet when he had called to make the arrangements – not a detailed explanation, just the elements: looking to finance the final stages at Trillium Lake, need $35 million, would rather not go back to shareholders at this stage, prefer something non-dilutive. However, before getting down to business, he had to endure several minutes of monologue from an excited Edward. He was told of "the strong platform for growth outside the UK in continental Europe", "leveraging the platform by adding new customers in existing geographic areas and by achieving greater geographic reach", "generating greater value from customer relationships by applying our relationship-driven model, which has delivered greatly superior revenue per customer and revenue per employee metrics". At 46, James should have recognised bullshit when he heard it. Unlike Edward, he had been through a cycle or two, seen some downs after the ups. Later on he would recall all the relationship-driven guff with disgust. At the time, however, he reported back to Peter on a very positive meeting.

"They'll do the lot. In fact, they felt we should add a contingency."

"What, all $35 million? Plus some?"

"Yep. Edward said that emerging young companies like Rareterre were exactly the kind of clients RBS is keenest on. Building relationships for the long term."

"But…" Peter did not want to break the spell. No call on shareholders! Just a big, simple loan facility. No dilution, just an interest bill. He said it anyway. "But we are still loss-making. What about interest cover[8] tests and so on?"

"Well, our projections show a nice cash flow from the old deposits at Trillium Lake, and once the feasibility is done and the processing kit is up to scratch again, all of which is seen as an investment, capital expenditure phase rather than a loss-making one – well, we should be extracting new ores and generating cash in a far from unsatisfactory manner."

"Yes, we should, but what about in the meantime, during the 'investment phase', as you call it. What about the covenants, how will they deal with that?"

James had been through this with Edward. Banks like to keep their customers under control, they want a weather forecast built into their agreements with borrowers so as to spot the rain coming, the better to know when to start demanding their umbrella back: this is one purpose of the covenants in the loan agreements.

"We discussed that. They are talking about inventing some new measures to take all that into account. We'll have interest cover and all that sort of thing, but based on the profit and loss account after adjusting for the spend at Trillium."

It was not signed and sealed, far from it, but Peter, James and Olivier were confident enough to embark on their road-show with their couple of Complicated Truths to deal with: the timing and cost of the final stages in bringing their key Oregon mine asset on stream. Confident, because they also had a super, elegant solution in their back pocket. RBS would simply fill the gap at no cost to shareholders. It was supposed to be a simple truth, not a complicated lie. But circumstances change.

The road-show: a week or so of meetings with institutions who have invested in the company or might do so – the people who manage pension funds, investment trusts, hedge funds and other collective investment vehicles. The princelings of fund management. Most people who have a pension, insurance, or an investment portfolio of any sort, which is most people, are more or less unaware that these princelings are "managing" it on their behalf, skimming off a fee for the service. If those unwittingly passive customers of this hugely lucrative self-regulated industry were more aware, they would probably object that so much remuneration was attached to so little performance.

Of course, the princelings of finance require fitting accommodation. What conference rooms they all had, these custodians of lesser mortals' hard-earned savings! Palatial high-rent offices clustered in Mayfair and the City, complete with marble-clad receptions and irritating, time-consuming security measures. RBS's set-up on Bishopsgate was a prime example, requiring a mugshot and a printed visitor's pass before access was granted even to the waiting area with its plush leather sofas and massive wall of interlaced TV screens, displaying brave RBS bankers out diligently doing business, advancing credit to worthy companies such as Rareterre. All that security was intended to prevent competitors from stealing RBS's brilliant, fail-safe money-making business secrets, no doubt. Or their list of client companies, whose financial needs they serviced in order to make the bank its honest profits in a contentedly and mutually advantageous relationship, diligently nurtured by RBS's excellent, client-focussed staff. It was not really believable, even back then.

"Remind me why we do this, Peter," said James as he settled back in the seat of their lovely dedicated taxi, theirs for the day, a necessity given the back-to-back schedule of meetings oscillating between the West End and the City, but one that felt like a luxury. "Remind me why the hell we have to go to five different places a day for five solid days in a row?" He waved the printed itinerary of their week-long road-show at Peter. "Why is it even allowed? We might fail to resist the temptation of saying something interesting to some of these people." He sighed resignedly. The taxi swerved to avoid a cyclist running the red light.

"These people, as you call them, just happen to own our company, James. They like to be told how their investment is doing."

"Yes, and we will be telling them all the same thing. Otherwise we'd be unfairly offering unequal information to some shareholders and withholding it from others. There are rules about that. Stock exchange rules." He said this in a passably good imitation of Julian, one of their nominated-advisor minders. Old Etonian Julian Marian-Smythe, their constant conscience.

"Well, not exactly withholding it, James. I must say though, I have often wondered why we can't just get everyone together and tell them all at once. Think of it! One 90-minute meeting, then a nice lunch and back to the office and get some work done. Or we could hold the meeting somewhere interesting. Blackpool Tower maybe. In a pod on the London Eye."

"Not big enough."

"First come, first served?"

"Dream on. But surely they wouldn't ask for individual meetings if they weren't hoping to get something out of it that the others, I mean the ones not present, didn't know? If we weren't so well-disciplined it might lead to insider trading, and then what would Julian say?"

"It's a grey area."

"A fog bank."

"And we have to navigate in it."

"We have to navigate the fog bank of ambiguity generated during our cosy one-to-ones over chocolate digestives, trying to avoid the de Tocqueville reefs!" James regretted that Olivier was not in the car; extended metaphors were nearly as dear to him as double negatives.

"Every company has its Complicated Truths and their associated Simple Lies, both good and bad, James. Although I sometimes think we have more than our fair share."

The great grey truths take time to explain and involve non-binary outcomes; all the while the Simple Lie is crouched like an idiot hobgoblin on the fund manager's shoulder, whispering into his ear in black and white. The truth always comes out eventually, of course, but to express it in sufficient detail takes too long. For all their huge remuneration, their 1.5 percent fees picked annually out of other people's pension pockets, the princelings liked it kept simple. The Complicated Truth would deprive them of their simple clarity. They might have to think, when what they really want is a fix of the unthinking exuberance which gets them buying, or of the equally reactive dissatisfaction, which starts them selling.

Peter was just reflecting how the de Tocqueville conundrum ends up with incomplete information all round and unnecessarily volatile markets and how he, the reluctant ringmaster, hated the semi-mendacity, the spin, the careful crafting of half-truths and the message-management demanded by his investor relations activities, when the taxi arrived at its destination. The drizzle had turned to rain. Their briefcases bloated with presentations, Peter and James got out onto the wet pavement where Olivier was waiting for them. The Rareterre team's first appointment of the road-show was with Viking Victor IV, a hedge fund from somewhere Scandinavian. The offices were in a lacquered Mayfair terrace conveniently close to Le Gavroche. The building's exterior had the appearance of a townhouse, the interior was all exposed brickwork and disturbing art. In the entrance-cum-waiting area there was a large vase of flowers pickled in refrigerated formaldehyde or something. It was not pretty, and the refrigeration unit made an annoying hum, but it achieved its objective of declaring the financial success of VV IV, and implying that edgy, modern, iconoclastic thinking permeated its management. In the meeting room, to which they were ushered by an unusually tall and intimidatingly trendy girl – high heels and a floor-length kaftan of some sort, in violet velvet – there was a painting of what looked like a butcher's counter displaying human body parts in place of meat. James grimaced and bagged a chair with its back to the art, retrieved three copies of the PowerPoint presentation from his briefcase and slapped them down onto the glass-topped table.

It was the first meeting of a week-long schedule, so there were as yet no little habits formed amongst the team – no prescribed seating geometry, no tired little set phrases. Peter sat on James's left at the head of the table and Olivier on James's right, back also to the charnel scene. Judging by her accent and manner when asking whether anyone wanted coffee, the tall girl had benefited from an English boarding school education; Peter, whose own three children were all in private fee-paying schools, wondered whether Daddy was happy with the return on his investment. He accepted the coffee offer on all their behalves.

"So, what d'you reckon?" he asked his colleagues when they were alone. "Looks like a niner establishment to me. Proper coffee, handmade from freshly ground beans in a stylish china cup, I'd say."

"Maybe. But remember the time we were in that room round the corner from here, the one with oak panelling from the chateau de somewhere or other, and they gave us each a mug of lukewarm Nescafé with floating undissolved granules? You guessed nine there as well, and it was a two. I'm going for a not unreasonable five. Or maybe six." As a conservative accountant, James's guesses were always low. Olivier participated mainly to humour his colleagues. He thought it a childish English schoolboy-type game.

"Just as long as you don't say out loud 'It's a one!' like you did at…"

The door burst open and Jens, a diminutive bespectacled tieless and tireless young man, strode in. The Rareterre team got to their feet and introductions were made.

"No Jim?" Jens asked, somewhat redundantly looking around the small room.

Jim Spratt was an equity sales team member from Rareterre's Nominated Advisor,[9] NOMAD Securities, and the corporate broker assigned to Rareterre. Jim and his colleagues on the sales desk had the job of introducing investors to client companies, promoting the investment attractions of their shares, and facilitating the process by which information flowed both ways, transactions took place and capitalism worked –

money transferred, share prices rose and fell. By knowing the companies and investors well, the brokers hoped to generate "trading volume" – on which their employing bank would earn a commission – and, ideally, advise on occasional large fundraisings where the fees were much more sizeable. In good times, the equity salesman's job is easy. As a relationship job it requires personable, affable, sociable people – not always the sharpest, in fact seldom the sharpest. Jim fit the bill perfectly: a slightly Estuary-English accent, no sign of too much education, ready smile, prone to statements of the obvious or the unverifiable – mainly related to the functioning and condition of "the markets". Apart from as a chaperone, and to secure his claim to any business emanating from individual investor institutions, Jim's presence served no apparent purpose. Peter had not noticed his absence.

"I'm sure he'll be along soon. He normally is," he answered, somewhat nonsensically. "Shall we start anyway?" One of the practical problems with road-shows is keeping to the tight back-to-back schedule to allow travel back and forth between the City and the West End. Miss Lofty came into the room with three caffè americanos in stylish white triangular cups on saucers (definitely a nine, Miss Lofty at least putting to good use the domestic science component of the curriculum of her pricey British boarding school). For Jens a jokey personal mug: "I survived the Hamlyn Securities Minerals and Mining Conference San Diego 2004", in red lettering above a cartoon picture of a man slumped over a lectern, crosses where his eyes should have been, tongue lolling. Peter winced inwardly.

Hamlyn was one of NOMAD Securities' main competitors, and the only brokerage whose equity analyst held a negative view of Rareterre. Their "house view" had switched to negative with their earlier "Medium Rare or Half-Baked?" note and Stacey East, the analyst in question, had unhelpfully produced another report a few days before the road-show started. Distributed as widely as possible to institutional investors, it highlighted potential cost overruns resulting from the development delays at

Rareterre's all-important Trillium Lake mine and suggested that a further funding looked inevitable. "Rarely Rarely Expensive" was its irritating title. It was annoying for three reasons: first, its timing, guaranteed to spoil the road-show; second, its undiluted negative conclusions, not giving Rareterre the benefit of any doubt; third, and mainly, because Stacey was right on the key new Complicated Truth facts. *God knows how she does it*, Peter thought grimly.

Jens was one of those annoying undisciplined people who flip to and fro during a presentation, denying its presenters the logical narrative they hoped would run through the meeting, one they had laboured to create with the expensive help of bankers and investor relations advisors. He could do this as he was clearly the brightest person in the room, and because he had what the presenting team wanted: the investment funds. The Rareterre presentation started out with Peter introducing the team (to Jens' slight irritation as he had, after all, just shaken their hands) and quickly going on to the background of rare-earth elements, their qualities and many uses. Page three of the presentation had a semi-transparent picture of a Toyota Prius, its intestines visible and marked with the names of the various rare-earths involved:

- Battery technology, Neodymium
- Electric motors, Praseodymium
- Catalytic converters, Lanthanum

Peter was pointing out how the green tech economy was dependent on rare-earths, and had just quoted "green technology comes from black earths" when he noticed that Jens was studying page 15, concerned with the operations at Trillium Lake, which highlighted all the steps to commercialisation, the first eight smugly ticked. Early stage proof of the resource (big tick); define process for beneficiation, extraction, separation (tick); initial feasibility studies (big tick); pilot plant (tick); environmental impact assessment (smaller tick); environmental and other approvals (tick); bankable feasibility studies (ongoing); letters of intent with customers (tick); finalise concentration plant and staff training (ongoing). Peter stopped and looked at Jens. Viking Victor IV was not yet an investor in Rareterre, so the story Peter and his team were trying to tell was new to Jens and, like any other story, benefited from being told in the intended sequence.

"If you want to go on to that page, fine, Olivier here can take you through it." Olivier murmured his assent. Peter wondered if he had sounded as irritated as he felt. He had just noticed a copy of Stacey East's "Rarely Rarely Expensive" analyst note under Jens' notepad.

"That would be great. I was just wondering about the feasibility studies and the last point, the 'finalisation' of the concentration plant and staff training. Am I right to think that actually you have not finished the feasibility study or the concentration plant?"

"Yes. We have not followed a traditional path, because of the age and standing of Trillium Lake," said Olivier. "The mine was in production for years until 1998 or so. Then the Chinese really racked up production, prices fell, and we..."

"Yah, I got that, I know that. The whole world knows that China is dominant, that for various reasons they can produce more cheaply than we can in the West. I was asking you about the timing and cost of getting to the finish line, getting to full production."

This was a bit much, Peter thought. There were important, carefully crafted slides which Jens had skipped over in his rush to reach Stacey East's "Rarely Rarely Expensive" point. Listening with half an ear to Olivier answering Jens' questions, Peter mentally itemised the best bits that Jens had skipped over. Maybe he would be able to slip them back in, better late than never.

"'There is oil in the Middle East; there are rare-earths in China.' So said Deng Xiaoping in 1992. This has been going on for decades! China dominates the world in rare-earth metals, 95 percent of global production is Chinese…" In his head Peter was showing graphs illustrating the fall to near zero of non-Chinese production, the line for China zooming upwards. In the room, Olivier was still plodding through the outstanding tasks required of the feasibility team.

"These minerals matter too much for us to remain wholly reliant upon China. Chinese export restrictions are already putting at risk exactly the sort of high value-added, high-tech and green manufacturing that Western governments like to think will become a driving force in the 'knowledge economies'…" Peter liked this point, it had a nice Sino-symmetry, now that nearly everything else was being manufactured by cheaper, harder-working people living further east, toiling in factories run with far fewer scruples about the environment. Surely Rareterre would benefit from this geological–political situation – surely developing independent sources was the sensible thing to do? Surely there would be a ready market at high prices for Rareterre's output? Amongst the rare metal extraction community, the positive implications of this situation and line of thought were warmly embraced. Peter wanted Jens to know these things, that any investment in Rareterre would be riding a globalisation wave. But Jens was noting down the capital expenditure Olivier was describing, totting up total costs for individual machines. Peter's mind was still on the global big picture, whilst everyone else in the room was doing elementary arithmetic.

What James called, in his characteristically knotted way, "a tacit mutual vow of silence" surrounded the reverse side of the Chinese supply-dependency coin: almost complete Chinese control of the market also brought great dangers for would-be competitors, and potentially fatal disruptions in the markets; markets the state-owned Chinese mines could easily manipulate. In the conversation taking place in

Peter's head he dismissed this with ease. Now prices were healthy and prospects bright, thanks in no small part to the efforts of Al Gore and the green revolution.

The Green Thing was definitely a big plus for Rareterre. Peter wondered if Al Gore had ever been to grim Baiyun-Obo, the immense opencast rare-earths mine in Mongolia, source of many materials vital for wind turbines and hybrid cars and such things. "The black heart of the green economy" someone had called it. Peter *had* been there – he had the photos on his telephone to show people – and to the clay deposits in south-eastern China, where a mafia-operated artisanal extraction using the most rudimentary opencast acid techniques made Baiyun-Obo look like a Swiss mineral-water plant in comparison.

Rareterre and other Western competitors would employ far more environmentally acceptable methods which, although much more expensive financially surely represented a huge potential advantage when the objective is green? But no one wanted to draw too much attention to this matter either, because all rare-earth extraction, all mineral extraction of any sort, has its environmental cost. Massive amounts of energy are used, carbon emitted, acids and other chemicals employed, rivers-full of water consumed. And yet, in the rush to address environmental and climate change issues, taxpayers' money and political capital by the bucket-load were being expended to promote the development of technologies requiring rare-earths. The mining of these was leaving tracts of rural China poisoned, uninhabitable wastelands with abandoned, contaminated rice paddies and water tables, and scarred barren topsoil pockmarked with acidic extraction pits.

The half-ear Peter had still trained on the proceedings in Mayfair, worlds away from Baiyun-Obo, noted that Olivier was still boring to Olympic standard on the difficulties of coordinating approvals, investments and finance. James was about to speak, Peter could tell. He could also sense that Jens and VV IV were a lost cause – the man was about as likely to invest in Rareterre as he was to pay PAYE income tax like a normal person.

Jens was getting to his feet. He held up Stacey's "Rarely Rarely Expensive" note.

"It looks like she might be onto something here, guys. Come back when you do the financing; I might like the pricing better then. But I still think you are miles off getting everything lined up to start production."

"Well, one couldn't exactly disagree with the observation that that could have gone better," said James, outside on the Mayfair pavement between an art gallery and a shoe shop, dedicated to such expensive footwear that apparently they could only afford to put one pair on display in the window.

"What was the narrative? Rare-earths are getting more important – there's a supply/demand imbalance coming which will favour producers like us – we have a great and established resource in a stable political environment – we are nearly ready to restart supplying the market – buy our shares?" James was ticking off points on his fingers. "What did young Jens, intense Jens, hear? – Hi, here we are – rare-earths are important – Stacey's right, we've got timing and finance issues – better to invest in C. Brown!"

Their major competitor, C. Brown Pty., the big rare-earths operation based in Western Australia, was a listed company several orders of magnitude larger than Rareterre. In the starkest contrast with their published work on Rareterre, Hamlyn seemed to take the attitude in their analysis of C. Brown that they were innocent until proven guilty; Rareterre was always guilty as charged, no trial.

"Yep, that was about it. Bloody Stacey! I wonder – do Hamlyn have a relationship with C. Brown? I mean, might they be angling for some M&A work, a London listing, something like that, with nice fees attached…?"

"You're surely not suggesting that they are being unfair out of simple self-interest?" said James in exaggerated mock-horror. "Inform the *FT*: stop press! Bankers Motivated by Greed!"

The road-show was not a success, largely thanks to Stacey's note, a copy of which seemed to be on everyone's desk. Peter, Olivier and James wrestled with the facts surrounding the company's financing needs, unable to reveal the solution in the form of the highly innovative, but as yet unfinalised, RBS loan. There were, of course, encouraging meetings with loyal share-holders who had consistently followed the company and its management, especially Peter, and were interested in the long-term fundamentals of their business. People like John Wellbeloved, who ran a small portfolio of discre-tionary money for private clients, and who invested his own money in the same fund.

"I see Stacey still loves you, boys!" said John with a mischievous grin, waving the Hamlyn "Rarely Rarely Expensive" note under their noses. "Keeping up her new-found imbalance. Did one of you, you know, do something to her? I mean, it almost seems like a personal thing here. 'Hell hath no fury' and all that..."

It had occurred to Peter that someone inside the company might have had some sort of relationship, a liaison with Stacey, and it had not ended well, or at least not to Stacey's satisfaction. Or maybe it was ongoing, this affair, and whoever it involved was somehow not well-disposed to Rareterre? That would explain Stacey's annoying ability to identify the things most on their minds and publish them in her particularly slanted analysis. As he was thinking this it occurred to Peter that James had once voiced similar thoughts.

"You don't suppose Olivier is, y'know, enjoying inappropriate relations with Stacey?" he had said with uncharacteristic directness. They were at the annual Rare-Earth Minerals Conference the preceding year, which had taken place in New York. Peter and James were sitting in the semi-darkness of the conference hotel bar after a long day listening to other companies' presentations, and both had observed Olivier accompany Stacey through the lobby. Had his hand made contact with her lower back as he appar-ently ushered her in the direction of the lifts?

Peter emerged from his thoughts and examination of Olivier's reaction (there was none), in time to respond to John Wellbeloved after an imperceptible delay.

"Attractive though she is" – he had to admit this, although he tried to make the admission sound like sarcasm – "we all know better than to take any risks with people in her position." But did they all know better? Did Olivier know better? "Besides, we're all happily married men!" Another questionable statement. There were rumours about Olivier's marriage. And could he really describe the current state of affairs in the Mount household as "happy"? That morning he had left a silent house, breakfastless and without the peck on his cheek he was accustomed to receiving. Ivy had slept in Harry's empty room, such had been the magnitude of the previous night's row. Cruel things had been said – mostly by him, he knew – and now he could not even recall what had sparked the dispute. He vaguely remembered having felt snappy, maybe having actually snapped, when Ivy had been describing some inconsequential disagreement she'd had with some inconsequential person – a friend or a neighbour or a shopkeeper or something. He had things on his mind, was tired, had experienced several quite unsatisfactory interactions with other people that day himself, but would not waste either of their time in recounting them. Ivy seemed to enjoy making mountains out of these little social molehills. He remembered it all now. He had told her to bloody well stop getting on people's nerves if she wanted not to have these "problems", that he had real problems to resolve, and she should grow up and deal with it. He might have told her to stop bothering him with trivia. She might have responded that if he cared for her at all, he would see that it was far from trivial. His answer to this might have been unkind and, with the smallest amount of hindsight, unfelt.

Central London, February 2007

Rareterre had many good shareholders like John Wellbeloved. But far more investors and potential investors that they saw on this road-show, enough to be seriously irritating, were largely unconcerned about the timing of their efforts in Oregon – it was the financing that obsessed them. If Rareterre was going to raise more money in equity, from share-holders like them, including them, it would depress the share price. Firstly, there was the discount to the market at which the new shares would be issued – traditionally something in the region of 10 percent. Why? No one on Planet Finance ever explained this, it simply served their greedy purposes. Then there was the supply/demand equilibrium – more supply equals a lower price; especially if lots of new shareholders have shares bought at a discount, shares they can simply sell quickly and crystallise their unmerited gains.

Nearly everyone that Peter, James and Olivier met quickly became fascinated by the prospect of a fundraising by means of a new share issue. Try as they might, without being able to talk about their attractive deal with RBS, none of the Rareterre team was able to offer a satisfactory answer to these concerns. Over the course of the week the share price dropped steadily, until it breached the "psychologically important" 100p mark.

"Psychologically important!" Peter had exploded when Julian, their director at NOMAD Securities, had used the phrase for the first time. "Psychologically important!? What the hell's psychology got to do with the price of our shares?" Peter suspected, with more accuracy than he would have believed, that Julian enjoyed winding him up.

Maybe psychology was irrelevant, but apparently neurology was not. The stock market was clearly suffering from bipolar disorder. There had been times in the past, when something triggered a manic phase in the patient's condition, and the price of Rareterre shares rose exuberantly on the slightest stimulus. But right now, even after a hard week of "investor relations" activities, arguably because of it, the depressive phase was definitely predominant. As with a moody teenager, nothing anyone said was interpreted positively. James pointed out that the revenue stream from the old stockpiles of ores was increasing year-on-year at a healthy 20 percent rate. A grumpy shrug. Olivier reported that, although delayed, the preliminary findings from the feasibility study were all very encouraging, and there was data suggesting even greater probable reserves on the Trillium Lake property than had been thought. An insolent insertion of earphones. A slammed bedroom door. But it was Peter who manifested the equivalent of an adolescent temper tantrum.

Towards the end of the week, when everyone had more or less had enough, when they were getting on one another's nerves almost as much as they were failing to impress their audiences, there was a meeting with the fund manager at Dreadnought Investment. Dreadnought, one of the biggest fund managers in the world, with billions of dollars under management, was also one of Rareterre's major shareholders, owning just under 10 percent of the company. The manager, Piers Frobisher, was relatively new to the account, having been moved to manage the small capitalisation "Minnows" portfolio from somewhere more prestigious in the organisation, as a punishment for some unspecified misdemeanour. The lucky investors in the Dreadnought Investment Minnows fund had their pension savings hopes pinned on a youthful yet disgruntled and miscreant manager in post as a penance. Although not actually an adolescent, he was not long out of the LSE, and had been granted a first-class honours degree in economics recently enough for him to think it actually meant something.

Dreadnought Investment's offices were, like so many of the City-based institutions, in a modern high-rise building of bland appearance. However, such was their scale that the entire building belonged to Dreadnought, and so valuable the fund-management expertise contained within the rough granite-clad walls that there was a two-stage checking-in process. Three stages if you counted the uniformed "guard" at the door who, if ever anyone addressed him – which they only did if they were neophytes of the first degree – would simply point helpfully in the direction of the reception desk.

Because it was late in the day, Peter, James and Olivier had accumulated a sizeable unpunctuality. The ten-minute security procedure ("I'm glad we didn't have to remove our shoes and belts," Olivier had said loudly enough for the severe-looking lady at the desk to hear) only made things worse.

The similarities to airport administration did not end with the thoroughness of the check-in procedure. Once in the departure lounge, visitors to Dreadnought were informed by means of an electronic destinations screen which meeting room to attend, and on arrival at the gate the company's identity and that of their Dreadnought host were displayed, along with the agreed meeting times. Peter tried to imagine the capital investment proposal that justified the expense of this system, but could do no better than "we've got loads of money, so let's just have it. That and the cigar-smoke extractor in the board room".

As they progressed down the corridor en route to departure gate 14C, he turned to Olivier: "Y'know, all this" – he gesticulated around him, taking in the thick carpet, the modern art punctuating the walls, the impractical long-legged darkwood table bearing an ovoid sculpture in a pool of halogen light at the end of the corridor – "this stuff, ostentatious luxury, it seems all wrong when you think of the conditions we work in, and I'm sure it's the same for most of the investee companies. We come here and get kicked in the arse if our cost ratios deteriorate, and here they sit in judgement in a—" He was going to say "Fort Knox of excess", but Piers appeared at the open meeting room door. Peter wondered how much he had heard.

"Hello, Piers. Sorry we're late. Hopefully someone from NOMAD called ahead to warn you?"

"No, they didn't. Well, never mind, let's get on with it." He gestured them into the room. Enough space for 20. Dark shiny table set with embossed notepads and branded biros. Coffee (a six or seven, Peter recalled from previous experience, but cookies, double chocolate chip, which scored 10) was available from a large vacuum flask, milk and sugar beside, in a niche at the end of the room. Piers did not offer them any.

Hands were shaken. They took up their habitual places, Peter at the head of the table on James's left and Olivier on James's right. Piers sat down opposite Olivier, but one chair further down the table. He had a copy of Stacey's "Rarely Rarely Expensive" note on top of his pile of papers.

"Thanks for sparing us the time," Peter began, as usual, pushing a copy of the presentation down the table towards Piers. "We —"

"Can we just get straight to the point?" Piers asked rudely, ignoring the presentation. James knew what "the point" was going to be. Financing. Peter knew. Even Olivier knew. Piers was consulting his notes.

"Last time we met you told me that, and I think I am quoting you accurately, 'Rareterre is funded through to profitability'." He rolled his eyes ceiling-ward, pursed his lips disapprovingly as if, in uttering the words, he had tasted something unpleasant. Piers was what James called a "young fogey", someone with all the traits of an old fogey but not the maturity. He was almost certainly a member of the Young Conservatives and probably shot and killed small feathered and furred creatures for pleasure. He was now giving Peter a decidedly old-fashioned look. Peter felt like reminding him of the quarter century that divided them, but resisted the temptation. For rather too long he resisted the temptation to speak at all. He had once given evidence in a trial, and been advised by the barrister not to answer questions that had not been asked, that the defence silk would be trying to undermine his credibility. It had been easy in court to heed this advice, leaving long silences whilst the defence waited for him to be tempted to offer unasked for but revealing explanations. In the context that Peter now found himself such a course was not appropriate, but Piers had asked no question and Peter was tired and angered by the impoliteness and, in truth, by the embarrassing accuracy of Piers's quotation – so, foolishly, he said nothing. The silence lasted perhaps ten seconds, but they passed with the heavy tread of an under-strength pall-bearing team in a muddy graveyard. Finally, James broke the silence. Unfortunately, he too was tired.

"We don't necessarily feel we can't confirm that statement today, I mean we can't be definitive on the matter, but we are not idle and recognise the not unjustified concerns of shareholders..." Poor James, unable to mention the RBS deal because it might never happen, but keen to impart the message that the financing issues were under control. He could have gone on like this for God knows how long, but Peter chose this moment to pour fuel on the already healthily crackling flames of Piers's dissatisfaction.

"You know what, Piers? In the real world, in the world where people actually do things – I dunno, make widgets and build power stations and, yes, extract minerals – in that world where all the wealth of this country is generated and hard decisions are made daily, complicated decisions which go beyond 'buy' and 'sell' and 'should I get a new Ferrari with my bonus this year?' and 'could we get Tracey Emin to hang some soiled bed-sheets in the reception area?' Well, Piers, in that world sometimes things don't turn out quite as they were expected to. Shit, Piers, happens in that world, for all sorts of complicated reasons you would not have the faintest chance of understanding, and you probably don't care to understand anyway. Yes, we are behind schedule with the refurbishment and the feasibility is over budget; yes, Piers, well done for remembering that we were hoping things would be different 12 months ago, well done for being able to read the unbalanced so-called analysis from Stacey..." He was fizzling out. "Bravo." The full stop at the end of his rant was addressed as much to himself; bitter congratulations on a job bloody well done. Excellent work, Peter. Pat on the back for that one. Way to go, Mr CEO.

Piers, stiffly for a man of his age, got to his feet and, with a slight nod of the head to a desolate James and a horrified Olivier, left the room without a word. He took the Hamlyn Securities note with him. He had shares to sell and was going to need the telephone number on the cover.

CHAPTER 7

When Peter and James next met with the RBS team lead by Edward Bald at Rareterre's Hammersmith head office, it was against the rather depressing backdrop of a share price down by 20 percent, and with Dreadnought half out and still actively selling their shares whenever the chance arose.

The RBS bankers, three of them, had come to discuss the detailed terms of the proposed loan and the due diligence enquiries they would be expecting to complete. Peter was dismayed to learn that the bank's pre-loan investigations were to involve a great deal of subcontracting to an army of professionals: battalions of lawyers with various specialisations, corps of accountants – both Rareterre's own audit firm and an "independent" – and brigades of geologists and mineralogists. Naturally, Rareterre was to pick up the costs for RBS's little mercenary army, whether or not a loan agreement was actually signed.

"But, Edward, isn't all this due diligence something for your benefit? I mean, we know our books are accurate and our auditors are just as reputable as Masondo, who you want to engage – why the separate accountants' report? Plus, surely you have your in-house experts to support you on the geology and so on? RBS is, after all, 'one of the biggest lenders to the mineral extraction sector', that must result in some internal expertise?" Peter intentionally emphasised the "biggest lenders to the sector" bit, which was a direct quote taken from the RBS pitch presentation Edward and his sidekicks had made at the start of the meeting.

James was beside Peter at Rareterre's diminutive conference table in their cramped meeting room – no external windows and so narrow that if someone wanted to leave, everyone between him and the door had to suck in their stomachs and squeeze their chairs close to the table to let them past. James was not a man for a fight; he would describe himself as a "realist". James had those essentially British qualities of a slight distaste for money, or at least for haggling over it – possibly a disadvantage in a chief financial officer – and a deep, visceral dislike of a "scene". The episode at the meeting with Dreadnought had been pure torture to James, and they had not discussed it, beyond a muttered apology from Peter to him and Olivier on leaving Dreadnought's building. Yet here was Peter, all brimstone and flashing eyes, ready to take on RBS when, in James's opinion, they repre-sented something not unlike a saviour, apparently willing to advance the funds they were missing, on good terms, and without the shareholders or the diminished share price mattering a jot. He jumped in before things deteriorated: "Oh, it's quite normal, Peter. All banks do it. No doubt Ed has his credit committee paperwork to complete, and they'll certainly be wanting to know which experts have signed off on our financials and business fundamentals."

James looked Peter in the eyes and Peter saw there the plea "don't let's look a gift horse in the mouth". In fact, Peter was as keen as James to do the bank financing – RBS had indicated very keen pricing in terms of the interest rate, only a couple of percentage points over one of the interbank rates, and a repayment schedule long enough to allow for some future slippage in the plans.

Early in his tenure as CEO, Peter had attended a course at the London Business School entitled "Corporate Finance for the non-financial Executive". It is well established that most people recall only three key messages from any such course, and from nine weeks of Thursday night attendance at the Regent's Park campus, one of these three things for Peter was: "equity is the most expensive form of capital". It made sense – it was the riskiest and therefore should win the greatest return. Peter was also persuaded by the attractions of filling their funding need from the deep, single pocket of RBS and not from the equally deep, but much more difficult-to-access, pockets of his unruly group of shareholders. The thought of another road-show, which was inevitable if they were to do an equity fundraising, was too horrible to contemplate. Bank debt was also supposed to be much cheaper in upfront arrangement costs than equity, with its discounted pricing, shareholder documents, brokers' fees and commissions and legal expenses. But, he was now beginning to wonder just how much the loan was likely to cost as he mentally totted up all the partners of accountancy and law firms with their by-the-minute charging.

Edward did indeed have his credit committee to satisfy, and the structure of the covenants in the Rareterre loan was certainly unconventional and would require explanation. Edward had little doubt that the deal would be approved, and he let James and Peter know as much. However, there was a process to observe, even in the heady, aggressive, balance-sheet leveraging environment that prevailed at RBS amid its hubristic dash for growth, its unseemly at-all-costs scramble for the global top-dog-bank slot.

Peter and James knew that it would be corporate finance madness to issue new shares at less than 100p each, when cheaper loan finance was available. The RBS proposals were just so neat, so eye-catching in their simplicity and innovation – they would establish Rareterre as an exceptional company amongst its peers because of its ability to win the support of a major "relationship bank" with a long tradition of corporate banking in the UK. In short, on the basis that the RBS deal was not only cheap money but also prestigious, James and Peter recommended to the board that Rareterre set aside the resources required to make the preparations for the RBS loan.

Accountants duly came in from the bank's preferred firm of Masondo, one of the "big four", consisting of Partners (charging £600 an hour for their insightful services), Managers (£300 per hour) and "the ones who actually do the work", as James referred to them, paid an hourly rate of £15, but for whom Masondo charged its clients ten times that. Lawyers rolled up their sleeves and activated their time-clocks. An extravagant geology consultancy was engaged to "give RBS comfort" – a turn of phrase about which, uncharacteristically, Olivier cracked a crude joke.

There followed several extensive negotiations of professionals' engagement letters, each containing its disclaimer of any responsibility incongruously nestling amongst astronomic fee demands. For some reason James had circulated the draft letters to the whole board, probably thinking that so big a commitment required the full board's approval, or at least its being informed and offered a chance to object. And Frits did object. He called James.

"So, let me get this straight, James. Masondo charge us £600 per hour, that's £10 a minute, A MINUTE, yet they have the effrontery to tell us that neither we nor anyone else can rely upon any of their work." James's heart sank. He recognised the symptoms; Frits was winding himself up and James knew he was in for a marathon.

"It looks worse than it is, Frits," he began, hoping to head him off, maybe get it down to a 400-metre sprint or perhaps even a 110-metre hurdles. "They always put in language like that. It's something not uncon-nected with their professional indemnity insurance. Or something." Like Franco-German Olivier, Dutch Frits found James's phraseology both chal-lenging and annoying.

"Not unconnected? Insurance? But they say…" With a sinking heart James heard the rustle of paper. Marathon, not steeplechase. "'Our work is to be based primarily on internal management information, which we will not verify or corroborate'." He was quoting from the letter. *Bloody hell*, James thought, *he almost knows it by heart.*

Frits was just getting into his stride. "They won't verify or corroborate our information! What the hell are they doing for their six hundred quid? And why in the name of God do they need insurance, and us to indemnify them when they are explicitly not doing anything?" James distinctly heard multiple question marks, probably intermixed with exclamation marks. Frits was still going. "So as well as doing nothing they explicitly tell us that they take no responsibility!" More rustling. "They want us to indemnify them against third-party claims, but they have no equal obligation to us! I mean, did you read the bit about 'gross negligence'? We can make a claim, limited to the totality of the fees we have paid them, but only if they are *grossly* negligent and not if they are just plain vanilla negligent? I mean, how much negligence is 'gross', and how much negligence is acceptable at £600 per hour?"

James had to admit that Frits had a point. James was also aware that Masondo were not going to accept any changes, that the bank would back them up, that to do the deal they would have to accept. RBS and Masondo enjoyed a close and mutually beneficial relationship. There was really no point in fighting it. It was nearly an hour before he had calmed Frits down enough to get these unpalatable truths through to him.

With something similar to the inevitability of a hangover, Rareterre agreed to the unreasonable terms of engagement for RBS's subcontracted army. With the same inevitability, a huge team of expensive but not answerable professionals descended on Rareterre's modest office and staff, seeking out information, facts and data, all of which would return to the same offices and workforce in the form of beautifully presented, graphic-rich, landscape-format, full colour, brochure-style documents, ultimately destined for the bank but requiring prior verification. Employees' real work was relegated to after-hours and inter-meeting opportunities, the masters of the RBS team noisily requiring precedence. An old saying about hiring consultants to tell you the time, and their borrowing your watch to do so, was given a wide airing.

Health club, Hammersmith, London, April 2007

On the evening of a particularly trying day of skirmishes with the bank's mercenary detachments of accountants and lawyers, Peter made his way to the underground car park where he kept the Fireblade, down through a draughty urine-scented cement stairway of that sort unique to car park architecture, helmet in hand. The sight of the big bike, resting muscularly at a slight angle under the neon strip lights, did not have its habitual effect of lifting his spirits. Wearily he slid his head into the helmet, fired up the bike and eased it up the ramp and out into the damp Hammersmith streets. He had decided rather than going straight home, as he usually did, to go to the gym.

Several years earlier, when his brother had been warned of high blood pressure and high cholesterol following a routine medical, Peter had joined the gym near his house in Chelsea, one of a large nationwide chain of health and fitness clubs. Their grandfather and two uncles had died young of what was at the time called a "heart attack", but which today would enjoy far greater diagnostic specificity; the generality of the risk and the genetic probabilities of the underlying condition had forced Peter into the welcoming arms of the fitness industry, without any investigation of his own cardiovascular health. He normally went to the gym three mornings a week; an evening visit was rare, but today he felt a need for the mindless, repetitive physical satisfaction of a workout.

Leaving the Fireblade illegally parked in an alley close to the club, Peter took his biking stuff to the changing room, opened his locker and quickly changed. There were five or six men in various stages of undress padding around from shower to locker, or struggling into or out of clothing. Peter wondered why a naked man carrying a towel back from the shower did not wrap it around his waist, what motivated this act of voluntary exposure. The man had an enviable body, admittedly, but what was this deliberate exhibitionism trying to achieve? Was this some sort of homosexual invitation? Was the man merely lazy, indifferent, or did he want to show off? Whatever the case, as usual no one spoke, observing the strict unwritten rule forbidding partly or fully naked locker-room conversation. Other unwritten gym rules included: never look, other than fleetingly, at a member of the opposite sex, the more attractive they are the less time your glance can rest; never talk to anyone on the gym floor, unless it is your trainer; never make eye contact with anyone; if you meet someone you recognise from the gym on the street, never acknowledge them and certainly never use the line "sorry, I didn't recognise you with your clothes on"; never return the free weights to their rightful place on the stand. Peter tied up his Nikes with careful attention to the laces, avoiding raising his eyes to an embarrassing line of sight.

The club was very different in the evening, the clientele was older and a bigger proportion were men. In the mornings, Peter was accustomed to being outnumbered by younger and, most agreeably, by lycra-clad female members. It was, as he told Olivier, an uplifting way to start the day. Olivier had not seen any pun, *kein Wortspiel*, which may have been as well, all things considered. Humourless Hun. With little enthusiasm Peter climbed onto an elliptical cross trainer machine and punched the buttons, selecting the required time, programme and difficulty scale. He inserted his headphones – a further protection from unwanted social intercourse – and began his 25 minutes of fruitless energy consumption. Not for the first time he wondered why these machines were not somehow wired up to the national grid, as part of the government's green renewable energy feed-in initiative. Maybe they were, the gym making a sly additional profit, unknown to its members, literally from the sweat of their brows. Extortionist bastards.

The room was vast, with six lines of cross trainers, each of about 15 devices interspersed with running machines, set out in two opposite rows of three. Like opposing armies, these ranks faced one another across a barrier of back-to-back ceiling-hung flat-screen television sets. Members labouring on their machines gaped at the screens through sweat-clouded eyes, some of them hooked into the associated sound channel, others just hooked on moving colour pictures out of numb-minded habit.

She was not staring at him but at the third television screen from the left, which was suspended from the ceiling directly between them. She was at one end of the second south-facing row, 25 minutes into her habitual half-hour on the running treadmill. He was at the back of the north-facing block, about 15 metres from her. It was her breasts that first attracted his attention – they were, as it happened, the part of her body most familiar to him. He scarcely had the time to make the connection between this physically perfect form and the Italian girl in the Underground before he made his mistake. His gaze having risen from the constrained bouncing of her chest to her face, he realised, with a sudden rush of adolescent-redolent recognition, that she was looking directly at him. Her face was flushed and shining, her hair bobbing in time with her breasts, which were encased in an elastic black sheen beneath a loose cotton top. She was achingly desirable, and she was looking his way. Without any thought, driven by Darwinian impulses from deep within his selfish gene, he broke just about all the unwritten rules of the gym. He returned her gaze, smiled, and waved.

But she was not looking at Peter. Of course she wasn't; she was in her late twenties and superb in every respect, he was in his early fifties and "looked after himself well". Her skin was the colour of acacia-blossom honey and the texture of silk satin; he looked weather-beaten and leathery. Her hair was raven-black, luxuriant, shoulder length and in a ponytail swinging in time with her loping stride; he had a grizzled head of hair, not quite unkempt, long for someone his age. She was wearing a tight black lycra bodystocking with an oversized, artfully weathered white cotton boat-neck shirt off one acacia shoulder; he was in old tracksuit trousers and a baggy T-shirt bearing the legend "Caterpillar Heavy Equipment – Accessible Power", a freebie from a mining conference five years previously. No, she was not looking at him, but she did see him. Beyond the screen she saw the wave, the smile.

Being a polite and agreeable girl from northern Italy and therefore either ignorant of any unwritten rules or totally unconcerned by them, she waved back. Despite not sharing the genetic tendency to cardiovascular ill health of his male relatives, and despite the blood flow requirements of his exercise, Peter's heart paused as if briefly held in the grip of a fist; he felt a hollowness in his gut, a feeling he had not experienced for decades.

Ridiculous, he thought. And he was right. There is nothing quite so ridiculous as a middle-aged man who still commits himself to the folly of hope with a young and attractive female. No one is more likely to humiliate himself and not know, or if he knows, not to care; no debasement is too profound. Intelligent, educated, mature men become their ignorant awkward adolescent selves once more, but without the peak physical condition, or the hormone-bathed excuses for their behaviour. The ageing would-be Lothario often has the advantage of money, or is perhaps encouraged by the phenomenon of those men who really do have money – film stars, bankers, successful industrialists – who trade in their first wives for younger, more nubile versions, better able to confirm their social status and financial success, even whilst simultaneously attesting to an emotional bankruptcy.

A few minutes after the unlawful eye contact her half-hour was up and she slid neatly off the back of her treadmill, walked to the water fountain, mopping her face and neck with her towel, filled her bottle and left. Peter still had 20 minutes and 43 seconds to go on the cross trainer. He briefly thought about following her, to seek an opportunity to build on the vestigial foundations he hoped were constituted by the appreciative look on the Underground – could it really have been? – and the exchanged salutations across the gym floor. Was that stalking? There must be an unwritten gym rule about stalking. Besides, where was she going? Probably the changing rooms, in which case he would be thwarted at the door.

He finished his session as normal. He followed 25 minutes of dull exertion on the cross trainer with a sequence of exercises at one of the weight machines – the sequence varied monthly and was noted on his card by an earnest, muscular young man called Garth, the only person in the gym Peter was authorised to acknowledge with a "morning" or, more often, a tacit nod. Having been unable to conceive of a way to pursue the Italian girl, he told himself that he was behaving responsibly. He was a happily married man whose eldest son was close to her age, for God's sake! The implication that there was an irresponsible alternative course that he might actively pursue but was consciously avoiding, that some sort of relationship with the Italian girl was a possibility, remained, quite unshakably, in Peter's delusional lustful middle-aged head.

He went down to the changing room, showered and dressed, feeling physically and morally virtuous.

The gym had a "club room", essentially a snack bar with a scattering of leather armchairs in clusters around low-level coffee tables that were slightly battered in the way of all shared property. There was a bank of computers at one side, where members could access the internet and check their emails, and a few dog-eared newspapers – the idea being that members would generally hang around there and, the management of the club hoped, spend money on the selection of high-priced healthy light meals and fruit-based smoothie-type drinks or, at equal profit margins, the less healthy coffees and chocolate-based snacks. The club room was positioned adjacent to the entrance, so members walked past but not through it on their way into and out of the club; somebody clever at head office had specified this arrangement in all the group's branches, as the result of scientific testing to determine the income-maximising layout. The aroma of sinful coffee was present in the entrance as a reminder to members of the club room's delights; a sign by the stairs to the squash courts informed customers that the club room café, part of a nationally franchised chain, offered "the best espresso this side of Milan".

Kiara Molinari came from a suburb of Milan, and hence was well-placed to make a judgement on the comparative quality of the coffee, which was why she normally had a smoothie whilst she waited for Massimiliano – Max – to finish his more muscle-building oriented gym activities. Kiara was the only child of a widower, a Milanese pharmacist, whose own death had coincided with her arriving in London to study ten years earlier, at the age of 18. Her three years at UCL had passed with a rapidity that spoke of an enjoyment in the city she knew meant that she would never go back to Settimo. Having tried a variety of jobs – she never had much trouble finding work – she had ended up working at a specialist Anglo-Italian travel agency. There she had established her own successful niche by building a loyal and growing clientele amongst universities – her own UCL, other London colleges Kings and Imperial, but also Oxford, Cambridge, Durham and their equivalents in Italy. Kiara would arrange travel, of course, greeting and orientation and also lodgings for students on the Erasmus programme and other exchanges.

It suited her well, this work, allowing her to capitalise on her own experience of initial homesickness and bewilderment at the vast cosmopolitan City of London and its extraordinarily expensive and inexcusably shabby accommodation, and allowing her to communicate some of her enthusiasm for her adopted home city. So successful was her "Falling in Love with London – *Cadendo nell'amore con Londra*" service, that it came to underlie the largest part of her agency's revenues and two years previously she had become a partner in the business. At about the same time she had met Max, a beautiful boy from Padua, physically the male equivalent of herself. It was through the extensive London Italian network that they had met, at a dinner party where the two of them were so dramatically differentiated from their fellow diners in terms of age and attractiveness that their coming together was almost preordained, as the hostess, Max's aunt, had clearly intended. Arranged marriage in London is not limited to the populations from the Indian subcontinent, it is simply that they are more honest about it.

Max worked in his uncle's law firm as a junior solicitor, his lack of talent or dedication – to firm or clients – only just compensated for by the importance of blood relations amongst the Italian middle classes. Max and Kiara did not marry and never would, but on the very day they met had begun an intense, fiery, physical and essentially unstable relationship, the sporadic existence of which was more a testament to the quality of the sex they enjoyed than anything more substantial.

Kiara had been at the beginning of a day's student orientation on that sultry August morning when she had first met Peter – if you can call being thrust up against someone on the westbound Piccadilly Line "meeting". At the time she had been aware, naturally, of the physical contact they had made, and of its inadvertently intimate nature. But what had struck her more than anything else was the astonishing resemblance between this stranger and her father. Peter had seen something in her eyes that he labelled "appreciation", which was laughable, but for the rest of the day she had wondered at her reaction. A more traditional response for a healthy young Milanese woman, or one from anywhere else really, to having a stranger's face a quarter century older than her breasts plunged between them, would have been revulsion and possibly violence. She was aware that the incident in the train had not been his fault, that if anything she was to blame for not having instructed her undisciplined flock of newly arrived students to move down the carriage. He had seemed like a kind man; certainly an offended slap would have been an injustice.

But she had not only failed to slap him, she had – what? – she had looked into his eyes and known that whatever message she had given was not, as it should have been, one of simple displeasure. Kiara had seen enough TV, read enough tabloid newspapers, been to enough plays to know of, if not in any detail, the Electra complex. Most people do: Oedipus, Electra, Narcissus – the great uninformed popular success of Freudian analysis is its appeal to the prurient lowest common denominator, and its provision of easily remembered if over-simplified and misused labels. So, during that August day and occasionally afterwards she had asked herself about this man on the train and his similarity to her father, about her self-imposed exile in London and her unsatisfactory if sporadically satisfying relationship with Max.

It had been months since that meeting on the Piccadilly Line yet she had immediately recognised the waving man at the other side of the gym. Unlike him, however, her brain had not been temporarily replaced by a little pressure cooker of hormones. She knew who he was, or rather where she had seen him before and in what circumstances, knew he had made a mistake and waved to her on the basis of a misunderstanding. But why had she waved back? Why had either of them waved? They had shared a very brief and somewhat embarrassing moment, surely better just forgotten. These things were on her mind when Max appeared, flushed and newly showered, looking and smelling great, his thick hair slicked back, and his muscular torso easily discerned beneath his slightly damp shirt.

Kiara had never spoken to anyone, least of all Max, about the Piccadilly Line incident. She found it almost impossible to imagine how she could explain it at all, and not only did experience suggest that any attempt at meaningful discussion with Max was unlikely to be a success, but in addition he was prone to extreme jealousy, quite unreasonably in the light of his own infidelities during their frequent "off" periods. Now, here in the club room, half-finished smoothie before her, she attempted to describe the whole thing, from getting on the train at Barons Court to waving across the gym. As she had predicted, it was not a successful conversation. Max was more obtuse than normal, quickly jumping to the conclusion that she had been sexually harassed and demanding to know why she had not reported the incident. When she corrected this interpretation, explained she had herself unwittingly put herself in such a position, he had angrily accused her of offering herself up to strangers. Old strangers at that. In his view this was confirmed by his wave and her response. And he, Max, was in the same gym at the same time! It was an insult. An affront to his masculinity.

The conversation was conducted in increasingly voluble Italian, understood by no one else present. Had it not been in a public place it might have ended in blows, as had once happened before in her Earls Court flat; on that occasion like children they had immediately made up and, very unlike children, fornicated where they were in the hallway. On this occasion he angrily grabbed his bag and stormed out of the club room, whilst she, in a very Latin way, hurled some final words about his being a self-obsessed pig at his retreating back. She had not even mentioned Electra, which was probably just as well.

This was the scene Peter partially witnessed as he came down the stairs from the changing room. The sound of angry Italian voices, the sight of Max's form storming through the turnstile gate to leave, Kiara slumped in a leather armchair in silent tears of fury, frustration, disappointment. He could not know what had caused the row, but the sight of a distraught, vulnerable Kiara, placed in the context of his unsubstantiated fantasy brought out in him a deep-rooted instinct to protect. That, at least, is how the virtuous, happily married, old-enough-to-be-her-father Peter told himself the story. Others might have been less charitable. But here was a damsel in distress and the newly invented chivalrous knight Peter made his move.

"Hello... I just wanted to apologise... Oh, what's the matter?" He had never been much good at small talk, and was quite pleased with the idea of an apology. After all, his flimsy foundations began with that incident on the Tube, and he hoped she realised that he had not been responsible, had nothing to apologise for, except circumstances beyond his control. The distance between this cold calculation and the New Sir Galahad was totally invisible to him. She raised her head, wiping away tears with her sleeve in a disarmingly childish way.

"Nothing. My boyfriend. He's a pig," she stated simply, "and you don't have to apologise, it was not your fault." Someone less guileless would have feigned ignorance of the reason for his apology. She spoke with a slight accent. She looked at him, straightened herself in the chair. Even tear-smeared, her face was beautiful. She passed a hand through her hair, a movement she often made when thinking. She was looking for, and finding, similarities with her father. He realised he had to speak but could not find anything to say, now that the Piccadilly Line was neatly dealt with, never to be mentioned again, or at all in fact.

The barista arrived with a tall glass cup of frothy liquid, a spoon standing up in it. They both looked at him blankly. He had witnessed the whole Italian altercation but had already started his espresso machine to make Max the cappuccino he had ordered. In keeping with his employer's profit-maximising ethic, he decided to take the drink over to the table where his customer had previously been in the hope of receiving payment for it, choosing to ignore the very ostentatious storming-out climactic part of the scene.

"Just the thing!" said Peter, who disliked cappuccino, especially in the evening, reacting quickly. "Thank you. Would you like… ?" he looked at Kiara, and her half-finished smoothie. She shook her head. The barista placed a small stainless-steel saucer with a scrap of till roll on the table and left.

"I hate to see you unhappy," he said, truthfully, but somewhat incongruously in view of the fact that he had only actually seen her twice before, briefly, including an hour ago in the gym, and neither time had they spoken. "I take it the pig in question is the handsome young man who just left the club. But you know, you should be careful about maligning pigs; they're very much misunderstood creatures. Did you know that pigs are as intelligent as Labradors?" This odd and assumedly unverified fact about pigs had been provided to Peter by one of Ivy's annoying vegetarian friends, as an argument against eating them. Presumably this was why she had chosen the Labrador, which obviously only a monster would contemplate eating, as opposed to, say, a pit bull terrier.

"This one isn't as intelligent as a Labrador! He has nothing of the Labrador! They are nice and loving and… faithful." She smiled weakly.

So that was it, Peter thought, an unfaithful boyfriend. In no way could this explain any of his imaginings; the edifice he was building upon its flimsy foundations. But the eager-to-be-convinced mind requires little proof. And he had made her smile and somehow compare a man he baselessly saw as his rival, unfavourably, to a dog.

"If he were a dog, then, which would he be? An Alsatian? A Rhodesian Ridgeback? One of those ludicrous huge poodle things, with curly hair?"

"I've told you, he's a pig, not a dog." She was smiling properly. Lovely white, even teeth.

They had an enjoyable conversation. He was witty and charming. He made her laugh. Max never made her laugh, he just was not an amusing person; when his cards were dealt he had received an exceptionally strong hand, but no ace in the personality suit. She was vivacious, quick and intelligent and, although aware of her attractiveness, not arrogant.

After 24 years, sex with Ivy had become infrequent and Peter always had the impression that she was doing him a favour – as indeed she was. The idea of sex with Kiara, no matter how improbable, dominated Peter's thoughts, at least in some lobe of his brain preordained to ignore facts and concentrate on procreation. It was one of pure earthy delight, an impressionistic fusing of pornography and tenderness. But they had a pleasant conversation, no more than that. At quarter to nine she looked at her watch and jumped.

"*Merda*, it's nearly nine! I was supposed to be home at nine to meet my cousin. She's 16 and from Settimo and can't speak English. The taxi will just drop her on my doorstep. In the dark! In Earl's Court!"

"I'll take you." Peter nodded at his biking gear on the floor by the armchair. "You'll be home before she gets there." He was keen on her seeing his Fireblade, a young man's toy, evidence of his continued youth and vigour. This was perfect; he would impress her and also learn where she lived. Of course he should have known that a motorbike does not impress a girl, only boys are impressed by loud, shiny, fast dangerous things, but the cranial lobe in charge was not wired up for reflection. Although even that lobe knew better than to become a stalker, a sad obsessive loser whose prospects of sexual gratification, already vanishingly small, would certainly be extinguished completely by such a thing. But knowing her address would be good anyway.

"Without a helmet?"

"I'll drive carefully."

"Okay, *andiamo!*" In her childhood she had often accepted bareheaded lifts on friends' scooters and motorbikes, and she kept a scooter in London herself, a bright-red Vespa. It was the quickest way to get around town, she knew that. They got up quickly and he led the way out of the club – nice chirpy Kelly on the reception desk gave him a quizzical look – to the bike, still safely parked in the alley. Kiara did not appear impressed, surprised rather, and climbed on behind him as soon as he had the bike on the road, engine purring. She put her arms around his waist, as you must as a passenger, especially one without a helmet. He had forgotten this, was stupidly taken by surprise. The little pressure cooker of hormones in his head, which had continued to simmer since she had waved back to him from her running machine, briefly reasserted its dominance. He could feel her chest against his back, her hands were inches from his groin. That adolescent hollowness in the pit of his guts, the brief clench around his heart. Ridiculous.

He rode quickly but carefully to the street name she had given him, a square he knew near the prep school his children had attended. She squeezed his arm when they arrived at the right number; a substantial mansion block just off the Earls Court Road. It was three minutes to nine. She jumped off the back of the bike. He, helmeted and leathered, remained astride the grumbling machine, all his senses inhibited by clothing, noise, and the need to keep the bike steady.

"Thank you, Peter. And thanks for making me forget the pig." She put her hand to her mouth, kissed it, and placed it on his nose – the only part of his face accessible through the helmet visor. She did this because she was Italian, demonstrative, because she was nice, because she was grateful.

That's all. A nice conversation from inauspicious beginnings, and a useful lift home. Yet the little pressure cooker nearly blew its safety valve.

The Mounts' House, Chelsea, London, April 2007

He got home at 9.15. Quite late, but Ivy knew he was busy with financing a bank deal of some sort, and although she did worry more when he was late home since he had bought the motorbike, she had learned by experience not to nag for information – just as he felt he had learned from experience to keep her informed. Neither was wholly right. She did, if not nag exactly, solicit information for practical and emotional reasons (which he, unreasonably, continued to find cloying) and he did not keep her as well-informed as he imagined. This evening he had texted to let her know he was planning to visit the gym, but still 9.15 was late. She was in the kitchen, already in her dressing gown, hair still damp and lank from her bath, pompom slippers on her feet. She was not looking her best.

"Hello. You're late. Good workout?"

"Hi, Ivy." A peck on her cheek. "Great, thanks. But the bloody bank's people are driving us all mad at work."

"You texted at half six to say you were off to the gym. I expected you an hour ago!"

"Oh, we got bogged down with the accountants and didn't get rid of them until quarter to eight."

Peter, still stuck somewhere between Sir Galahad and Bill Clinton, did not consider for a moment telling Ivy about Kiara. How could he possibly explain it? Certainly not the whole thing, from his close acquaintanceship with the deliciously perfumed perfection of her breasts in the steamy Underground train the preceding summer to his getting a kiss on the nose, and ascertaining her address, this spring evening. Even his having consoled a distraught young fellow gym-member and seen her safely home would probably require more explanation than he felt competent to give. Instinctively he was certain that Ivy must never know about Kiara. He had done nothing wrong, yet, to quote another American president, he had "committed adultery in his heart". But surely every man on the planet, being honest with himself, would have to plead guilty if charged with this crime? He had done nothing wrong, yet dissembling seemed so much like the right course that he never questioned it for a moment. There really was no alternative. Thus began a clandestine new corner in Peter's life in the shape of a secret from Ivy which made his relationship with Kiara seem much more guilty than it need to be. A secret from Ivy, especially in the form of a single 28-year-old Milanese girl of appalling beauty, was a departure for him, somehow putting Ivy and their marriage in a different perspective, somehow introducing an unfair, pernicious and wholly theoretical comparator. And he had done nothing wrong, yet.

Rareterre Plc's Offices, Hammersmith, London, April 2007

The warning signs were there. Edward Bald broke the news to James on the telephone, halfway through RBS's "due diligence" process: there would be additional fees payable to the bank. Conflict-avoiding, realist James did not think it quite right to suck a client in, get them half-pregnant with accumulated non-reimbursable fees and expenses, and then suddenly announce a major change to the cost of the deal. It was James's nature to tread carefully anyway, but now he had to: Rareterre was already becoming dependent on RBS in a premature foreshadowing of an imbalanced relationship.

"You say your committee will require additional arrangement fees and a boosted non-utilisation fee, and only now you tell me this, Edward? If you don't mind my saying, that strikes me as a bit less than wholly fair. I don't like to think how Peter is going to react." James was sitting in his small, untidy office, papers piled up on most of the horizontal surfaces. Amongst them was a picture of his family, squinting out from some sunny holiday beach, the children near-comical miniature copies of their father, especially as concerned the prominent ears. His was two doors down from Peter's slightly larger but still decidedly tawdry office – both south-facing, with the same unprepossessing view of an architecturally uninteresting part of Hammersmith. In the summer the sun assaulted those south-facing windows and made of their offices little saunas, but without the pine scent and the nakedness. But this was a dull early April day, with low cloud and drizzle, in keeping with James's mood.

After a few minutes of self-serving explanation from Edward, which James unconvincingly resisted, he got to his feet and ventured the five metres to see if Peter was in his office. He was, with his back to the door, feet on the blond wood desk, staring apparently aimlessly through the window at the small 1960s block opposite. James and Peter had a good but professional-only relationship; it would never have occurred to James to remark on Peter's increasingly frequent quiet and introspective episodes. The outburst at Dreadnought had also been very uncharacteristic. He tapped on the open door with a forefinger.

"Sorry to disturb."

Peter quickly swivelled his chair around to face James. "No, you're not disturbing. Just having a little think."

"I've just been on the phone with Edward Bald at RBS. He told me that the bank will want to up its fees."

"What, now? At this stage? When those Masondo clowns have nearly finished telling us what we have told them? When Klaus just got back on his first-class flight home to New York?"

Klaus Katz, "Club Class Klaus" as James, who saw his expense claims, called him, was the senior geologist at the specialist consultants called in by RBS to give them "comfort".

"Yes, quite. I told Edward that it was a pretty shabby do."

"How much?" Peter interrupted. He hated to think how James had expressed his displeasure. "Pretty shabby do" was probably the extent of it. Just not on, old chap.

"They want a 'Further Fee', additional to the arrangement fee, of $1.6 million."

"What?" Peter barked. He was standing. The arrangement fee had been hard-fought, with Edward initially asking for 3 percent, or $1.2 million. In the end they had agreed on $1 million payable in two tranches, one immediately on signing the agreement, the other 12 months later. The idea of deferring part had been Edward's. It had not been explicitly discussed, but Peter and James had clearly understood that the straddling of a financial year-end would be "presentationally advantageous" – in other words, the true cost of the loan would be obscure to investors. Anyway, James had reasoned, 2.5 percent spread over a seven-year facility, if you equate it to an interest cost, is not much – less than half a percent per annum. Not the greatest bit of analysis, but Peter had let it pass. But now, here was RBS asking for another $1.6 million.

"Total fees $2.6 million on a $40 million loan! And before you say it, the fees can't really be spread out over the seven-year life of the facility, because maybe the full $40 million will never be drawn and – perhaps more importantly – upfront money is really worth more than future, contingent money. It's daylight robbery!"

James could have objected to a finance lecture, since he was the chartered accountant, Peter a mere geologist. But he had more bad news, and judged that objecting would not necessarily be the wisest course of action. Besides, Peter hadn't finished.

"And how do they justify it, at this stage? Bloody hell, Masondo and Klaus and everyone's lawyers must have clocked up half a million by now!"

James knew the professionals had already reached £700,000, but thought it better not to mention that either. He had something else to mention.

"It's justified, apparently, because the credit committee are not going to like the innovations, you know, the covenants and so on. Oh, and there's to be a non-utilisation fee. Apparently it's normal, he says. They just forgot to mention it before. Apparently." James trailed off. He had avoided a conflict with Edward but was not so optimistic about avoiding one with Peter.

"You know what, James? We should bloody well have done as I said and looked for an alternative lender, run two in parallel. Those bastards at RBS would think twice about gouging us if there was another bank in the picture. But now it's too bloody late. We need the financing soon or we'll have to put the refurb at Trillium on ice. They know that as well, of course. Thanks to fucking Masondo. That's why they insisted on our having them – they're spies, not due diligence support! We're paying £600 an hour to harbour a viper—"

James interrupted before Peter started frothing at the mouth. "I don't think there are any other providers for this sort of loan, Peter. It's really cutting-edge stuff. If we get this done, we're definitely doing the right thing for shareholders, for the company; we're going to look like heroes! The fees, well, no one will notice them. They'll be 'financing costs' in the accounts. Over two years. It's still very cheap money. Senior debt where normally equity would go! I know it's hard to accept, the way it's all happened, but let's keep the objective in mind."

"How much?" Peter seemed deflated, defeated.

"What?"

"You just mentioned a 'non-utilisation fee'. How much is the non-utilisation fee? You haven't said. And what the hell is a non-utilisation fee anyway?"

"Oh, 0.65 percent. You pay it, like interest, but on amounts you have not borrowed. I mean, unutilised facility amounts. On our $40 million, if we only draw ten, we pay this percentage on the other $30 million."

Peter was beginning to feel greater sympathy for Olivier and Frits, and the others whom James regularly confused with his apparently complex formulations.

"Let me understand. We pay interest even without borrowing the money? Marvellous. I want to be a banker. Someone else does all the work, the poor bastard who is your client pays all the costs, you pretty much name your price, then you up it, and you get money even when the loan stays safely tucked up in your own safe!"

"Well, Edward claims that Masondo's preliminary report suggests that the original term sheet mispriced the risk, to use his words, and so these proposals are required to put it all back in line."

"Bloody hell, James, and you bought that crap? RBS has known us for ten years now, and last I saw Masondo was in line with our own auditors and the published figures – published figures, James, for which you take responsibility as finance director, which you should have been willing to defend. And don't talk to me about the 'downsides', I've seen those Masondo 'downsides'." At this Peter made annoying mid-air inverted commas. "They are pure worst-case fantasising! It's all about squeezing more money out of us, and they're in it together, RBS and Masondo."

All across the spectrum, lenders – from supposedly reputable high street banks to loan sharks, via credit card balances, the rate of interest on which rivals the sharkiest of them – make their livings lending money to people and businesses who need it. For a small company borrowing money, as with anyone in need of money, the greater the need, the fewer the alternatives the borrower has and the greater the cost. It is one of the immutable laws of finance that lenders charge small companies high fees and interest, because supposedly the risk is higher there, but mostly just because they can.

When it came down to it – and it did eventually come down to it – the biggest risks the banks took in 2007, when RBS was arranging the loan to Rareterre, were not with the little businesses like them. Far bigger were the unthinking, wholesale acceptance of huge-scale commercial property lending and supposedly investment grade, rating agency-approved, "low-risk", industrially packaged retail real estate loans, securitised for convenience and obfuscation. The biggest risk of all, ultimately, was the exposure each bank had to other mindless banks like themselves. The mispriced debt, not the diversity of small company loans to borrowers like Rareterre, was where the existential risk to the banking industry originated.

Of course James and Peter ended up agreeing to pay the additional fees demanded by RBS. It was the right decision they told one another and, anyway, there were by that time no alternatives. All those fees for arrangement, commitment and non-utilisation, all those costs however unjustifiable they may have seemed, were indeed justified because of what they bought: financial security for the company. The loan facility was arranged, fees were paid, the bank was committed, the funds were available and Rareterre could proceed with its plans.

California, April 2007

In sunny California, three lawyers representing New Century, a bank focussed on mortgage lending to higher risk borrowers – what the world would come to be familiar with as "sub-prime loans" – filed for Chapter 11 protection from its creditors: bankruptcy. As befits the seriousness of their task, the three men were soberly dressed in dark-grey suits. A young photographer, out trying her new camera, saw the three lawyers walking abreast as they reached the top of the grey granite steps of the administrative building, three large black crows perched on a line. She took a monochrome picture of the scene, selecting a narrow depth of field – the men's black backs in sharp focus, the building and steps a soft grey backdrop. It was a striking picture, atmospheric, slightly threatening. Like the beginning of Hitchcock's *The Birds*.

Royal Bank of Scotland Offices, London, April 2007

Having spent the requisite ten minutes applying for and being presented with their plastic-sheathed individual identity cards-cum-visitor-passes, complete with photo and name of host, Peter, James and Frits were sitting on the white leather sofas in RBS's plush reception area, trying not to look at the huge TV-screen displays, but failing. Frits happened to be in London at the time and rightly observed, "Hey, the signing of a $40 million loan facility doesn't happen every day of the week at Rareterre!" It wouldn't be right for the chairman to miss it, especially as he was in town.

James, who was wearing the Churches traditional Oxford brogues he kept for special occasions, was wondering why it was being estimated that the introduction of ID cards to Great Britain would cost nearly £5 billion, when apparently a spotty-faced teenage RBS receptionist could achieve 90 percent of the task for three of them in ten minutes, with nothing more than a desktop computer linked to a webcam and a colour inkjet printer. Peter was thinking about Kiara. Frits, ever the workhorse, was leafing through the loan agreement one last time.

"Are we sure about these covenants, James?" He fixed James with his trademark steely gaze over the top of his half-moon glasses. "I mean, looking at this, and from what the lawyers were saying, if we get any of this wrong they get to call the loan, demand repayment, right? It's all quite complicated, all these adjustments to the financials."

"Yes, I mean no, that is, the adjustments may seem complicated but they're not necessarily that bad. We've done some simulations and agreed them with the bank. Exchange rates can be a bit of a pest. But we're not unaware." James sensed a slight tensioning in Frits's face, even though the said steely gaze had been drawn to the massive moving images of brave RBS bankers meeting clients in their bakeries and engineering-shop floors, shaking grateful yeoman customer hands. He corrected himself. "We are very aware of the risks associated with default of any sort, not only covenants but other breaches."

Frits tore his eyes from the screens. "Like what, James, what other breaches?"

"Oh, there's no end of ways in which we could breach this agreement. Covenants, of course, failure to observe any one of the ongoing obligations, from provision of routine information to the sale of an asset without consent..." Peter seemed to awaken from some sort of reverie.

"Don't worry, Frits, we'll take the greatest care. James has appointed a senior member of his team to monitor all our obligations." On the screens, which covered an entire wall, a smart besuited young man was climbing into a helicopter, which quickly took off and offered a vertiginous aerial view of a vineyard. "Unparalleled International Reach" flashed briefly across 20 metres of the wall. Peter was talking to Frits but looking at an image of what appeared to be a New York skyline, but was in fact a city he had never heard of in China. "She will liaise with the bank frequently and make sure we stay in compliance all the time. And there is no condition anywhere which relates to the share price." This had been a concern of Frits's, that the bank would insist the company's stock market value must remain above a minimum – he had seen such a clause at a US company where he was also chairman.

Edward Bald appeared at the end of the cavernous hall.

"We're honoured," Peter muttered from the corner of his mouth. "Fetching us in person!" It had never happened before, and would happen only once more.

After so much effort, so many expensive hours of due diligence, negotiation, legal advice, consultation of Nominated Advisors and auditors, board meetings, simulations, more negotiation, preparation of PR and investor relations campaigns, after over three quarters of a million pounds in expenses, the signing of the agreement ended up being something of an anticlimax. Edward had tried to make an event of it, booked an impressive room – all the meeting rooms were named after mainline London stations, and this one, the Liverpool Street room, had the advantage of a view of its eponymous station, or at least part of it, from one end of the huge plate-glass windows. The lawyers were there in force, of course, one final bite of the cherry. All Edward's RBS team members were there, looking proprietorial and pleased with themselves. They took their places around the massive meeting table, Frits at the head on one end, Edward at the other; the distance between them a polished wooden tennis-court length. The lawyers each had piles of final version documents in front of them for signing. At each end of the room was a huge vase containing a massive bouquet of long-stemmed lilies interspersed with orchids, one behind Edward, one behind Frits. *Someone here could actually rival Ivy for her monthly bill at Millefeuilles of Kensington*, thought Peter grimly. Beside one of the vases was a silver tray with two bottles in ice buckets and a collection of champagne flutes.

"Well, welcome to the closing of this exciting and innovative medium-term debt facility." Edward was speaking at public-meeting volume to be sure Frits, seated in the distance, would hear him. Probably that was why he spoke public-meeting platitudes. "I think I speak for all the team when I say that RBS is very proud to have been able to respond to Rareterre's needs so flexibly."

Maybe it was the use of the church hall prize-draw voice, the platitudinous pronouncements, or perhaps the size of the room and its clear intent to impress; perhaps it was the smirking bankers or the size of the document pile beside the lawyers, but suddenly James felt depressed. As finance director he should have been elated, this signing would seal the financial future of his company for the foreseeable future. The deal was a good one, and it was indeed innovative – Rareterre was financing development capital expenditure with debt, not equity. Their competitors would be impressed, even jealous, at the size of the loan and its terms.

James was a chartered accountant, not a profession known for its *joie de vivre*, but there was more to it – deep down, James just knew that this deal should not be happening. RBS was living a period of hubristic excess. It was the biggest bank in the world, its insouciant bankers were pigmy-brained Titans riding high. Credit was readily available, whole nations were financing their every wish through increasing amounts of debt, and so were their citizens. Unlike Peter with his mushrooming mortgage, James had not participated in this folderol; unleveraged, he was condemned to feeling a fool, throughout years of hearing smug friends' tedious dinner conversation on the buy-to-rent property portfolio they were accumulating, with the help of an overeager lending industry. Certainly, he would take his share of the glory for this financial coup but James, in his cautious conservative heart, knew that the deal was a mistake. Loss-making companies don't fund feasibility studies with debt, they just don't. Edward was still speaking.

"We at RBS like to think we combine the best of the treasury-driven Dynamic International Money centre and the client-focussed Working in Tandem business models," he said, emphasising the contrasting nature of these two by extending his long arms sideways.

Never one to be out-platituded, Frits cleared his throat. "And we are pleased to count RBS, a dynamic bank indeed, amongst our most important relationships. We have been impressed throughout the process at the professionalism of your teams," he affirmed. Peter, wondering on what Frits could possibly base this statement, nodded his insincere agreement.

The mountains of triplicate documents were signed, everyone shook everyone else's hand, the champagne was opened and mostly drunk. Rareterre's bank account – with RBS, of course – was credited with the first $10 million draw on the loan and simultaneously debited with $1.7 million, the first instalment on the arrangement and commitment fees. Everyone quickly ran out of platitudes, and the meeting broke up half an hour after the first bottle had been opened.

The following morning, at 07.00, Rareterre issued a statement to the London Stock Exchange Regulatory News Service. It ended with a quote from Peter, as CEO of the company; words he never uttered, words which had been "wordsmithed" and placed in his mouth by the fluent, fashionable boys and girls at Scottish Spinsters, the financial PR agency.

> **Peter Mount, CEO of Rareterre plc, said: "I am delighted to be able to announce the arrangement of this medium-term financing with RBS, one of the world's strongest banks and a great British relationship bank. With this facility in place, Rareterre is securely financed through to full production at our key Trillium Lake asset."**

Such statements are made to comply with stock exchange regulations, the AIM[1] Rules and good corporate governance, in the laudable interests of complete shareholder information. They are not only wordsmithed, but checked by all parties involved, double-checked by the Nominated Advisor, and approved by the board of the issuing company to avoid any possibility of misinformation. The resulting committee-speak dullness is supposedly a fair price to pay for uninspiring accuracy. They are not, therefore, meant to be misleading at all; quite the reverse.

Carl couldn't understand it. Stacey was not returning his calls. Since their Parisian encounter she had not discouraged him, despite her wedding, which went ahead not in the god-awful northern mill town where she was brought up, but somewhere sunnier, more costly and less accessible for her relatives, in the eastern Mediterranean. There had been phone calls, quite flirty, and the occasional text. She seemed a good sport, Stacey, and Carl preferred married women: far less likely to expect any sort of commitment from him. Okay, he had been a little vigorous in the George V but she had not complained, not really. In his opinion, girls often quite like it that way; not an opinion, of course, based on any actual evidence beyond the bragging he and his friends at his amateur soccer club enjoyed in the changing room.

Stacey had not liked it, not one little bit, and was angered and ashamed to have been foolish enough to acquiesce in going to Carl's room, convinced by a combination of his undeniable wit and the drudgery of the afternoon's programme at the Fifteenth United Congress, but most of all by her own doubts about her forthcoming convenient marriage. It would never happen again, but she was cynical enough to consider what possible advantage she could gain from this regrettable lapse. As Carl was an insider at a mining company and she was paid to publish insightful research and analysis on the sector, there was an obvious if one-sided synergy; one-sided suited her just fine.

Sure enough, she had extracted some interesting mining and mineralogy gossip from him over the course of several excruciating phone calls, where she had pretended to like him. However, nothing in any way important enough had been gleaned from these conversations to make her feel any better about him or, more importantly, about herself. Then Dan and Montagu Montagu had returned a couple of times to Australia, and Stacey had scarcely needed the unsubtle hint Dan had dropped that, of the rare-earths players quoted on the stock exchange, Hamlyn Securities rather favoured "the equity story" of C. Brown. Stacey did not know that MNM's unlikely mate Bruce Shaw, CEO of the Australian company, had engaged Hamlyn alongside its regular bankers to advise on the increasingly pressing issue of the interest expressed by the Chinese in acquiring a controlling stake in C. Brown. She didn't need to, she simply guessed that MNM's corporate finance interest, promising as it did hallmarked kilobars, had trumped the bread and butter sell-side analysis with its laborious accumulation of little gold clippings.

Dan and Stacey co-wrote an annual "sector analysis", covering all the rare-earth companies, looking at their specific issues and the overall market, its prospects, possible competition, the influence of the macro-economic outlook. Amongst the more diligent, trainspotting type investors, the Hamlyn Annual was eagerly read. Dan came back from one of his Antipodean trips and suggested that they write their annual analysis early – he said he wanted to use the information he had acquired down under whilst it was still fresh. When Stacey proofread his section on C. Brown for errors and omissions, she was struck by the newly upbeat tone and the changed recommendation – from "Hold" to "Strong Buy" with a price target of A$28, over 50 percent above the current market price. She knew that, if only for sectoral balance, they would have to disfavour one or more of the other companies they covered. And she knew exactly which one she wanted it to be.

CHAPTER 8

Health Club, Hammersmith, London, May 2007

Acknowledging Kiara at the health club had been in strict contravention of both unwritten gym rules one and two, but there was an unwritten rider to unwritten rule two, which permitted eye contact and even voice communication if you knew the person in real life, from outside the gym. Peter's rescheduling of his frequent workouts was unconsciously intended to take advantage of this, on the basis of his having driven Kiara back to her flat on his motorbike. He told himself that an evening workout was far more convenient, as it allowed him an early-morning Fireblade ride into work through the less busy streets, a considerable reduction in the risks of the journey, and to get plenty of work done before the interruptions of the normal office day intervened. But, of course, Kiara's habit for evening rather than morning gym attendance, rather than any work-related diligence, was what really brought Peter to the club, almost daily, at 7pm instead of his previously habitual 7am.

It was a few weeks though before he was rewarded, sighting her emerging from a spinning class as he laboured on a seated machine designed to work the abdominal muscles, involving repeatedly bending forwards and pushing against a padded bar at shoulder level that offered variable resistance. It was not a dignified procedure. She was still slightly breathless from the static bike, flushed, her smooth skin radiant with heat and perspiration. She took his breath away.

"Did she turn up okay?" he croaked, leaning back in the seat of the machine, inclined at an unnatural angle as if seated in a low-slung sports car. His head was a good metre below hers, an angle of view which, if anything, enhanced her sensuousness. She squatted lithely beside him.

"Ciao, Peter. Who?"

"Your cousin. The 16-year-old alone in wicked Earls Court."

"Oh! Yes, she was there already, at the lobby. Thanks again for the lift. She's decided to stay a few weeks. The cousin."

"And the *Schweinehund*?" A brief hesitation.

"Ah, Max. I told you, just *Schwein*, no *Hund*. I don't know, Peter, I haven't heard from him. I don't think I want to, just yet."

Just yet. Max was not definitely out of the picture, Peter concluded sadly. He realised he was still awkwardly reclined, having to keep his head uncomfortably rotated to the left so as to talk with her, pinned in by the shoulder-level padded bar.

"Coffee later?"

"No, thanks, Peter."

Despair swept over him. Max is still an element; she is refusing to see me again except like this, by chance, a prisoner of some diabolical machine.

"I prefer a banana smoothie after gym. It's full of potassium." She smiled brightly. Peter could not have hidden his pleasure had he tried.

Midtown Manhattan, New York, June 2007

In a New York meeting room, a small mob of angry, mostly shirt-sleeved financiers were trading recriminations and blame. The air was thick with disappointed greed. The Bear Stearns High-Grade Structured Credit Strategies Enhanced Leverage Master Fund: the name should have been a giveaway. It sounded too complicated for its own good, for anyone's good, and it was. It was also bust.

Some of these angry financiers, the Lenders, had lent money to the Master Fund and its sister, the Bear Stearns High-Grade Structured Credit Fund. The other angry financiers, the Managers, managed these funds and used the money borrowed from the lenders to invest in packages of sub-prime mortgages – big bundles of low-grade debt. The sub-prime mortgages paid interest at a higher rate than that charged on the borrowed money, the difference being the Spread. All the angry, shirt-sleeved financiers made money because of the Spread: in particular the Managers were paid a percentage of the total value of the Funds annually and a bonus based on the profits from the Funds – 2 and 20, a one-way bet just like Jay's friend Dick Veroof. These percentages were explained to the trusting investors in the Funds by reference to the skilled financial engineering the Managers could bring to bear, magically reducing the risk. They were all very clever, these sweaty shirt-sleeved financiers, but until today none of them had spotted the fatal flaw: the Spread could only exist if risk also existed. In well-functioning markets the Spread was *confirmation* of the risk.

The financiers, both the Lenders and the Managers, were all confronting a bleak truth: the sub-prime packages were not worth what the Funds had paid for them. Because of this the Lenders wanted their loans repaid, but the Managers could not repay them, because to do so they would have to sell some of their sub-prime investments and every time they tried to sell, the price went down further, making the problem even worse.

It was a mess. Like an unruly rabble of seagulls squabbling over the remains of a rotten fish, the irate financiers noisily joined the New Century lawyers in their cawing murder of crows.

Health Club, Hammersmith, London, June 2007

Maximiliano, muscular macho Max, Kiara's sometime boyfriend, came into the club room at the health club one Wednesday night about three weeks into Peter and Kiara's "smoothie relationship".

They would meet up, never by arrangement but always at about 8pm after each had exercised and showered, about twice a week. Peter's routine was to detour through the club room every time he left the gym, hoping to see her there sipping her smoothie. Kiara too hoped to see him, there was something hugely comforting about talking with this man who resembled her father and made her laugh. No matter what her mood, she always felt better after they had relaxed together and chatted over a yoghurt and banana-based beverage. She had not called Max after their big public row, and was increasingly feeling that she never would. Peter was, in her mind, no sort of substitute for Max, her super-ficial self-analysis and the Electra complex long forgotten. He was just a friend, an older male friend.

Peter's brain was functioning completely differently – when it func-tioned at all in Kiara's presence, other than to enable his performance as some kind of highly accomplished clown/counsellor. He was witty and charming, he was wise and experienced, but he never asked himself the question "where is this leading?". The answer would have been more than he could bear, for the instinctive bit of his being that desired Kiara, lusted for her, did so in background mode, never making its intended destination clear but controlling the vehicle anyway. Any answer that did not result in a sexual relationship was never considered by the hormonal pressure cooker part of his head, for it could not contemplate such a reality. Peter was an optimist in more ways than he consciously knew.

He was just telling Kiara about an experience he'd had involving a misunderstanding concerning chocolate biscuits in a station waiting room – actually not his own experience, but one he had heard on the radio recounted by a celebrity wit – a good story which he told well, and she was enjoying hearing it, smiling, eyes bright, when Max made his striking entrance. He was impossible to miss, even from their corner table. He was a truly impressive sight as he swept through the club room – tall, dark-haired, square-jawed; a Burberry raincoat draped over his shoulders, loose-sleeved, swinging behind him like a nobleman's cape. As he stopped before their table a thought crystallised in Peter's brain, one which had been seeded there when he had first seen Max, leaving this same room, also to some dramatic effect. Gaston. Max resembled Gaston from Disney's version of *Beauty and the Beast*, a film he had taken his children to see 15 years previously and all had enjoyed so much he bought the video. Big handsome hunk, arrogant, unintelligent Gaston. He said it out loud. He did not mean to, really not, but it slipped out.

"It's Gaston!" Surprise, a moment of recognition, not an attempted insult.

Beauty and the Beast was also a favourite of Kiara's, a fond childhood memory. Max had just launched into an angry and animated monologue in Italian, with much gesturing in Peter's direction. Kiara looked at him, his slightly cleft chin, his muscular arms and firm pectorals, and burst out laughing. She was a kind girl, not one who would willingly hurt anyone, but the image Peter's "It's Gaston!" had conjured was pure comedy, sharpened by the tension. Max was not familiar with Disney, and anyway had no sense of humour. He raised his voice further, his words bitter and threatening. Peter saw Kiara had understood, that they shared the point of reference.

No one's slick as Gaston
No one's quick as Gaston
No one's neck's as incredibly thick as Gaston's

Peter quoted quietly – not singing, but nearly. A high risk, given that he was seated in a low armchair in front of a coffee table, Max towering over them both. Max gave him an uncomprehending look. Kiara could not control herself, the harder she tried the more she snorted with ill-contained mirth. Max looked at her then at Peter, a mix of hatred and contempt. He spat one final word in Kiara's direction, possibly not a very nice word, before he spun on his heel and stalked out. Kiara wiped her eyes.

When I was a boy I ate two dozen eggs
Every day to help me get large

Now I'm a man I eat three dozen eggs
So I'm roughly the size of a barge
She recited, inaccurately.

Mount Hood, Oregon, July 2007

In early July, as the anonymous telephone voice had suggested, the Oregon State Assay and Mining Authority called at the Trillium Lake mine unannounced, four men in an unremarkable and unmarked grey sedan. Splitting into two pairs, one went with their sampling equipment to the waste water pipeline, the other to the area neighbouring the creek downhill from exploratory drills 70 and 71; laser-guided missiles. They left with their samples but without any explanation.

Rick called Olivier. When Olivier called him back two days later, Rick told him about the Authority's visit. "They came, four of them, no prior arrangement. I guess they have the right to do that, it's just that it's never happened here before, not that I know of. They went to the evaporation pools and down towards the creek. Then they left, they didn't even come back into the office to say they were through."

In a heavily regulated industry the regulators have life and death power, both men knew that. Olivier should have known to take it more seriously – very seriously. But he thanked Rick, hung up and got his raincoat. It was his daughter's birthday and he had promised to be home early for the party.

The Mounts' House, Chelsea, London, July 2007

Peter's got a lover, a mistress. The thought did not strike her, it crept up on her.

Ivy had not voiced this notion, not even permitted it to form fully in her mind until earlier that afternoon when she was soaking steak in marinade. Perhaps it was the commonly made connection between sex drive and red meat that insinuated the possibility of infidelity into Ivy's thoughts, as, mixing olive oil with soy sauce, she gloomily compiled a mental list of Peter's recent failings, their recent quarrels. As a young wife with small children she had often imagined it likely, indeed almost normal, that he might at least be tempted to stray – he was attractive, funny and successful, and she felt increasingly worn out, domestic and unsexy. But despite several suspicions, which proved if not baseless at least impossible to substantiate, she had concluded that he was not the philanderer her friend Odile assured her he probably was.

She crushed a clove of garlic into the marinade. Why was it, she wondered, that as the years had advanced she gradually no longer considered the possibility at all? Because it seemed to her increasingly unlikely? Did she care less? Was her love for him changed, diminished, less prone to fuel a jealous reaction, less liable to assume other women would be attracted to him because her own attraction had declined? Had he in some way gradually won a deserved level of trust? Or was this just a natural mellowing with age, a comfortable accepting of the permanence of their marriage? If so, why did she suddenly feel it so uncomfortable, so impermanent? She ground some pepper into her mixture and realised she was weeping.

Ivy held an Independence Day supper every year. Weather permitting, it was a barbeque, in their tiny bijou Chelsea garden. Peter played the role of reluctant chef, but she, of course, did all the work. So ridiculous, she thought, that barbeque "cooking" was somehow a male preserve, as if it was too difficult or risky to leave in the hands of those without Y-chromosomes, who were nevertheless successfully entrusted with cooking the rest of the time. It was Ivy who made the salads and parboiled the potatoes for roasting on the barbeque. Ivy who prepared the *amuse-bouche* nibbles and the French fries, the sauces for the meat, the vegetarian option for Odile, the corn on the cob, the ice-cream-based desserts and the all-American apple pie. It was Ivy who selected and purchased the steaks from Randall's, Rolls Royce steaks from organic farms connected, it was hinted, to the Prince of Wales. Peter had become a tight-fisted bore, constantly nagging her about the smallest indulgence. She wrongly imagined that she was successfully containing her costs – but one thing one should never economise on is meat, she thought.

Ivy selected the guests and issued the invitations, ordered the wine. She even bought some little star-spangled banners for the small teak table, with space for eight, just accommodated between large pots of expensively maintained plants. The whole garden squeezed in behind the house was not much bigger than her dining room, and slotted between the identical gardens of the houses on either side and the brick wall of the house behind; that's all you got for your two million pounds.

She was expecting Peter home half an hour before the first guests were expected to arrive, swanning in from the gym, still glowing from his exercise. With her usual efficiency, she had even ensured that they had enough of the right type of charcoal for the barbeque so that he would be able to create a fire sufficiently established, smokeless and emitting the right heat to cook the meat.

Ivy had not asked herself, although maybe she should have done, why Peter's morning gym routine had recently become an evening event. She assumed it had something to do with his work schedule, and didn't mind. Nor did she mind when, by dint of putting a match to some charcoal and flipping seven steaks with an average modicum of male skill, he garnered and accepted full credit for the entire meal. Ivy was not searching for reasons to be discontented, quite the reverse.

As a Catholic, marriage for Ivy was a permanent institution, more an island in the stream than the series of stepping stones many of her friends seemed to consider it to be. If the stream was in flood and the stepping stone became submerged, these friends skipped apparently lightly on to the next. If you are on an island and the floodwaters are rising, your best course is, Ivy believed, to stay put. Now she had the impression of clinging to a tree as she watched the roiling brown waters rise.

She did understand that their family budget had something to do with it, Peter had made that clear, but she was utterly incapable of economy; she had never had to exercise it. Her upbringing had been without financial concerns of any sort. Her father was a stockbroker in the years when it was a gentlemanly and undemanding pursuit, affording a comfortable income easily augmented by access to market rumour at a time when insider trading was, if not exactly legal, benignly ignored. There was inherited money on her mother's side, and a chateau in Normandy. Her education was in selective establishments that accepted only pupils capable of meeting their intellectual demands, with parents capable of meeting the financial ones.

Ivy spent her school years surrounded by the clever and indulged offspring of the well-heeled during term time, and by her extended family of French uncles, aunts and cousins at the chateau during the long holidays. She grew up with so little exposure to material need that university, even Cambridge, had been something of a shock to her. Her mother was one of those French oddities, a wealthy socialist proud of her country's revolutionary past and the *égalité* that went with the *liberté* and the *fraternité*, and she ensured Ivy was equally aware of this heritage. Cambridge was her first real opportunity to express herself as being on the left of the political spectrum, and there she had met boys from Manchester with full maintenance grants, clever but resentful boys who made it their business to complete her education in the economic privation that spawned the Co-operative and Labour movements, and the progressive politics she favoured. Such deprived conditions being rare in Cambridge in the 1980s, one of the Manchester boys, Jed, had taken her up north and shown her his native pre-regeneration Salford. Ivy had been deeply impressed by the squalor but had adopted her mother's political position, espousing the need for greater equality without sacrificing any of her own continuing material advantages. Jed had succeeded in one of his objectives, shocking her at how the poor lived, but not the other of inveigling her into a class-barrier-defying relationship. She already loved Peter.

Her life protected from need, and her commitment to lifelong monogamy, had led her to entrust all her financial affairs to her husband, and once she had left full-time employment to give birth to and bring up Harry, Emma and Kirsty, her dependence on Peter became more and more complete as the years passed and her employability and her inheritance both declined. It was an exposed but consistent arrangement. Now, with the marriage seeming less solid, their relationship suddenly a fragile thing, she was acutely aware of the precariousness of her position. She had explained all this to Odile, whose response was a snort of disgust.

"Ivy, this is the twenty-first century, for God's sake! What the hell were you thinking? You should have kept at least some money in an account that only you can access, in case of the worst! And instead of that, you let him control the lot, like some sort of Victorian little woman, like chattel."

Ivy had actually thought about it – having an emergency fund – but it had seemed to her almost an act of disloyalty, planning for the unthinkable, and perhaps making it more probable. In any case, it was too late now.

She knew that the problem went further than disagreements over the household budget. Peter was changed, changing, and it could not all be explained by a silly overdraft or mortgage, or whatever. She knew that there had been some difficulties at work, progress with his precious Oregon mine had been slow, the share price disappointing, the City hard to please. But Ivy had been Peter's wife for 24 years, and she knew her man very well. So far as she was aware Peter had never been unfaithful, until now, when she was convinced that there was more than work and money worries behind his recent moodiness, irascibility, the apparent departure of his sense of humour. She felt exposed, stupid. Afraid.

Jerry, Fulki's undeserving Jerry, was the American most frequently invited to Ivy's events, so of course he and Fulki were top of her list for the Independence Day dinner. Jerry was someone whose popularity owed perhaps more to his spouse than to anything in his own character. A combination of his Texan loudness, vulgarity and certainty in his own rightness on almost everything could make him awkward to deal with, but in his favour he did take a joke and normally came as a packaged deal with Fulki, whom it was impossible not to like. Ten years earlier, with no relevant qualifications except an enormous sense of self-belief, and lacking anything better to do, Jerry had acquired a tired retail pharmacy in Brentford that he had subsequently transformed, through hard work and a keen eye on costs, into a mini-chain of ten outlets spread across the unfashionable parts of west London. Ivy knew that Peter liked him, respecting his achievements; Jerry was also the only regular Chatterer whose politics were somewhat right of centre, although as an American it was sometimes difficult to categorise him. She had also invited Brett and Norma, a quiet couple from Chicago she had met through one of the children's schools, whom Peter did not know, and Odile and Margot, whom he did, perhaps too well.

It was a hot evening, quite muggy in the small garden, the heat and greenhouse gases emanating from the barbeque making things more airless. Jerry, revelling in his role as American-in-chief, had brought with him a large beer cooler in the form of an inflatable Uncle Sam top hat a metre high of questionable taste; he had also provided two large bags of ice cubes and a selection of cans. Ivy, who had selected four bottles of Stag's Leap Fay cabernet sauvignon from the Napa Valley as part of her economy drive, feigned delight.

Peter was wearing an apron over his work shirt, open at the collar, sleeves rolled halfway up his forearms; he was slightly sweaty from his proximity to the fire and the aftermath of his workout. Ivy, looking out at his flushed face from the kitchen, suddenly wondered whether the cardiovascular strain that produced the flush three evenings a week was indeed the consequence of an honest gym workout. Or something else. He had already consumed two largish glasses of Stag's Leap before Fulki and Jerry arrived with their load of American beers, and was now most of the way through a can of Bud Ice, blithely ignoring the advice he had received consistently throughout his adult life concerning the inadvisability of mixing his grapes with his grain.

"This" – he waved his can at Jerry – "tastes inoffensive enough. American, is it? How inappropriate, considering George Dubya's foreign policy. And is 'inoffensive' quite what we strive for in a beverage?"

"Well, we'll leave the offensive beverages to you Brits." Jerry was drinking a fizzy lager-type beer himself, from the can, and helping himself to handfuls of Ivy's carefully composed *amuse-bouches*, little bundles of prune wrapped in bacon. "I was in a pub near Staines the other day and I swear they were serving something called Gnat's Piss. Or was it Dog's Breath? People were lapping it up, literally."

"That would be Australian probably. But I was going to make another point. Don't you hanker after the days when the USA was not the only superpower, and you had to exercise just a bit of circumspection before starting wars in other people's countries?"

"You were going to segue from a can of Bud to the War on Terror, Peter? Wow, that's impressive." Jerry pulled a completely unimpressed face. "Anyway, they started the war in our country, actually, maybe you remember, something to do with a couple of big buildings in Manhattan?"

"Does that excuse Iraq? I mean, the invasion of Iraq and all the death and destruction we have rained down on them, shocking and awing them, peasants who have probably never even heard of—"

"Oh, Peter, really, don't give me all that shit, you Brits were there alongside us, eagerly kicking your share of Iraqi Ass. Tony and George are bosom buddies. They pray together, for Chrissake! I'll bet that, proportionally, you Brits committed an equal number of atrocities."

"I don't think you'll find that's the case," said Peter in his most superior manner, which meant: when you take the trouble to be so well informed as me. He continued, "But what about my superpower point? That the Russians, the Soviet Union, were in the end good for the world as they kept you lot more or less honest."

Jerry enjoyed this sort of thing. He was just about to point out that the same beneficent Russkies had invaded Afghanistan before most Americans even knew it existed, when Ivy led the Bernsteins, Brett and Norma, into the garden.

After they had each been given a can of beer from the top hat, Jerry said to Brett, "So, Chicago eh? Mayor Daley. No wonder you fled to London! What's your view: Soviet Union, force for good or evil? US of A: fighting for freedom or Great Satan?"

Ivy had warned Norma when she invited them that there might be some vigorous debate, and she should give as good as she got. Or pay no attention. One or the other, Norma couldn't recall. Ivy fidgeted with the hors d'oeuvre tray.

"Devil on horseback?" She held the plate out to Brett.

Norma looked confused. Was this a third descriptive option for her homeland? Brett was a visiting professor in sociology at Kings College and in this stuffy little garden he knew only Ivy, whom he liked, although he categorised her as "confused bourgeois".

"Actually, the Soviet Union had some very enlightened policies, as do most regimes of the left, regarding the developing world..."

Peter glanced over at Jerry. They were going to have some fun tonight.

Odile and Margot arrived together, for once, both late. Both were in their work clothes. In Margot's case this meant a pinstripe trouser suit, which Peter assumed to be some sort of ironic statement, and in Odile's, jeans, substantial black shoes which looked like they might have reinforced toes, and a bright-red T-shirt. Odile was frosty to Peter, which was not unusual, whilst Margot was hyper because she was on a new deal.

"Of course, I can't tell you much about it," she said excitedly. "But it will be announced tomorrow morning at seven so there's no harm really, no risk of..."

"Insider trading, Margot? Do you really think we would?" Jerry looked genuinely offended. Margot worked in the Mergers and Acquisitions department of a minor London investment bank.

"Oh, no, of course not. It's just the rules, you know. Anyway, my client is this dynamic little company, really good management team, and they're bidding for a competitor four times their size! It's so, well, exciting! Venture capital backed my client, well, private equity really, they are going to fund the whole thing with debt! Citibank. Can you imagine, they are going to quintuple their business with no dilution of their ownership. None." She burbled on happily.

"Do you think that wise, ascribing so great a proportion of the surplus value to the money capitalists?" asked Brett Bernstein, who had just spent 20 oxygen-starved minutes in this hot little garden being baited like a medieval bear, hearing from his host and this Texan, who seemed to be some sort of regular, about the superior outcomes to be expected from an unfettered market economy. Brett was a good communicator, but had the professional tendency of resorting to lefty intellectual catchphrases, which seemed to enrage Peter. A quick learner, Brett had begun to include more and more of these irritators. Margot looked at him quizzically.

"I mean, in the capitalist paradigm, the returns on economic activity have to be divided between interest and profit of enterprise, which are both fruits of capital, legitimate or otherwise, but determined by particular laws. Your client will be giving too much to interest, not enough to productive capital."

"I think he's saying you're borrowing too much, Margot," suggested Peter helpfully. "Overleveraging your client's business and the one he's buying." He turned to Brett. "Marx: he was pretty successful in business.

Did he have a view on the appropriate level of debt to equity? What would he make of what's going on today?"

"As I told you earlier, I'm not really a Marxist; who is these days? But I do think that, poor at managing his own affairs as he was, his intellectual frameworks may yet offer a useful way of trying to understand the neo-capitalist economic world. Especially, as it happens, the division of the spoils between money capitalists and active capitalists, which we can interpret today as the bankers and Margot's venture capitalists respectively. Love him or hate him, one thing Marx got pretty much right was the tendency for different parts of the capitalist class ferociously and wastefully to attack one another, and I think that applies today as much as when he was writing."

Margot was impressed. She was used to meeting left wingers like herself of one sort or another at Ivy's house, but they were normally softies who just wanted everyone to be nicer to the poor and for the unemployed to get bigger benefits, or sometimes merely the envious who just wanted the rich to pay higher taxes. This was something else.

"Private equity," she corrected, "and they're not mine. Anyway, Peter here could teach us all a trick or two about dealing with money capitalists!"

Margot was not referring to his personal indebtedness, which was considerable but not public knowledge, but to Rareterre, where the mould-breaking $40 million loan was very much so. Nevertheless, Peter felt an unpleasant sensation in the small of his back that he could not identify. Earlier that evening he had, between futile attempts at slaking his thirst with premium Californian red, glimpsed an email on his Blackberry from Freddy Lee with the words "Permit Withdrawal" in the title. Freddy was a non-executive director of Rareterre, a brilliant Hong Kong Chinese geologist, educated in the USA and with a lifetime of experience in the mining and mineral extraction business. Peter had invited him onto the board with the vital importance of the Trillium Lake mine in mind: if anyone knew the business of mining and its regulation, it was Freddy. And here he was emailing Olivier, cc Peter and Frits, about "Permit

Withdrawal". It was probably nothing, Peter reasoned, there had been frequent false alarms from Olivier in the past and he had no time to deal with another imaginary crisis at Rareterre. He did not read the email, went back to the barbeque and put it from his thoughts – or had done until Margot mentioned his familiarity with money capitalists, which uncomfortably reminded him about all sorts of vulnerabilities.

Peter found now that Freddy's email remained at the front of his mind, nagging like an approaching migraine. Making an excuse, he went to the lavatory, Bud Ice in one hand and his Blackberry in the other. He sat on the toilet with the lid still down and keyed in his security code. He noticed in an almost distracted way that he also had three missed calls – Freddy and Frits (twice). He also noticed, equally distractedly, that his heart rate was elevated and he had an unaccustomed nervous feeling in his belly. Odd. He scrolled through the junk that had accumulated since Freddy's message. The title in the subject line was "US mining Permit Withdrawals: often a manageable experience". Heart thumping now he quickly scanned the text of the email. Freddy and Olivier had been in correspondence a couple of times that day. The thread started with Olivier forwarding an email from the Oregon State Assay and Mining Authority shutting down the Trillium Lake mine, rescinding Rareterre's Conditional Use Permits with immediate effect.

A conference call was proposed. Freddy and Frits, both in the States, could not manage anything before 4.30pm EST – 9.30pm in London. Freddy's mail, the one which had first caught his eye, was a more or less anodyne account of how such permit withdrawals can be temporary formalities, not necessarily anything to worry about, to be discussed later… Freddy was wrong, playing it all calm, plain wrong. It was a potentially devastating development. He checked himself. Let's hear the details first.

The Conditional Use Permits, which they all unimaginatively referred to as the "CUPs", covered a few amendments to the collection of land use permits governing the activities at Trillium Lake. The rare-earths extraction plans relied on the CUPs. Without renewed extraction at Trillium Lake, Rareterre plc was an uninteresting, dwindling stream of residual cash flows from the accumulated ores already piled up in Oregon. The company's share price would halve if the permits were not immediately reinstated, maybe worse.

Peter disappointed himself with his initial response. His first thought was of his large and burgeoning mortgage, now in excess of £1.1 million of personal indebtedness, efficiently accumulated by Ivy, ably assisted by him, basically in an effort to appear wealthier than they really were. Subconsciously he balanced this monster mortgage against the asset side of his domestic balance sheet, which comprised mainly shares in Rareterre – value: who the hell knew? His second thought was the bigger bubble represented by the deeply indebted Rareterre, where it was he who called the shots, made the tough and the easy decisions. Peter was positively a debt-junkie, a veritable poster-boy for the live-now pay-later culture he often loudly decried.

He drained his can, crushed it painfully in his right hand and sauntered back into the garden.

"Sorry guys, it looks like I have to take a call in about half an hour."

In fact, the decision for Rareterre to borrow $40 million from RBS had been an easy one because Peter was an optimist. The beauty of leverage and the optimist! If you own an asset worth $100 and it goes up in value by 10 percent you are $10 better off; if you borrow $400 and, putting it together with your $100 to buy a $500 asset and it goes up in value by the same 10 percent, you are notionally $50 better off, a neat 50 percent return on your $100 because you still repay the bank the same $400 – all the increase in value belongs to the equity. That's the great thing about debt – it only wants its interest paid and itself back ultimately. That's why house mortgages are so popular in good times. Rareterre needs an additional $35 million to bring the Trillium Lake mine back into commission, to the great profit of all concerned. RBS wants to lend the lot at an attractive interest rate, and to throw in an extra $10 million for contingencies.

Why would you do it any other way? Why not go for the 50 percent return rather than the 10 percent? Karl bloody Marx could say what he wanted, it was a no-brainer!

But perhaps a no-brainer for brainless optimists for whom there is no contemplating the downside. Just as the upside brings the 50 percent story, so the downside brings its own asymmetry. Worse still, if you fail to "service" the debt, if you produce figures which breach the covenants laid out in such loving detail and all too greedily agreed by the 50 percent-case optimist, if you step into the world of the "troubled credit", if you cross the threshold of the lender's "workout department" – should you do all those things then woe will, really will, betide you. It will come rushing in like a frothy, soiled, red-brown briny sea and cover you, smother you. You will not have any say, any control whatsoever; that bank will fucking OWN you, own you, man…

"Peter." Ivy was talking to him, solicitous hand on his forearm. Jerry, seated opposite, was looking uncomfortable. What had he been doing? Muttering under his breath? Ignoring his friends? Frothing at the mouth? Everyone was looking either nervous, intrigued, or both – in the way people who have had an unexpected glimpse of some private sorrow are either uncomfortable or intrigued. Intrigued as people are by reports on the secret lives of celebrities who, despite beauty, wealth and fame, end up in the divorce courts or rehab, or in public toilets in a homosexual clinch with a complete dreg-scum stranger. Schadenfreude-intrigued.

In his gut, Peter knew what was coming. He had not yet had the conference call, but he knew. His friends' puzzled, worried faces were an early portent of the changes he was about to endure in his professional and personal lives. He looked at his watch: 21.25. Without a word he got up and stumbled into the house, went to his study, picked up the handset on the phone and, consulting his Blackberry, dialled.

Freddy Lee was already on the line when Peter called the Rareterre conference call number. Freddy was chairing the call.

"Hi, Freddy. No Olivier? Why's he not chairing this? He's the executive." Only in very small part thanks to the inadvisable mix of Bud Ice and Stag's Leap, Peter was not himself enough to question why he was starting out so aggressively, why he was interested in the administrative detail. On his desk the digital picture frame the children had given him at Christmas, pre-loaded with images of themselves and their mother in a variety of happy places, started dutifully to scroll through its pictorial record of family harmony.

"I called the meeting, Peter. Olivier didn't seem to want even to attend. I guess it's quite late over there?"

Bloody Olivier. Forever defending his right to a private life, even when crisis struck in his area of direct responsibility. But Peter checked his anger; he didn't really know yet whether this was a crisis or not. "I saw the email thread, something about our permits up at Trillium? Sounds serious enough to me to merit Olivier getting off his arse."

"Oh, it's serious right enough, Peter. We need to get to the bottom of why this has happened. The CUPs are local permits and the problem may be a bureaucratic issue at the Mount Hood or the Salem level. But it could stem from the federal level, an EPA matter, or anything between. The thing is, today's the fourth of July. We heard from the Assay and Mining Authority yesterday, on Tuesday. They had a technical complaint about the water leaching from the Trillium mine into the water course which feeds the lake."

There were two beeps in quick succession as Frits and Olivier joined the call. Peter found himself checking his watch. 21.37. The digital picture frame silently transitioned from a picture of Harry, aged three, giggling in a paddling pool, to one taken ten years later of Ivy and all three children on a wet Lake District hillside.

"Hi, Frits. Hi, Olivier. Better late than never." Why so acerbic? "You were saying, Freddy?"

"I was just saying that it's a shame we didn't get a response to the Assay and Mining Authority before everyone over here cleared off for the

Independence Day weekend. Now we don't get to respond until Monday, they will probably assume we really have a problem…"

"And don't we?" Frits was on edge, his voice a semitone higher than normal.

"We don't think we do." Olivier spoke for the first time. "I have tried to get the local management to check it out, but they're all out of contact for the long weekend."

"When on Tuesday did we hear of the problem?" Peter felt his heart pumping.

"At about 4.30."

"Our time? Evening?" Of course evening. Of course our time. Peter remembered that Olivier had gone home early for a parents' night at his son's school.

"Well, that would have been fairly early morning in Oregon; plenty of time to contact them and sort things out. What exactly is the problem and what did we do?" Freddy and Olivier both started to talk; Freddy won.

"The problem is a high concentration of arsenic, cyanide, barium, copper, lead and other things, including nuclides, in the leach water from the mine. Oregon's local mine regulation programme has periodic checks. We are not sure why we got one, we were not due to have another for a year or so, and the readings look all wrong…"

"And there is a federal angle too," Olivier butted in, stung by the implied criticism that action had not been taken swiftly enough. "The Federal Clean Water Act underlies the permits, although ours are kind of grandfathered…"

"Well, yes and no." Freddy was trying not to be too openly contradictory. "The CUPs were awarded following a public meeting and the continued protection of the water was one of the conditions of approval, a so-called general welfare standard."

"A public meeting?" Frits, an additional semitone higher. "Hell, will we need a public meeting to reinstate the CUPs? I hope to God not!"

"Hang on, hang on – did Freddy just say the readings look wrong?" *Christ,* thought Peter, *there's so much emotion sloshing around we're at risk of missing the big points.*

"Yes," Freddy said hesitantly, "it's odd to see arsenic in there – as far as I am aware arsenic was never used up at Trillium Lake – it's not a gold mine. Plus, the concentrations of these materials are a bit strange." Peter was wondering how relevant these facts might be, whether they were looking at a situation where the toothpaste was out of the tube and getting it back in would be a near impossibility, regardless of the facts. He thought it best not to mention this gloomy possibility.

The discussion ebbed and flowed. Freddy and Olivier did most of the talking, with Frits occasionally making helpful suggestions, and Peter irritably trying to establish a clear position that Olivier was unable to provide.

"In summary, as things stand we are stopped from any further development of the mine. We don't know why, or for how long, but we think we can supply data that the authorities would need to reconsider their position, even though we don't know right now which authorities it is – community, state or federal. We're going to look pretty daft when we announce this to the markets." There was a sound rather like a walrus surfacing after a long and unsuccessful submersion in hunt of fish. Frits.

"Why on earth would we announce this to the world? The share price would tank."

"That's kind of the point. You do think this is price sensitive information? Eh? What do you think, Frits? You know the stock exchange rules. You know what Julian will say. Our biggest asset, the reason nearly all our shareholders invested in us, has been put on hold."

As Rareterre's Nominated Advisor at NOMAD Securities, and as such guardian of the board's conscience and arbiter concerning the company's disclosure of information and adherence to other provisions of the AIM

Rules, Julian had the laudable task of trying to ensure as fair a market in shares as possible.

"Yes, but it's easy for His Sanctimoniousness, he will go for the easy option and blurt it all out in its current half-digested form – less risky for him, no chance of the FSA or stock exchange or whoever criticising them – but as you just said, we know too little to give the market a clear and sensible picture. We can't just go scaring the horses without full information."

"And what about people who buy the shares tomorrow morning for 104p, and then the day after we tell them we can't continue to develop Trillium and the price drops to 50p. Won't they have a justifiable claim that they were not fairly informed of the risks in the investment?"

"Okay, we make a half-arsed announcement tomorrow and the price drops to 50p. People sell. Then we get a full understanding of what those EPA bastards are really after, find out it's all a storm in a teacup, and the price bounces back up again. Aren't the shareholders entitled to assume we are at least partly on top of our Exploration and Mining position when we make a public statement? Won't that lot of shareholders, the ones who sold at 50p, have a valid complaint too?" Peter could not help it. He was multiplying the number of shares he owned by 50p. The Mount family balance sheet was barely solvent at that level. Frits was still talking.

"… need to talk with Julian in the morning, and Olivier, get off your ass and get someone in Oregon, someone with half a brain at least, to start collecting samples of our own. I think you should go out personally and take charge. I'll bet you don't even know the EPA guys! Well, do you?"

"No, of course I don't, but…"

"Well, you bloody well should! Who's our top man out there? Does he have the contacts to get this sorted quickly?" Olivier had a mental blockage. He could not recall Rick's name; his contact with him was infrequent. Olivier preferring to deal with high-cost, customer-focussed, university-educated consultants, not rough and ready learned-on-the-job night school roustabouts like…

"Rick! Rick Stone." He said it too loudly, after too long a gap. He sensed all the others on the call concluding he was not close enough to his operations, too aloof – an easy enough impression to give when you look like an SS *Sturmbannführer* and speak with an indefinable European accent. Besides, Olivier was aloof, there was no denying it. "I'm pretty sure he knows the local officials, but no one at federal level – why should he? It's nonsensical."

Frits was barking now, Olivier was snarling. Peter wanted to howl. Instead, with a superhuman effort, he intervened in the dog fight and terminated the call with the proposal that Freddy and Olivier should work together on getting to the bottom of the actual problem, reporting back to the whole board in 24 hours – Friday evening. He, Peter, would hold off St Julian with a call emphasising the current uncertainty, on which he was beginning to see Frits's point of view.

As Peter hung up, the mini slide-show on his digital photo frame displayed a picture of the whole family taken recently, seated around a table at the Manoir aux Quat'Saisons, celebrating Harry winning a place at Oxford. Vainglorious excess, expense met by a further increment to the mortgage – improper ostentation for a man with over a million pounds of debt. The stupidity of his life with its unjustifiable spending was horribly clear to Peter as he sat in a bitter pool of doubt about his business, the value of which was his last resort of justification for all the unfunded swagger. As the happy family in the picture began to fade and make way for the next image, Peter found himself counting his blessings, irreligiously thanking God for this healthy family filled with love and support, gifts, he told himself, that transcended any material problems he might have.

In the hallway behind his closed door, Peter heard the Chatterers taking their leave of Ivy, very early, subdued, as if she was a newly bereaved widow, and the door concealed a coffin.

Rareterre Plc Offices, Hammersmith, London, July, 2007

Olivier slammed the phone back onto its cradle. In addition to the more or less explicit criticism from Frits, Freddy and Peter, he had just had a frustrating conversation with an obstinate Rick Stone at his home in Rhododendron. Yes, it was important, that's why he was calling at 10.30 in the evening. Yes, he was aware that it was Independence Day. Yes, he knew it was a big national holiday. Yes, you guessed right, Rick, it was to do with the permits. Yes, he was aware that it was over two weeks since Rick had first called about the authorities' visit. No, of course he'd always taken it seriously.

Rick was angry that Olivier, a man he saw far less frequently than he was entitled to expect, had been so unresponsive to the warning sign that had been the unscheduled visit from the Oregon State Assay and Mining Authority. He felt that Rareterre had missed an opportunity to head off trouble in advance. This specific anger was anchored in a more general sea of discontent at Olivier's apparent lack of interest in the detail of the running of his company's biggest asset. Like most people, Rick was taking Thursday and Friday off, making a nice five-day break of the Independence Day holiday, and he had planned a hiking trip with his wife and some friends. Activity during this period at the mine was scaled back, allowing most of the staff to plan trips of their own. It was therefore with great reluctance that Rick agreed to take a team the following day to various spots on the mine's extensive site to collect some water and soil samples, when he had planned to be trekking up the Cooper Spur Trail. No one was going to like it.

Saint Julian started work late, Peter knew, so his new early-morning office routine gave him plenty of time to prepare for his call. He rehearsed carefully, even making a bullet-point list of the key messages he wanted to convey, struggling with the biggest Complicated Truth yet. *It really should not be like this*, he thought. *NOMAD are supposed to be on our side.*

At 09.30 he closed his office door and dialled Julian Marian-Smythe's number, remaining standing and looking out at the busy and slightly down-at-heel Hammersmith street. He pictured Julian, impeccably dressed, white handkerchief peeping from the top pocket of his pinstripe suit, Churches-shod feet up on his desk. Julian's view was of St Paul's Cathedral.

"Good morning, Julian. How goes it?" For some reason Peter always found himself talking like some faux eighteenth-century parson with Julian.

"First rate, thanks. To what do I owe the pleasure…?"

"Well, there've been some developments out at Trillium Lake of which I want to apprise you."

"Not positive ones, I gather from your tone." Peter could hear in Julian's voice that he was removing his feet from the desk, sitting up and reaching for his Montblanc.

"It's hard to say too definitively right now." Nonsense. The developments were unquestionably bad, the hard thing to say was the degree of badness. "We received notification yesterday that the Conditional Use Permits at the mine have been temporarily rescinded." Tendentious. They'd heard two days previously and there was no basis for the emphasis on the word "temporarily". "We are still assessing the situation and seeking clarification from the authorities." True, although his wording suggested a greater degree of progress and control than was the case.

"I see." Julian's tone effectively communicated as yet unfounded moral disapproval. "If I recall correctly, the CUP is the permit that allows you to expand your operations at the mine, yes?"

Peter hated it when people ended statements with "yes?", which, despite the questioning intonation, did not require an answer so much as serve as a confirmation, hard to contradict elegantly, especially when there was no break in the flow for a response, as was the case here.

"Your hope was that the existing permits, this CUP and a negative declaration regarding the revised plans you are preparing, will suffice as far as operating the enlarged mine is concerned, yes?" Still no break in the flow. "How temporary is 'temporarily'?"

A real question at last. Unfortunately Peter, who had indeed used the word, had no clue of the answer. "We can't answer that until we get the clarification I mentioned. You know how these authorities can be. High-handed." Peter was hoping Julian would not ask which particular authority it was, because the answer "I'm not sure" was so unsatisfactory.

"Did they give any reason for the rescindment?" The other question he was hoping to avoid.

"Oh, apparently there was an unscheduled inspection and they claim to have found some contamination, but frankly, Julian, I'd rather not speculate until we know more." Less than informative. Then Julian said what Peter had been really hoping not to hear.

"We must issue a statement, of course. At least a holding statement." Peter pictured Julian, with great accuracy, inspecting his manicured finger-nails. They had debated the timing of statements to the stock exchange before. Julian was open to criticism, formal censure even, if an avoidable false market in the shares of his AIM-listed clients developed. Because a false market most often involved the incompleteness of the information available, Julian almost always wanted to reveal every negative piece of news; yet he was reluctant to announce positive developments for fear he might be accused of hyping the shares. The resulting tension with opti-mistic management could be ugly. Peter opted for decisiveness.

"No, Julian, really that would be horribly premature. We know too little. It's Independence Day weekend, so let's wait until close of play Monday and decide what we need to say then."

They had the same debate, but in more civilised terms, as Peter had endured with Frits, Freddy and Olivier the night before. Neither barked or snarled, but in the end Julian growled, "Very well, Peter, but Monday at the latest."

Mission accomplished, Peter thought, like George W. Bush on the deck of an aircraft carrier, unwittingly at the start of a protracted war.

Trillium Lake Mine, Mount Hood, Oregon, July 2007

It was Albert Einstein, via Friedrich Hegel, who made the most useful observation. Rick had chosen Friedrich and four of the other geologists and mineral analysts on secondment to the Trillium Lake site because they were scientists of a sort and, anyway, distant from their families and friends and so had less planned for the holiday weekend. "Come in your hiking boots." Rick had told them, bitterly.

As instructed, they all turned up at the mine on Thursday morning wearing clothing they considered suitable for hiking, in each case pretty much indistinguishable from their daily work-wear. It was a lovely, fresh, sunny Mount Hood morning and Rick's sampling team were as excited as children on a school outing. Rick and Friedrich had prepared the sampling equipment and laid it out on the long table in the canteen, like some sort of highly specialist bring-and-buy sale. Friedrich had some relevant experience of environmental testing from a job in Alaska the preceding year; Rick had spent half the night reading the US Government's Field Guide. Beginning by swearing them all to secrecy, Rick and Friedrich briefed them on the purpose of the next couple of days' activities.

"Thanks, guys, for taking on this extracurricular task. As most of you are probably aware, a couple of weeks back the Oregon State Assay boys paid us an unannounced visit and took away some soil and water samples. Well, on Tuesday they sent us notification that they'd found contaminants in those samples, and as a result they suspended one of our key permits. That there's confidential by the way; none of you guys is allowed to trade company shares until I tell you otherwise. And nor can your mothers or anyone else connected with you."

A murmur passed around the team: this was indeed unusual, it made them feel special.

"We're planning to go out and take some samples of our own, to double-check what they are telling us because, frankly, I don't believe the bastards. I know where they went to collect their materials," he indicated a large-scale map pinned to the wall, the evaporation ponds and the drill field marked with yellow Post-it notes with arrows drawn on them, "so we'll split into groups of two. One guy collects the samples, the other records everything – including taking pictures with those cameras over there – and we'll go back to those same places and do just what they did, see what we find. It all has to be done and the samples analysed by Sunday night, so the quicker we collect our stuff the faster we can get the samples off to the labs. Okay? Now Friedrich here will brief you on using some of this equipment."

That was when Friedrich made his useful observation.

"Albert Einstein's definition of insanity was 'doing the same thing over and over again and expecting different results'. Well, it occurs to me that we don't want to get the same results, so we should not do the same thing as the Assay boys. Not exactly the same thing anyway. We should sample where they did, sure, but we should also take samples from other logical places like this," he pointed to a place a few hundred yards upstream of the drill field, "and this," a few hundred yards downstream. "That way, if their results are, by chance, local anomalies, we'll be able to demonstrate it."

Rick was nodding. Obvious. It didn't take a genius to spot that.

Kiara's Office, London, July 2007

Kiara had put together a version of her trademark *Cadendo nell'amore con Londra* package – travel, accommodation, orientation and evening activities – for a group of students from Rome and Naples. She had sent them lists of approved accommodation for the term time and booked a hotel for those who had not yet made their longer-term arrangements. She would take them on one of her well-tried routes, sightseeing and teaching them the geography of the sprawling city. They would go to a West End show, a musical preferably, and a typical British pub. Theoretically the package was two days of intense activity, then they were on their own – except that she often found herself providing an unofficial after-sales service when things went wrong. She didn't mind. She switched on her desktop computer and, whilst it was booting up, checked she had the right number of Oyster cards and the correct time of arrival for the students' flights. Online, she saw that neither flight was delayed and flipped to her emails. An apologetic message from one of the students lengthily explained that he would no longer be coming to London, for personal reasons linked to his girlfriend's mistrust of loose Englishwomen and their morality, sentiments based, it seemed, on observations made at one of the more down-market beach resorts on the Amalfi coast. Eleven places booked and paid for, ten students coming; last minute change being an Italian speciality, Kiara was unconcerned.

"Ricardo, where have you booked in today's group? Hotel and theatre, I mean? One's not coming." Ricardo was born in Mile End and known as Dick to his family and friends, but he saw having Kiara call him "Ricardo" as one of the best perks of working at the agency. He was generally able to purchase or sell theatre tickets with ease, something Kiara put down, correctly, to his East End connections.

"The usual hotel in Russell Square, got the discount rate again, and *Beauty and the Beast*. They're doing a revival. Bloody crap, most likely, but your little Italian friends'll love it. I'll offload that ticket no probs."

"*Beauty and the Beast*? On stage? In the West End?"

Despite his accent and background, Dick was something of a cultural snob. "Yes, Kiara, they keep doing this, y'know, remaking stuff. Here's how it goes: European folk-lore fairy tale from time immemorial, normally earthy and honest and quite bloody, gets written down sometime in the eighteenth century, gets redone and redone and increasingly banal over the years, until finally Disney get their hands on it and complete the process of sugar-coating. Then this is the version perpetuated, that the Lloyd-Webbers and so on make into stage musicals."

"Oh, but it's a great film!" Kiara was genuinely shocked. "I'm not so sure the bloody original version would be much good. I loved the Disney film when I was a girl. Maybe people like sugar-coating, Ricardo." She hesitated for a moment. "Don't – how did you say – 'offload' the ticket, Ricardo. I think I know someone who might like to come." She would call him on the way to the airport.

"Would I like to come, Kiara?" Peter pressed his Blackberry against his ear as if to trap in the invitation; he could scarcely contain his excitement. Twice-weekly chats over smoothies in the gratifyingly sweaty environment of the gym were one thing, but this sounded like a date, even if there were going to be ten other Italians present. He nearly referred to bears shitting in woods, but thought better of it. "I'd love to, Kiara. Tomorrow night? I'd love to. I'd…" With difficulty he stopped gushing. "I love that show!"

CHAPTER 9

The Mounts' House, Chelsea, London, July 2007

Ivy knew Peter better than anyone. Better than he knew himself. That morning she had seen him pick out his favourite suit, an Oswald Boateng she had helped him choose the year before, nothing too extreme but definitely fashionable and youthful. Maybe he was planning a surprise outing for them all, to celebrate Emma's birthday.

"Something special planned for today?" she asked, hopefully, gesturing at the suit. Peter had given a lot of consideration to the matter of what he should say to Ivy. One thing continued to be clear in his mind: the truth was not an option. He felt, however, that something close to the truth, something containing elements of it, would be preferable to a complete fabrication. He would be more convincing that way, and there would be the possibility of credibly claiming confusion later. Not that he was thinking about dealing with "later". He wasn't really thinking at all.

The absolute truth would be: "There's a gorgeous Italian girl 20 years my junior I've been chatting up at the gym for months. I seem somehow to have come between her and her boyfriend. She's invited me out to see a West End production of a children's film made into a musical. I think I'm in love." Unlikely to go down well. A complete fabrication would be: "Some boring old fart at RBS invited James and me to the opera. Boys-only do. It'll be dire, but, you know, one does what one has to." Massively open to failure in verification – so, in answer to Ivy's question he said: "There's an Italian I met at the gym; he's got a spare ticket to this show, I'm not sure which, I just hope it's not a musical! Given that it's Tuesday and you'll be out with Odile and that crew anyway, I thought I might as well go along." Nearly true, one deniable gender change, offhand.

"In your Oswald Boateng?"

"Oh, is it? I mean, yes, there's a potential investor, an institutional investor, coming to the office today."

Ivy smelled a rat, she had been smelling rats for weeks. She had considered investigating further, employing the well-established methods of searching his pockets, gaining secret access to his mobile phone and rooting through the text messages – actions which seemed somehow degrading for both her and him. Would he really be so careless? Yet so many cheating spouses seemed to be exactly that – careless. She felt sure that whatever he had done – or was doing – he did still care for her. Mostly though, she felt that she would be better off not knowing, but Peter was so very bad at dissembling. Right now he was behaving slightly jumpily, like a nervous cat who thinks it might have heard a dog enter the house. She looked at him and, despite everything, could not help feeling affection for the poor incompetent fool. He quickly left, foregoing breakfast, leaving so strong an odour of rodent behind him that she forgot to remind him of his daughter's birthday.

Central London, July 2007

Until 11.15 the evening was a great success for Peter; it could not have gone better. Kiara and her garrulous group of students were in the theatre foyer as arranged. She gave him his ticket and quickly introduced him; no one seemed too interested. Seated chastely beside her in the darkness of the theatre as the cast sang and danced their way through an agreeable show, enjoying her innocent pleasure, feeling her warm arm and, occasionally, her thigh against his, had been delightful to him. He had ordered a half-bottle of champagne for the interval and they had abandoned the students to go to the pre-appointed spot in the bar with his name on a scrap of paper beneath the two glasses. She had appreciated the convenience of this arrangement and marvelled that it worked when theft would have been so straightforward. She was wearing a tight pair of black trousers made from a discretely shiny material, short black boots with heels and a simple dark grey cashmere V-neck sweater. Peter realised with sudden pleasure that people were looking at them: women disapprovingly, men with envy.

Kiara had a favourite pub for after the shows – traditional Victorian, very British, more than slightly scruffy, variable service – where she liked to take her student groups and show them this important component of English culture to round the evening off. It was a short, disjointed walk along the thronging pavements of Shaftesbury Avenue from the theatre. Kiara walked along with a young man who seemed to be called Dolfo, whilst Peter tried with no success to make conversation with what he understood to be Dolfo's brother, but could have been anyone. When their ill-disciplined group finally all congregated in a gossiping gaggle in front of the pub, Kiara told Peter:

"They want a night club, Peter, not the pub. Rodolfo was here last summer and says he knows a place not far. They like to dance."

Peter was momentarily excited then disappointed; he too liked to dance, dancing with Kiara would be beyond even his most wildly optimistic expectations for this evening – but he was not sure whether he was invited, or if so with what degree of sincerity. He was, after all, a stranger to these youngsters, and old enough to be their father. He reluctantly went for the option with the lowest risk of embarrassment.

"Oh – okay, fair enough. I'll perhaps see you at..." But Kiara was talking quickly to Dolfo in Italian, pointing, and the students moved off as a group, Dolfo's brother (or whoever) waving to Peter as he hurried after them. Peter may have seemed hesitant and confused, perhaps Kiara was thirsty, maybe she just wanted to show friendship. For whatever reason, she took him by the hand and led him, through wooden doors glazed with ornate bevelled frosted glass, into the busy pub.

A beautiful woman must get used to the effect she has on groups of men, especially those at the end of an evening in the average British boozer. Peter was thinking this as, still hand in hand, they dodged their way to the bar. Kiara did not seem to notice anything, not even the bearded man sitting with two others in a corner, at a small round table damp with beer and laden with empty glasses and crisp packets. The man's look, first admiring then astonished, could not have been more overt or pronounced had Sophia Loren in her prime just walked in leading Peter by the hand. Neither of them noticed this man. Jerry Chimer. Texan Jerry. Jerry as in "Fulki and Jerry".

They had a great time, Kiara and Peter. He was on top clown/counsellor form and there was the show to talk about. She was sitting on a bar stool, the last remaining, facing Jerry's corner, feet on the stool's footrest, knees bent; he stood close beside her in the crush, between her right knee and the bar, leaning on the counter with his right elbow, torso swivelled towards her. The crowd thinned but they remained in place, close. Occasionally she would touch his upper arm in appreciation of a joke or to emphasise a point. They had a great time, Peter and Kiara, until 11.15. Then the group of three men sitting in the corner got up to leave. It was not the exit closest to him, but Jerry crossed the room to the door facing Peter. As he passed he caught his eye and winked salaciously. A sharp vacuum filled Peter's gut, his fingers and neck tingled as from the adrenaline rush associated with a near-miss driving a car at speed.

NOMAD Securities' Offices, The City, London, July 2007

Peter and Olivier were alone in a conference room at NOMAD Securities' offices. It smelled faintly of stale beef, a luncheon two days earlier perhaps.

From the window the wet front steps of St Paul's Cathedral were visible through the drizzle, thronged with cagoule-wearing tourists. On the table in front of Peter were a half-empty cup of cold coffee and two sheets of A4 paper.

"Bloody hell, we pay NOMAD what, 40 grand a year, and the clever boys and girls at Scottish Spinsters about the same, for their professional input at times like this. And this" – he held up one of the A4 sheets, a draft of the Regulatory News Service announcement to the London Stock Exchange, between index finger and thumb as if it were damp with rat's urine – "this pathetic effort is the best we can communally come up with after half a day's concerted effort."

"It's not an easy message to deliver."

"Made a damn sight more difficult by Julian's compulsive need to disgorge everything from the authorities but nothing of our own findings!" Olivier knew better than to try to defend Julian, whose stance he actually thought quite reasonable in the circumstances. Peter carried on: "I mean, listen to this. And I quote. In fact, I quote myself, apparently. 'Peter Mount, CEO of Rareterre, said: "We are convinced that the Oregon State Assay and Mining Authority's data overstate the contamination and look forward to working with them to resolve the matter to our mutual satisfaction."' Close quote. What a dickhead, that Peter Mount! 'Convinced they overstate the contamination'!" He spoke the words in the nasal tones of a slightly camp bureaucrat from Lancashire. "Can't they see I appear to be confirming that there is contamination at Trillium Lake? It's not right!"

Olivier drew a breath, inhaling a little courage. "Julian says we can't ignore the fact that our own samples showed traces of uranium and thorium. The complete absence of..."

"The *ground* contains uranium and thorium! It's in the earth! It's bloody supposed to be there! The mine was originally found by prospectors *looking* for uranium, Olivier. But isn't it odd, the cyanide and arsenic concentrations are around the sampling points the Assay Authority used but nowhere else! And Julian won't let us say that!"

"With due respect, Peter, I think he's right on that one. The last thing we can afford is to alienate the Authority by implying their bad faith in any way."

"With due respect". Has that expression ever been used other than to state quite clearly that very little if any respect was due? Peter tried to avoid audibly grinding his teeth. "But I am quoted as saying that they 'overstate the contamination'. Surely that also suggests we think they are wrong?"

"We 'are convinced' 'their data overstate'." Olivier imprecisely circled the text on the page in front of him. "It's sort of passive. Anyway, you wanted that part in there." Peter wondered grimly if Olivier, who had a 12-month notice period in his service agreement, was trying to get himself sacked. He replied with exaggerated patience.

"Rather than not mention wassisname's, Rick Stone's, data at all! Because it was not third-party, independently generated? Remember? It was you, Olivier, who sent Rick to do the work."

"Yes, over the Independence Day weekend, and if it hadn't been for Rick we'd have no alternative data at all with which to counter the Authority in time to make an announcement today."

"Yes, but as Julian is not letting us use it that's not much use to anyone, is it? Oh, this is futile, we're going in circles. Where is Julian anyway? He said he'd be back by now."

Both men looked at their watches. Half past two. Julian had left two hours earlier to attend an uncancellable lunch, sorry, chaps, too late notice, by the time I'm back you'll have the announcement finished, humourless laugh. In fact, Julian's lunch was with a headhunter, an "executive recruitment consultant" as he preferred to be called. Julian liked to get his ducks in a row well in advance of bonus time; a few offers of plum positions at competing banks had served him well in the past. As if on cue, a cursory knock and the conference room door opened. Julian walked in.

"So, gentlemen, progress?"

"No!" said Peter, with some force, just as Olivier started to say "Yes." Julian looked at Olivier, as if appealing for reason to prevail. He had accepted several glasses of claret from the headhunter but was not feeling mellow.

Peter carried on, "I know we've been over it all a dozen times, but I can't accept that we cannot mention our own findings: NO contamination, NO unusual concentrations of any of the harmful substances the Oregon State Assay and Mining Authority found, except from the sampling points they used. It just does not stand up to scrutiny!" Julian made a theatrical effort to gather his patience and reason to him.

"Point one. You can't call the American authorities liars or cheats. Not if you ever want to get your CUP back and drink from it." He winced at his own clumsy joke. "Point two, your measurements are your own, not compliant with the requirement for independent third-party validation, so officially these data do not exist at all. And before you ask again, no, we cannot delay the announcement until after you get an independent report done. Frankly, we've already waited too long."

Peter suddenly felt an almost physical depression, as if transported to the bottom of a deep swimming pool. Wearily, he began to swim for the surface. "Well, we can't make any announcement until the board has approved it. The market closes at five. That gives us a little over two hours to get to a text we can recommend to the board, have them respond by email and issue the statement. It's a shame you couldn't cancel your lunch, Julian, but I think we are now running out of time. I still think we should make the statement tomorrow morning. That allows us more time to get it right and set up a conference call for analysts immediately after the announcement goes out." As he said this the frowning face of Stacey, the equity research analyst at Hamlyn, appeared in his imagination, pushing him back into deeper water.

The text was finally agreed at ten o'clock that night, but not before Frits had insisted on a conference call in which he had rehashed all the arguments Peter had been making all day. The announcement factually revealed the withdrawal of the Conditional Use Permits and the precise findings of the Authority's sampling. So much was known, anything else surmise, the board had been persuaded.

Peter was quoted as saying: "From our own preliminary research, we are convinced that the Oregon State Assay and Mining Authority's data overstate the contamination and look forward to working with them to resolve the matter to our mutual satisfaction." The five additional words, "from our own preliminary research", had taken the involvement of 12 people over an additional seven hours.

After all that, and precisely as Rick had predicted, no one was going to like it.

Hamlyn Securities Offices, The City, London, July 2007

Stacey was having fun.

Everyone enjoys success and she was having plenty of it. In the months since her unpleasant encounter in Paris with Carl, an experience that, as time went by, she increasingly saw as coercive on his part, she had issued three notes covering Rareterre plc and its sector. There had been "Medium Rare or Half-Baked?" suggesting that Rareterre had problems managing the timely progress of its development at Trillium Lake; this had seen the share price fall from the 120–130p range to 100–110p, at which value the board of Rareterre were unhappy to issue new shares to finance their final Trillium Lake investments.

When these additional financing needs were prematurely revealed to her by Carl, she had taken great pleasure in penning "Rarely Rarely Expensive", beautifully timed to precede their road-show by a couple of days, which exposed the spiralling costs of completing the work in Oregon. The shares had dropped further, following what she heard was a pretty underwhelming road-show performance, to below 100p for the first time in years, aided on their way by Dreadnought Investment Management selling a huge block of shares. Her colleagues on the trading desk were happy to ease these into the market and make their commissions, icing on the cake so far as Stacey was concerned.

The company had certainly pulled a rabbit from the hat announcing its loan facility with RBS, true, but she had quickly published "Polonius: a Rare-Earth Element?" quoting Hamlet and explaining why "Rareterre should neither a borrower nor a lender be". She recycled Carl's point about the heavy rare-earths produced at Trillium Lake Mine costing more to extract and process, hence making the operations more exposed to market fluctuations, arguing that the debt would only exacerbate this exposure – "for loan oft loses both itself and friend", she had sagely if disconnectedly concluded. That had seen the share price settle at about 80p. She assumed, but never explicitly checked, that Montagu Montagu and his new client, C. Brown Pty. Ltd. were pleased.

And now this. What a gift! Stacey picked up the stock exchange announcement and held it to the light, as if checking a banknote for its watermark. "Rareterre Conditional Use Permits Suspension" was the heading. She scribbled on her lined yellow notepad. "Rareterre's broken CUP?"; "Repaired CUPs rarely hold water?"; "Many a slip 'twixt CUP and lip – Rareterre's environmental disaster?" She deleted everything except "'twixt CUP and lip", then crossed that out too.

The announcement of the permit suspension saw Rareterre's share price fall by half to 42p. When Stacey published Hamlyn Securities' extremely pessimistic view of the situation – CUPs were hard to secure, requiring public meetings and local support; Oregon State Assay and Mining Authority data looks damning and may involve costly remediation; new exploitation at Trillium Lake probably stopped for years if not forever –

under the title "CUPs and Poisoned Chalices", the share price started a gradual decline that would end in October 2008 with it hitting bottom at 6p. This was one twentieth of the price two years earlier, when Stacey had followed Carl into a Paris hotel bedroom because she was bored and did not want her potatoes.

The Simple Lie was indeed very compelling; the withdrawal of the Conditional Use Permit was a huge and potentially irreversible setback, a loud, shouty, attention-grabbing fact, like a drunken uncle noisily refusing to leave a family party. The Complicated Truth did not have any chance of being heard over this fascinating scene. Rick's sampling was quickly confirmed by independent experts: the contamination at the mine was perplexingly localised and made up of some unlikely components, the State Authority's results appeared to be aberrations. Someone should have cared. But look! Uncle Joe has just thrown a punch at the head waiter!

Rareterre Plc Offices, Hammersmith, London, August 2007

After Jerry had salaciously winked his way out of the pub, leaving Peter almost winded with apprehension, the evening had quickly come to an anticlimactic end. Kiara saw his inexplicable sudden change of mood, but he quickly gathered himself sufficiently to straighten up, disengaging himself from her silky legs, and make what felt distinctly like a getaway. Stiffly, he had thanked her for an enjoyable evening, she confusedly reciprocated with thanks for the company. She had lent quickly forwards and kissed him on the cheek uncomprehending – neither dry and business-like nor a lover's kiss, not a daughter's nor a friend's. It was an awkward, British end to a Mediterranean evening. They took separate cabs to their separate homes.

Kiara was therefore surprised next time they met at the gym over smoothies. Inexplicably, Peter was exactly as he had been prior to the evening in theatreland, which was not mentioned. Her years in London had prepared Kiara for this British sort of disjointed social behaviour, but she could never get used to it. Meanwhile, their gym-and-smoothie relationship continued along its enjoyable track, somehow still teetering at one extreme edge of platonic, somehow to both their satisfaction. Somehow.

When his Blackberry rang Peter was returning to his office from a lengthy conference call with one of the task-forces he had set up, their objective being recovery of the withdrawn permits as quickly as possible. His heart sank as he saw the name on the little screen of his beeping phone. Jerry. Nearly two weeks had elapsed since their sighting in the Shaftsbury Avenue pub and Peter had started to hope he had imagined it, salacious wink and all. All the same he had been expecting to hear from Jerry and had feared that it might be at some social event – he wouldn't put it past him to make a stupid joke of it, careless of who heard. In some ways taking the call was a relief, but it didn't feel like it. He opted for pretending not to know who was calling.

"Peter Mount speaking."

"Peter, you old dog! You're certainly the dark horse! My God, you randy old…" Peter interrupted before he could be likened to any more animals.

"Hello, Jerry." He quickly entered his office and closed the door. "Do I take it you are referring to our encounter in the Marquis of Granby, where you saw me with a young associate? It sounds like you have jumped, as I feared, to all the wrong conclusions." Jerry made a snorting noise.

"I love it! Encounter! Brief, was it, Peter? Young associate! Ha! What sort of 'association', exactly? The mind boggles; mine's not stopped boggling for days! And don't try telling me that she works at Parterre, it's just not feasible that a girl like that would get her hands dirty." Peter's mind was reeling; he did not know where to start on this list of irritating inaccuracies, far less the components which contained, more irritatingly still, seeds of accuracy. He elected to adopt diversionary tactics.

"It's Rareterre, Jerry; 'parterre' means something else altogether, as I suspect you know. We may be having our problems right now, but we're only temporarily down. And do you really suppose that all the employees of a mining company spend their days scrabbling around in the earth?" It failed; Jerry had observed Peter's debating style too often.

"Diversionary tactics if ever I heard them! Come on, we know one another well enough, Peter, you can trust me – who's the raven-haired beauty and does she have a sister?" Peter's mind was as crowded as the bar in the Marquis of Granby had been, and just as noisy. He remembered the rumours about Jerry and his bookkeeper, rumours he had found hard to credit when he thought of the lovely Fulki. He did not think of Ivy at all, even though the whole thing was about her – or about Ivy not finding out. In Peter's mind it was not personalised, it was a general need for secrecy, even though theoretically there was no actual need for secrecy, his relationship with Kiara being still innocent. But in the real world he knew that no one would believe that; even if the facts and probabilities based on age and appearance were all strong arguments in his favour, most people, like Jerry, would assume the worst. Or the best. There was the annoying little truth: that a small, highly influential self-deception pressure group from the noisy crowd in his head was keen on pursuing a less innocent path with Kiara. He had another go.

"She's a friend, just a friend, Jerry, nothing more. We'd been to the theatre – she had a spare ticket for *Beauty and the Beast* and offered it to me at the last minute."

Jerry exploded in mirth, part derisive, mostly genuine amusement. "*Beauty and the Beast!* Priceless!" he finally coughed out. "Look, Peter, we're friends, we go back a ways. I saw how she looked at you. Her body language was not at all 'just a friend' body language. If you don't want to tell me about it, fine, but you're one lucky old goat." He was gone.

Peter winced and placed the phone in the middle of the small circular table in the corner of his office. He was sitting straight-backed on one of four chairs squeezed around it. Elbows on the surface in front of him, he arched his hands together, fingertips to fingertips, and looked at the inactive Blackberry. Was Jerry right about the body language, the way she looked at him? Would Jerry be more trustworthy if he put his trust in him, explicitly? He was pretty sure Jerry would not tell Ivy directly, but what chance was there that he would speak to Fulki or – God forbid – Odile? It seemed unlikely, especially if the bookkeeper rumours were true. Why had he been so cagey with Jerry, why had he denied it? But denied what exactly? Why had he not said, "Okay, I'm a lucky old goat – but let's keep it between ourselves, eh, old chap?" It was admitting more than existed, outside his imagination, and even in formulating this sentence he seemed to have completed a transformation into some kind of pre-war cad.

Idiotically, he fleetingly wondered if Kiara did have a sister.

CHAPTER 10

Hotel Conference Room, South Kensington, London, September 2007

Rareterre's board met on alternate months, normally gathering in a hired meeting room at a London hotel, the company's Hammersmith premises being both too small and a bit too depressing for Frits's taste. As well as Frits and Freddy, there was one further non-executive on the board, Austin Roach. Frits was chairman and Freddy a well-connected expert in mining and mineralogy; Austin's added value was more financial. His demeanour was generally one of weary disappointment, a sense of "I've seen it all before so don't try it on" quickly pervading any space he occupied. He and Olivier provided a useful counterweight to Frits and Peter who were definitely "glass-half-full" guys.

Austin was a qualified company secretary as well as an accountant, and enjoyed a good "City reputation", or so he believed, backed up by St Julian who, as Nominated Advisor, should know. To Peter, Olivier and James, the executives who had to run the company day-by-day, Austin often appeared more an impediment than a help. It was Austin who had most vociferously backed Julian's stance on issuing the news of the CUPs withdrawal, with Olivier taking his habitual passive position. Austin was a professional non-executive director, on several company boards, and had close relations with RBS from having worked with them at other companies. James had

238

to admit that this had been useful during the negotiation of the loan and finalisation of the documentation.

Austin was a tall, angular man in his late fifties with a long angular face, a stoop and thick glasses, the result of years spent scrutinising the small print in financial documents and miniature-font notes to accounts, snuffling out inconsistencies and infelicitous attempts at concealment, like a trained pig finding truffles. A minor English public school education and a business degree from a second-rate university partly explained his long-windedness and desire to be seen as a member of the Establishment, which he was not and never would be.

At the September board meeting, in the nondescript conference suite of a nondescript South Kensington hotel, Austin was standing looking down his long nose and addressing the board. He had proposed item six of the agenda: "The Banking Environment".

"In the five months since we signed up for our loan with RBS, things have been changing in the financial world quite quickly. We saw the bankruptcy, or rather Chapter 11, of New Century in April, around the same time as we closed our deal. At the time there was some concern about contagion – that the problems with bad debts on their sub-prime book and their inability to liquidate their balance sheet, to sell their assets, would in turn cause other banks problems, push down asset values, and it would all escalate into a banking crisis."

The other members of the board stared at him blankly, all except Olivier who was texting his wife holding his Blackberry under the table. Frits and Freddy both lived in the USA and had experienced first-hand the TV coverage around the revelations of apparently crazy loans being made to wholly un-creditworthy individuals to buy overpriced homes, but life went on despite what had increasingly seemed to be media hysteria. Even James, who paid more attention to the financial press and goings on in the City and on Wall Street, was wondering how any of this could be relevant to Rareterre. The sound of laughter from outside the door told them that the youthful team of pharmaceuticals sales reps who had hired a neighbouring room were taking a coffee break. Frits perked up, but everyone knew Austin was going to plough on. He did.

"You may recall that back in July there was a further scare when the big American investment bank, Bear Stearns, refused to support two hedge funds bearing its name; they too were deeply involved in the sub-prime loans business, investing in financially engineered bundles of debt, the so-called Collateralised Debt Obligations or CDOs. A mate of mine" – Austin liked to use this demotic type of expression, but he was neither working class nor posh enough to carry it off – "works at one of the big New York law firms, a partner as it happens, and he was involved in the whole sorry mess. He told me that it looked like the contagion so many feared had really started to spread. Contagion was his word. Lots of banks were exposed to those hedge funds, they had borrowed hundreds of millions. Many more are directly exposed to CDOs. The thought that a bank thousands of miles away, with no direct loans to the Bear Stearns funds, might be at risk too, was looking more and more…"

It had been a long and depressing meeting. The board had spent much time discussing their plans to recover the lost Trillium permits and gloomily contemplating the gradually but uninterruptedly declining share price. Frits was a man naturally wired for positives, and all this negativism was draining him; now Austin seemed determined to depress them all further with this talk of someone else's problems. Plus, he wanted a cup of coffee and would have welcomed the chance to mingle with the bright young reps outside, whose energy and enthusiasm he currently envied. He interrupted Austin.

"Okay, okay, Austin, we get it. Contagion. Those idiots on Wall Street have screwed up. But I'm struggling to see what this has to do with us, frankly, and I am gasping for a cup of caffeine." Austin drew himself up to his full height, which was considerable, and adopted his most disappointed look, which was very disappointed indeed.

"Well, if you permit, Mr Chairman, I'll finish, but I'll be brief," he said, resorting to formality. Peter, Frits and James all nodded encouragingly: be brief. "It's simply this. Suppose RBS had lent money to Bear Stearns' hedge fund and lost a couple of hundred million – that would be bad for them, tough. They haven't, at least so far as I know, but actually we don't know, there's no transparency, which is another big part of the problem. But they almost certainly have lent money to one or more of the other banks that lost money when the Bear Stearns funds went under. And they definitely have plenty of sub-prime exposure, I mean they own vast quantities of those risky CDO packages of dodgy mortgages themselves. The problem is interconnectivity. All the banks are exposed to all the other banks because they all borrow and lend between each other." He glanced at Frits who was fidgeting. Outside, the pharmaceuticals reps were returning chattily to their meeting room. "All right. Bottom line: I'm worried about RBS and so I'm worried about Rareterre. We rely on RBS for pretty much all our future financing needs, especially with the share price so low. That's all." The fog of gloom that had characterised the meeting from the start thickened. James broke the silence.

"That certainly cheered us all up! Looking on the brighter side, RBS is the biggest bank in the world by some measures, so Edward Bald was telling me, and there has been no talk that I have heard of their being at any sort of risk. It really is an American problem. And our needs are so small – we've already drawn all but seven million of the facility. Things would have to be pretty dire before seven million dollars poses a problem to RBS!" Austin pursed his lips but said no more. He did not appreciate being painted as a Cassandra, and RBS's expensive headlong dash to ill-considered market leadership was one of the main reasons for his concern.

Everyone else was pleased with James's alternative view but somehow no one was fully convinced. They adjourned for coffee and found that the carefree young pharma reps had drunk it all, and eaten all the biscuits.

The Mounts' House, Chelsea, London, September 2007

The small TV screen in the corner of Ivy's kitchen was filled with pictures of admirably patient people forming a long queue outside a bank somewhere in northern England. An interviewer stepped forwards brandishing a microphone. The voice-over was describing the "chaotic scenes" as depositors "rushed to withdraw their savings" from the bank, Northern Rock. "The first so-called 'run' on a high street bank in the UK since the 1930s," it intoned, before the interviewer, an aggressive-looking man of about 30, thrust his microphone towards a young couple in the very un-chaotic line.

"So, why are you here today and how long have you been queuing?" The woman looked confused and on the verge of tears. The man, presumably her husband, stepped crossly forwards and the interviewer pointed the mike at him, as if to ward him off. His hair was so short that he appeared bald, he wore a single earring and a tattoo was visible on his neck beneath his tracksuit top. He spoke in a thick regional accent.

"All our life savings, and we've come to get our money out, like." The interviewer moved on down the line, not really in any hope of finding someone who would actually answer the question asked. He did not much mind the series of non-sequiturs he was collecting, his main objective being to give an impression of this incoherent and fearful crowd.

Peter came in, back earlier than normal from the board meeting; no one had been in the mood to socialise. As he gave Ivy an unreciprocated peck on the cheek he was just in time to hear an elderly woman tell the aggressive-looking interviewer that she had been there since mid-morning, and that now the bank had closed without her getting anywhere near it. "It's not fair," she said plaintively. "They ought to have stayed open until we all had our turn."

"Maybe they ran out of cash, so there was no point in staying open," suggested the interviewer helpfully. The old lady looked distressed. "It's not fair…" she repeated.

"It's not fair!" Peter mimicked, in a whining Geordie accent. Ivy turned on him with venom, eyes flashing.

"Peter, that poor woman might lose all her savings because that bank, Northern Rock, well, it looks like it's bankrupt. She's bound to be upset! People like her need protection! You should be ashamed of yourself, mocking her!"

The scene on the TV had moved to a studio. An expert from the *Financial Times* was explaining the cause of Northern Rock's problems. He had a big, domed balding head that reflected the studio lights, a caricature sci-fi boffin. The backdrop was a large still photograph in black and white of a queue outside a Northern Rock branch somewhere, snaking back into the distance like the famous political election poster "Labour isn't working".

"She won't lose her life savings, Ivy! She's stupid enough to put her money in a dodgy bank chasing an extra few quid in interest, no doubt, and she's stupid to queue up now to get it out, but it's a waste of her no doubt precious time. The government, sorry, the taxpayer, guarantees depositors' money."

"Stupid! Peter, she's just an ordinary hard-working person, who couldn't possibly know that this bank was about to go under, or that there is a scheme to protect her… It's only her right—"

"Bloody hell, Ivy, a minute ago you didn't even know there was a guarantee, now suddenly it's her right! Of course she could know; you'd think that before entrusting what you assure me are her hard-won life savings to any institution, she would read the small print! I don't know anything about this Northern Rock or why they're in trouble myself, but no well-run bank would suffer a run like this. Generally I'd say that if you put your hard-earned life savings in an unknown bank, you're stupid. I don't know why we're so keen to protect stupid people." Ivy made a sort of frustrated roaring noise at the back of her throat.

"Easy for you to say, with your degree and your education and your lawyer and accountant and banker friends. But her! Look at her! Surely there is some government regulation of banks to prot—" She stopped herself before using the word "protect" again, "that would allow her safely to make the assumption that she can trust the system."

"'The System'? She's an individual who made an individual decision, a bad one by the looks of it. What is this 'System'? And what's it got to do with that silly woman?"

The *FT* boffin was outlining the sub-prime phenomenon. "The originating bankers, those who actually loaned the money, became slapdash. They didn't care too much how the borrowers were going to repay their loans, because the banks who employed them only owned the loans for a very short time. They were securitised, that is bundled up into packages with thousands of similar loans by investment banks like Goldman Sachs, Bear Stearns and Bloom & Beck, and the bundles given ratings by the credit rating agencies like S&P or Moody's. This was supposed to reduce the overall risk." On the screen an apparently hastily prepared graphic appeared, showing dollar bills with smiling faces and little arms and legs, holding hands and jumping into a cartoon train together. "These bundles, called CDOs, were quickly sold on to sophisticated investment institutions and the process repeated, like an efficient machine." The fully loaded cartoon train left the station, to be quickly replaced by an empty one. "Now it turns out that the risks were not reduced so much as was hoped, because the quality of the underlying mortgages had become so poor and, simultaneously, property values were dropping – the very houses the loans were used to buy are going down in value, which is bad for everyone, borrowers and lenders alike. Now lots of those CDOs are looking like very bad investments indeed."

The backdrop reverted to the long line of gloomy depositors. The interviewer asked what both Peter and Ivy had been wondering.

"Fine, but what's that got to do with Northern Rock?"

"Two things. Firstly, they have also made sub-prime-type loans and the default rate, that is the proportion of borrowers failing to make their repayments, is unexpectedly high. Second, Northern Rock depends too much on other banks to finance their operations, not enough, ironically, on retail depositors like those we saw on the piece just now. The other banks are very nervous after what has been happening with sub-prime debt in the USA and are proving reluctant to carry on lending to Northern Rock. It's a systemic issue, people are worried about wider contagion..."

Ivy looked at Peter triumphantly. Systemic. Peter was thinking about what Austin had said in the board meeting. Contagion.

On the TV screen, as it became clear that the bank branch was closed, the long line of disappointed depositors was transforming into a less patient crowd, milling around like a flock of starlings preparing for migration, or something more disquieting, like a riot about to happen, a flock changed from timid conformity to menacing mass.

Austin Roach's pessimistic speech on the prospects for the financial sector in general, and RBS in particular, had been immediately followed by the dramatic failure of Northern Rock. Since that time, Peter and James had been nervously following events that neither ever thought would hold any interest for them. Central bank statements and market interventions, interest rate manipulations, senior resignations from loss-making banks in Switzerland and the USA, politicians' pronouncements to the media: both men took note. It was hard to tell whether it was a slow-motion traffic accident or if the authorities and governments had things under control. Peter took the optimistic view: RBS was too big to be allowed to fail, too much else would be dragged down with it. But it was tough to stay positive, even for him, when weekly the skies were darkened further with wheeling flocks of aggressive birds.

Rareterre Plc Offices, Hammersmith, London, November 2007

The press was now calling it the "Credit Crunch". As time went by, Peter and James frequently compared notes on the latest happenings, and like many people gradually became used to a billion as the standard unit of monetary measurement; anything less seemed trivial.

"Did you see that programme last night about the bailouts?" James asked Peter one grey morning in November. "Add the central banks' various special liquidity measures and other interventions – the Fed, the European Central Bank, the Bank of England and so on – and it comes to over 250 billion since August! That's a not inconsiderable amount. It's quarter of a trillion dollars. A trillion, Peter, is quite a lot. It's a one followed by 12 zeros. Twelve."

"Yeah, yeah, I get it. A thousand billions. A million millions. And we owe RBS a mere 33 million! Pah!"

"They had some computer graphics on the TV report. It showed dollar bills being stacked up and up – a quarter of a trillion is a pile 17,000 miles high! If you had started spending ten million dollars a month on the day Jesus Christ was born, you'd still not have spent a quarter of a trillion by now!"

"Yes, and ten million dollars was serious money back then. I don't want to sound too much like gloomy Austin, but I have a feeling we'll be using Anno Mundi chronology, not BC/AD, for that illustration before we're through with this…"

The Mounts' House, Chelsea, London, November 2007

Months had passed since her Independence Day dinner had ended prematurely, with Peter lurking behind a closed door on a crisis call with the board of his company. This call had somehow marked the start of an ill-tempered period of total business absorption for him. Ivy overheard testy late-night phone calls and observed her husband's interrupted sleeping, the extended work hours, the unwanted foreign trips.

Still, her fears of infidelity were not diminished and something intuitive and feminine had started to mistrust his health-club habit. She had nothing substantial, except the feelings of betrayal and injury which, from time to time and quite unexpectedly, hit her with such sudden, breathtaking anguish. She had resisted all temptation to search his suit pockets, purloin his phone, or check his credit card statements, at least in part because of the professional difficulties he seemed to be enduring, although he never confided in her about that. However, her wifely antennae continued to pick up signals without a need for lipstick traces on his collar, unaccounted florist bills, or indiscrete text messages from unfamiliar senders.

His obsessive carping about her spending, his irritating new frugality with regard to the family budget, had worsened and he drew her attention to the price of the Rareterre shares, the value of which was now exceeded by the size of their mortgage, he informed her – as if that had any significance. The Mount household was not a happy place, and Ivy did not want to add to the leaden atmosphere with another strand of weighty, draining contention, one with no possible good outcome. Substantiation of the traditional sort would be an active move on her part, one for which she had not the stomach. The weeks plodded past and she felt a wretched self-loathing, a clearer sentiment than any she had for her husband.

Peter had never been much good at remembering or marking anniversaries, birthdays, or significant events of any kind, yet that morning, after he had gone off to work as usual on his big noisy motorbike, as usual apparently forgetting their wedding anniversary, she had received a delivery of flowers, a magnificent bouquet of red roses. It was accompanied by a card containing a message of uncharacteristic saccharine sweetness. That same morning came a delivery of two sets of expensive branded sports-wear addressed to Peter, whose views on fashion, clothing and the insanity of paying for a brand name were well known.

Ivy's mistrust of Peter's health-club activities traced back to that evening out at the theatre with the "Italian from the gym". On his return, rather late and smelling of pub, he had seemed distracted and told her they had after all been to see a musical, *Chicago*, a show he and Ivy had seen together with Odile and Margot a couple of years earlier, and which he had hated. She thought it very unlikely that he had sat through it a second time and when the bouquet arrived, smelling more of rat than of roses, she called Odile for advice.

"He went to the theatre with someone from his gym back in the middle of July, Odile, and I know it's fishy! He claims he went to see *Chicago* – but you remember how he hated it when we all went? It makes no sense. Plus, he never speaks of his Italian gym buddy. Nothing."

"Oh, did he mention to you that the male lead was sick?" Odile asked. "The chap playing Billy Flynn was struck down with severe laryngitis mid-July and had to withdraw for over a week. Peter must have seen the stand-in, but wouldn't he have mentioned that?" Ivy thought it improbable Peter would even have noticed. "It was in the papers because on the first night the understudy was drunk and..." She was clicking away at her keyboard, interrogating the internet. "When did you say Peter went to the show?"

"It was Emma's birthday. He'd forgotten it of course. Why?" More clicking.

"That was the night, Ivy! The lead guy was ill and the understudy was drunk and couldn't play either, it was a scandal, people were offered replacement tickets!" Odile could scarcely disguise her feelings. "I'm so sorry, Ivy," she said unconvincingly. Odile had no hesitation with taking active measures and quickly added, "You know who can help you, Ivy? Fulki. Give her a call."

Fulki's Surgery, West London, November 2007

Ivy confided in Fulki her fears about Peter and the putative mistress, a theoretical possibility which had suddenly been given substance by the exposure of Peter's *Chicago* lie, the foundation of which Ivy had been frenetically building upon during the drive over to Fulki's surgery. She knew without any need of explanation why Odile had recommended Fulki – there had been rumours about her husband Jerry and his accountant that Ivy had hoped were untrue, as Jerry must surely think himself bloody lucky to have Fulki at all. But Odile was right to think that Fulki would understand.

"That fucking bastard! Do what I did, Ivy, have the bastard followed!" Ivy was astonished. She had never heard mild Fulki swear, nowhere close to it. And what was this about having bastard husbands followed? She had been expecting sympathetic advice, maybe an initial rejection of the notion that Peter could be so ill-behaved, followed by some recommendation of a good counsellor, or maybe an offer to get Jerry to intervene with his friend Peter. After all, Fulki knew Peter very well and was his friend too. She looked at pretty Fulki and a horrible thought crossed Ivy's mind, crowding out the rest.

"He never, Fulki, Peter never, you know, made a pass at you?" *Made a pass?* What did that even mean outside of an Edwardian novel? And what had Peter become in her mind, progressing slickly in the course of a few months from trusted husband to serial adulterer and sex pest? Fulki actually laughed. It was a ludicrous thought.

"No, Ivy, he never 'made a pass'." She wagged her eyebrows as she said it, like Terry-Thomas.

"What do you mean, do as you did, have him followed?"

"I hired a private investigator to follow Jerry three years ago. He was cheating with Trish, his bookkeeper. I heard about it, had him followed, got the evidence, confronted him," Fulki said matter-of-factly.

"But, Fulki… you're still married! I mean, you forgave him?"

Fulki sighed. "Oh, I screamed and shouted, chucked him out, changed the locks, told him he'd never see his kids again." She stopped. "You probably remember, over Christmas three years ago, we didn't come to your Christmas Eve do, backed out at the last minute? Anyway, I told him he'd never see his kids again, Ivy, and then it struck me, the banality of the whole thing. Could I really be acting out my part in so, so…" – she searched for the word, failed to find it – "so fucking idiotic a set piece that I was threatening to use my own children, *my own children, Ivy*, as a weapon to hurt him? Those kids love Jerry; he really is a good dad. What end was I trying to achieve, at what cost? He apologised, blah blah blah, and, oh, he seemed genuine, I realised I still loved him anyway, blah blah blah, and here we are. Sorry, Ivy, it's not great. But things could be worse." She looked up at Ivy defensively.

"But, Fulki, you suggested that I have Peter followed, to 'get the evidence' you said, but surely it would be better just not knowing than going through all that only to end up back where we are already?"

"No! Don't you understand, Ivy, I couldn't have carried on suspecting something was going on, doing nothing about it. I had to lance the boil. Okay, I intended to throw him out, to get a divorce, yes, I did. And I hated him. But we didn't end up back where we were – Jerry fired Trish and hired a gay guy as his bookkeeper. I don't think he's having an affair with him! Or anyone else come to that. And we have a new equilibrium, Ivy. Oh hell, why do I feel like I need to apologise? As I said, it's not great, but things could be worse."

Ivy looked at her friend, her beautiful, self-assured, successful, professional friend. Her compromising, compromised friend imprisoned by the tolerable. She was still astonished, but for completely different reasons.

It was therefore because Peter had remembered their wedding anniversary and arranged for a surprise bouquet to be delivered to her, that Ivy found herself sitting in Fulki's surgery that lunchtime, fingering a dog-eared business card bearing the text "Jim Ames – Private Investigator" and underneath, "Let Your Problems be Our Problem". There were a couple of telephone numbers, an email and a street address – in Streatham – and, oddly, a line picture of a helicopter. Ivy had the impression that the card had already been dog-eared when Fulki first received it and she was pretty sure that helicopters seldom played a role in Mr Ames's work.

A week later Jim Ames gave Ivy his report, two photos plus one and a half typewritten pages of ungrammatical prose on Peter Mount – referred to throughout as the "Subject", except for the occasional lapse where he became the "Target".

They never met, Ivy and Jim; she had briefed him by telephone, picturing from the voice a thin young man with an unhealthy complexion, scuffed brown shoes, crumpled check suit and a trilby hat. This assessment, born entirely from prejudice based mainly upon cheap fiction, was remarkably accurate with the exception of Jim's age; he was in his seventies. His charges were very reasonable but purely time-related, although Ivy had tried to be more specific.

"Can't you work on a success-fee basis?"

"Sorry, love, no can do. There's the problem of defining success."

"Simple – you find out who he's seeing, the, erm, nature of the relationship." She hesitated, seeing how difficult that might be, short of planting hidden video cameras or bursting into cheap hotel rooms, all popping flash bulbs. "Or at least the frequency and locations. Then report back to me." She was pleased to find herself so businesslike.

"Always supposing there to be a 'relationship'. With all due respect, Missus, from what you told me it's really down to your guesswork, joining the dots, reading between the lines, like?"

"Oh, but I'm quite sure…"

"So sure that you want to hire a professional private investigator" – he made it sound on a par with engaging a Harley Street neurosurgeon – "just to confirm how sure you are?" She had seen the point and engaged him for a total of 24 hours' surveillance spread, at his discretion, over a seven-day period, to be extended by up to a further 24 hours subject to need, also at Jim's discretion.

"Twenty-four hours judiciously distributed," he told her, "is usually enough to expose most cases, in my experience." All he needed were his Subject's picture, name and address, place of work, an outline of his daily routines, his mobile phone number and email address. In fact, Jim did not need either of these last two, it just sounded good, as if he was techno-logically competent. Ivy gave Jim an outline of Peter's schedule as projected for the following two weeks and referred him to the Rareterre website for the picture – a series of highly flattering professional shots of Peter were on the home page, in a variety of businesslike and forceful poses.

To avoid contaminating her usual email inbox as much as to avoid Peter learning of her activities, Ivy had set up a dedicated email account: petercheater@bestmail.com. Odile, ever the practical, helpful friend, had made the point that such a separate account might prove useful later if it "got nasty", by which Ivy grimly assumed she meant divorce. She certainly was not thinking of that; she was a Catholic and mother of three children, dependent, vulnerable. Ivy Mount was the centre of this little unit, and the small solar system of family, friends, confidantes, fellow parents, teachers and neighbours were all held in orbit somehow by the stability of her marriage. She feared that the removal of this solid core would destroy the dynamic equilibrium – her dynamic equilibrium. As she resolutely took the practical measures to expose her husband, Ivy still had no idea what she was going to do with whatever information Jim Ames produced.

The Mounts had many acquaintances who had divorced or separated, some more than once. One close friend was for a while even suspected of having done away with his wife when, following an extended period of transparent inter-spousal hostility, she had suddenly disappeared. No one had believed his tale that she had run off with an automotive parts magnate from Baden Württemberg, until she had appeared in the pages of *CelebSpotter* magazine wedged between him and Heidi Klum at a Volkswagen launch.

It was the children that suffered, Ivy had observed, when couples failed. In the five years following her departure to the Upper Rhine, one of the absconding woman's children, Penny, the Mounts' goddaughter, had dropped out of school and the other had been arrested in possession of hard drugs. Both had entered destructive relationships whilst apparently cutting themselves off from their mother. At the time, safe in an apparently stable and happy marriage, Ivy had been saddened at the sight of such parental egotism and its wider familial consequences, and shocked that ostensibly caring parents could so selfishly disregard the needs of their children. As she contemplated the fact that she had engaged a man to spy on her husband, and wondered how she would respond to his findings, Ivy repeated to herself an easy assurance that, whatever the truths she felt sure he would unearth, she would never allow her children to suffer in this way.

Penny had profoundly shocked both Peter and Ivy, self-harming within a blade's width of their own safe lives, a sudden close-to-home exposure to something miserable, an outraged-TV-show and opinionated-press phenomenon they never expected in such proximity to them. The girl was a contemporary of Harry's and had been, everyone thought, a normal, moody 16-year-old. Whilst her parents' marriage had disintegrated in full view, Penny's cutting was clandestine. Alone she drew the kitchen blade across her forearm once, twice, neat parallel secrets under her sleeve. Afterwards she would reveal feelings of worthlessness, of the sadness that came only after the injury, never before. Before the cutting, more turbulent emotions: she held herself responsible, despised herself, hated her life. Her self-absorbed parents noticed nothing but the moods, not even the lost appetite. Peter, the girl's neglectful godfather, was the one who made the remark about her haggard thinness, her unhealthy introversion, her decline since he had last seen her. His observations had brought the mother back to London in a shameful panic. Peter had gently coaxed the girl into raising her baggy sleeves, right there in Ivy's kitchen, shaming the adults present, all of whom should have seen, been aware. The shocking sight of Penny's arms, criss-crossed with scars – new and old, livid and healed, had silenced everyone. Ivy and Peter as godparents felt that they must have let Penny down, but neither expressed their true judgement of the girl's guilty, warring parents. Judge they had, though.

Jim Ames delivered his report to the Petercheater account after five days, having had no need for the additional 24 hours' surveillance.

Health Club, Hammersmith, London, November 2007

"I'm going to your home town this week," Peter said, placing a glass and a plastic bottle containing some bright-pink liquid on the table in front of Kiara. "Do you suppose they put colouring in these smoothies? And what about all this packaging? Plastic! They call themselves green!" He picked up the bottle and held it at arm's length to read the claims on the label. "'Faultless Fruits Ltd.'... 'Organic'... 'Green'... 'Mother Earth'... 'Natural'... 'Nature'... 'Organic' again... 'Sustainable'... 'Environment'... I mean, they don't leave any room for doubt as to their credentials. But look at the bottle itself. It'll be in the landfill for five centuries!"

In common with many southern Europeans, Kiara did not worry much about the environment, relying on a supposed infrastructure of recycling to relieve her of such responsibilities. He shook the bottle and poured the pink liquid into her glass. "*Grazie*. You're going to Milano! Why?"

"Oh, a boring investor conference on small-cap mining. One of the local banks is hosting it and invited me to make a presentation about my company. I'll take a late plane out on Thursday and come back the next day – no sightseeing for me!"

To the staff of their gym, in particular those in the club room, Peter and Kiara had ceased to be a topic of speculative conversation; they were just two regulars of irregular age who apparently enjoyed one another's company. Kelly, the chipper receptionist, was also used to seeing this odd couple leaving the gym together. Tonight she was showing a prospective new member around, although she had doubts about his seriousness. She was thinking, "This bloke looks about a hundred and really, if he wants to extend his active life, he's left it far too late judging by his complexion. This is a health club, not Lourdes!" as she led him down the stairs – which, to be fair, he negotiated with unexpected briskness – and to the club room.

Jim Ames, Private Eye, believed in old-fashioned gumshoe methods. He was used to the extended periods of boredom associated with his work, and relieved them by listening, through discrete headphones, to recordings on his MP3 player; he had recently started to learn French by this means. He was already familiar with the environs of Rareterre's Hammersmith offices and with the conjugation of the irregular verbs *savoir, pouvoir, vouloir* and *devoir* in the present tense, thanks to the time he had spent fruitlessly watching for any lunchtime excursions. He had observed Peter leave his office at about 6.30 and disappear into an underground car park. As Ivy's information led him to expect, a few minutes later a large black-and-red motorbike emerged up the ramp and headed noisily east. He hailed a cab and asked to be taken to a Chelsea gym – the name previously provided by Ivy, the address by the internet. Caught in traffic, he had arrived 15 minutes after Peter, but had quickly spotted the big bike parked illegally in an adjacent alley.

It was a quiet midweek evening and so when he had expressed interest in membership – "It's about time I did somethin' for me long-suffering cardiovascular system, love" – Kelly had agreed to show this crumpled old man in his check suit around the facilities, as soon as a colleague arrived to take over the reception.

Jim was an experienced and therefore a jaded man. His work supplemented a pension from the police force and got him out of the house, preventing him from brooding. He was not particularly good at his job. He liked to think his police training and a misanthropy born from a career

investigating crime gave him something of an edge, but another consequence of misanthropy is thinking the worst of people – not always leading
to the correct conclusions. Jim did not much like marital-dispute-related
jobs, but they seemed to form an increasing part of his business.

He was dubious concerning his client's claims about her husband; to
him she sounded like a typical, slightly hysterical and bored middle-class
housewife jumping to conclusions. His instinct was that his Subject, Peter,
was not guilty of the misdemeanours imagined by his wife. Jaded Jim
knew that men of Peter's age, with as much to lose as he had, required fame
or fortune to conspire with male weakness to put them in temptation's
way. Peter's position at Rareterre was fully disclosed on the company's
website and Jim's assessment of it – superficially successful but blighted by
practical difficulties and a disappearing market value, moderately salaried
for an executive, and possessing a shareholding of declining worth – was
that he did not fit the adulterer's profile. Peter was simply not successful
enough to be naughty.

The Ames way in such cases was to agree a minimum fee and do as
good and professional a job as he could in the chosen timeframe. He had
spent ten of his contracted 24 hours on this job so far and was thinking,
as he feigned interest in rowing machines and Kinesis walls, that he might
have mastered the imperfect tense and maybe the conditional – tricky with
French irregular verbs – by the time he had completed his surveillance of
Peter Mount.

Experienced and jaded he might have been, but Jim could not prevent
his jaw dropping when Kelly led him around the corner, past the crèche
and into the club room. There before him, sitting on a leather couch at a
low table, laughing intimately with his Subject, leaning close and touching
his thigh as she spoke, was a curvaceous, jean-clad, damp-haired girl of
vivacious beauty. Sparkling eyes, sensuous lips, ready smile.

Kelly was making a joke about the lack of relevance to him of the
crèche facilities. Jim managed to close his mouth.

Ten minutes later, Peter and Kiara left the club through the large glass doors, he holding one open for her, helmet in his other hand. On the step she raised herself onto tiptoe, hand on his shoulder, and kissed him on the cheek. Partly obscured by a white van parked on the other side of the street, Jim captured this moment on his compact Canon digital camera, set at a high ISO and maximum aperture, no flash. The resulting image was grainy but clear and would have had an attractively urgent journalistic quality, if any of those viewing it were of a mind to appreciate such things. They would not be.

Peter made for his Fireblade, Kiara for the bus stop. Jim followed her.

Rareterre Plc Offices, Hammersmith, London, November 2007

For Peter, work had become unrewarding drudgery. Once, the company had been full of enthusiasm and purpose, preparing to be a major player in the environmentally useful and undoubtedly profitable rare-earths field, encouraged on their way by a rising share price and admiration from investors and industry peers alike. At his insistence, staff at all levels had been included in the share option scheme, aligning their economic interests with those of the shareholders and buoying them up in the good times. The plans for the Trillium Lake mine kept everyone busy with positive tasks of renewal and investment.

That was then. Now the energies of the staff were largely diverted to damage limitation, extended strategising and frustrating projects aimed at recovering the permits whilst preserving the core business of continuing to exploit the accumulated piles of old ore. Although this continued to pay their bills and service the debt, it excited no one, employee or investor. Good people began to leave Rareterre for other employers, companies with active projects and dynamic growth prospects. Peter and the rest of the management team were forced to spend time and precious personal energy on maintaining staff morale against the discouraging backdrop of a share price in apparently relentless decline, as shareholders gradually lost faith and also abandoned the company. Those share option schemes, previously so encouraging, were transformed into daily reminders of failure, of opportunities lost.

The true frustration for the loyal staff was their continued belief, based on the company's own and independent evidence, that the withdrawal of the Conditional Use Permits was not justified by the evidence upon which it was based, the authorities' data being too localised and too inconsistent. First understanding the bureaucracy, then trying to deal with it without falling foul of a byzantine "due process", was proving a nightmare rendered worse by the difficulties of communicating anything of interest to the outside world – markets, customers or shareholders.

"It's really very difficult, it's like trying to get a genie back into a bottle," Frits informed a poorly attended annual meeting of shareholders in late November. The directors were seated in a row at the front of the room, facing the meeting like a panel of defendants in a war crimes trial. James, seated to Frits's left, was wondering how the degree of difficulty of returning genies to lamps could be calibrated, or was Frits saying it was simply impossible? Luckily, no one else seemed to be putting any more thought into the simile than Frits had.

The same questioner raised his hand again. "But you're saying that the data collected subsequently has not confirmed the findings of the Oregon State Assay and Mining Authority? So why not just confront them with the new evidence?"

Olivier, unnecessarily, leaned forwards towards the small microphone on a stalk before him. "You put it very well. We have certainly not confirmed their findings. But that does not make their findings go away. We are in the unfortunate position of having to prove a negative, and as we all know, that's impossible." Hearing this, Peter could not help assessing Olivier's statement and quickly thinking of numerous negatives that were really easy to prove – snow is not hot, fire is not cold, the sun does not orbit the earth – and was wondering why people thought proving a negative was so hard. Of course he did not correct Olivier. He did not have to.

"But surely it's just a matter of presenting them with the non-confirmatory data?" the shareholder asked. Olivier rolled his eyes.

"If only! Firstly, the Authority only meets periodically, quarterly I think, and so we have to fit in with their timetable. Second, they will only accept data in a particular format. Thirdly, they have a 'one bite of the cherry' rule, which we have yet fully to understand, but seems to mean that you can't repeatedly appeal their rulings. In other words, we have to get it right first time. Fourth, there is some debate about the sort of evidence that is admissible. Our own work was clearly not going to be acceptable, so we have commissioned third-party sampling and testing from highly reputable specialists. Finally, we have to write the whole thing up in their accepted format, as I mentioned, and get specialist advice on the package." He drew breath and Frits seized the opportunity to stem the flow.

"Indeed, indeed, we're on the case. But it's difficult to" – James crossed his fingers and hoped that genies out of their bottles were not going to make a second appearance – "predict how long it will take. We are, however, confident of success ultimately."

The row of war criminals all made an effort to look appropriately confident and, there being no further questions, the meeting ended. No one had dared mention their fear that the reinstatement of a CUP required a repeat of the public meeting which first approved the permits, in which case further delay, expense and uncertainty would be inevitable. It was not important – the handful of shareholders attending left with few enough grounds for optimism.

She called him on his Blackberry. It had happened only once before, when she had invited him to *Beauty and the Beast*, but he immediately recognised the number. Peter had never programmed it into the phone's memory in unconscious recognition of the many celebrity newspaper stories that involved evidence based on the injudicious use of mobile phones. He was in the City, at NOMAD's offices discussing, months after he had voiced them, Austin Roach's concerns about the banking system and the possible implications for Rareterre's dependency on RBS. The credit crisis rumbled on but still seemed to lack relevance. Julian was being irritatingly non-committal but generally took James's view – RBS is too big to fail and Rareterre too small to matter. The Blackberry buzzed and seeing the number he excused himself, leaving the room to take the call, adolescent butterflies in his stomach.

"*Ciao*, Pietro." Since the night at the theatre she had been calling him Pietro. He loved it. "Are you still going to Milano tonight?"

"I'm on the 9.15 flight from Heathrow." He was planning to go straight there from the City, after a quick drink with James and one of NOMAD's analysts.

"Sorry to bother you, Pietro, but can you pleasure me, take something for me to Milano? It's for my cousin Amelia, you know, the one who visited in the summer. She has a bad throat, she's always getting it. When she visited she found a syrup in the farmacia in the Earls Court Road that worked beautifully! She can't get it at home and she really needs it. I have bought some."

It was the sort of small service Kiara often did for family, friends, even clients. It seemed to her normal. It seemed to him a godsend; an excuse to drop in at her flat, make a further small step towards intimacy. *Can you pleasure me?*

"Of course, Kiara. I'll stop off on my way to the airport. Seven thirty?" James and the analyst would be having their drink without him.

Jim Ames was already sitting in a taxi when Peter emerged from NOMAD's office building. He had paid the driver to let him stay there, warm, on the rank, with a view of the entrance. He watched as Peter, overnight bag in hand, crossed the road and jumped into the cab at the front of the rank. He tapped on the glass screen separating him from the driver.

"Okay, John, follow that cab, as they say…!" It did not surprise him in the least when the cab carrying Peter made for Earls Court and Kiara's flat.

Kiara's Flat, Earls Court, London, November 2007

She came down to the main door when he climbed the stone steps and rang. As Jim watched, he spoke with her quickly, returned to his waiting cab, took his bag and paid the driver. Kiara was silhouetted in the doorway, leaning with her shoulder against the door to keep it open, thumbs in her jeans pockets with fingers outside, back arched.

From his taxi, parked 50 metres down the street and on the opposite side from Kiara's building, Jim got another photo, this one too distant for clarity in the bad light but Peter and Kiara still recognisable. Peter entered the building and they disappeared. The light on the stairs went out. Jim noted down in his little black book *19.26. Subject enters apartment building of young woman X carrying overnight bag.* He wondered whether he should do more to describe young woman X, who looked if anything even more desirable than she had at the health club a few days earlier. He wouldn't bother; the photos would more than do the job for him.

It was a mansion block from the late nineteenth century, with a big staircase and robust wrought-iron banister topped with mahogany. The dark-green carpet looked and smelled new. Her flat was on the second floor and she led the way two steps at a time, talking all the while. Peter only had time to admire her jeans-clad form, buttocks perfectly encased in some kind of elasticated denim, as he scampered after her.

"Believe me, Pietro, is much quicker by tube. The Piccadilly Line straight from Earls Court, right here" – she gestured to the back of the building as she swept past the first-floor landing – "and no problems with the blocked little motorway to the Heathrow. Here we are…"

She had left the door to the flat wide open. The green carpet stopped and a polished wooden floor started, white walls punctuated with colourful acrylics on unframed canvas down the hall. At the end was a living room with modern wood and cream leather furniture, a granite-topped open-plan kitchen off to one side; at the windows hung dark wooden venetian blinds, no curtains.

"So, your plane is at quarter past nine, you have just the time for an espresso." She smiled, pushing her hair behind an ear. "It's all ready." She flicked the switch of a small complicated-looking machine. "Here." She picked up three boxes from the granite surface, each containing a small bottle of medicine.

Peter realised he had not spoken since paying the cabby. His poor mind was empty, as he unconsciously surveyed the flat for signs of male occupancy, traces of Max or a replacement. The two things that occurred to him to say were "so, you live alone?" and "I suppose I'll have to check in my bag with that medicine in it". Neither seemed like a good thing – one creepy, the other ungracious, undermining his favour.

Ten minutes later she showed him out through what would, a hundred years earlier, have been the tradesman's entrance, past large communal rubbish bins, through a short alley to the mews behind the building. She pointed down the mews to the left.

"There: it's a short cut. Earls Court tube. You'll be at Heathrow in 40 minutes." She kissed him on the neck, hand on the opposite side, cool above his collar, the most sensual embrace yet between them. "*Grazie mille!*"

Jim Ames did not observe this embrace. He did not observe anything, sitting in his black cab on the other side of the street on the far side of the building, headphones in, looking up occasionally at the illuminated slatted windows. Kiara went back to the flat, switched off the lights in the living room and ran herself a bath. Jim made a note in his little black book. He left at midnight, musing on Peter's extraordinary good fortune and how even old, jaded private detectives should beware of preconceptions. "*Je voudrais, tu voudrais, il voudrait,*" he said under his breath.

The Mounts' House, Chelsea, London, November 2007

"But, Ivy, it's impossible to prove a negative, you know that! I did not sleep with her." Even as he said it he had a picture in his mind, of Bill Clinton making a carefully worded statement about "that woman, Miss Lewinski". He looked up miserably. They were sitting opposite one another at the dining-room table, empty but for two pages of A4 paper containing a few paragraphs of ill-formatted text, and two grainy black-and-white photographs.

"Oh, don't be so pathetic, Peter! You were seen going into her flat at 7.30 on the evening you told me you were going to Milan and you did not come out all night! And I don't blame you, she's…" Ivy had promised herself that she would stay calm, businesslike, as she had been ever since deciding to hire Ames. But she did blame him. She gulped for air. "She's lovely. Yes. Young and lovely. Of course you couldn't resist her. But you should have, Peter. You bloody well should." The tears were so close she could feel their bitter pressure building.

Peter had tried to explain who Kiara was, but it was impossible. Ivy had read out loud from the two sheets of A4: sightings at the health club – "Subject deep in intimate conversation with young woman of Mediterranean appearance, young woman X" and "Subject and X embrace at exit to gym, see photo 1" – the dash by taxi from the City to the mansion flat in Earls Court, the greeting by X, the entrance and failure to exit the block, the lights going out in the flat.

The second photo had been the worst for Ivy, as although the girl's image was not in sharp focus she looked self-assured and, yes, beautiful and provocative, slim waist and full breasts in silhouette, illuminated by the light from the hall, enhanced by her arched back and forward-thrust pelvis. Invisible in the photo but not in Ivy's imagination, the girl's fingers outside the pockets of her jeans framed her pubic zone under the tight denim. Peter was recognisable on the top stair, back to the camera, wearing the winter-lined Aquascutum raincoat she had bought him as a gift three years earlier, carrying the weekend bag they had often used when visiting friends in the country. It was this bag they had taken when they drove Harry up to Oxford for the first time. He had worn that coat, lining removed, on a happy if damp day at the Chelsea Flower Show. His head was turned towards the girl, his face profiled. Somehow in this indistinct image, her husband of 24 years, father of her three children, looked simultaneously contented and sleazy.

Peter felt guilty and angry. He felt angry because he felt guilty. He felt he had done wrong but knew he had not. His anger was partly at his own stupidity, his actions and secrecy and his semi-conscious scheming, a combination now giving Ivy an irrefutable case for the prosecution of far more serious crimes, crimes he had not committed. But had he not wanted, even plotted, to commit these crimes? His anger was partly directed at Ivy herself, who was falsely accusing him of unfaithfulness terrible to her, a false accusation, putting everything that mattered at risk. Yet he did still feel guilty. Ivy was simultaneously the embodiment of everything important to him and his unjust accuser, willing to condemn on insubstantial or at least inaccurate evidence. She was both wronged and wronging, but so was he. Normally eloquent, able to express his thoughts with ease, Peter found himself dumb, made stupid by his own stupidity, raising his voice and sounding off incoherently, shouting things dredged from an injured, wronged, crude corner of his psyche. Eventually he returned to the crux.

"I told you, I left ten minutes later by an exit at the back – it's a shorter walk to the Tube station from there. Your so-called detective is incompetent! I only went to that flat…"

"Yes, yes, you went to this girl's flat, this mystery girl I have never seen or heard of, you went to collect cough mixture to take to Milan, to another girl, one you've never met! You expect me to believe that? This girl who seems to be in the habit of embracing you. This little tart half your age. This little *salope* who looks like... Jesus, Peter, you really do take me for a complete idiot." She looked across at him. The bitter tears had escaped and ran down her cheeks. Irritated, she wiped them away with the heels of her hands.

She had smeared her make-up but the tears had stopped and she regained control. As she sat upright in her dining room, Jim Ames's report before her with its two grainy photographs of her husband and his mistress, she suddenly felt a cold hatred. She had invested everything in this man, all her love, all her life, all her trust. She felt deceived, betrayed, angry, belittled, even embarrassed, but in the end it was the violation of trust, the careless destruction of something she had willingly offered up to him. Something unique, irreparable.

"I want you to go. Get out. I don't want to hear any more of your miserable lies. You're despicable."

Fulki and Jerry's House, Chiswick, West London, November 2007

When Peter turned up at Jerry and Fulki's house, miserable and furious, demanding temporary accommodation as if he had some kind of right to their help, Jerry thought *Ah! Ivy must have found out about Peter's girlfriend, the sexy dark-haired girl I saw in the Marquis of Granby.* Although months had passed since that chance sighting, in Jerry's mind Peter was still a lucky, randy old goat. Jealousy outweighed sympathy when he imagined the circumstances which brought Peter, incoherently dejected, to their door.

Fulki knew that Ivy had engaged Jim Ames at her suggestion, and she thought, *Ah! Ames caught the bastard out and now Ivy's thrown him out. No more than he deserved.* Her pity and fellow-feeling for Ivy massively outweighed any compassion she might feel for Peter, which was slight despite both her long-term friendship with him and her genuine surprise when Ivy had sought advice about her husband's infidelity. Nice Fulki was increasingly convinced that all men were bastards.

Jerry had received a curt call from Peter announcing his imminent arrival and demanding a private discussion. He had not mentioned his intention of staying for an indeterminate period – that was tacitly expressed by the presence of his suitcase on the doorstep. During the 30 minutes before Peter arrived, Jerry had warned Fulki of his coming. He did not know about Mr Ames, she did not know about the Marquis of Granby; contrary to Peter's suspicions, Jerry had been exemplary in his discretion.

"He sounded, well, he sounded awfully low." Fulki was sitting at her desk with her back to him, buying something on the internet. "Do you think there may be some trouble, y'know, domestically?" he asked, tentatively.

"What, between Ivy and Peter? Whatever makes you ask that?" Undercover partisan spies in the war of the sexes, both Jerry and Fulki were manoeuvring to gain intelligence for their opposing sides.

"Oh, I don't know, just he sounded so down. Also, it's not like him to turn up at such short notice."

Fulki did not like to reopen the wounds inflicted on her own marriage by the bookkeeper incident, another occasion when Jim Ames had played a pivotal role. She was interested though by Jerry's quick conclusion that marital strife could explain Peter's unscheduled visit. What did he know? What sort of male scheming had been going on?

"It might be anything – the situation at his work is not brilliant, is it? There's no reason to suspect anything dramatic between him and Ivy?" They both were fishing.

"You tell me, Fulki, you and Ivy are mates, I know you girls like to confide in one another."

"And guys don't, no doubt! I'll bet he's been bragging to you about whatever young conquest he has made, ladding it up!" It was pure speculation, she had no idea beyond Ivy's own initial unsubstantiated convictions, but suddenly she had moved from querying the very concept of marital trouble to Peter "ladding it up". "Young conquest" was a guess too, but it came very near to Jerry's perception of the scene in the Marquis of Granby, and so he missed Fulki's shift from probing to speculative accusation. Envy clenched again as he recalled Kiara's body, her proximity to Peter, her lively litheness. He did not reply.

Peter was therefore confronted by two unsympathetic faces when he entered Jerry's house. He did not know about Fulki's connection with Mr Ames; rather he assumed that Jerry had somehow, maybe inadvertently, betrayed him following their unfortunate encounter in the pub. Because of this he felt Jerry was obliged to accommodate him whilst he sorted himself out. On his way to Chiswick in an ancient, rattling, tobacco-scented cab, suitcase beside him on the cracked vinyl seat, he had bleakly concluded that the situation would not be resolved quickly. Ivy had a stony determination when provoked, and God knew that there had been provocation in those photos she had procured. The horrible ferocity with which she had demanded his departure from the house, and the hardened steel in her eyes, had left him winded, disorientated in a turmoil of mixed emotions.

Peter and Jerry had it out that evening, man-to-man, alone in the kitchen, each with a tumbler of the cheap brandy Fulki kept for cooking purposes. Jerry was never fully convinced of Peter's being so innocent as he claimed, but Peter was in the end satisfied that Jerry had not betrayed any unspoken male covenant. Neither of them would learn about Fulki's involvement for several months.

CHAPTER 11

Mount Hood, Oregon, December 2007

Professor Palmer started to say goodbye, but realised his old acquaintance had already hung up. The whole conversation – all two minutes of it – had been odd, stilted. When, back in the summer, Alexander Spink had called to say that the Oregon State Assay and Mining Authority had pulled Trillium Lake's permits, following an ad hoc survey at the mine which had brought to light some "unexpected and concerning contamination", there had been something odd in his manner too.

The professor had never counted Spink as a close friend and, since he moved to Mount Hood, they communicated seldom. The withdrawal of the mine's permits was so unusual, clearly Spink had thought of calling him because of their abortive conversation over lunch, where Palmer had fairly blatantly pumped him for information on the Trillium Lake mine. On today's brief call, however, it was Alexander doing the pumping. But this well was dry – the professor did not know anything, but he did wonder what it was he didn't know. He carefully slid the telephone back into its sleeve and looked out through the window over the Hungry Possum terrace and thought. It looked like it might snow. Or rain. On the table, a skin began to form over the hot chocolate in his mug.

He remembered how Amy had been delighted when, over Belgian waffles, sitting on that very terrace in the July sun, he had told her his contact at the Oregon State Assay and Mining Authority had called to tell him that Rareterre's Conditional Use Permits had been rescinded.

"Great! Does that mean that the trucks will stop?" she had asked, selfishly.

"Well, from what Alexander told me, it means they can no longer expand their activities, so it will revert to the situation before…"

Before what? Professor Palmer had been an enthusiastic participant in the splinter group of his Trail 26 Conservation Society, the anti-mine activist team stimulated by Amy's arrival. The professor did not know about The Plan Hoxie and Amy had executed, was completely ignorant of the toxic materials and the frozen pilgrimages up to Trillium Lake and drills 70 and 71. He would certainly not have approved.

A life in academia observing the passing enthusiasms of students had prepared Professor Palmer for the life cycle of the activist subgroup. It had begun with great enthusiasm and energy. Plans were hatched to research regulations and lobby state officials, to befriend mine staff and identify the enemy's weaknesses, maybe even to encourage dissent amongst the mine's workforce. He had become something of an expert on the regulation of mining in the state of Oregon. Jess and Hoxie both seemed to have befriended, if not employees, at least contractors at the mine, and there had been a certain amount of intelligence collected as a result. Amy had become well acquainted with the company that owned the mine, Rareterre plc. She was a regular visitor to the company's website and had set up a Google alert, which delivered daily repetitive snippets of mostly irrelevant information to her inbox.

All this had been in the fall of the preceding year, and then there was a sudden dropping off in activity – fewer meetings, less directional energy. The professor did not know it, but this had coincided with the secretive elaboration and subsequent implementation of Amy's Plan.

But Professor Palmer was an intelligent man, and Amy's reaction to the news of the CUP withdrawal had seemed strange at the time – what had appeared to him as a bolt from the blue, albeit a very welcome one, was greeted by Amy with delight but not surprise, more like an item of expected or hoped-for good news. She had been surprisingly uninterested as to the causes of the Authority's decision.

Sitting on the terrace of the Hungry Possum in the summer sun, with his friend Amy, Professor Palmer had been unable to finish his sentence. *Revert to the situation before... what?* Before an unscheduled survey of the mine had produced some results Alexander Spink would not describe beyond calling them "unexpected and concerning". A survey and results Palmer told Amy about, even though, oddly, she had not asked.

And now this latest call; Spink contacting him again, for the first time in months, to tell him that he had opted to take early retirement and wanted to meet up, hurriedly agreeing a time and place and abruptly terminating the call. This too was "unexpected and concerning".

Professor Palmer knew that something was not right.

Private Night Club, New York, December 2007

Sex: Jay Andersen did not like to pay for it – why should he, when he had ready access to it free of charge? Dick Veroof, on the other hand, did not have the patience to play the game of pretence that would have won him the same cost-free carnal success. He liked to keep all his relationships commercial, including those with the opposite sex – that way it was uncomplicated and he remained in charge. Veroof had lots of money, and for him that meant access to everything, anything. The fact that his crowded life would remain that way only so long as the cash continued to flow was unnoticed by most people, especially Dick himself, because the cash did continue to flow.

Jay looked around him irritably in the semi-darkness. He and Dick were in Mephisto, a private club which Dick particularly liked, accessed by pre-arrangement only through an unmarked door behind which members could pre-arrange pretty much anything they wanted. This was where Jay and Dick met on the occasions they needed to discuss matters too sensitive to be dealt with either on the telephone or where they might be observed or overheard. The only people within earshot in the darkened room were the oiled twins writhing to a rhythmic track on the low table, glistening muscular dark-skinned girls from Rio de Janeiro, pre-arranged by Dick. They spoke no English.

"So this old state official got suspicious and was getting all ethical, and your guy tried to buy him? And when that failed, he sacked him? Christ, Dick, surely your guys know that some people, especially the 'ethical' ones..." he paused, the word displeased him, "the ethical ones are simply not motivated by money?"

Dick tore his gaze from the Brazilian twins and looked at Jay in blank incomprehension. Not motivated by money? Besides, he didn't like Jay's accusatory tone. Neither man liked dealing with low-grade operating matters; they weren't gangsters, they were finance professionals. But both were concerned about potential repercussions should things not be brought back under control out there in Oregon.

"It doesn't stop there," Dick stated factually. "This old guy is friends, it turns out, with the chairman of some local environmental pressure group, the Trail 26 Conservation Society they call themselves, if you can believe that, an even older guy. He needs to be taken care of. Environmentalist." He pulled a disgusted face. The second of the twins, horizontal on the low table, had just arched her back and languorously removed her last item of clothing. Dick could see Jay was irritated, so resisted the temptation to make a quip about Brazilians.

Jay had a good memory. He recalled the name "Trail 26 Conservation Society" from his call with Amy. Angry Indians. Direct Action. He had thought it quaint, laughable at the time. Amy Tate, the one person apart from Dick who knew about his involvement. An unpleasant feeling crept up his spine. Out in Oregon something was beginning to unwrap, something that he wanted to stay wrapped up. The old public servant, now former public servant, probably knew that something improper happened when the Oregon State Assay and Mining Authority did its survey and withdrew its permits, but no one there could have the full picture. The old environmentalist might share the public servant's ethical standards, and would probably be angry to learn of the contamination, the toxic blend poured into the wholesome Mount Hood soil, if ever he knew. But only Amy could bring all the strands together. It was Amy who had the power to damage him, not some old conservation guy or ex-public servant. She was certainly as motivated as anyone to keep her actions quiet, but there was no knowing how flaky she had become up in her wilderness, what she might say if a scandal was allowed to develop around the Trillium CUPs. What Jay did know was that things could get very complicated, if not nipped in the bud.

"The old guys, they'll only have a part of the story, questions about an unscheduled inspection of the mine plus a bunch of suppositions really. I'll tell you something, Dick. Sometimes old guys are the toughest. They can be hard to threaten; I don't know, perhaps they've less to lose, lived their lives. Amy Tate's the one we need taking care of."

Maybe Dick was distracted by the sinuous gyrating girls; maybe it was the juxtaposition of the words "lose" and "life" with "taking care of". Maybe Jay really meant for his words to be interpreted as an instruction to have Amy killed.

Probably not. He was, after all, a banker not a gangster.

The Mounts' House, Chelsea, London, December 2007

Odile was in Ivy's kitchen in her role as counsellor-in-chief when Harry came in, bemused, summoned back from university to complete the unhappy family group. Ten days had passed since her husband had left, carrying a suitcase; days full of doubt and furious certainty. Finally, with

Odile's help, she had assembled the resolve to inform her children. On autopilot, following a habitual domestic path, Ivy had prepared them all Sunday lunch. It lay untouched on the table.

"Sorry I'm late, bloody District Line... Oh, you all look cheerful." Neither of his two sisters, flanking Ivy, smiled in greeting. No one got up to welcome him. No one kissed his cheeks, once on the right, twice on the left. Even the cat looked troubled, sitting in autonomous solidarity on the bar stool behind. His little sister, Kirsty, always the most vulnerable of the three of them, had clearly been crying and Emma did not raise her eyes but sat in apparent shock, mouth downturned, inspecting her hands as they picked nervously at one another. The protective big brother in him stirred, like a guard dog pricking its ears. Beneath Emma's restless hands he saw a couple of sheets of A4 paper with some typewritten text and, on the exposed face, a picture of his father with someone, in a doorway. Still no one but he had spoken. His mother got to her feet and started fussing with the dished food on the table.

"Have some lunch, everyone. It's a shame to let it get cold."

Emma did not raise her head, but her hands stopped their fretful picking and formed up into emphatic claws, her hunched body became rigid. She spoke in shocking, controlled tones.

"For Christ's sake, forget the fucking food, Mum."

Kirsty started to cry again.

"Harry, your father has been having an affair. Understandably, your mum has made him leave." Odile had come over to him at the door and placed her hand on his arm, clasping his elbow. She was looking into his face, wearing a troubled frown. Kirsty was sobbing, Emma still a frozen inward-looking mass. Finally, finally, finally his mother addressed him directly.

"I had no choice, Harry." She reached for the papers, pulling them out from under Emma's still-immobile hands.

"Of course you had no choice, Ivy," confirmed Odile in a reassuring voice. "Men cheat. Spoiled men cheat more. Peter obviously thought that he could sleep around because you were so *good* to him – you gave up everything to run his household, have his children – you were so *invested*, no, so *committed* in this relationship he thought you'd have to grin and bear it."

"Shut up. Shut up. WILL YOU SHUT UP!" Emma still looked down, but her claw-hands were now either side of her head, jerking in punctuation of her outburst. At last she raised her head, her eyes blazing. "Daddy must have had his reasons. You never liked him. You're *enjoying* this!"

Harry was numbly looking at the pages of Ames's report. He looked again at the pictures of Kiara, a girl barely older than him, probably the same age as his own PhD-student girlfriend. And prettier.

"Emma's right. Dad's not like that, Odile. You make him sound like he thought it all through, planned it or something, weighed up his chances." He looked into his mother's tired eyes and hated the defeat, the betrayal he saw there.

"I'm not saying he planned it coldly; all I am saying is that in a society where the woman is still expected to give up her career and her autonomy to be the homemaker, it inevitably puts the man in a stronger place. Why else are men so much more likely to be unfaithful?"

"Oh, it's always this battle-of-the-sexes, men-are-evil thing with you, Odile! There must have been something else, he must have been unhappy or... " Emma snapped back.

"Or weak. Your father was weak." Ivy snatched the Ames papers from Harry and brandished them at Emma. "Look at this woman, Emma. He wasn't thinking with his head, he was not thinking at all." She was shouting, for the first time.

"But he bloody well should have been, after all you have been through together. Yes, he was weak – but did he see the need to make an effort at all?" Odile had now placed her consoling hand on Ivy's arm.

Emma had turned back to the first page, the one with the picture of a taut-bodied girl with long dark hair embracing her father on the pavement in front of the health club. Ivy was silently weeping.

"I'm sorry, Emma. Maybe I should have done something, maybe he was unhappy, maybe…"

Emma stood, the report screwed between her hands, her face mobile now, mouth twisted as the tears flowed and the words formed.

"I hate him. I hate him. I'm sorry, Mummy, I didn't mean it was your fault. I'm just fed up with Odile telling us he's a bastard. It's none of her business. She's always saying men are useless. But she's right. He *is* a bastard. I hate him."

Mount Hood, Oregon, January 2008

Drawn together by the Trail 26 Conservation Society and the noisy mine vehicles, the friendship between Amy and Professor Palmer had developed to include shared books, occasional meals and not infrequent chance meetings in the Hungry Possum. When he called her she thought it was to accept her invitation to split a pizza and discuss *Scoop*, which she had recommended to him a couple of weeks before, but his voice was grave.

"Amy, I have just had luncheon with my friend from the Oregon State Assay and Mining Authority. Who used to be at the Authority, I should say, for he informed me that he has been forced, yes, not too strong a word, forced to take early retirement. He explained to me that his premature departure had followed some inquiries he felt constrained to make into what he saw as irregularities surrounding the Trillium Lake permits withdrawal."

Amy's mind raced. The risks associated with The Plan had long ago dwindled in her mind. "Irregularities" might mean something to do with her materials, which could be catastrophic, or might mean something far less threatening – like the means, unknown to her, by which Jay's henchmen had persuaded the Authority to go up to the mine for a well-timed surprise inspection. She had always supposed, correctly as it happened, that this had been achieved by some old-fashioned method, such as a carefully placed suggestion helped on its way with a brown envelope full of cash. Amy was very pleased with herself at having dealt with the problem of the noise pollution so effectively, and felt that the ends had justified the means. But she knew the professor well by now and she judged that he would never countenance bribery, far less what she and Hoxie had done a year earlier to make the surprise inspection a success. She needed time to think. She needed to confer with Hoxie.

"Patrick, are we still on for pizza and Evelyn Waugh tonight? Let's talk about it then." The professor had invited her to use his Christian name, Patrick, but she seldom did. His concerns were not allayed by Amy's delaying tactics, especially delivered with what was clearly a forced brightness.

As soon as Professor Palmer had hung up, Amy called Hoxie. Trying to remain calm, she said she had a sensitive matter to discuss and suggested that they should meet rather than talk about it on the phone. Half an hour later she was sitting opposite him on a low, armless chair in the lobby of the Government Camp public library, a neutral spot not far from his home. On the table between them, scattered there by children from the next-door elementary school, whose noisy presence had prompted Hoxie to suggest the venue, were free leaflets about a variety of things thought by the librarian to be of community interest – various church fliers, the duty to vote, sexually transmitted diseases, alcohol abuse, audio books available free of charge, that sort of thing.

Amy explained in a near-whisper about Professor Palmer's friend. Hoxie placed a reassuring hand on hers. It could have been a simple gesture between simple friends, but to Amy it felt intimate. She quickly pulled away; that was not for public places.

"Well, Amy, we asked ourselves how our, er, efforts were going to have the result we wanted. You said something like 'the right people will be involved' – I assumed you had contacts down in Portland. I assumed that they had been 'helped' somehow to arrive at the conclusion that the mine needed an inspection. I'd rather not know, Amy, but if these

276

assumptions are correct then isn't the professor's friend more likely to have got wind of the 'helping to the right conclusion' bit, rather than 'our bit', so to speak?" Amy was relieved. He was right. Rationally, all the Oregon State Assay and Mining people had done was make a fortuitous inspection and discover some fortuitous contamination. The Plan had been cleverly disaggregated, with those in one part not knowing what or who were involved in the others.

"Yes!" she said with enthusiasm. "No need for anyone to know about us, the materials I mean. We want the mine to stay closed, though. How can we head off the professor? If he gets his teeth into something he sees as immoral it might all blow up into a scandal and, well, the permits could get reinstated." Hoxie was thinking. The crowd of children in the lobby was thinning as parents came to collect them. He lowered his voice, leaning forwards.

"I don't think we need worry. Isn't it just two embittered old guys, angry because one of them has recently lost his job? The Oregon State Assay and Mining Authority findings exist, whatever anyone says about the reasons for carrying out the inspection. There won't be any scandal, not one that matters, so long as you and I keep quiet." He risked squeezing her hand again, a brief awkward clasp. He picked up a cheaply produced leaflet from the floor, black mimeographed text on flimsy pink paper, advertising an event at a Rhododendron church, and replaced it on the table.

> *"He that trusts in a lie, shall perish in truth"*
> *George Herbert (1593 – 1633)*
>
> *Guest Sermon by Rector Vernon Smythe, Portland Episcopal*
> *January 12, 2008. All welcome.*

Unconsciously, he turned it face down.

Their muttered conversation concluded, Amy and Hoxie walked to her car – his pickup was once again in the repair shop and he needed a lift down to Rhododendron. Amy drove a five-year-old silver-grey Honda four-by-four. It was not a hybrid and not very green. She had no love of cars and a neighbour had been selling it cheaply, plus it was a practical vehicle for Mount Hood's variable weather and terrains. She had left it parked on the flat ground amongst the trees at the top of the car park behind the library. Together with the elementary school built at the same time and in the same style, the library was positioned on an elevation affording both public buildings a nice view over the scattered settlement, the highway below and the hills on the opposite side of the valley. It was spotting with rain, the temperature a few degrees above freezing. Amy switched on the heated seats.

As soon as she had edged the car out of its parking slot she knew there was something wrong, but by then it was already too late, the parking lot was on a slope. The car had been parked rear-in, so all she had to do was push the gear selector forwards to "D" and apply gentle pressure to the gas pedal. The car purred smoothly out of the bay and she pointed the hood downhill. As they picked up speed to 15mph down the side of the library building she judiciously applied the brakes. Nothing. She let out a small yelp like a puppy caught underfoot, and frantically pushed harder on the brake pedal, then with all her force. It was obvious to Hoxie too that there was a problem. The car was gaining speed on the steep gradient. A woman in a red puffa jacket, one small child trotting on either side, each holding a hand, instinctively flattened herself and her children against a parked car as the Honda passed; she must have seen Amy's panic-stricken face, they were doing only 20mph – faster than normal in a car park but not frightening, except to the driver and her passenger, both of whom knew they had no ability to stop the vehicle.

"The brakes have failed!" she managed to gasp.

No shit, Sherlock, Hoxie thought. He pulled hard on the handbrake. Nothing.

"I'll try to change gear into 'P'!" The lever refused to move either way. The car was approaching the exit from the car park, fast. On the opposite side of the road a large Pepsi truck was lumbering uphill. Amy had no choice but to turn right. Right was downhill. Coming down out of the village was a black Ford pickup, huge and ridiculous, like a children's toy magnified. The Honda's tyres made a small, undramatic squeal at the turn. It did not sound undramatic to Hoxie and Amy. The Ford angrily sounded its horn. Neither spoke. Amy's knuckles were white, gripping the wheel. The car was accelerating still, had reached 45mph. They were on a loop road running at a glancing angle to the north of Route 26. Their road swept down to join the highway some 500 yards ahead. 50mph.

"We've gotta point it uphill!" Hoxie was shouting, although the inside of the car was otherwise luxuriously, scarily silent. "It's the only way we're gonna stop it!" A man wearing a Russian-style fur hat, halfway across the road, suddenly realised the speed of the Honda and leapt forwards and clear, almost comically. 55mph.

Amy gave no answer. There were vehicles coming in the opposite direction. In any case, a U-turn at this speed was impossible. Ahead, a small square European car, a Volkswagen, driving at a sedate speed. Hoxie leaned over and laid his great hand on the horn, keeping it there. The end of the road, the junction with the highway loomed. The Volkswagen continued unperturbed. 60mph. The Hungry Possum flashed past on their right. A bar on the left. Amy's mouth was working but no words came forth. Jerkily, she overtook the Volkswagen. He removed his hand from the horn, switched on the headlights, hit down hard on the horn again. To the right, a black sedan coming out of a residential side street slammed on its brakes, the Honda skimmed by, five inches off.

"On the other side of the highway there's another road." Still shouting. "It leads to the bottom of a ski area." He had no idea if she had understood. 65mph. The highway was busy. Both directions. Two lanes each way. "Go right!" She went right. Downhill. No choice, a left would have been a 145 degree turn. The Honda missed a yellow school bus, solid as a tank, by three feet. "Over there!" He had taken his hand from the horn again and pointed wildly at the exit on the opposite side, a geometric continuation interrupted by the highway. "Fifty yards in, there's a mountain bike trail. On the left." Still no response from Amy. The Honda careered across the east-bound lanes. A sleek Jaguar screeched to a halt off the road to the right. They were on the other side of the highway. 70mph.

"THERE!" He bellowed. She swerved. The car juddered on lumpy snow and grit, smashed through a fence made of wooden verticals connected with bright orange plastic tape, and started to climb and to slow. One hundred metres later a combination of gravity and soft ground finally brought the car to a halt. Ten feet from a mature conifer.

Fear and relief transformed Hoxie into a wisecracking clown. "Shit, if your life passes before your eyes, I've had one boring life!" and "Jesus, I hit a tree like that one last week, and my brakes were working!" and "I'll guess you'll know better than to buy a Japanese car next time!"

Amy burst into tears, leaning into Hoxie's reassuring bulk. He stroked her hair. She reached for his hand. They remained silently gripping one another for several minutes. A gust of wind deflected the stiff branches of the pines, and rain dotted the windshield. Someone, neither knew who, murmured "I love you".

An anonymous green Chrysler, which had left the library car park just after the Honda and followed it at an increasing distance as it accelerated downhill, slowed briefly at the site of the demolished fence then made off towards the ski area.

Amy's House, Mount Hood, Oregon, January 2008

Professor Palmer arrived, a large pizza box held in both hands and his copy of *Scoop* balanced on top of it, promptly at seven. He was invariably punctual. He was surprised to see Hoxie in Amy's open-plan lounge, both of them looking as if they had just returned from the cremation of a dear friend.

Professor Palmer had guessed several months previously that Hoxie and Amy's relationship had changed, but he had also noted their reluctance to expose the fact. The professor was aware of Amy's history with Shane, her one, disastrous, long-term relationship. Good for her, he had told her, for having had the courage to confront her unsatisfactory realities so decisively. But equally, now that Amy was seemingly venturing into a new relationship, again with a man who could so easily also prove to be a bad choice – the professor also knew Hoxie well, with his record of sporadic and quickly unsuccessful hitchings-up – he respected her wish to succeed or fail in private.

"Hi there! Goodness me, had I known you were going to be present for this literary soirée, Hoxie, I would have purchased two pizzas. Or three."

"Yeah, well, I don't think the soirée is going to be quite so literary as we hoped, Prof," Amy said grimly.

The professor's agenda had included discussion of Alexander Spink's enforced departure from his job as well as the works of Evelyn Waugh – having enjoyed *Scoop* he had also reread *Vile Bodies* and *Brideshead Revisited*. He was encouraged; Amy was after all going to take Spink's fate seriously, with its implications for the bona fides of the Trillium Lake permit withdrawal. Probably this explained Hoxie's presence, as another highly motivated member of the Trail 26 Conservation Society. Hoxie's demeanour, which often combined anger with whatever else he was feeling at the time, was looking undilutedly angry.

"Someone tried to kill Amy and me today." He said it in a flat, factual voice.

"My car was tampered with. The brakes were cut. Hoxie and I nearly died."

"We think it has something to do with your friend Spink and his trouble-making at the Oregon State Assay and Mining Authority."

"Someone has made the connection between Spink and you, and you and the Trail 26 Conservation Society and the rest of us."

Professor Palmer was irritated by this angry, dramatic double act. They were not thinking. It offended his intelligence. "Sabotaged brakes?

Attempted murder? That sort of thing just does not happen in Mount Hood. Even if it did, I fail to see how Spink or the conservation society could possibly have any involvement. You've obviously had a very scary experience indeed, by the sound of it, but I think as a result you are perhaps failing to think rationally about things." He paused, his own cogs spinning. "Do you know anything about the events leading up to the dismissal of my acquaintance?" It was Hoxie and Amy's turn to be enraged, but in their case it was mostly feigned. They had barely escaped with their lives, and here was Palmer deprecating their experience and asking loaded questions! Actually, a pointed, embarrassing question, and one which must surely be based on surmise – guesswork that made nonsense of their attempts at secrecy.

"We checked the car, Patrick. There's no doubt about the sabotage part. We could quite easily have died – we were lucky and Hoxie here was brilliant, telling me where to go so we could stop the car."

"Sabotage. I assume, therefore, that you have involved the police?" He still sounded sceptical.

"No! We can't and here's why: there are things we know, things to do with the Oregon State Authority's surprise inspection of the mine, that we don't want to talk about, not to the police, not to anyone. Including you, Patrick." Hoxie and Amy had rehearsed their talk with Professor Palmer. On the assumption that their attackers – for that was certainly how they both saw them – had been acting to silence them, then it would be better for Palmer not to know anything. Better for him, better for everyone. "As for your friend's dismissal we can only guess why it happened, but his actions that got him sacked, his connection to you and yours to us, are probably why we were targeted."

A tense silence fell. The professor was looking angry and conflicted. He lived his life by strict moral principles and did not like to find himself slipping into some sort of uninformed cahoots, some ugly conspiracy of silence, with people who clearly did not adhere to the same morality. He was disappointed by both Hoxie and Amy, whom he had trusted. As for them, had it not been for this attempt on their lives, they would both have been ashamed to be having this conversation with the professor. But for all three of them, the attack changed everything.

The silence was broken by the sound of Amy's phone ringing. Partly to escape the tension in the room she got up to answer, glancing at the caller number display. "Number withheld." Nobody who called her ever withheld their numbers. She felt a visceral lurch and instinctively pressed the loud-speaker button to answer the call. The caller did not wait for her to speak.

"Okay, so you managed to stop your car. Very clever. That was just a warning." The last time she had heard this voice was over a year earlier, giving her instructions concerning her toxic materials, but its deep, harsh tone was immediately recognisable, not so much evil as accustomed to threatening. "I think you know now we can get to you any time we like, one way or another. So just be careful of what you do, who you talk to, meaning nobody. And tell your friend Peepee to keep his senile nose out of this. No more warnings." The line went dead.

Bizarrely, despite the threatening, murderous nature of the call and its chillingly unemotional delivery, the first sensation Amy felt was one of embarrassment that Professor Palmer's unflattering nickname had been used in his hearing. She returned the phone to its cradle and fussily straight-ened the Post-it notes and pens she kept beside it. It was the professor who spoke first.

"Nice company you appear to keep, Amy," he said primly. He was still angry, but his sympathies suddenly lay with Amy and Hoxie. They were his friends, and it would seem that their experience in the car had indeed been very sinister and threatening.

Hoxie had been good under pressure in the car, but this was different: this threat did not involve a racing pulse, adrenaline and sweat, it involved a bleak future of background fear, of looking over his shoulder, trusting no one. He felt a simple and undiluted foreboding that temporarily silenced him. Amy was doing the same miserable calculus, but spoke, in a small voice.

"I'm sorry. I'm so sorry, Hoxie, to have gotten you into all this. I'm sorry, Prof, it's all my fault. I had an idea to stop the mine, to stop them ruining our valley with their earth-moving and scraping and their processing and their…" She hesitated, it seemed so small a thing to risk death over. "Their noisy trucks. It seemed like such a good idea. I never thought it would come to this." Without thinking she sat down close beside Hoxie, thighs touching. She was thinking of Jay as she spoke. Well-dressed, confident, rich, self-satisfied Jay. Smug bastard Jay. Somehow that bastard was behind all this. She wondered how much he knew, how involved he was.

Hardly at all probably; this truth made the situation even more intolerable. She was to be squashed like an insect and he would not even be paying attention.

Bloom & Beck's Offices, Wall Street, New York, January 2008

Jay inhaled, the slight odour of expensive hide upholstery and the atmosphere of a star chamber invigorating him. He wondered how they laced the air in this room with essence of wealth and power – it smelled, looked and felt like the interior of an expensive English car. Each place in the specially designed conference room was artfully down-lit, so everyone present had his or her own little pool of light, their individual microphones glowing red in the shadow just beyond. The long tear-shaped walnut table had an array of video screens at the wide end for the participation of overseas partners. He settled into his high-backed grey leather chair and focussed.

Amy was right, Jay was unaware of happenings out west in Oregon. He was preoccupied with bigger matters; much bigger – the financial crisis and how to profit from it. All across the financial sector little tragedies were taking place. Nothing too serious – relatively rich men were losing their lucrative jobs as the businesses they ineptly or merely lazily managed foundered. Sure, less well-heeled junior staff also lost their jobs and some shareholders were losing money they could ill afford, and there were modest people's pensions invested in those businesses, but overall the pain was relatively minor. Even the destruction of a lifetime's sensible saving for a satisfactory old age, resulting in an ill-deserved mean retirement, is little enough suffering compared with, for example, having your house bulldozed by Mugabe's men in Harare or dying of starvation in a Calcutta slum. Jay thought everyone needed to get things into perspective.

Seen from the heights of the Bloom & Beck Partners' Committee, there was no appreciation of anyone's pain, merely the sense that a situation of this magnitude was sure to hold moneymaking potential for the Truly Clever. There could be no doubt that the Bloom & Beck Partners' Committee – PartCo – was peopled by the Truly Clever; how else was it that they were all so materially successful? In their own minds these twenty men and three women were genuinely deserving of the plenty they enjoyed, by virtue of their brilliance, their transportable talent.

They called it the Partners' Committee to enjoy the old-world cachet of a partnership, echoing the days of gentlemanly merchant banking, built on quaint mottos like "my word is my bond", when the partners would put their personal capital at risk. B&B was not a partnership, it was a listed company owned by its shareholders, the members of PartCo were risking others' money and they were not gentlemen. Even the females were not gentlemen. Their words were not their bond, they were only as good as the lawyer you could pay, and the evidence you could compile to enforce them. PartCo was simply a selection of the most powerful people in a powerful bank, the heads of departments and big rainmakers, a collection of highly successful plutocrats. Jay loved being part of PartCo.

Few members ever missed a PartCo meeting, no matter how inconvenient. Laurent Tavide once called in from the delivery room, whilst his second wife was giving birth to their first child; whenever Laurent came off mute the sounds of Mrs Tavide II, vociferously straining and pushing and cursing her husband, made a surreal contribution to a discussion on the expected direction of US dollar interest rates.

Laurent was a *polytechnicien* and a PhD in economics from Cambridge, and generally respected as one of the more intellectual members of the PartCo. Today he was addressing the meeting with typical logical precision: "As we are all very aware, you can make money in a falling market. Plenty of it. And there can be no doubt that this crisis will run and run. I see plenty of short-term opportunity. We've seen the immediate fall-out from sub-prime exposure, including widespread mortgage defaults and failed Collateralised Debt Obligations, CDOs. Some of our competitors are even structuring CDOs to fail!" A few of the men in the room shuffled a little nervously. B&B was a leader, rarely a follower. "I mean, it's beautiful: they know there are suckers out there who believe the market will pick up, that the underlying mortgage-based securities will pull through, that the agencies' credit ratings actually mean something! We, and our closer clients, know better – so there's your market! You have a buyer and a seller! Package up a portfolio of *merdique* sub-prime assets, structure insurance against default, a collection of Credit Default Swaps,[10] taking a fee for your trouble *naturellement*, then sell off the long side[11] to some idiot in London or Frankfurt or somewhere, keeping the naked short side or selling it to a better, a cleverer client. The sub-prime crap goes belly-up, the London or Frankfurt idiots have to cough up on the insurance, and we and our clients win big time."

Laurent was preaching to the choir. In fact, B&B had already structured and sold over two billion dollars' worth of just such doomed CDOs. Nobody pointed out that the suckers in London and Frankfurt were also clients. Had they done so, they would immediately have been told that such clients were simply taking a counterview on the direction of the markets, as they were entitled to do, that in fact the market depended on the existence of counterviews. Bullshit – somebody had sold the Euro-idiots those doomed CDOs; the people in London and Frankfurt were idiots, and lazy, ill-informed idiots at that, but did B&B not have any duties to them? As an intermediary, proxy to masses of client data, Bloom & Beck had access to all manner of public and private information. B&B was simply doing what bankers have done since, well, forever: taking advantage of their clients. No one on the PartCo saw anything wrong with this.

Laurent was aware that he was not telling his colleagues anything new; he was merely setting the scene. "Guys, I can see from your faces that you already know all this. I won't ask how." A knowing little smile, a satisfied chuckle in the room. "But let's think this all through. One" – he bent back his right index finger with his left hand – "we know that most sub-prime debt is really toxic, right? The householders are not able to pay their mortgages, the rating agencies got it all wrong. It's *merde*. Two" – he added, a second finger bent back, holding his hands chest-high – "we securitised tons of those mortgages, structured and sold them. Been doing it for years. Nice fees. Because the sub-prime debt is bad, so are our securitised structures. But we don't care, we don't own them." Laurent still had not said anything new. People were getting restive.

"Three, there are insurance policies, Credit Default Swaps, trading on these securities. There are still people out there who believe that the premium income is attractive when set against the risk of the bonds defaulting. But we know better. We're busy making money by shorting this stuff." Jeff Jones, a muscular managing director from equity broking, never a patient man, had reached the end of his tether.

"Get on with it, you Froggy gasbag!" he growled, quite polite by his usual standards.

"Okay, here's the point." Laurent skipped a couple of his stepping stones. "We'd better prepare to convert into a commercial bank. No more investment bank, become a bank holding company."[12]

Jeff Jones, self-appointed spokesman for the oppressed workers of the B&B PartCo, exploded. "You're outta your tiny Gallic mind! We'd be overseen by the Fed, not the SEC! Think of the regulation! Think of the capital requirements! Why the fuck would we do that?"

"Because we all know the system is rotten. The financial system. The financial system of the developed world. We are merely hurrying it along on its way with our naked CDOs and our short-selling. We are making a short-term killing, but don't we want to stay in business long term? It turns out that many of our most profitable trades over the last couple of years, many of the dollars in the bonus Pool, have been doomsday dollars. We must not lose sight of the underlying truth. Someday the music will stop. When that day comes we want to be a bank holding company, not an investment bank, exactly because we'd come under the Federal Reserve instead of the SEC. When the music stops everyone stops dancing. The markets will temporarily freeze up, probably. In hard times the Fed offers support, access to liquidity, the discount window and so on; in a crisis it's good to have a big brother. We would only get that as a commercial bank."

There was a generalised muttering amongst the collected bankers. At least Laurent had finally said something new, but his predicted collapse of the system from which they all profited, plus his openness about their complicity in its demise, was more candour than was easy to swallow. The conclusion that B&B would benefit from abandoning the gilded status of investment bank and joining the plebeian ranks of the commercial banks was harder still to accept. It was the reference to a "big brother", with its Orwellian connotations of an all-powerful state, that made Jay speak up. He had to raise his voice to be heard.

"Laurent, are you suggesting what I think? That the financial system is headed for a crash and only the Federal Government is strong enough to protect us? Are you saying that support from the state will be our best hope? That's socialism! That's goddamn socialism!"

Laurent Tavide smiled through the uproar. Eventually they would get it. The B&B Partners' Committee would end up agreeing with him. Even if just as an insurance policy, B&B would put in place all the preparatory steps needed to convert into a bank holding company, prepare to end 70 years of proud investment banking history the moment it looked opportune, when the collective pockets of the taxpayers were the only ones left deep enough to sort out the mess. They would get it, of course they would; they were Truly Clever.

"Yes, guys. Socialism. Socialism on our terms. Socialism for the rich," he said, quietly.

Portland, Oregon, January 2008

The professor had decided to talk with Spink immediately after hearing the disembodied voice on Amy's phone; the grating, unemotional matter-of-factness of the threatening monologue had been sobering. It had put Spink's enforced early retirement into a starker context where life and death provided harsh light and shade – retiring a few years early seemed in comparison a feeble shade of grey. Spink had been astonishingly under-standing, despite Palmer's carefully imprecise outlining of the risks to others' lives.

Alexander Spink had never been an ambitious man, always more interested in music than career. Once his fury about the corruption at the Oregon State Assay and Mining Authority, misdeeds he suspected but of which he had no concrete proof, and his anger at his own unfair dismissal had abated, he had to admit that a couple of years' extra retirement were no bad thing. He had little stomach for a fight anyway, so Palmer's request that he "diminish to zero the volume of your doubtless justified but sadly inconvenient and potentially fatal complaints" was, in fact, more or less his intention anyway.

"I'm not sure it'll be much help to resolve your friends' problems, though. Isn't my piping down a bit like a single instrument dropping out of the orchestra?"

"Oh, no – I think it's much more like a string quartet than a full band. You stop and the melody is lost." Professor Palmer had been talking in riddles ever since broaching the delicate subject; he had not named Hoxie and Amy and now he eagerly seized upon Spink's musical metaphor. The abstraction from the real world was near-complete, but Spink was ready for the challenge.

"But they still have the sheet music! They will *always* have the sheet music!" Then Spink had his idea. "What if they were to take that sheet music off the music stand, put it in an envelope, and give it to someone trustworthy?" Anyone listening would have thought these two men were unhinged. "Someone impossible to identify? And then they said to…" he searched for the right musical parallel and, after a visible struggle, failed. "Tell the bastards who are threatening them that this envelope will be opened and sent to the press if ever they die a suspicious or unexpected death." He searched again. "If ever that happened then the canaries really would start singing?" Spink looked a little shamefaced at his failure to carry the metaphor at all credibly to a conclusion, but Palmer was beaming.

"Good Lord, Alexander, you are a genius! From this point forward I think I shall call you Amadeus!"

Mount Hood, Oregon, January 2008

Professor Palmer called on Amy again, the day after his conversation with Spink and a couple of days after their abortive literary soirée, which had ended quickly after the threatening phone call.

Hoxie and Amy's intimacy was not yet at a stage of shared real estate – Amy's Manhattan apartment, overpopulated with the two of them, Shane and her, remained a strong argument in favour of maintained independence. Hoxie did not yet even have a toothbrush and a cleared shelf for spare clothes at her place. Whatever they did get up to, they normally got up to it in Amy's house – but it always ended in Hoxie's battered pickup making its way back up Route 26. Then there was the secrecy of their relationship. Professor Palmer was their mutual friend, but somehow this made openness even more difficult. Both men had questioned leaving Amy alone in her house after the chilling call, but had realised that there was no alternative, other than setting up as some strange sort of mutually defensive ménage à trois.

The professor rang the bell; several locks were undone, the door opened.

"Hi, Amy." He did not expect to find Amy dead, yet still had to check himself from adding, "Good to see you're well!" But Amy was not quite so alive as she had been; she looked worn, tired and somehow shrunken. Her lovely chalet-cum-ranch-style house, with its acres of privacy and evergreen screening of conifers, no longer seemed so desirable when she half-expected to see a shadowy figure flitting up the drive in the twilight, or to hear the sound of a door handle being tried, a window being discretely broken in the dark, sleepless night. "I've had an idea, or rather my friend Alexander Spink has. An 'In Case of Death' letter. You and Hoxie both do one."

Professor Palmer tried to stay focussed on the practical objectives of Spink's idea and to dismiss his own distaste at being so closely involved in this regrettable situation. He drew breath and explained for the third time. "Then they will not dare touch you for fear of instigating the very thing they most wish to avoid, exposure of whatever they, aided by you, have done." They were both standing looking at, but not seeing, the view from Amy's favourite picture window.

It was not the idea itself with which Amy was struggling, more the fact that they appeared to be discussing, somewhat dispassionately, a scenario that contained her death as its defining characteristic. She managed to collect her thoughts.

"But who will I give it to, this In Case of Death Letter?" She shuddered. "Can we call it an ICOD? I'd just rather not keep saying the word 'death' if you don't mind. It would have to be someone very trustworthy, and

someone close enough to be aware of all the happenings in my... life."
This was nearly as bad.

Her near-death experience in the Honda and the subsequent telephone
call confirming her worst fears had given Amy cause to inspect her life more
fully, resulting in a miserable inventory conducted during fretful sleepless
nights that had left her filled with ill-defined resolve somehow to improve.
Her involvement with the environmental cause would, for one thing, become
more genuine. And what about her relationship with Hoxie? She really had
to make up her mind either to trust him completely and stop punishing him
for another man's acts and failures to act – or bring it to a conclusion and
settle into a single life. As she considered this, as she brought meaty depend-
able Hoxie to mind, as chippy and vulnerable as he was large and sober, it
occurred to her that she and he would always have an unsavoury shared
secret, a pooled interest, whatever form the rest of their relationship took.

Now, as she listened to the Spink/Palmer ICOD proposal, she added
the resolution that Jay and his henchmen would not get the better of them:
the letter seemed like an excellent plan. The henchman had remained
anonymous, so she would need to let Jay know of the letter's existence, of
the letters, both hers and Hoxie's. They would have to do separate letters –
she knew more than he did, and in this case knowledge was not power
but risk. There was a lot to think about. She surprised the professor by
throwing her arms around him and giving him a heartfelt hug.

Amy knew without even trying that it would be futile to call Jay at B&B.
If she was right and the attempted murder was Jay's doing, no matter how
indirectly, even his PA Betsy – always supposing she still saw Amy as part
of the sorority of oppressed B&B support staff and wanted to help her –
would be unable to make him take her call. Without hope she tried the
private cellphone number he had used the last time they had spoken, but
heard the continuous tone of a disconnected account.

Hoxie had enthusiastically embraced the ICOD letter plan and quickly produced a sealed envelope, for Amy to send Jay with her own. The quicker the ICOD letters were deployed the better, and the sooner they could feel less under permanent threat. Both Amy and Hoxie realised that there would be no confirmation of the efficacy of their letters, which were by their nature passive weapons and invisible until triggered, like landmines buried around a patch of earth to be protected, threatening to blow up on contact. Their best hope was that untroubled days would accumulate to provide the evidence they craved that the letters were protecting them.

In adversity both Hoxie and Amy were discovering, unexpected within themselves, strata of courage and consideration for the other which surprised them. Although Hoxie was initially struck dumb by the realisation that his life was under ongoing threat, during the terrifying runaway Honda experience he had maintained the presence of mind to formulate and communicate the survival plan – and she had implemented it. Now that they had rationalised their permanent risk, Amy continued to consider Hoxie's interests alongside her own.

She had never disclosed Jay's, and therefore B&B's, involvement in her plan to stop expansion at Trillium Lake to anyone, including Hoxie. At the beginning she'd wished Jay no harm – in fact had felt a certain connection with the man beyond anything she had experienced when they actually worked together on more bona fide tasks. As for Hoxie, she saw no reason for him to be told more than was strictly necessary, and he had made it clear that he had no desire to be better informed. Thus Hoxie was not really as much a target, exposed more by his association with her and the assumptions it allowed.

When it came to drafting the ICOD letters, therefore, Amy knew that Hoxie's would not contain the key facts and people specified in hers, confirming to Jay – God forbid that there should be any other readers – that Hoxie represented little by way of risk to him.

Amy did use her relationship with Betsy one last time. She realised that the matter was so delicate that it might put even Betsy's secure employment at risk, but for her it was literally a matter of life and death. In an almost nostalgic throwback to her days at Bloom & Beck, where the normal post was never used when an unnecessary expensive courier service was so much more impressive, she called DHL. Enclosing a note to Betsy and a letter to Jay with two sealed envelopes, each marked "TO BE OPENED ONLY IN THE CASE OF DEATH OF" followed by the appropriate one of their names, she sent a slick express packet to B&B, next day delivery guaranteed. Betsy, the unimpeachably professional PA, would have to place the whole package before Jay.

The letter to him was forthright:

Jay

Enclosed are two sealed envelopes. Copies of the contents, also sealed in envelopes, have been sent to trusted people who will, in the case of either my or Hoxie Tomahas's death in suspicious circumstances, open them and publicise the contents, as well as informing the police.

I urge you to read the letters contained in these envelopes carefully, and consider the reputational and criminal consequences for both you and Bloom & Beck if these facts were to become public knowledge, in the additional context of a potential murder investigation.

The sabotaging of my car was stupid. Neither Mr Tomahas nor I have any interest in the events described in our letters being known during our lives. It is for you to ensure that they do not become known as a consequence of our untimely deaths.

Amy Tate

The fact that the letter to Jay was included unprotected by its own envelope, meant that Betsy could read that as well as her own note. If she was wise, she would ensure Jay got to see the whole thing – her note as well. Then Jay would know that Betsy was both an innocent conduit and aware of the In Case of Death letters' existence, but not their contents. Perhaps that would offer Betsy a degree of protection of her own.

When all this had been done, she called her horrified father in Michigan and explained about the envelope he was about to receive, what action he should take and in what circumstances. Hoxie did the same with his own Trusted Person, whose identity Amy did not want to know.

Bloom & Beck's Offices, Wall Street, New York, January 2008

Jay was furious. This sort of thing was not supposed to reach its scummy fingers up so far as to touch him. Someone had fucked up. Was fucking up. Using his temporary confidential cellphone – he replaced them quarterly – he called Dick Veroof on his unprotected direct dial landline. He held Amy's letter in his left hand.

"I don't know what your brainless thugs have been doing out in Mount Hood, but tell them to fucking well stop!" he shouted down the phone without any preliminaries. "Let's meet. Mephisto, 8pm." He pressed the red telephone button so hard the handset made a cracking noise.

Veroof's bemused PA repeated it all, word for word, to Dick when he returned from a "business meeting", with one of the lithe, oiled Brazilian twins, he wasn't sure which.

CHAPTER 12

London, March 2008

Peter kept seeing his daughter. Everywhere he went, there she was, little Kirsty, always the most sensitive of his three children. In the milling crowd at St Pancras station, looking small, furtive quick eyes, dank hair, on edge, dodging and disappearing before he could get close. Standing at a bus stop in the rain, half-obscured by discontented ill-dressed people huddled unwillingly together – there he had been able to cross the road and check, but the small hooded form he had taken for his own 14-year-old was in fact a malnourished boy of about that age whose main similarity with Kirsty was his height and the jacket he wore. The people at the bus stop had their own problems, familiarity with insufficiency, month-end lackings, but they still looked at well-heeled Peter with pity. Reason told him that Kirsty was not wandering the streets of London, she was protected in her plush school surrounded by green home-counties acres, fed and dry and supported. This was easily confirmed. Yet still he saw her, glimpsed amongst the city's masses. She haunted him, as did the memory of his goddaughter Penny's damaged arms, suddenly revealed, lurid in Ivy's halogen-lit kitchen, self-inflicted lacerations born of adult problems, domestic cruelties of which she was innocent collateral damage.

Peter did not know it, but it was not Kirsty he should have worried about.

Later he called them "the limbo months", but there was more of purgatory to this period than ever he admitted. Communication with Ivy was near-impossible. Communication with anyone in his personal life was near-impossible; he had never been a communicating type, and for over a quarter of a century his support had been provided efficiently and invisibly by his wife, a monopoly supplier. When it came down to it, he had no infrastructure of support at all. Ivy, on the other hand, was surrounded by a clucking coterie of sympathisers. It was like a laughable stereotype from *Men Are from Mars, Women Are from Venus.*

Ivy was glad that none of the children had been at home to witness their father's departure, complaining but compliant in a way that, to Ivy, confirmed his guilt. There had been an ugly scene, words were used that Peter forbade in his offspring, the parental unity they were accustomed to relying upon messily shattered. She wondered how long he had been betraying her trust, whether there had been others, how many others there had been. She wondered to what extent their whole lives had been a miserable fiction. Who else knew, whilst she was playing the gullible loyal wife? Who was laughing at her, who was feeling silent compassion for her, which of her relationships were tainted by asymmetrical knowledge? She asked herself whether it was possible that any of the children knew what she herself had just discovered, secretly pitying their mother – worse, maybe siding with Peter, sneakily conscripted by him. How poisoned were they? How confused? Briefly, horribly, a picture came to her mind of them all, Peter and the three children, in that girl's company, happily sharing a chatty pasta meal. Having children educated in various distant live-in locations had the advantage that the unedifying final scene had not been acted out before them, but what about its repugnant, deceitful cause?

Studio Flat, Hammersmith, London, March 2008

Following his brief stay at Jerry's, Peter had rented a studio flat in a small 1970s Hammersmith block. Two rooms, one containing a kitchenette and sofa bed, the other a cramped bathroom, all painted tasteful magnolia, slightly sooty in the corners and carpeted in a looped synthetic material the colour of wet cardboard, flattened and discoloured in the high traffic area by the door. There he spent a miserable winter, shunned by Ivy and his children, all three of whom were old enough to understand his supposed crime and their mother's fury, especially when presented with Jim Ames's photographic evidence, and Odile's able assistance in interpreting it.

Peter realised that he was condemned without his day in court, that no one would ever hear his side of the story unless he made some sort of contact. He tried to reach them all, his wife and his children, directly and via intermediaries. In some ways it was impressive, that so solid a wall could be constructed so rapidly along the new internal boundaries of his fissured family. Calls to school were politely converted to messages taken without response; calls to mobiles passed automatically to voicemail where they languished. In the hope that they would at least be listened to, Peter composed these snippets of communication with care, tried to recall a jokey persona that had made his children giggle in the past, whilst observing the seriousness of the situation that had befallen him, befallen them all. It was a tough balance and, for all he knew, a wasted effort. He even resorted to calling from anonymous phones – in hotels, offices, borrowed from friends – in the hope that the absence of his name on the mobile screens of his children's phones would gain him guileful access; to no avail.

He thought about physically approaching them in places he knew they would be – the girls returning home for exeat weekends, participating in sporting events; Harry at his lodgings in Oxford, outside lecture theatres. The picture this generated of a lurking, disowned adult trying pathetically to clutch at the children as they busied themselves on some bona fide activity was too demeaning. But he became increasingly desperate as the weeks passed with no contact with the people he loved the most, each day marking a tacit confirmation of whatever binary, black-and-white version of events had been impressed on their sensitive minds, an incremental setting in the cement of a false oversimplification.

In Peter's defence, he did not plan to steal his goddaughter's telephone, and it did seem to him afterwards that this act might mark some sort of moral low point. Penny's father was one of the few people who appeared to see things from Peter's point of view – cold comfort given that he was already separated from the woman he had taken up with when his wife, Penny's mother, had abruptly left for the Rhineland. Peter was not in a position to be choosy. Slumped on this fellow outcast's sofa watching a football match, he spotted Penny's bright pink Nokia, misplaced behind a cushion, and a thought struck him. For telephonic success he did not need to be anonymous but rather the reverse: he needed to be someone else, a SIM-card-listed trusty. He would return the phone as soon as possible. Needs must. He pocketed it.

First, he tried Harry. He was the same age as Penny and probably had a closer relationship with her than Emma. Kirsty was too young. He waited until lunchtime, Penny's phone weighing guiltily in his pocket. It had rung twice in that time, and Peter refrained from looking to see who was calling, confusedly virtuous. When Harry did not pick up, Peter scrolled through his goddaughter's contacts and selected Emma's mobile number. He realised his heart was beating fast, he felt like a concert soloist mounting the stage.

"Hi, Penns. Thanks for calling back – sorry to bother you again." His daughter spoke first, her voice sounding slightly strained; in the background, the noise of a school canteen. For a ghastly second, Peter forgot his script; he nearly pressed "end".

"It's not Penny, darling, it's me. Daddy." There was a pause. She did not hang up, a wonderful thing.

"Oh." She was caught off her guard, but not for long. She lowered her tone as she left the refectory, her voice edging to anger. "How come you're on Penny's number? Penny, of all people?"

Peter was not prepared for this, he was ready for all sorts of recriminations but not specifics relating to Penny. It made him feel suddenly sick and stupid as he quickly joined dots, making obvious connections. Emma was the same age as Penny had been back then. He decided to ignore both questions.

"I'm so glad to hear your voice, Emma. I've been missing you and…"

"Well, whose fault is that?" She snapped back.

"Mine, mine, Emma. But it's not as it appears. No doubt you've been told that I had an affair, but it's not true! You've got to let me explain it all."

"I haven't got to do anything, Dad. The photos don't need any explanation. Do you think I'm stupid? Do you really think all women are so, so…" Emma had raised her voice.

She's seen the photos, Peter thought. *Why am I surprised?* And then, *"all women"? She's my 16-year-old daughter. Where's this "all women" stuff coming from?* Pacing around in the corridor beyond the canteen, Emma found her words, dominated her anger.

"Men like you still expect women to give up their careers and autonomy, and when they do, instead of being grateful you take advantage of their dependency to cheat! CHEAT, DAD. You're a CHEAT!" She was channelling pure Odile, she knew that. So did he.

"Don't be angry, Emma, don't, until you know the facts. Don't just fall into these easy feminist arguments, things are more complicated…"

"HOW exactly is what you did COMPLICATED?" Emma was shouting, people were staring, she did not care. "It's the oldest thing ever, disgusting old men fucking younger women, taking advantage of them just as they abuse their wives. And their wives' commitment."

Peter was not prepared for the depth of her anger. He was horrified by what she said, and how. He almost forgot that her accusation was unjust, that he had never actually done it. At the back of his mind niggled the knowledge that, had things varied but a fraction from the path they took, had opportunity arisen, he could so easily be guilty as charged. He silenced the haunting thought with the more likely reality that it was never an opportunity that had any probability of being offered. He was being unjustly punished.

"That's rubbish, Emma. Rubbish straight from Odile. I – did – not – do – it. I was not unfaithful to your mother. The pictures you have seen prove nothing but an overactive imagination operating a good camera." He was departing from his script; he took a breath and regained his conciliatory tone. "I can explain it all. You've got to let me—"

"I've told you, I don't have to let you do anything at all. And before you tell me I'm not thinking for myself, you should know Odile defended you, she DEFENDED you! She said it was male nature to be polygamous. It's Darwinian. I disagree. I think there's no excuse. No excuse." She had quietened but only because she was crying. With no further words, she hung up.

Peter sat and looked grimly at the stolen handset. Bloody Odile, filling his daughter's mind with trite generalisations. Bloody Ivy, showing her those pictures. How could the call, so often rehearsed, have gone so badly? How had he misjudged his own daughter so? As he brooded the echo of an incongruity came back to him. What had she said at the start, when he was almost overcome with nerves, when she had first answered? "Thanks for calling back – sorry to bother you again"? With trembling hands he navigated Penny's phone to the call register.

Why had Emma called Penny, the self-harm survivor, five times in the last three days?

It was really hard to look on the bright side, but Peter tried. He was now able to read in bed as late as he liked, without Ivy beside him complaining about the light; it was a short walk to work rather than a short Fireblade ride, so that was safer and involved less protective clothing. By May he was very busy with the efforts of responding to the bank's unexpected request that Rareterre find a means of repaying part of their loan, which involved a punishing schedule of meetings in America and across Europe. Life without domestic responsibilities was far better suited to this disruptive programme.

Jammed between the door of his mini-bathroom and the avocado-coloured wash-basin, Peter looked at himself in the mirror. Not a pretty sight and getting steadily worse since he had stopped going to the gym and was eating mostly pre-cooked ready meals and takeaways instead of Ivy's organically sourced home cooking.

He was lonely, only a low-energy sadness always with him. Ivy continued to deploy her credit card like a high-powered automatic weapon, if anything firing with increased ferocity since his departure. All correspondence arriving at the Chelsea house not hand-addressed on nice stationery was forwarded weekly to Peter's office in an impersonal brown manila envelope. The mortgage continued to grow. He sold the Fireblade.

But worst of all, he was desperately worried about his elder daughter – sweet, smart, skinny Emma. Dear, vulnerable, distant Emma.

Rareterre Plc Offices, Hammersmith, London, May 2008

If you put a frog in a pan of cold water and heat it gently, the frog will remain, unconcerned, until the water boils and it dies, so we are told, although it would be a pretty mean thing to do. The creeping-up of the great financial crisis of 2007/8 on Rareterre plc, would later strike Peter as analogous to the experience of this hapless amphibian.

Austin's "Banking Environment" concerns were neither alarmist nor unfounded, but the impact of the financial crisis upon RBS, at least as was revealed to the outside world, was initially gradual, more an acidic erosion than an explosion.

For most people, the big events were just too esoteric to register as important. After all, they had their own lives and troubles – financial difficulties, health problems, work problems. Marital problems. And it went on for months, the news of more bank failures in the USA, of dramatic government initiatives, interest rate cuts, of toxic time-bombs of ill-rated CDOs being uncovered on the balance sheets of banks and institutions across the globe – all this seemed, as James described it to Peter, "dramatic but not serious" with respect to Rareterre.

Coming into the office one morning, late, Peter overheard the end of James's attempt at explaining to Olivier the latest twist in the Credit Crunch, which he saw as crucial and, more importantly, had produced a paradox. James loved a paradox. James was explaining the demise of the monoline insurers. Olivier, who had little enough understanding of anything non-geological and an increasingly justified Germanic view on Anglo-Saxon finance – little better than socially acceptable gambling and cupidity – was struggling. The conversation had already lasted over half an hour and could have gone on until one of them died of exhaustion. Fortunately though, James had just got to the paradoxical point of his story, and so it ended thus:

James: "So, you see, the rating agencies rated the insurers who used their strong ratings to write insurance for financial products, like the sub-prime mortgage packages, their customers wanted to insure, essentially 'wrapping' the packages with their high rating. They rented their ratings, Olivier! But the rating agencies were everywhere; they also rated the financial products themselves, which was how the insurers priced the wraps. And the ratings were wrong for the packages, wrong for the wraps!"

Olivier: "They were lazy, the insurers, to rely on the ratings from these agencies?"

James: "Yes, but they paid the price! The mistakes of the rating agencies made them, the insurance companies, look incompetent. When the agencies downgraded the financial packages they then downgraded the insurers too, making them look bad, you see, because they had more risk. The insurers had mispriced the wraps but it was because of the wrong ratings. Downgrade led to downgrade, the rating agencies were both cause and effect. And cause again. But by downgrading the insurance companies, *all* the wraps sold by the monoline insurers were downgraded, even the ones covering good financial products. We're talking trillions of dollars here. Everyone suddenly had more risk than they thought."

Olivier: "They were crap, the wraps?"

James: "The financial packages were crap, the ratings on the packs were crap, the wraps on the crap packs were crap, the insurers were..."

Olivier: "Let me guess: crap. Let's face it, the whole system is crap at this stage."

Peter interrupted because he could see that James's attempts to synthesise the problem for Olivier were ineffective, likely to consume a large part of the working day and depressingly dependent upon allusions to excrement.

Olivier's character contained a major Teutonic component that required the punishment of the guilty. He frowned. "They've a lot to answer for, these agencies! Can't they be downgraded too?"

No one was unaffected, including Rareterre, as Austin had foreseen. Although insignificant in the bigger picture, in its own terms Rareterre owed RBS a large amount of money, having drawn $33 million of the $40 million loan total, and its plans depended on the final seven being available.

Rareterre Plc Offices, Hammersmith, London, July 2008

The first anniversary of the loan had passed in April, and, by July, RBS had already "become uncomfortable with their exposure to the company", and asked Rareterre whether they could "see a way to deleverage".

Nice Edward Bald explained it to James: "No pressure, you understand. Completely accept that we have a commitment and still stand by that commitment. It's simply the credit committee feels it inappropriate to have a $40 million exposure to a company with a market value of $10 million. It's just not the same as when we signed the agreement and Rareterre had a value on the stock market of over £100 million. Completely take the point that share price played no role in the lending decision or the formal agreements. It's just a question of confidence within the credit committee."

In ways not apparent at the time, it was the beginning of Austin's predicted difficulties. The board had considered the position and mandated Peter to go out on a special road-show, one aimed at unearthing equity investors who might be willing to make a sizeable investment enabling them to repay part of the RBS loan. A quiet, confidential road-show. An international road-show, targeting sophisticated specialist financiers who understand mineral extraction and have access to large pools of capital. Show the bank good faith, do the right thing, if nothing comes of it (and Peter feared that nothing would come of it, given the fragile state of the markets and their continued lack of progress with the Conditional Use Permits) too bad, back to situation *ex ante*, RBS honouring its loan agreement commitments. All the same, it was a huge undertaking of a quasi-clandestine nature, because the Simple Lie was so unappetising: Rareterre has lost the confidence of its bankers! Emergency fundraising inevitable!

"Our legal position is the same as before, right? I mean, RBS has to honour its obligations in the loan agreement? Lend us the remaining seven million?" Peter was in his office with James, preparing for the investor road-show without enthusiasm, a draft PowerPoint presentation printed out in mini-format on the table in front of them. James recognised a rhetorical question when he heard one. Peter carried on, making an amendment to a slide in biro as he spoke.

"I mean, what a waste of effort. Investors are ultra-cautious these days, what with all the uncertainty. And there is the CUP position. I hope you insisted that they cover our costs for this. I feel like charging for our time!" James had not insisted that RBS cover the costs; it had not occurred to him.

"Yes, things are unchanged legally. We haven't breached anything in the loan agreement. Bald said as much when he called. In terms of investor interest, at 20p the shares are really good value, so maybe it's not completely hopeless. I agree that the bank ought to cover our costs, as we are really just doing all this to meet their needs, but I don't think they would necessarily look kindly on your charging for your time. How much would you charge? £750 an hour like Klaus?"

"James, I was joking about charging for my time. But did you tell Edward that they have to cover our direct out-of-pocket costs?"

"No, and I don't see them doing it, to be honest."

Irritated, Peter had already swivelled to his desk and was reaching for the phone, looking up RBS on the contacts in his computer. Five minutes later, after an ill-tempered conversation with Edward Bald, Peter had their agreement to cover all the travel and incidental costs and, should a refinancing be arranged, all Rareterre's legal fees and other expenses associated with it. James, who believed in never making enemies and had witnessed the call, was both impressed and concerned. Peter got back to editing the presentation, cracking his knuckles and smiling to himself grimly. James elected not to voice his feeling that having Edward onside would probably be worth all the costs of this exercise; having him against, feeling bruised, might come back to bite them.

Peter had been brittle since, without explanation to any of his colleagues, he had moved alone into a studio flat in an unattractive part of Hammersmith. He had few people in whom he could confide, and none at work – there people knew better than to pry or try offering support. In fact, he was in a state of passive-aggressive denial as things piled up

– his mortgage, Rareterre's unstable debt, and now the unjust ejection from his home based upon inaccurate allegations of an infidelity he had half-wished into being. British reserve, embarrassment, dislike for openly expressed emotion, contempt for the rush to pseudo-psychological senti-mental incontinence so often to be witnessed on the TV – these things increased Peter's isolation. So much confusion prevented him from identi-fying priorities and led to inaction; errors of omission piling their weight onto his errors of commission, real and imagined.

Studio Flat, Hammersmith, London, BBC Radio 4, August 2008

The man on the radio made another attempt to speak.

"It's a global crisis which started in Ameri—"

"Oh! Nothing to do with you then! The UK government had nothing at all to do with regulatory failures in the British banking system." Bill Boot, the interviewer, interrupted for the third time. "Let me quote something to you, from the Bank of England. They say in the UK we 'failed to strike a balance between burdensome regulation and excessive risk-taking', and as a result this crisis will be 'the biggest financial shock since the Great Depression'. The IMF agrees."

Peter was in his Hammersmith studio hurriedly packing his bag for another trip to see East Coast American private equity investors, a further attempt at enticing someone to invest in Rareterre. He was on to second-tier prospects now, the most promising ones had all either declined or rudely failed to respond at all. Hardly surprising, considering the turmoil in the financial markets everywhere. Had he paused to analyse it, he would probably have seen that his frenetic international funding efforts, under-taken really to appease an undeserving bank, were better understood as a distraction, an escape from his broken personal life and the depressing drudge of daily work at stricken, post-CUP Rareterre.

He was no supporter of the politician on the radio, but Peter felt that a current affairs programme should contain rather less from the interviewer, more from his guest. Although no question had been asked, the man spoke again – probably because Bill Boot had finally stopped.

"Well, of course, given the scale of the financial shock to the system, probably no amount of regulation would have—"

"So, nothing to apologise for in the past then. Can we assume, therefore, that you will not be making any plans to avoid another crisis like this one? The Governor of the Bank of England is proposing that the banks be forced to contribute billions into an emergency fund to be used to protect savers against future bank failures. You don't support that idea, I take it?"

"It's complicated. Bank balance sheets are weak at the moment, they've had big write-offs, so it may not be a good time to—"

"So, you propose to put taxpayers' money up as guarantee, as we saw with Northern Rock, rather than demanding that the banks themselves resolve their problems? Well, that's all we have got time for, thank you, Chancellor. Over to Molly and the weather forecast."

Peter angrily snapped the radio off. He did not know what annoyed him more. Boot had treated with disdain both the listeners and his guest, a man who had, after all, risen to one of the highest public offices in the land, so was perhaps owed some respect. More annoying still was Boot's failure to let the Chancellor say enough to damn himself. Worse still was that he, Peter, thought the bullying Boot had a point.

The fact that Boot was right and taxpayers would be forced to support the banks was troubling for Peter as a taxpayer but reassuring to him as CEO of Rareterre. The time was approaching when his company would need the final $7 million of their loan. Their private equity road-show was not looking promising. It was reassuring to think that RBS would still be in a position to provide the rest of their agreed loan, no matter how that was achieved.

Midtown, New York, August 2008

NOMAD Securities had an office in New York. It was really a one-man operation staffed by Dylan Winslow, a presentable Connecticut Brahmin in his early fifties whose mainstream investment banking career had come off the rails for reasons unknown and therefore about which everyone speculated. Peter's personal theory was that it had been drug-related – citing Dylan's soft, slow delivery, his often distant and borderline dreamy disposition, as a sure sign of fused synapses, cannaboid-induced cerebral short-circuiting. For Peter, Dylan's presence chaperoning him around US business meetings was a pleasure. Dylan was fun to be with not least because he was so unusual – the offer of a shared joint never materialising but also never seeming totally out of the question.

Their first day's appointments were all in Manhattan. The following morning they would venture to Dylan's native Connecticut, home to many billions in hedge-fund money, the specialist peripheries of which they hoped to access. Neither man was very optimistic. Many fund managers, people who had experienced years of easy credit, benign upwards-trending markets and low interest rates, were either too young or too amnesic to remember the dot-com crash with any clarity, and were enduring the near-daily market disturbances associated with the crisis with great difficulty. The stock market was jittery and so were they. As Dylan put it, "at times like these folks stay close to their money", conjuring up an image in Peter's mind of a pale, skinny miser sitting cross-legged in a safe surrounded by piles of banknotes.

And yet, despite all this, when Peter arrived at NOMAD's New York office – a small, slightly shabby serviced affair in one of the brick-built old-school midtown skyscrapers, 30 floors up in an ageing lift – he found Dylan in a state of rare excitement.

"I've just had Julian in London on the line. Bloom & Beck have requested, *requested*," he savoured the word, "a meeting with you. They heard we were on a funding road-show and want to meet." Peter let pass the implied breach of the confidentiality he had hoped surrounded the road-show and above all its purpose. There was a bigger objection.

"But, Dylan, they are big investors in a competing business which owns the White Crag mine. We'd have to be really careful." Dylan gave him a look which said, "beggars can't be choosers, man". He was too polite to voice it, but if he had, Peter would have objected that Rareterre was not a beggar, the company was funded, their plans could be financed from the agreed bank facility, the road-show was merely a gesture to please RBS.

"And careful we shall be!" said Dylan. "We can rip out any pages of the presentation we think might contain competitive information. But Bloom & Beck, Peter! They certainly have the means to make a sizeable investment. Man, they could take out the whole RBS loan!"

Peter was painfully aware that the loan with RBS had been arranged to avoid a fundraising below 100p per share. Here was Dylan, his financial advisor, getting excited at the prospect of refinancing the lot at – what would they have to settle for, with the market price at 20p and still inching down? – 15p probably. Peter had been in the habit of bench-marking financial proposals by reference to Dreadnought's 10 percent. Had Rareterre, instead of borrowing the money from RBS, done the $40 million financing by issuing shares at, say, 80p, Dreadnought's 10 percent would have been diluted to 8 percent – bad enough to make the RBS loan a more attractive idea. But now, after Oregon State's inspection and the withdrawn Conditional Use Permits, plus the writings of malevolent Stacey, 80p per share was a distant memory; financing the same amount at 15p would leave Dreadnought with just over 4 percent. Peter was an old-fashioned CEO who took his responsibilities to shareholders seriously; diluting their stakes to less than half seemed to him something better avoided. Mellow Dylan's idea did not look good for shareholders. Peter explained this.

"Wow... the ethical CEO! I thought Darwinism had eradicated that species long ago. I mean, like, didn't Dreadnought sell their whole holding?

Man, I bet you feel great about protecting their interests so diligently," Dylan replied mildly.

"Oh, I'm only using them as an example, Dylan! The principle is the same for all shareholders."

"Ah! The *principled* CEO! See my earlier comments re the big CD, Charley Darwin. All I'm saying is that the shareholders might equally sell if they don't like the deal on offer. It's kinda one of the good things about capitalism."

"Anyway, if B&B invested $40 million they'd have to make a bid for the whole company – it's one of the London Stock Exchange rules." Dylan looked unfazed. Dylan always looked unfazed.

"Options, man, options; people like to be offered choices. It's way better than having no choices. I mean *way* better. Why don't we just go on over there and hear what the nice people have to say?"

Nice people; Dylan had never met Jay.

Bloom & Beck's Offices, Wall Street, New York, August 2008

But Jay was nice, very nice. He could turn the charm on when it pleased him. He had monitored Rareterre since the early stages of B&B's interest in the rare-earths business and the large mine at White Crag. He was on Stacey East's mailing list and watched closely the share prices of Rareterre, C. Brown Pty and REM AS. He had seen, with uncontained satisfaction, the catastrophic effect on Rareterre's market value when the Conditional Use Permits had been suddenly withdrawn thanks to his inspired actions. When he met Peter, who seemed to have brought along a short-haired hippie dressed in a suit, he saw him almost as a victim. Not that Jay was a compassionate man, his conscience was not in any way a well-developed faculty, but Peter was a businessman and his adversity, for which Jay was in large part responsible, was something he could at least understand if not sympathise with. He also understood that there could be much to gain for Bloom & Beck by White Crag doing a deal of some sort with Rareterre, especially whilst its share price was so very low. This understanding was all that really mattered. He flipped the charm switch to "on" and, assuming Peter to be a normal heterosexual man, invited Lori Taylor to join the meeting for good measure.

Peter and Dylan came to B&B's offices directly from meeting an eccentric and highly focussed fund manager in one of the downtown office blocks that Peter labelled "Lidl offices – pile 'em high, sell 'em cheap". They were certainly piled very high, these huge impersonal blocks, apparently designed simply to pack the greatest amount of rentable space possible on their square of compressed land, accommodating hundreds of tenants, small and large, whose employees, despite shared facilities, clearly felt no sense of community. Termite hills with the work ethic but not the social cooperation.

Bloom & Beck of course shared nothing. Their dedicated building off Wall Street was B&B branded through and through, a purposeful palace of accumulation, dedicated solely to the enrichment of its employees. The atmosphere, immediately notable on entering, was one of successful teamwork. It was a façade naturally. There was plenty of rivalry and back-stabbing, which, whilst not actively encouraged, was certainly seen as healthy, and became increasingly prevalent as one climbed the steep invest-ment banking career ladder. Team B&B had a successful formula, and all the staff, including the receptionists (racially diverse, all female, all attrac-tive) and the fatigued young business-trip executives wheeling expensive cabin luggage across the lobby, were in on the secret. Dylan checked them both in at the reception desk with such extreme mellowness that Peter almost expected to hear the words "Peace, man" in conclusion.

Within minutes a pretty, tired-looking young woman, in a tight tailored white cotton shirt and charcoal-grey business suit, came down to collect them and show them up to a plush 32nd-floor meeting room, the swift, silent lift causing their ears to pop. During this brief journey Lori amiably and knowledgably exchanged industry scuttlebutt with Peter.

Jay was waiting for them. After the preliminary courtesies he launched into an entirely hypocritical expression of sympathy for Rareterre's CUP misfortune. Lori thought it insincere, she knew Jay well enough to know that when he was in charm mode his true feelings could often best be expressed by simply adding the word "not" at the appropriate place in each of his sentences; she found herself silently doing it.

"Peter, that was [not] bad luck with the, who was it, Oregon State Assay and Mining Authority. We do [not] feel for you. These things can [not] be so unpredictable. Of course, if there's anything we can do we would [not] be glad to help you. In many ways we are [not] all in this together."

Lori did this purely for her own amusement. She had realised that her active contribution would not be required, her presence in the room being not necessarily for her sector knowledge. She had not been involved with White Crag since the deal had closed two years earlier, although she still kept herself informed of developments in the rare-earths area. But this deciphering of Jay's insincere assertions suddenly placed something she had overheard, the butt-end of a telephone conversation two years previously, in its required context. That weekend in his Long Island beach house, to which she had attributed her receiving the highest bonus of the entire 2005 associate intake, he had been talking about a "toxic blend" and Rareterre, and had guiltily hung up when he saw her.

Lori saw clearly that her reinterpretation of Jay's words revealed the true extent of his insincerity. The loss of the Conditional Use Permits had not been a matter of bad luck. It had not been unpredictable. Jay would not help. And they were far from all being in it together.

The meeting proceeded amicably enough, focusing on the issue of Rareterre's financing needs – which Peter presented as a discretionary matter, a preference for less debt – and how Bloom & Beck might participate. Lori looked at Peter, whose face was showing signs of strain and appeared much older than his image on the company's website. Unlike her boss, she did feel compassion.

On leaving B&B's air-conditioned building, Peter and Dylan were met by a brutal, humid New York August heat that assaulted them like a cosh. Their senses were attacked by the noise of traffic, of massive buses that seemed to make as much noise stationary as they did when moving – until they did move, when the effect was deafening. The air was heavy with that unique New York odour, combining exhaust fumes with street food and occasionally, lurking in dank shadowy corners, a rank smell like uncooked chicken giblets. Peter normally loved this edgy city, but their meeting with Jay had depressed him.

"Do you have the expression 'he would sell his own grandmother for a fiver' here in the USA?" he asked Dylan, who could guess what a fiver was and also understand the expression without it being part of his own repertoire.

"Oh, he was all right. I get the impression he was doing his best to be nice."

"That only makes it worse."

"The black chick was cool though. Plus, I think they might invest."

"Strictly on their terms, I'd say. But I don't know that we want them. We'd end up with Sharky there on the board and nowhere else to go but them if we ever wanted to sell the company." Dylan was giving him the "beggars can't be choosers" look again. It annoyed him.

Peter decided then, in the shimmering noisome heat of Wall Street, that enough was enough; he'd done his bit. If the best they could achieve was selling a majority stake to a direct competitor, and hobbling themselves forever as a consequence, then RBS would just have to do what they had signed up for, stick with their loan, and advance the last $7 million when it was needed.

"Dylan, I've just realised something. I'm going through all this, performing like a circus elephant across two continents to please RBS. To try to satisfy their fickle needs, respond to a change of mind on their part. It's not been a success – the financial system going into crisis has not been a great help, of course. Anyway, I've just made a decision. Sod them. Cancel the rest of our meetings – I'm off back to London. RBS were happy enough to take arrangement fees and non-utilisation fees from us, and signed up on commercial terms satisfactory to them at the time, less than 18 months ago. I'm going to tell them they should bloody well grow up and stick with our deal. It is a legally binding contract, after all."

Dylan's "beggars can't be choosers" look had transformed into a "good luck with that one, baby" look, surprisingly cynical in one so mellow.

"How people treat you is their karma; how you react is yours, man." He said elliptically.

Guggenheim Museum, New York, August 2008

Peter rearranged his flights and found himself with a spare afternoon, which had previously been scheduled with futile meetings with self-satisfied yet fearful potential investors. He gratefully decided to treat himself with a visit to the Guggenheim. Peter loved the Guggenheim and everything about it, from the cylindrical stacked-disc exterior to the airy, spiralling beehive interior. He loved the atmosphere of barely suppressed pretension, the democratic accessibility to tokens of great wealth, the train-station bustle in the ground-floor rotunda, named for a private-jetting corporate barbarian. And the people there, similarly contradictory: artsy materialistic millionaire hedge-fund managers; armchair levellers with PhDs in obscure corners of luxury; team leaders of socially inclusive educational programmes exclusively enjoyed by the bored wives of wealthy men. And tourists, tourists, tourists – great herds of box-checking, guide-book-wielding plodders getting under everyone's feet. It was New York, encapsulated.

Peter did not love the art, so artfully spread across the creamy flawless walls, not all of it, but a visit to the Guggenheim was always a pleasure to be savoured. His visit coincided with a spectacular temporary exhibition of explosion and projectile-obsessed work by an acclaimed Chinese-born artist, but if the art was not always to his taste, the people-watching opportunities more than compensated for that.

Peter had been there for an hour, starting at the top and rolling slowly downhill, past walls bearing blasted black images created by gunpowder ignitions on paper. He had no time for this kind of thing, which (he could not help thinking) could be executed equally effectively by any delinquent teenager with time on their hands. Maybe they had been. To his delight, he heard a short, earnest middle-aged man with a neat white goatee and a paunch, say: "He uses explosives to manifest the pure force of energy, not as a means to art but as an art form itself."

Whilst Peter tried to unpick this sentence the better to mock it later, he realised the man was reading from the museum's notes of the exhibition to a companion, obscured by a dangling installation, who had just replied: "I think he expresses the violence of our still male-dominated society perfectly. Violence and futility – but in a way that invites the viewer to share in a critique. It's very witty, in a post-ironic way."

Peter did not even have time to savour the quality of the tosh. The voice was Odile's. Ivy's head-friend, counsellor-in-chief Odile. Corrupter of the Mount youth Odile. She emerged from behind a giant lantern, which appeared to be made from two large hessian sacks roughly stitched together, and saw Peter. For a moment she seemed to consider dodging back behind the installation.

"Odile!" Peter's voice reverberated off the smooth, curved walls. "Odile Callow!" Odile stepped closer to her goatee-bearded friend. "How fortunate. I've been wanting to have a talk with you."

"Not now, Peter. Maybe back in London? I'm here with a friend." Odile was edging towards the rotunda slope. Mr Goatee looked crossly at Peter, confirming the validity of Odile's statement.

"Not so fast, Odile. I think you owe me an explanation, don't you?" Odile was walking away now, in the downhill direction, the friend in slightly nervous lockstep. They each carried a maroon shoulder bag sten-cilled with "Feminism NY 2008", and beneath, in smaller lettering: "The Radical Idea that Women Are People". Behind them, suspended at angles from the domed roof, Peter could see two exploding white cars, sparks radiating in arcs of alternating coloured multichannel light tubes, the top of a huge installation comprising nine continually combusting cars cascading up from ground level five sweeping storeys below. It was as if Jeremy Clarkson had been given carte blanche and a big budget.

Peter followed Odile and her friend. "Odile, surely you're not going to *run away*?" She did not stop walking but Mr Goatee, flustered, loudly asked her in strained jokey tones "who's the looney-tunes?"

Exceptionally, to accommodate the scale of the temporary exhibition, half of each downwards-spiralling rotunda was inaccessible. Odile found herself cornered short of a plexiglass screen upon which a fantastic pack of full-size levitating wolves, flying in a long swift rank, were crashing to the floor. She had to turn and face Peter.

"Listen, Peter. I don't know what you think needs explaining. I'm just another innocent bystander in the mess you've made. I've no need to run away, but surely you are not going to *pursue me*?" A sign to her right informed them all that the flying wolf installation was titled "Head On".

"Another innocent bystander?" Peter was enraged. The other innocents would be who? His children, his wife? "*Innocent*, Odile? You have poisoned my children against me. God knows what effect you have had on Ivy. You're not innocent, Odile, you're an odious, interfering, opinionated…" The Guggenheim is an open-design space with little to dampen the transmission of sound. Peter was speaking both loudly and in tones that demanded the unwholesome attention of the uninvolved. A young couple from Milwaukee, sneaker-clad and each carrying a bottle of water, stared. Goatee-beard looked like he might say something, then thought better of it.

"All I have done is offer support to my close friend, answer her calls for help. You're the one who cheated, remember! Even you can't somehow twist that to a scenario where you're the victim, Peter." She moved towards the curved interior wall to pass him, back uphill to the lifts. He stepped into her path.

"I'm not saying that I am the victim. But I'm not guilty of cheating on Ivy, even if no one believes me. Too bad. I know perfectly well who the victims are, thanks to you, Odile. They are Harry, Emma and Kirsty. Mostly Emma. She phoned me up, Odile, spouting a load of man-hating feminist crap that must have come straight from your over-simplifying prejudiced mouth." Peter felt himself losing control. The thought of Emma and what had happened was, of all the miserable recent history of the Mount family, the hardest to bear. People were gathering at the opposite inward-facing walls of the rotunda layers above and below, disinterestedly interested. The couple from Milwaukee continued to gape. Peter did not care. Odile's companion, lent courage by the unthinkable concept of a feminist accused of prejudice, chose this moment to make a stand.

"I think it's time you took a couple of deep breaths, brother, and calmed down a little."

Peter looked down at him, the six-inch height advantage very slightly augmented by the sloping floor, and, keeping his own eyes firmly on the man's, said to Odile, "He thinks I need to calm down. Tell your snivelling little mate to shut up, Odile." She ignored that. The snivelling little mate got the message anyway.

"Emma did not phone you, Peter. You called her, tricking her into answering by using Penny's phone. You stole your own goddaughter's phone to spin the truth of your sleeping around. Jesus, Peter, don't you see you need *help*?" Odile's voice had also risen by several indiscreet decibels. She smiled. She knew that it would infuriate Peter to be told that he was in need of psychiatric support. The sophisticated Guggenheim audience also understood the nuance and held their collective breath. Many even wondered whether this loud English-accented altercation was itself some sort of artwork.

"You can smile, Odile. Proud of yourself, are you? Pleased at the effects of your intervention in my family's problems? Do you know what my daughter said to me, Odile, just before she told me she hated me? Emma said, 'Men like you still expect women to give up their careers and autonomy, and when they do, instead of being grateful you take advantage of their dependency to cheat'." His voice had dropped now, as he recalled the conversation. "Does that sound like a 16-year-old to you, Odile? Because to me it sounds like an embittered, jealous, barren middle-aged woman with a restricted, prejudiced view of the world. Like you, in other words."

"So, she hates you? Well, you should have thought about that before you undid your zipper, before you betrayed Ivy. And the rest of the family."

"Yeah, well, she says she hates me and maybe she thinks she has every right to; but I love her. I'm still her dad. I'll always be her dad." Peter was horrified to note that tears were creeping down his cheeks. His voice cracked with emotion. "You think you know all about it. But there are things I'm sure Ivy has not shared with you, no matter how close you think you are. I picked up Penny's phone by sheer chance. Lucky for me, eh? Lucky. It gave me time to react, to intervene. Because Emma was burning herself. Cigarettes. Odile, Emma was harming herself. All down her thigh. All down her thigh." His voice had become small. He paused to swallow. "She thought Penny could help her out. Lucky me! I took the one person's phone that Emma was most likely to answer."

Jolene's Apartment, Mount Hood, Oregon, August 2008

Jolene heard them on the stairs, stamping their nasty booted feet as they laboured up, foreclosure papers in hand. She knew they would come, these heavy, mean men, red-faced and breathless from the three flights to her front door. She had received enough threatening letters, horrid impersonal things signed by a computer, warning her of the consequences if she remained in default, calling her "delinquent". She had looked it up. She was not a delinquent, she wanted to pay, but how could she when the bank was asking for $1,100 a month and her gross take-home pay, even in a good month when tips were plentiful, amounted to less than $1,300? She wanted to pay, she wanted to keep her apartment, her furniture, her independent life. Her dream.

She had tried calling Brad, but he never answered his cellphone and the woman at the number on his card seemed unable to decide whether Brad had been promoted out of the area or Millennium had gone out of business. Or both. Jolene had always known, deep down, that as soon as her mortgage was arranged Brad would be back out of her life again, and so it had been. She had always known, but still it was another disappointment added to the accumulating catalogue of disappointments that weighed down her spirit and subtracted from her previously sunny disposition. She sadly concluded that Brad saw her only as a piece of business like any other. Stupid of her to dream anything else. Stupid.

But she remembered his reassuring words in answer to her worries about what would happen once the two-year "introductory period" was over. He was so convincing, so clever. He always had been. Surely he would not let her down, he would help her now that they were threatening to come to her apartment and evict her, warning her she should not attempt to detach any fixtures or fitments, "properly the property of the mortgagee"? She looked that up too. It was the bank, although she did not recognise its name at the head of the threatening letter. Did they mean that she could not unscrew the scales from the kitchen wall? Her mom had given her those as a house-warming present, visiting soon after she moved in, her dad proudly closing the front door with a flourish saying, "Who would have thought it, our little Jolene, a place of her own! Man, ya gotta love America."

Brad did let her down though. He was gone. He had sold his house, fearfully cashing in when prices looked like they were softening. Unlike Jolene, Brad got out at a nice profit, before his own mortgage exceeded the declining value of the house. As the red-faced, heavy, out-of-breath men with their foreclosure papers were banging angrily on Jolene's Oregon door, Brad was sitting on his father-in-law's sunlit Florida porch drinking beer and telling his teenaged brother-in-law how he had become a dollar millionaire before he was 30, had made the most of it whilst the party lasted.

Jolene had been sold a dream and it was beyond her means. She was not a delinquent, she wanted to pay. But she couldn't. Not in money. She paid in shame, in bitter tears, in sleepless nights. She paid in stress, in worry. She paid a heavy price but it was not enough for them. The mean, meaty red-faced men evicted her.

Her failed mortgage joined the stream down the river network to the reservoirs of Wall Street, where her delinquency mingled with thousands more, apparently surprising all sorts of people even cleverer than Brad.

As Peter flew back from New York to affirm his karma versus the Royal Bank of Scotland, that same bank announced the largest half-year loss in UK banking history. At £700 million it was chickenfeed compared to the widespread slaughter happening elsewhere in the world, and laughable in light of the tidal wave of blood-red ink that would subsequently sweep so much away, including RBS. The flocks of malevolent birds swirling around the banking and finance industry, hungrily cawing, perceived a new target, another vainglorious megalith to be brought low. But as Peter read about it mid-air in the *Financial Times*, uncomfortably squeezed in an economy-class seat, the main consequence of RBS's loss as reported appeared to be that the bank's share price fell below the 200p, at which a rights issue had been sold just six months earlier. Bad news for investors perhaps, but for customers, depositors and borrowers, a bit of a "so what?".

Austin Roach did not consider it a "bit of a 'so what?'" at all. He was of a naturally pessimistic disposition, a trait that in good times inhibited his effectiveness and constrained his participation in the generalised well-being;

a corporate party-pooper. Exuberance was one of the many things of which he disapproved. In difficult times, however, Austin was at his most cheerful – which was really not very cheerful. Nearly a year had passed since, in his capacity as non-executive Cassandra, he had forced the board of Rareterre to sit through a doom-laden discourse on the potential for credit contagion infecting RBS and hence its vulnerable, dependent customer, Rareterre. During that year much had happened to confirm in Austin's mind the validity of his concerns and the superiority of his pessimistic analysis, although Rareterre's continued survival for so long had the opposite effect on most of his fellow directors, seemingly confirming Austin as an alarmist. When RBS announced their comparatively piffling yet still record-breaking loss, Austin was moved to email Frits as chairman of the board.

From: \<Austin@apollo.com\>

Date: Tue 19 August 07:27 AM

Subject: Banking

To: FritsV@rareterre.co.uk

Frits

You probably saw the recent announcement made by RBS regarding their half-year results – the biggest half-year loss ever at a British bank, the consequence of £6 billion of debt write-downs. Their core tier 1 capital ratio is down to 5.7 percent – meaning that at a time of great volatility this bank has a cushion of just £1 for every £20 it lends. More write-downs could be disastrous, wiping out this thin capital base altogether. As you know, I am concerned about their desire, even their ability, to continue to support Rareterre.

Last September, at my instigation, we discussed the risk of our position vis-à-vis our dependence on RBS, and the discussion was duly minuted. Since then we have seen great turbulence, numerous bankruptcies of banks and investment vehicles, the US Fed injecting massive amounts of liquidity into their economy to prop up banks, the stock market fall by nearly 20 percent, interest rates slashed, and a general air of crisis.

RBS's request in May that we consider ways to recapitalise was of course no good sign, no matter how gently put. I believe it is high time to revisit, at board level, the issue of our future financing needs.

Regards

Austin

As an afterthought Austin copied in all the board. He liked to cover his back.

When Frits read the email his first reaction was to question why Austin had not simply called to discuss it – these banking concerns had already come up several times in other conversations. Then he saw the reference to minutes and board level discussion, and he saw the formal side of Austin's message. The board takes shared responsibility, matters raised have to be properly discussed and the discussion properly recorded. As chairman, Frits realised Austin's widely circulated email was a warning shot across his bows. An image of himself as captain of a buccaneer ship and Austin as commander of a nineteenth-century Royal Navy frigate flashed briefly across his mind. When he considered it, he wondered about the board of RBS. Here he was, chairman of a small AIM-listed business, concerned about the proper governance of his company. What on earth were the board at massive RBS thinking as they apparently let their management team run wild in an orgy of ill-controlled risk-taking? If he was captaining a privateer, they were on the bridge of a massive sci-fi space cruiser, bristling with conning towers, sensors and docking ports. How could they attempt to justify their considerable remuneration?

He decided to reply with a one-liner proposing the agenda for the next board meeting be amended to include the topic of future finance in the Credit Crunch. James had got there first:

From: <JamesS@rareterre.co.uk>
Date: Tue 19 August 07:37 AM
Subject: Banking

All

RBS has a balance sheet total of £1.9 trillion. We owe them $33m (£18m) out of a $40m (£21.5m) facility. By all means let's discuss it, but let's keep this in proportion.

James

As Frits typed out his response he saw in the bottom corner of his screen a new message arrive from Peter:

From: <PeterM@rareterre.co.uk>
Date: Tue 19 August 1:17 PM
Subject: Banking

Dear Austin

You say "I am concerned about their desire... to continue to support Rareterre".

There is no question that RBS no longer has the desire to support us – that's why I've been hawking myself around the private equity investors of the world for the last several weeks; but RBS's desire does not come into it. We have a legally binding seven-year term loan agreement with them. Last time I checked RBS was a British bank, not Sicilian.

It does seem a bit far-fetched to think RBS might go bust, but by all means let's have the discussion.

Regards

Peter

Frits still sent a non-participatory one-line email agreeing to add the topic to the board agenda for the 15th September – exactly a year after Austin first raised it.

The Restaurant at Harvey Nichols Department Store, London, August 2008

Back in London, Odile did give an account to Ivy of her encounter with Peter at the Guggenheim museum in New York, but only a partial one. She described Peter's furious, uncontrolled verbal attack, but as time passed she had increasingly rationalised the whole thing as the consequence of a damaged male *amour propre*, an instinctive lashing out against the situation as much as against her as a player in it. She never approached the subject of Emma's self-harming. Odile told herself that she was respecting Ivy's desires in this regard; all the same, she felt a certain irritation that she had not been deemed close or trustworthy enough for this final confidence. She did not know that Peter and Ivy had skilfully colluded, without direct contact, over the management of what both tacitly considered to be a shared problem of importance far beyond their own wounded relationship.

Odile pushed her plate away and looked across at Ivy, exasperated. She signalled to the waitress for the bill.

"Ivy, I can't believe you mean that. He runs around behind your back with a young, a young..." She searched for a suitably derogatory but also non-sexist and non-judgemental noun, to describe the girl whose image Ivy had shown her, grainy pictures of stolen embraces. She failed. "Young *tart*, not to say that sex workers do not have a valid place in our society, of course." With relief she regained safe terrain, the object of her disdain being a middle-class white heterosexual male. Safe. "Anyway, that bastard Peter runs around behind your back like the slimy worm he is, you quite rightly kick him out, and now you tell me you miss him?"

Ivy struggled briefly with the impossible image of a slimy worm, running. She did not admit to herself that she had been moved by Peter's quietly efficient handling of the Emma problem, dealing with it in the teeth of their soured relationship, so arranging things that they could jointly address a shared challenge whilst respecting her strictures forbidding direct contact. Somehow, he had operated behind the scenes, marshalling the resources that needed to be deployed in support of their daughter. He had remotely provided a reassuring presence – like before. Between them they had succeeded – like before. And now she was struggling to explain a new set of sentiments to Odile, to herself.

"It's just that I seem to have so little to do with him gone. And he used to make me laugh. Before, well, before his work got so difficult and stressful." Before the value of his shares dropped to a point where our family finances were stretched, making him an expenses bore, she could have added. Before he started running around behind my back. Like a slimy worm.

"Don't start making excuses for him! He betrayed you, Ivy. You have to be strong – otherwise you'll only get hurt again." The bill came. Ivy automatically took it and, without glancing at it, handed it back to the waitress with her – Peter's and her – credit card. Odile made no attempt to pay; lunch at Harvey Nicks was expensive. "If you don't have enough to do it's because you used to spoil him, doing everything around the house. He treated you like a domestic, Ivy."

Ivy knew this to be unfair, Peter had a full-time job, which provided for her and the family, she furnished the caring side of the partnership. Their traditional division of labour, perhaps exploitative in Odile's view, was an explicit and functioning understanding she had willingly entered into. Besides, she had enjoyed her domestic life, but with all the children away, one at university the other two at boarding school, there was less to do. She had been happy to partly fill the time with socialising. But since Peter left she had quickly found any kind of entertaining pointless. She could provide great food and was not dull company but without Peter there, keeping everyone debating, laughing, sometimes squabbling, it all seemed too much like mere catering.

The fact that her group of regular guests had not commented on the reduced frequency of her invitations seemed to her confirmation that they too felt it less enjoyable, even though at one time or another they had all found Peter frustrating, sometimes worse. She had begun to realise that after a quarter century of marriage, she and Peter had become a double act. Laurel and Hardy. Or more like Robin Hood and Maid Marian. Without the outdoor camping lifestyle, obviously.

"If you haven't enough to do, you should get a proper job, Ivy."

A proper job. Get a proper job. As if her life so far had not been a proper, respectable occupation. As if bringing up children was not a proper job on a par with any other. What exactly did Odile have in mind? A proper job like that of a sex worker, whose valid place in society she had just acknowledged and clearly respected more than hers? Ivy wanted to scream at her friend that if more mothers did a proper job of bringing up their offspring, then perhaps society would have fewer problems, fewer sex workers and less demand for them. But that sounded too Tory. She wanted to tell Odile to fucking fuck off, but that sounded too Alastair Campbell. But she wanted to.

"Charity work, you mean?" she asked, controlling herself. They were standing waiting for the lift.

"Or what about that?" Odile pointed at a notice-board screwed to the wall. A list of available vacancies had been posted there offering staff their statutory right to apply for internal advancement. Odile was pointing at the top vacancy on the list: "Buyer, women's luxury goods."

"What, a rare example of a proper job I'm actually qualified for, you mean?" Ivy nearly said. Again, she controlled herself.

She applied for the job that afternoon. She really was ideally qualified for it, knowing all the brands, including the newer, less well-established ones, and the tastes of her fellow high-spending consumers, as well as having excellent taste herself, along with an eagle-eye for hand-stitched quality. She was not at all surprised when asked to start the following week.

CHAPTER 13

Rareterre Plc Offices, Hammersmith, London, September 2008

One of the most annoying phrases in the English language, Frits van Steen was thinking, was, "I hate to say 'I told you so', but I told you so." It was asinine and self-satisfied whilst pretending not to be. It was somehow worse that Austin did not actually say the words, but his entire disapproving, pessimistic presence shouted them out loud.

Austin's repeat of his board item on Rareterre's financial exposure coincided with the collapse of Lehman Brothers, owing $650 billion. Austin had no need to outline for the board the dangers of contagion a second time: as he was speaking, stock markets around the globe collapsed, and central bankers and finance ministers started taking the sort of action that only extreme crisis and extreme fear could justify.

Fear did play a role in the discussion Frits chaired at the September board meeting in Rareterre's inadequately sized conference room, but not a major one. Within Rareterre's boring little loan agreement with RBS were provisions for the loan to be drawn in chunks, subject to certain tests, up to the maximum total of $40 million. The company had planned to draw their final $7 million mid-December and this timing had been discussed with the bank, an expectation based upon projections for cash flows and investment, an indication but not a firm draw-down timing. Access to that final $7 million draw was critical to Rareterre's plans and, they all knew, probably its survival. The sentiment around the table was more prudent concern based on changing circumstances than any thought that the final $7 million would not be available.

"Peter, James, remind the board of the terms of our loan agreement with RBS," Frits said after Austin had selflessly avoided repeating "I told you so" for the fifth time.

"It will of course count for little if RBS does go under," Austin remarked.

Number six, thought Frits.

"But we really should not be basing a board discussion on the premise that the biggest bank in the world will go bust!" protested James.

"Tell that to the boys down at Lehman Brothers."

"But that's my point, Austin. Lehman was NOT too big to fail, that's why they were allowed to go under; RBS's balance sheet must be at least three times the size."

"And MY point, James, is that no one at Lehman really thought they would be bankrupt today. We have not seen the consequences fully unfurl. No one knows who had exposure to Lehman – directly and indirectly probably everyone. We can be sure that RBS is a leading creditor, who has more to lose than most. That's why we're at risk." *Number seven.*

"Because they are more incompetent than the others, or what?"

"Because it is a very big bank and has been very aggressively managed. Big means widespread exposure. Aggressively managed means perhaps a higher risk profile than most."

"Incompetent then…"

Austin had good relations with RBS, he had frequently done business with them and occasionally played golf with several of their bankers. He had disapproved of RBS's ill-conceived expansionism and its departure from simple, boring commercial banking for increased and growing reliance on the excitement of investment banking. He felt a mixture of loyalty to his acquaintances at RBS and, more importantly, to the potential of doing future business with them, confused with a belief in his own negative assessment of their business prospects. He felt James perhaps went too far with his charges of incompetence, yet part of him agreed.

"It really doesn't matter whether it's through incompetence, bad luck or whatever, the fact remains we need that final draw. The days when we could raise money easily from shareholders are over. We are reliant on RBS." *Number eight.*

As Frits sat counting Austin's implicit "I-told-you-so's", wedged between Peter and James in the cramped and depressing boardroom, he felt his energy seeping away. Frits was a high-energy man who charged at life's challenges with purpose, and he hated the sense of gloomy, impotent inevitability that Austin seemed to inject into the atmosphere.

"Okay, Austin. We get the picture: there's a risk that when we go to RBS in December for the final draw, that somehow it will not be available. Peter here says that is legally impossible. James here" – he held his hands apart before him, palm up, like a priest commencing the Eucharist – "tells us RBS is too big to be allowed to fail. But you continue to foresee doom. Fine. What the hell would you suggest we do about it?" He held his priestly posture longer than necessary.

"Make the draw-down request early. As soon as possible. Better that we have a few months' extra interest to pay than an unfillable $7 million hole in our finances."

"Won't that worry them?"

"If we are going to do that, we should also request a change to the repayment schedule," added James. "Thanks to our friends at the Oregon Authority the covenants are looking a bit tight in September next year – we might as well make life easier and ask to extend the interest-only period, start making repayments in 2010 instead of 2009."

"Won't that *really* worry them?"

"Shouldn't. It's only a minor alteration. Normally there would be no problem, just probably some additional fees."

"Of course. No opportunity missed for those RBS snouts to get into the trough!"

The board unanimously voted for an early approach to the bank.

Islington, North London, September 2008

Ivy was with her friend Ernest Fellden. She had not seen him for months, since she stopped her frequent Thursday night dinners. He lived as an ill-paid social worker in northerly Islington, miles from her home in Chelsea. He knew about Peter, Odile had filled him in on all the details, but Ernest had been too embarrassed to call either Ivy or Peter. What would he say? To her: "Sorry to hear about your loss"? She hadn't lost him, she'd booted him out. To him: "She'll come around and see reason, don't worry"? From what Odile had said, Ivy's actions had been completely reasonable. Hence it was Ivy who called Ernest – he was stable and serious and a man, maybe he would have a useful perspective.

"What did he say in his defence?" Ernest asked, when Ivy had finished explaining the events leading up to Peter's departure, showing him the photos of Kiara and Peter.

"Exactly what you would expect him to say. That she was just a friend; that they were not sleeping together. All so predictable."

"And the night at her flat?"

"Never happened of course. He claims he went there to collect something on the way to Milan. That my detective is incompetent." Ivy went on to describe Fulki's conversation with Jerry regarding Jim Ames's reliability. Ernest, whose daily social-worker's life revolved around failing, wrecked people with difficulties of a completely different order, found it hard enough to believe that one of his well-heeled friends had employed a private investigator, never mind that two of them had.

"But surely you can tell if he's been to Milan or not?"

"Well, he sent me receipts for his flight and the hotel but, as Odile pointed out, all they show is that he paid for a flight and a hotel, not that he used them."

"He sent you them? You mean you haven't seen him since, well, since he left?" Stable, serious Ernest sounded shocked.

"But what's the point, Ernest? I don't want him back, I'm not going to get hurt again. He had a relationship with that *salope*. I had no idea she even existed, of course I didn't, and he can't explain it away. I don't want to hear any more pathetic lies about her, that's all." Ivy realised that this had been her consistent position ever since she had first read Jim Ames's report, ever since she had first seen the pictures of her husband with that unknown girl. So why was she talking to Ernest about it, here, walking through a rough part of north London? Had the resolution of Emma's self-harming, with its resonances of their previous successful partnership pushed her towards a change of heart? Were these new doubts on the fundamentals of the case a cause on their own, or were they also an effect? Ivy realised that she was there in Islington talking with Ernest because she no longer felt secure in her deep, injured certainties.

"So, you're living alone in the Chelsea house; where's he living? With the *salope*?" It was a reasonable question in the light of her accusations. She shuddered.

"No, according to Jerry, he's by himself in a nasty little place in Hammersmith."

They were walking from Ernest's modest flat towards the high street, in search of a cab for Ivy. Ernest, a mild-mannered man in a stressful occupation, was feeling something close to anger at his friend and her wayward husband. They were passing along a street of once-prim, single-family Victorian houses, now mostly converted to multi-occupancy, with multiple vandalised doorbells and labelled letter-boxes, and basement flats accessed past overflowing bins down battered stairs. Someone had come up with the bright idea of installing thick cement planters on the windowsills, East-European utilitarian c. 1973, but no plants grew there except some straggling weeds. Most of the doors were painted the same bruised blue colour and the windows replaced with uPVC frames. The buildings carried the many neglectful signs of communal property, of a collective owner with more important things to worry about than architectural niceties. Loud reggae music could be heard thumping forth from one of the basements. This, and streets like it, were Ernest's place of work, the people who lived here his clients: unmarried mothers in abusive relationships, serial petty offenders feeding addictions, precociously mature children alternately caring for, and fleeing from, the adults in their lives. People with real problems.

Royal Bank of Scotland Offices, London, September 2008

The two bankers could hardly have differed more. Edward Bald was unchanged; slim, youthful, enthusiastic, eloquent. His colleague, Fred Judd, had the unhealthy look of a man who consumed too many meat pies, one whose mother had never taught him to eat his greens. Whilst Edward was tall and smartly dressed, Fred was short and shaven-headed, his shirt buttons straining, pasty flesh visible in the gaps between them every time his loud acrylic tie slid off centre. He kept tucking it back into the creased waistband of his trousers. James could not help but feel that the physical discomfort of his constraining clothing might explain Judd's irritability. When he spoke, despite his effortless use of banking technical-speak, it was like listening to a small-time East-End crook. Peter told himself not to hold his accent against him, but Judd did not seem like the kind of man who cared much for the opinions of others anyway.

Edward Bald and Peter had argued about RBS covering the costs of their unsuccessful attempt at refinancing some or all of the bank's loan, and Peter had been more assertive than diplomatic at that time, but there

was no hint in Bald's demeanour to support James's fears of poisoned relationships – except possibly this sudden appearance of Fred Judd, who was
inaccurately introduced as a senior banker on the Small and Medium-sized
Enterprises Team and who had enough demeanour for both of them. He
had an unconvinced look on his face as Peter and James went through
the presentation they had prepared, announcing the early draw-down of
the final $7 million and requesting the bank to consider extending the
interest-only period, during which Rareterre would not make any capital
repayments, explaining why this was a good idea. Peter and James were to
grow familiar with Judd's unconvinced look.

"You say that the draw-down request has formally been made?"
Edward asked.

"Notification," said Peter. It was not a "request", the word implied
RBS had discretion to consider and decline. This money was part of the
facility, the draw-down was a process agreed in advance which, as Peter had
repeatedly explained to the board, was legally binding.

"I have the papers right here," said James quickly, handing over a
plastic sleeve containing the draw-down notification and the signed decla-
rations from the directors regarding observance of all covenants. Was there
a reluctance in the way Edward accepted the papers?

"We are a little bit surprised at the timing of the draw-down request,
James," said Judd, emphasising the word "request". "Li'ul bih". Peter
wondered why he could pronounce the "t" at the start of the word
"timing", showing his mouth and tongue to be capable of the required co-
ordination, but not those in the middle of "little", where their presence
rendered the word so much prettier and easier to say. "Your cashflow
forecasts show Rareterre needing the money later, in December, not now."
"Lay'ah". Neither Peter nor James was keen to tell these bankers that they
were there prompted by fears for the financial viability of their bank. There
was no polite way of saying "we want the money fast whilst RBS is still
good for it". Judd had put on his most unconvinced face yet.

"And as for the request to extend the interest-only period." "In'erest". Judd again emphasised the word "request". "It seems early days to be saying that the covenants look tight when they were only agreed 18 months ago." "Eigh'een mumfs".

"Well, we needn't have mentioned it, but I'm sure you like responsible clients better, ones who confront matters, try to look ahead and avoid potential problems before they happen, Fred," said Peter lightly. "We don't need an answer on that point now, of course, but it would be great if you could process the draw-down without delay."

"What we like better, Peter, is not to have matters to confront at all," Judd replied heavily. There were so many glottal stops truncating the Ts in this short sentence that it sounded vaguely Arabic. Which was odd, given that what Judd most brought to mind was a bruiser from one of the nastier far-right, racist political parties.

The Restaurant at Harvey Nichols Department Store, London, September 2008

Ivy folded her napkin, pushed back her chair and looked at Max. Handsome, honed, arrogant Maximiliano. He bore a resemblance, she thought, to Gaston from Disney's version of *Beauty and the Beast*. He was also a crashing bore, that much was clear, although his social skills were wholly irrelevant to her specific purpose in meeting him.

"So, you're saying that my husband and your girlfriend…"

"Ex-girlfriend."

"My husband and your ex-girlfriend enjoy a purely platonic relationship. They are not having an affair."

"They are not having an anything. He does not see her. She is sad."

She swallowed, marshalling her thoughts. Clarity. Lack of confusion. Lack of the potential for confusion.

"They are not having an anything. When they did have a… a relationship, it was platonic?" She drew a breath. "No sex?"

Max gave her an impassive look, one eyebrow raised, which said "Are you mad? Have you seen her? Have you seen *me*?" Ivy could not be entirely sure whether he was confirming her purposely blunt description of Peter and Kiara's relationship, or merely finding it impossible to accept that someone of his majestic youthful beauty could possibly be usurped by anyone, far less a man in his fifties. She tried again.

"How would you characterise their relationship then? Father and daughter? Mentor and protégée? Gym buddies?" She added this last possibility although she had no idea what it meant. It reminded Max of the humiliating "it's Gaston!" scene in the club room, an episode that still angered and confused him. Since then he had told himself that he was finished with Kiara anyway, and indeed when they met, as occasionally happened in their small social circle of Italian expats, his coolness reflected this, his reality. But at the time, her clear preference for spending time with Peter, a preference that apparently went beyond the emotions of a recent row, had been hard to understand and impossible to accept. Drawing on the great inner strength of the truly arrogant, the egocentric analysis that cannot contemplate personal shortcomings of any sort but rather ascribes all negative outcomes to the failings of others, Max concluded that Kiara was deranged. "If she doesn't want me anymore, if she's keener on chatting and laughing over smoothies with that old man, she's certainly mad." He frowned.

"No. Not father and daughter." He had given little enough thought to the precise nature of their relationship; after all, she was mad and so her motivations required no further analysis. But now that Ivy was asking him, and clearly it mattered to her, he realised he had the perfect analogy in his own family. His uncle Francesco had remarried and started a new family with his second wife, creating four half-siblings, two sets of two. Not an unusual scenario, but as a result Francesco's eldest son, Leopoldo, who was 30, had a 12-year-old half-sister, Claudia, with whom he had an unusual, mutually doting relationship. Kiara and Peter were more like Claudia and Leopoldo, Max thought.

"They are like brother and sister who like one another, but different ages. Half-brother and sister, from the same father, different mothers, whose ages are also different." Max clomped heavily through this accurate description of part of his family, but even he saw how complicated and irrelevant it might sound.

It was because of his extended family that Ivy had managed to arrange this lunch with Max. Her boss in the buying department at Harvey Nichols was a middle-aged aristocratic Italian divorcé with whom she had immediately empathised, only partly due to an approximate shared marital status. This man was related to Max, for whom he had no affection – but they were family from a culture where family matters. In the months since she had started her "proper job", and once she had understood that his occasionally physical familiarity was not flirtation but rather simple Italian warmth, they had become friends and, ultimately, confidantes. In response to a tale of his wife's infidelities, Ivy had ended up showing him a copy of Jim Ames's report, and he had immediately recognised his cousin's girlfriend in the damning pictures. The mono-chrome image of Peter with Kiara never failed to induce anger, if not equal to that when the report had first arrived, still sufficient to keep alive the idea, persistently promoted by Odile, that divorce was the only honest way forwards, despite her religious beliefs.

But when her boss exclaimed, "But this is Kiara, my cousin's friend!" she had seized the chance to increase her knowledge of Peter's crimes. She felt confident Ames could have caught Peter *in flagrante* but recognised that her actual evidence, whilst convincing, lacked substance. At her request, it was arranged for Max to lunch with Ivy at Harvey Nicks' restaurant, and here he was pedantically identifying the genealogy of what seemed to her an unlikely comparator relationship for Peter and – knowing Kiara's name really did not help at all – that girl.

Max was just trying to be helpful. Ivy had invited him to seek an analogy that would explain his understanding, so she took his complex familial metaphor in that spirit, but thought better of exploring any further. Her judgement was that Max would never have been able to accept the fact of Peter and his girlfriend enjoying a sexual affair – he seemed to have found his perception of a platonic one insufferable enough. Besides, she knew her husband, she knew men, she had read Freud. Any relationship with that girl could never be completely sex-free in any heterosexual male imagination, whatever the realities. She had extracted all she was going to get from Max, she saw that. She looked at her watch and stood up.

"Oh, look at the time! I must get back, or your uncle will sack me!"

"Second cousin, once removed," corrected Max. "His great-grandfather was my great-great-grandfather." Ivy was not interested. Max had taken his jacket from the back of his chair, risen and was embracing her on the left cheek, stooping to do so, one hand lightly on her shoulder, his finely-honed musculature evident beneath his shirt. An innocent social gesture, if a fairly recent import to Britain from southern parts where the climate and the blood are warmer.

With a sudden flash of realisation, Ivy saw how a photo of this moment might appear.

Chiswick, London, September 2008

Ivy was enjoying her work and recognised that she had Odile to thank for the impetus that had driven her to apply for the job. She also understood that Odile as a counsellor was unlikely to support her in anything but the most hard-line handling of her marital situation. She went to see Fulki.

"It's just that *physically* he was perfect, Fulki, I mean, I felt almost guilty having lunch with him. He looks like, like... well, if I were the sort to search for a toy boy he would fit the bill perfectly."

"But boring, you say? Surely you wouldn't want a boring toy boy? You'd want to have a good time after, apart from, oh, as well as going to bed with him. Or is a toy boy just a piece of meat? Where's the interest in that? Besides, isn't it demeaning to use him for sex and nothing else? Wouldn't Odile count that as exploitation or 'objectivisation' or something, if the roles were reversed?" Fulki was no more the kind of woman to look for a toy boy than Ivy herself, and she was surprised to find herself defending their rights to be treated as human beings, not sex objects. Ivy sighed; Fulki was missing the point.

"Yes, boring. Fulki, I actually found myself *understanding* why that girl might prefer Peter. But Max told me that Peter and..." She still did not want to say the name, calling her Kiara made her more a person, saying "Peter and Kiara" turned them into a couple. "And his girlfriend, ex-girlfriend, were not actually y'know, *doing it*, that their relationship was platonic."

"Was?"

"Yes, that's the other thing he said. She has not seen him since..." Ivy realised she had not asked Max when the not seeing one another had started. "He said she was sad," she finished, sadly.

Rareterre Plc's Offices, Hammersmith, London, October 2008

In early October, Standard & Poor's downgraded its rating of RBS. Austin immediately emailed the board with the news, cut and pasted from their announcement, adding no comment of his own. Everyone on the board, with the possible exception of Olivier, knew and understood his opinion.

"The rating actions reflect Standard & Poor's expectation that RBS's financial profile may continue to weaken," he quoted them, citing "a combination of mixed earnings prospects, deteriorating credit risk in its key geographies, and difficult market conditions in which to shore up its capital."

"RBS have asked for another meeting?" Even down the telephone from his moving car in rural North Carolina Frits's voice sounded concerned. "And they have still not honoured the draw-down request? I hope there is not going to be a problem, Peter."

"Draw-down notification, Frits. I wish everyone would stop calling it a 'request'. And no, there can be no problem, as I've said a thousand times, they have no legal choice but to pay the money," Peter replied testily. "The delay is something to do with currency hedging, you know, the loan being in dollars and our books in pounds. James says that it is an issue at their end."

Frits wondered why Peter had called to tell him that there was no problem, and wished he had given more credence to Cassandra Austin and his perceived portents of doom. As his car swept past a ploughed field it scared up a crowd of migratory birds into a wheeling, complaining, airborne organism.

As he returned his handset to the cradle Peter also wondered why he had called Frits if there really was no problem.

Traversing London, October 2008

Fulki and Jerry were driving across London south to north, Chiswick to Finchley, no small undertaking at any time of day. Fulki knew that she had Jerry trapped, a prisoner behind the wheel of his Jaguar, unable to escape her interrogation for at least the next hour. She had in the past employed this means to secure his attention – not exactly undivided but impossible to withdraw – and Jerry was already feeling cornered as he pulled out onto the A4, heading east on the Great West Road.

"It's just that he's been so consistent, never shifting from a simple denial that he really had an affair, Jerry, but surely…"

"They should call it the Great East Road in this direction. Or perhaps the Little East Road for additional clarity." He looked pleased with himself. But he had not diverted Fulki.

"Whatever, Jerry. I saw Ivy the other day and she's quite miserable. Have you seen Peter in his bachelor pad recently?" As usual, the common friends of the divided couple had themselves split into camps. Peter's miserable rented flat in Hammersmith in no way merited the term "bachelor pad", with its carefree connotations of parties and concurrent superficial relationships. Jerry let this pass.

"It's like when you're going to Putney on the Upper Richmond Road. What's that all about? Going west to east they should call it the Upper Putney Road. Or maybe even the Lower Putney Road, for additional clarity."

"Oh, do shut up about road names, Jerry! Have you seen Peter?" She decided to risk a revelation. "Ivy is beginning to wonder if she has been altogether fair. She only has a few pictures of Peter with this girl, and although they look pretty bad, they are not really... conclusive." Since her chat with Ivy, Fulki had also begun to worry that Peter was being unfairly accused, and that her introduction to Jim Ames had been instrumental in this injustice.

Jerry had never seen the private detective's report himself, but remembered Peter saying that in addition to some photos it included an inaccurate observation of his entering Kiara's flat and not leaving again. Jealous Jerry had however seen Kiara across a busy pub, in his memory not just sitting close to Peter but almost entwined with him, attentive only to him, taken. So his friend's protestations of innocence had not really convinced him. But then one day in March when he found himself in the Earl's Court area – checking out a grimy, struggling pharmacy he was considering adding to his chain – he had taken it upon himself to confirm that the mansion block where Peter said Kiara lived did indeed have a mews-type exit behind, conveniently leading to Earls Court tube station. But even so, Jerry, the most dedicated warrior in Peter's partisan army, was not fully persuaded: his mental picture of Kiara with Peter in the Marquis of Granby was impossible to dismiss.

"Of course I have seen Peter. And of course he's unhappy. He's been unhappy ever since Ivy chucked him out. And yes, he has been consistent,

just as consistent with me alone as he is with you and the others on…"
he was going to say "on Ivy's side" but that sounded too childish. Fulki
pursed her lips.

"But what do you actually think, Jerry? Do you believe he didn't have
an affair with that girl? She was pretty bloody attractive. You haven't seen
the photos, Jerry, but she looks like Sophia Loren in that film you really
like, *La Ciociara*, 'Two Women'. It is hard to believe Peter is so innocent
as he says." Jerry, who had seen more than photos of Kiara and knew
her name from Peter, was shocked at the exactness of the image and the
sound of Kiara's name in the way Fulki pronounced *Ciociara*. He thought
it unlikely that this choice was made by chance.

"What do *you* know about Kiara? You and Ivy get together, with Odile
and the rest of the crew, and stoke one another up into a mutually confirmatory frenzy of condemnation, just because Peter knows a pretty girl!"
He was getting up a head of male-solidarity steam. "All your evidence is
circumstantial. You jump to conclusions and poor Peter is found guilty
without his day in court! Do you know how often he has seen Ivy, been
able to make his case, in the last – what's it been, eight, nine months? Zero
times!" He was conveniently forgetting his own assumptions, not fully
dismissed even now, concerning what effect the attentions of a woman like
Kiara would have on a man like Peter, like himself, like anyone.

"Kiara is it? That's her name? You know this girl too, do you, Jerry?"
It had been pure chance, but her mispronounced choice of *La Ciociara*,
and Jerry's naming of Kiara injected something new into this discussion,
something related to the far less exotically named Trish, Jerry's bookkeeper,
who had not looked at all like a sexy 1960s film star. Trust is a fragile
structure, easily damaged and hard to repair.

Jerry was trying to manoeuvre his Jag to the correct side of the
Hammersmith roundabout. "Do I *know* her Fulki? What are you implying?
Bloody hell!" A small man in a pimped-up car on his left, stony-faced,
edged forwards despite Jerry's indicator, to spite his shiny XK. Fulki was

unsure if the "bloody hell" was aimed at her or the small man. "I know a girl's name and suddenly I *know* the girl? I'm not sure what you mean, but you seem to be implying that I too have a relationship with her. It's ridiculous. You knew her name too, Fulki, so what are you... ?"

"I did *not* know her name, Jerry. Neither does Ivy. But this is not about you, it's about Peter. Peter doesn't deny knowing this girl, how could he, but he did keep her secret from Ivy for God knows how long, until she, she... found out about her." The little man in the pimped-up car had his little victory and Jerry finally made it onto the Shepherds Bush Road.

"I don't know what's worse, Fulki, your assuming that everyone who knows this girl's name is having it off with her, whatever that says about the sisterhood, about female solidarity, or that Ivy has chucked Peter out on such flimsy evidence that *she* doesn't even know the girl's name!"

Fulki thought about Jim Ames and the shabby world he inhabited, rooting around in other people's dirty laundry – sometimes literally, she imagined – and the possible inadequacies of his report to Ivy. She had introduced this unreliable element into her friend's life, blowing oxygen on the sparks of Ivy's suspicions. Yet it had all seemed so irrefutable, those photographs, that night-time observation of the girl's flat.

They were at Shepherds Bush, a miserable, tatty triangle of grass surrounded by multi-lane roads loaded with discontented, slow-moving traffic. The signal changed to green; ahead of them a car from the right had jumped the lights and was blocking the junction. Uncharacteristically, Jerry drove aggressively up to the side of the offending vehicle, sounding his horn and swearing.

"Jerry, what's the point... You know, the detective Ivy hired, well, he did see Peter going into the girl's flat and not come out all night." The traffic started moving again; Jerry belatedly took his hand off the horn.

"Hang on, Fulki, you're telling me that this bloke saw Peter *not* do something. Oh, that makes such sense, Fulki! What else did he see Peter not do? Solve Fermat's Last Theorem? Climb Everest without oxygen? Perform

Elgar's Cello Concerto?" He could have carried on but he was not making sense himself, he realised. Peter could do none of these things, observed or otherwise. Metaphors failed him. "Did he see Peter not go to bed with Kiara? Or did he just not see Peter leave by the back entrance ten minutes after he arrived?" Fulki was looking uneasy. "Well, did he, Fulki? Did he?"

They had arrived at an incongruous bit of elevated motorway striding over the town as though, propelled by its London-bound momentum, it had been projected beyond its natural end, the Westway. They were heading east. Jerry said nothing.

Royal Bank of Scotland Offices, London, October 2008

It was three weeks after James had handed over the $7 million draw-down notification that he finally heard back from RBS, although he had sent emails to Edward Bald enquiring, in his mild manner, when the final instalment on their loan would be available. Peter suggested that he bring the bank's attention to the terms of their agreement, which stipulated the timeframes for transfer of funds, but James viewed this as unnecessarily aggressive.

"If the boot was on the other foot and we failed to observe the agreement in any way, if we paid the interest late, for example, we would pretty quickly find out how aggressive RBS wanted to be," Peter opined. When Bald did finally respond, the tone of his message was quite unexpected; he did not so much invite as summon them to a meeting.

Obediently, Peter and James turned up at RBS's Bishopsgate palace on the date notified, rather than requested, by Edward Bald. It was a dull October day, the low featureless clouds seeming to press down on the City. In the vast reception area the atmosphere was similarly depressed; the wall of interlaced flat-screens, normally alive with images of successful, smiling bankers going about their lucrative business, was blank. In the days immediately preceding their summons, the RBS share price had dropped by half, to 85p; somehow investors had decided that what was worth over £30 billion days earlier should actually be less than £14 billion. James thought that maybe this was why the screens had gone dead, perhaps only companies worth over £20 billion were allowed such costly brashness, maybe there was a right-to-arrogance threshold that RBS had slipped beneath.

Markets are really little more than an apparatus for information evaluation. Liquid markets, where it is easy to buy and sell the commodities traded, are efficient, well-oiled machines which grind up and process all the information available to produce just one thing: a price. So much goes into the machinery, so much intelligence and energy, sentiment and analysis, greed and fear, 24 hours a day and all around the globe! Clever people, unorganised yet collaborating, industrious ants in the ant hill of capitalism, a massive disaggregated effort to produce just one intangible output. So much distilled into a number. In the days leading up to Peter and James sitting gloomily gazing at a wall of dead video screens in Bishopsgate, the machine had lurched, groaned and spat out a number for RBS's share price which was one half the value of a week earlier, one sixth the value of a year earlier.

The information evaluation machine may be highly efficient but, like any other machine, if the raw material fed into it is bad then so will be its product. Down the road from Bishopsgate, in the wood-panelled gentility of the Bank of England, real information was being generated and diligently concealed: nearly £40 billion of taxpayers' money was being provided to RBS just to keep it in business. Soft loans were secured against dodgy assets, loans that no disinterested third party would ever advance to so bankrupt an entity as the Royal Bank of Scotland. This toxic information had to be kept quiet, otherwise RBS would come tumbling down, all £1.9 trillion of it, and with it would come the whole economy. The desperate men in the wood-panelled rooms had good reason to be secretive, but they made a fool of the markets, they knowingly fed sows' ears into a silk-purse machine.

Over the following three months, the share price of RBS would divide by six again and only be saved from falling to zero by the further enforced generosity of the British taxpayer: businesses like Rareterre with their employment taxes and VAT and corporation tax, people like Peter and James with their income taxes and VAT and duties. Peter and James who sat, summoned as if to the headmaster's study, wondering about their seven million dollars.

Wine Bar in Fulham, London, October 2008

Of course Ivy knew Peter's improbable story of leaving Kiara's flat by the rear exit, bound for the airport, cough mixture in hand. When she had confronted him with the Ames evidence and he had angrily given her this explanation, his part-guilty/part-wronged demeanour combined with the photographs to submerge both him and the story in a sea of visceral, pressing certainties. She had given it no further thought, his having spent the night with that girl being so consistent with the undeniable (and undenied) fact of his having a secret relationship with her. Ivy's assumption was that many such occasions had existed, invented business trips with a clandestine carnal intent.

It was Fulki who had provided Ivy with the resolve as well as the instrument, Jim Ames, to act on her original suspicions. Odile, in her role of supportive friend, happily confirmed Peter's shortcomings and those of the male sex in general, and provided Ivy with the fuel to continue her journey through unresolved separation, a journey with divorce as the best destination. But it had been Fulki who started the engine.

"What do you mean, he may be telling the truth?" Odile snapped. She put down her glass with such force and imprecision that half the contents slopped out. The very idea was unthinkable.

"Jerry and I were talking about it…"

"Jerry!" Odile spat out the name. A Peter clone. "He's hardly the most reliable witness is he, Fulki? He and Peter are thick as thieves, they are both men, with all that that entails." The three of them were seated at a small round table, a bottle of Muscadet in the middle. Peter and Jerry might be as thick as thieves, Ivy thought, part of Ali Baba's gang, but she, Odile and Fulki could be mistaken for the opening scene of *Macbeth*.

"Jerry pointed out that Ames only had circumstantial evidence."

"You talked to Jerry about Ames? You, of all people?" Ivy was aghast. She had kept Ames's identity from Peter; it had been Ames's request, but anyway she did not want Peter pouring scorn on her source, nor – although it seemed unlikely – seeking reprisals.

"I'm sorry, Ivy, I don't know how it happened. We were in the car and I wanted to see if what Max told you, about things being platonic between Peter and that girl and it being over between them was, was... consistent."

Odile crossly picked up her glass. Three drops of wine from the wet table dropped unnoticed onto her jeans. She did not know where to start. "Fulki, how could you possibly imagine that talking to Jerry about anything, but above all anything to do with Ames, would confirm or deny or throw any light whatsoever on anything, anything... " It was worse than Odile knew. Fulki had not revealed Ames's identity to Jerry at the time of Trish the Bookkeeper either, nor had she since, until the car trip to Finchley. Odile was still spouting. "You might as well ask Newt Gingrich if he supports Christian family values." Bad example. "You might as well ask Tony Blair if Bush's invasion of Iraq was a sound and justified move."

"I didn't ask Jerry anything, not like that, I just wanted to get him talking." He had certainly talked, when the pieces fell into place, eastbound on the Westway. It had been three years since Fulki had confronted him with his affair with Trish – he had admitted it and faced the music. But the detective work delivered by Ames had been replete with errors and omissions – in fact, the bare, stark truth of the central allegation was almost all there was of any accuracy. The rest did not matter and, as things developed, mattered less and less. But no one likes false accusations, and when Fulki revealed to him that the same investigative genius had been behind his own problems, it opened in Jerry a sluice of pent-up injustice, which he redirected to the service of Peter's possibly more deserving, and definitely more contemporary cause.

They were nearing Finchley on Hendon Lane when Jerry, summing up his extensive case, said, "So you were so satisfied with the work of this chap, Ames – this man who assured you I was in Rio with Trish, when in fact she was in Crouch End General Hospital with her irritable bowels and I was in Bognor at the Pharmacy Investment Specialist Seminar – so satisfied with him that you recommended his services to Ivy? And his word is to be believed rather than Peter's? Give me a fucking break." He rarely swore to her. "Give Peter a fucking break."

Royal Bank of Scotland Offices, London, October 2008

Edward Bald, Rareterre's relationship banker, had always been punctual and polite. He was the man at RBS who knew the company best, the man who a year previously had invited Peter and James for a long weekend skiing in Val d'Isère – both had declined, not just uncomfortable to accept corporate hospitality on such a scale, but also worried about with whom else they would find themselves in enforced cheese fondue-sharing bonhomie – and that was before they had even met Fred Judd. But punctual, polite, corporately generous Edward kept Peter and James waiting nearly half an hour. He seemed on edge as he nervously accompanied them in the lift to a lower floor than normal.

Edward led the way not to one of the smart client-impressing conference rooms accessed via a further layer of reception-security, but through a busy open-plan office subdivided into cubicles full of unhealthy-looking young men and women, a battery farm of junior bankers, to a glass-walled internal meeting room. Between the gap-toothed, unaligned vertical fabric blinds four people were visible already seated at the table: Fred Judd was one, and Peter was surprised to recognise urbane, bald-headed Arthur Swallow, the Partner at Masondo who specialised in the extractive industries. As an emerging mineral extraction company in an exciting sector, in the good times Rareterre, and hence Peter and James, had been marketing targets for Arthur Swallow: invitations to industry events, mutual backslapper dinners in swish Park Lane hotels at which Masondo sponsored one or more overpriced tables, shiny unsolicited publications with the Masondo logo on every page, go-karting evenings. Arthur and his team had once even worked gratis for a time on a potential acquisition for Rareterre.

Bald showed them into the room. James and Peter both shook hands with Judd and Swallow.

"Arthur! What a pleasant surprise." Peter wanted to ask, "What the hell are you doing here?" but was inhibited by generations of British breeding. Also British, Swallow knew anyway that there was no pleasure in the surprise.

"Let me introduce you to Aaron Benz, my Partner in the corporate recovery department." Benz was a tall Dutchman with incongruously unkempt curly blond hair. Peter and James exchanged glances.

"Corporate Recovery? Isn't that a euphemism for bankruptcy?" James blurted out. Benz inclined his head slightly, his look assenting but implying that there was much subtlety lost in James's crude question. Peter wanted to say, "What the hell is *he* doing here?" but again, didn't. Judd was speaking.

"This is Sam Slight, he works with Richard." He gestured towards the satisfied-looking young man near the door, the only person to have remained seated. Neither Peter nor James knew who Richard was, but the tone in which Judd said the name suggested that they should. Bald had disappeared.

The satisfied-looking young man extended his hand. He spoke in a North American accent. "I work for Richard here full-time but until last month I was on secondment from Masondo, so I know Aaron and Arthur well," he said, comfortably.

Peter was feeling anything but comfortable. This meeting about their final $7 million draw seemed to be morphing into a Masondo/RBS corporate recovery family reunion. Everyone sat down, Slight and Judd leaving an empty place between them at the door end of the room; Peter and James facing them, flanked by the two Masondo partners. James remembered that the Masondo partners' charge-out rate was £600 per hour and glanced at his watch. Assuming them to have arrived half an hour before the time he had been told was set for the meeting, someone was already £1,500 in the hole for this.

With a palpable impact on the already uneasy atmosphere in the room, a lean stoat of a man wearing an expensive suit made an entrance, closely followed by Bald. Must be Richard. He was carrying an A4 black-bound notepad and a Mont Blanc ball-point pen. He sat in the empty seat between Slight and Judd and with precision placed his notebook square on the table, the pen neatly parallel. Sam Slight simpered.

"This is Richard Videur, Director of the Corporate Restructuring Unit here," he announced. Videur raised a pair of jaded, glassy blue eyes and gazed disapprovingly across the table. He had made no attempt to shake anyone's hand. An expectant silence fell, a few seconds passed, truculently.

"So, rare-earths. Not much interest in that. I mean, I hardly read about rare-earths in the newspapers every day." Videur looked around the table as if expecting a round of applause. His voice was nasal and his attitude was superior sneer. "Rare-earths does not seem to me to be a business for the future." He sounded poorly educated and what he was saying was ill-informed, yet the communal body language in the room loudly declared his authority. Swallow, the sector specialist, shifted awkwardly. Videur transferred his gaze back to Peter, eyes challenging yet uninterested. He expected a response but did not care what it was.

"Well, you and I obviously read different newspapers," said Peter, trying to correct Videur without implying that he was completely ignorant. "Arthur here can no doubt let you know about the importance of rare-earth elements to the modern green tech and communications industries." He looked over to Swallow, who remained mute. Peter continued, "And the strategic need for non-Chinese supply." He looked again at Swallow who was inspecting his biro.

"That's all very nice, erm..." Videur made a show of recalling the name. "Peter. All very nice. But we have a different problem. There is a credit issue. It goes to contractual solvency." Peter glanced at James who looked as mystified as he himself felt. Rareterre was not insolvent. At Bald's request they had brought with them financial projections under various scenarios demonstrating that the company could and was expected to remain able to meet its obligations as they fell due. Things were tight the following September certainly, tight but doable – subject to RBS advancing the final $7 million.

James cleared his throat. "Maybe you have not had the time to look at the cashflow scenario analysis we sent over yesterday. It quite clearly does not show a position of insolvency, meaning it does show a position of solvency..." Videur was making a dismissive gesture with his right hand, as if dusting dandruff off the table. He stopped when James ceased talking, and held his hand, palm up, towards Slight.

"It goes to solvency because Rareterre has entered into negotiations to reschedule its indebtedness." Slight was scrabbling in a pile of papers and pulled out a fat document bent back against its staple, open at a high-lighted section, and proffered it to Videur. Videur ignored him, he was looking at Peter in a contemplative way, an emperor considering the worth of a blooded gladiator. "Read it out to the gents, Sam."

Slight replaced the document, the loan agreement between RBS and Rareterre, on the table in front of him and started to read: "Clause 24.6 Insolvency. Sub-clause (a). A member of the Group—"

"Yes, Sam, no need for the whole thing," Videur interrupted.

Slight, lips moving silently, found the relevant sentence. "… Member of the Group… blah blah blah… commences negotiations with one or more of its creditors with a view to rescheduling any indebtedness." He looked up, triumphantly, a diligent schoolboy asked to read his essay to the class. "It's an event of default!" he affirmed severely, giving Peter and James a slit-eyed judgemental look he had been practising.

Peter felt a peculiar sensation, something similar to elation whilst being the opposite of elation. Self-preservation, fight or flight hormones flooded his neuroendocrine system. His pulse raced. Time slowed down.

An event of default meant that the loan agreement could be terminated by RBS, they had no further obligations under it. But there had been no event of default.

That was what this meeting was all about. RBS had no intention of advancing the final $7 million and thought they had found a legal excuse for refusing, putting the blame on Rareterre. That was why they had prepared a playground gang of Masondo partners and specialist bully-boy bankers.

It was RBS that was in breach of the agreement.

Excused with a lie.

"Commenced negotiations with which creditors?" Peter asked, knowing the answer, surprising himself at how unemotional he sounded.

Videur bristled. "With us. Last month, immediately after making a draw-down request you had a meeting with Edward and made this presentation." Unbidden, Judd held up one of James's PowerPoint slides detailing their desire for an extension to the interest-only period. They were like a synchronised swimming team, these three.

"Thought so." Still unemotional. "Two points. One: that discussion was just that, a client discussing the future with its bankers. Not a negotiation. Two: I very much doubt that the creditors in the clause Mr Slight just read out can include RBS. How would a client ever be able to discuss anything with you if that was the intended meaning?"

352

Videur looked at Peter with his best approximation of pity. Poor deluded soul. "That's not our legal advice. You a lawyer, are you, Peter?"

Peter and James did not know that RBS was bankrupt financially: few outside the panelled rooms at the Bank of England did. But morally? Morally this big, boastful, bullying bank was indisputably bust.

Rareterre Plc Offices, Hammersmith, London, October 2008

"What does Julian Marian-Smythe say about it?" Frits snapped, interrupting James's flow, part technical, part plaintive, explaining how Rareterre's financial life had been shortened to a few months by RBS's aggressive reading of the loan agreement. Frits was thinking about the 300 employees of the company, innocent workers who were entitled to rely upon their senior management to keep their employing company alive, who were dependent on them to continue to provide for their families. He was thinking of the shareholders, who devolved responsibility to the board, entrusting them with managing their investment, their savings. So much trust, so much responsibility.

"We have not talked to Julian." Peter cut across James's response. The four of them, Peter, James, Olivier and Austin, were sitting together in their horrible Hammersmith offices, everyone irritated at the hastily convened late-evening emergency board meeting, Frits and Freddy represented by the star-phone in the middle of the table. "The situation is too… unclear to discuss with Julian yet."

"What do you mean, unclear?" asked Freddy, a geologist whose tectonic world was one of rocks, geological formations and mineralisations laid down over millions of years, not unreliable bankers, legal interpretations, and vital loans that were there one minute, gone the next.

"Well, RBS did not declare us to be in default of the loan agreement. They just said they *could*. They claimed we *were* in default but they were not *calling* the default." James was not helping Freddy much. "Really all they did was establish a basis on which to refuse the final draw," he said, trying to summarise. Freddy was still bemused.

"Well, are we or are we not in default?" asked the geologist, reasonably.

Austin, who had predicted trouble and was more familiar with the workings of banks than anyone else present, was nevertheless surprised by the tale Peter and James had told. Despite being the sort of cynical realist that denies oxygen to any sort of optimism, leaving his more upbeat colleagues feeling stupid and naïve for daring to voice their aspirations, even he was shocked at the hostile route RBS had chosen to take. Unnecessarily leaning towards the phone and speaking in a raised voice, he tried to explain the miserable realities to Freddy.

"I am of the view that we are clearly not in default, but it almost doesn't matter whether we have defaulted or not. The reality is that RBS claim we have triggered an event of default by negotiating a change in the terms of the loan, so they are withholding any further payments under the agreement. In their reading of the situation, they are even entitled to demand immediate repayment, perfect their security, appoint reporting accountants and call in the receivers. In this relationship they are the strong ones, we are weak. I'm sorry, but that's the reality and we have to deal with it."

"But if we're not in default then they are acting illegally with this claim that we are! My God, they charged us enough in fees to enter into the agreement – that's theft, fraud… These guys should go to jail! Surely the law exists to make them perform their side of it? Or is the UK today encouraging gangster behaviour?" Frits, who did still retain some idealism in him, was spluttering.

"We are *not* in default then?" asked Freddy, still determined to establish some facts.

Peter was reliving the deeply disturbing organised crime vibe at the Bishopsgate meeting earlier that day: Sam Slight's rehearsed, slit-eyed condemning look, fat Fred Judd flatulently confirming the "negotiation" with a creditor – RBS itself, Richard Videur taking sadistic pleasure in introducing him and James to the realities of life as the small customer of a big lender in trouble. He wondered if Videur beat his wife. If he had a wife. The Masondo boys silent; Edward Bald missing-in-action; Sam Slight explaining, with further detailed reference to the loan agreement, that RBS was entitled to insist that Masondo conduct a review into the financial condition of the company, work to be paid for by Rareterre; the acrid smell of stitch-up, a solemn Bald showing them out of the building, an undertaker escorting the bereaved from the crematorium.

"RBS are stronger than us and what they have done is establish a basis on which to beat us up," said Peter. "They have not formally called the default – for that there would be a letter notifying us – as to do so would almost guarantee they'd never get back the $33 million they have already lent us. It's mutually assured destruction, so instead they take a weasel-word path." Richard Videur's stoat-like face haunted him, saying "you a lawyer are you, Peter?" in his sneering voice. "That's why we haven't yet talked to Julian. You know what he'll say, with his Nominated Advisor hat on. He'll insist we make an announcement to the market that we are, at the least, in dispute with RBS and do not currently have access to the final $7 million. That would throw into doubt our 'going concern' status. If we make that announcement we might as well throw in the towel. Our customers will start looking for alternative sources of supply, afraid we'll be going bust and unable to ship them the ores they need. Our best employees will send out their CVs and we'll quickly lose them. And the shareholders will panic and sell off, so the share price will drop to nothing.

"So, with their trumped-up event of default, RBS hope we will take whatever drastic action we can to fill the $7million hole and ideally pay them back into the bargain. As Austin has been saying, they have a shot balance sheet and putting us on the rack makes a small contribution to repairing it." He stated all this quite matter-of-factly, although he felt an impotent rage. It might be the reality, but it was wrong.

Austin added a bleak big-picture explanation. "We are experiencing a global financial crisis. The banking system is screwed, balance sheets have been destroyed. Governments are busy bailing out bust banks everywhere. The normal rules of capitalism do not apply. People are desperate. It sounds like the people at RBS are particularly desperate. We can apportion blame, put up a fight, but it's a bit like fighting a tsunami. It might seem unjust to us, but little Rareterre hardly matters."

Peter and Frits were on opposite sides of the Atlantic but on the same side in their inability to accept that anything excused RBS's illegal behaviour. Neither spoke.

In modern Britain it should not class you as a hopeless idealist to expect corporate law to trump the law of the jungle. It was all wrong.

CHAPTER 14

South China Sea, October 2008

Corporate law and the normal rules of capitalism have not applied in China since well before Mao Zedong pulled on a pair of hiking boots and set off on his extended walk. Neither mattered very much to Captain Fènnù, the Chinese master of an ageing blue fishing trawler that wallowed in the swell of the South China Seas, being circled by modern Japanese coastguard ships. He could have approached the disputed waters around the Senkaku Islands either to fish or to provoke; he might have been there by accident or with intent. Maybe he rammed not one but two government vessels of a supposedly friendly foreign power by mistake. Not very likely, but his government would later claim as much. Perhaps he had anger management issues and, being a fisherman from Fujian not a consultant from California, did not have ready access to vital psychiatric support. Maybe he just did not like how shabby those nifty modern Japanese ships made his own tired, rusting trawler appear in comparison, sharing the same shining sea. Maybe his catch was disappointing, his wife fat and unfaithful, his bones arthritic; maybe he'd just had a bad day. Maybe he was a radical nationalist.

Whatever the reason, in a welter of spray and black smoke, and to the furious and loudly amplified objections of the Japanese officers aboard his targets, he spectacularly rammed two Japanese coastguard vessels in disputed Japanese territorial waters and was, unsurprisingly, arrested and his ship impounded.

This small maritime incident and the travails of Rareterre, as it battled against a corrupt and bankrupt bank on the other side of the globe, were oddly connected; both ended up as precedents in the realists-law casebook of "might is right". And both would have consequences for the supply of vital rare-earth elements to the manufacturing industries of the West.

As Peter and Olivier had pointed out in countless presentations, China was by far the biggest producer of rare-earths, representing over 95 percent of global supply, a matter of great concern for those in the USA and elsewhere, where the strategic importance of these elements was all too well understood. Quite apart from the green and high-tech applications that were projected to consume rare-earths in ever-increasing quantities, there were the needs of the defence industry. All good reasons to invest in Rareterre and for Rareterre to invest in its Trillium Lake facilities, Peter and Olivier explained to investors.

Japan was the biggest importer of rare-earth elements, with its high-tech manufacturing giants gobbling them up to meet world demand for their shiny consumer goods and low-emission vehicles. Poor Japan, so chock-full of clever and hard-working people, so devoid of natural resources! Dependence on imported raw materials should not be a problem in a world where trade is governed by the World Trade Organisation, but then not everyone observes the WTO rules.

China and Japan both lay claim to the Senkaku Islands. As with all such territorial disputes it is an old story, and thus emotional. When Captain Fènnù suddenly and rather inexplicably decided to use his old ship as a battering ram and a blunt means of expression, it seemed likely that his motivation and his message must have something to do with sovereignty of the Senkakus. China's response to his arrest would confirm that view.

China was still getting used to the idea that it was massive economically as well as demographically, that its importance to the trading world was huge and growing. It was still getting used to mattering for reasons not associated with worries about dirty nuclear weaponry and an expanding population. Supposedly communist, openly capitalist, its economy an uncomfortably evolving system of pragmatic state sponsored capitalism – China was like the biggest boy in the class, an adolescent confused as to his sexual orientation, beginning to realise that the other pupils are frightened of him, but not yet decided that it is better to be respected than feared. This China responded to Japan's incarceration of Captain Fènnù by throwing a ham-fisted punch. They suspended all exports of rare-earths to Japan.

Such is the joy of operating a state capitalist economy – you may flout the rules of the WTO and those of the market, make disruptive decisions with one eye focussed on a territorial claim and one on the economic long term, and throw in a whole load of testosterone focussed on showing the world that you're not to be messed with. Through this, you can make whole foreign industries shudder, industries you would rather like to have more of at home.

Despite the rare-earths connection, China bullying Japan over mineral supplies and RBS bullying Rareterre over its loan agreement might seem very different, not just in scale. But both incidents involved the breach of some fundamental laws, the observance of which permits business to be transacted; the alternative law of "might is right" never has and never can result in long-term prosperity.

China had been using its monopoly over rare-earth supply with one eye on the economic long term for years, mercurially restricting exports, building stockpiles and trading favours. This was the reason the price of these materials had risen, the reason Rareterre and White Crag and the rest were frantically scrambling to reopen production, investing to the limits of their means, the reason governments from Japan to the USA were encouraging them.

Captain Fènnù was not even a pawn in this game, but when he was released, rare-earth exports to Japan recommenced. Chinese state capitalism had won another small victory and an antisocial behaviour pattern was rewarded. The real game was much bigger and had hardly started.

Lawyers' Offices, The City, London, October 2008

"I'm pretty sure that RBS have not had legal advice on this," said James to Jean Cape, the world-weary lawyer sitting opposite him. Peter nodded. The new characters on the scene at RBS seemed perfectly comfortable with their own sort of legal interpretation, without troubling to get it blessed by someone actually qualified in the law. They had all the qualifications they needed right there on the team – Richard Videur was Emeritus Professor of Client Maltreatment, Judd had an MA in Borrower Intimidation and Slight was studying at the Open University for a degree in Advanced Commercial Bullying.

"Actually, they are not really taking a legal position. It's more of a Realpolitik position. An 'I'm doing this because I can and what the hell are you going to do about it?' position. Oh, sure, they are basing their refusal to lend on a legal agreement and the whole argument is supposedly about enforcement – or not – of the agreement. But in the end, can we win a legal battle? Can we actually force RBS to lend us the money? Do we have the time or resources to take them on?"

Peter felt the energy drain from him; maybe Austin was right, perhaps they should just read the writing on the wall and devote their energies to meeting RBS's objective of having Rareterre fund itself through means other than by access to the RBS balance sheet.

Cape looked at the two men with pity. She had seen it all before many times. In fact, she had just seen it that very morning, when another angry and dejected finance director had sat exactly where James was sitting now and told a very similar story. She did not even feel the satisfaction she knew her partners experienced from the healthy flow of fees that the financial crisis was providing to lawyers like her, specialists in banking law. Once the banks had started to move into self-preservation mode, trying, by refusing credit to their more humdrum clients, to repair balance sheets damaged by ill-considered derivative exposure to exotic sub-prime mortgages and the like, a whole support services industry had quickly sprung up. Banking and corporate lawyers, accountants specialising in corporate recovery, company doctors, insolvency practitioners, outplacement agents: a pack of hyenas quickly forming to feed off the wounded creatures created by banks like RBS. Jean Cape owed a duty to her partners, but took little satisfaction from it.

"It probably won't surprise you to hear that you are not the only ones," she said. "RBS is particularly bad, they are getting a bit of a reputation, but they're all at it, the big banks. Credit lines are being pulled, overdrafts withdrawn overnight, perfectly good, well-managed companies are being put under. Of course, what Rareterre should do depends on the financial options open to you."

"We frankly don't have any currently," said Peter, thinking bitterly of Austin's year-long refrain about the risks of their sole reliance on RBS. "We never expected RBS to behave like this. We've been banking with them since the start, nearly ten years now. We've paid them millions for things with names like 'arrangement fee' and 'commitment fee': it's a British bank, not Sicilian!" His witticism, a comment he had made several times in dismissing the risks, now felt hollow; the Cosa Nostra could learn a thing or two from RBS. Nobody smiled.

"What about equity, issuing more shares?"

"With the share price so low it'd need to be too heavy, too many shares. Besides, until the permits situation in Oregon is sorted out there's zero demand, no one will invest."

"In that case you have no alternative but to fight. My advice to you is this: One: don't accept Masondo into the company to carry out their accountants' report for RBS; you deny the solvency point and so letting them in looks weak. Two: get a definitive legal view on the contractual position from the best QC in the field, I'll write a briefing and set up an audience. Three: write to RBS immediately rejecting their position and reserving your rights. I'll prepare a draft."

Wall Street and Midtown, New York, November 2008

Jay Andersen called Dylan Winslow, a short conversation across a small distance, Wall Street splendour to midtown down-at-heel.

"Hi, Jay Andersen here, Jay from Bloom & Beck. How's it hangin'?" Jay was too intense a person to do "laid back" well.

"Oh, hey, Jay. Everything's cool, thanks," Dylan replied guardedly, wondering to what he owed the honour of this call.

"I just noticed your client Rareterre's share price. It's in single digits! Man, that must hurt! You know what the market's saying at these levels? It's telling your guy Mount that he should have done a deal with us when he had the chance."

Jay's antennae were twitching; he had seen Peter Mount on a funding road-show and heard no more from him. He knew that the company relied on a large loan from a troubled Limey bank, the same bastard bank that he'd heard on the grapevine was trying to pull out of a considerably greater $300 million credit facility to his friend Dick Veroof. The Rareterre share price was that of a near-bust company. Jay sensed there was money to be made in all this misfortune.

"I hear ya, Jay, but you can, like, understand it from Peter Mount's point of view?" Mild Dylan made a question of the statement. "If they get their Conditional Use Permits back then the company will be worth what it was before. More even, given the way prices of rare-earths have been going."

"Yeah, well that's a big 'if', Dylan. A very big 'if'."

But Dylan was right. The mine at Trillium Lake alone would be worth 20 times the current value of the whole company if the CUPs were reinstated. Combine the business with Bloom & Beck's mine at White Crag and the cost savings and pricing power could multiply that by five again. A hundred-bagger! How often do you see a hundred-bagger? Jay's next call was to Dick Veroof.

He looked at the phone on his desk on B&B's executive floor and thought for a second. This was too good for sharing. He called Veroof from his anonymous cellphone.

Rareterre Plc Offices, Hammersmith, London, October 2008

Frits was worried. Sitting opposite Peter, he looked tired and stressed; he had been ever since the Oregon State Mining goons visited Trillium Lake and Rareterre's vital permits had been revoked. Frits would have worried even more if he had known about Peter's domestic problems.

"You propose refusing to let Masondo in for the review RBS have demanded?"

"That was the advice we got. Letting them in looks as if we accept their claim of a breach, because that's the reason they have the right to insist on a financial review."

"But we don't have anything to fear from a review, right? The numbers stack up, right?"

"Yes, it's all good." Peter was irritated; Frits should know that the draw-down formalities included a certificate from the directors affirming the company was still expected to be capable of meeting its obligations. "We are off budget, thanks to the impact on our plans of the lost permits and the costs of the work to get them back. But we're still compliant with the covenants. You know that. You know James and I had to sign a declaration. Or do you think we would have put our names to a lie?"

"Of course not. But you still think that a rescheduling of the repayments would be a good idea, right?"

"It would relieve the pressure, yes – but asking for that was the cause of this whole mess. It's off the table. Those bastards at RBS have very effectively taught us not to step out of line…"

"And the QC confirmed our legal position, right?" Peter was irritated, and not just because Frits had started punctuating all his sentences with an unnecessary interrogatory "right?" which was oddly offensive, but also because he was himself unsure how useful the QC's opinion would ultimately be.

Middle Temple, Royal Courts of Law, London, October 2008

Peter and James, accompanied by Jean Cape, went to see Justin Arche QC, who, Cape had assured them, was widely considered London's best barrister specialising in banking law. The cost was £5,000 for a one-hour audience. "But of course he has to read the brief and all the preparatory package we sent," she explained, "and write up his opinion. RBS certainly know Arche and cannot ignore an opinion from him." She said opinion with an implied capital "O". When the three of them turned up at the Middle Temple she was in a state of ill-contained awe.

"I love it, 'Middle Temple'," said James. "It sounds not unlike something from Tolkien. I wonder if it is ruled by the Dark Lord Sauron, or ever was?"

"Or will once again be," said Peter, more grimly than he intended. "Maybe we'll see Gollum slithering away under a bench if we keep our eyes open!"

"Actually, it's governed by the Masters of the Bench," said Cape, inattentively.

Masters of the Bench, Law Lords, the Lord Chief Justice, Inner and Middle Temples, Senators of the College of Justice: so much tradition, jurisprudence, so much infrastructure, so many acute and highly trained minds focussed on the rule of law! As he followed Jean Cape through the quiet gardens of the Middle Temple, autumn light filtering through the branches of mature trees, buildings reminiscent of Cambridge colleges, Peter suddenly felt that everything was going to be fine. The Middle Temple was physically a few miles from RBS's Bishopsgate headquarters, but morally it was in Tolkien's wholesome Shire. Bishopsgate in contrast was at the heart of Mordor, seething with malevolent powers. Rareterre were in the right, they would be confirmed in the righteousness of their cause, the smoothly running machinery of British justice would click soundlessly into gear. Everything was going to be fine.

James, Peter and Jean Cape were shown into a spartan vestibule, then through to a businesslike meeting room. James was a little disappointed that the table was not antique mahogany, and the walls not panelled and hung with oil paintings depicting generations of wise wigged heads. Exactly on the hour Justin Arche appeared. Jean looked as if she might faint. Arche had a thick file in his hands and Peter was pleased to note it was well-thumbed, bristling with yellow Post-it notes. Arche was a trim man in his late fifties, had unusually long hair and a neat beard, and looked not unlike the picture of Gandalf the White in James's boyhood copy of *The Hobbit*. James made an unsuccessful attempt to dismiss the image.

Arche spoke in clipped, precise tones and used fluent, precise language. He quizzed Peter and James on points of detail, flipping rapidly from Post-it note to Post-it note. Finally, he pushed his bundle to one side and clasped his hands before him, upright and symmetrical.

"There are three points to consider. One, is Rareterre solvent? You have told me it is. Therefore paragraph 24, upon which the bank seeks to rely, is wholly irrelevant, because it is governed by the heading, 'Solvency'. Two, and subsidiary to one, were negotiations entered into? What you have described to me and the materials you provided do not support an interaction with RBS that could qualify as a 'negotiation' as defined in the Oxford English Dictionary. Three, and subsidiary to the other two points, can 'creditors' be meant to include RBS? For the reasons argued by Mrs Cape here" – Jean looked like she was about to be transported to a higher plane – "it would be impractical for such an interpretation to pertain, and it should not. There has not been an event of default. RBS are in breach of the Agreement."

Fifty-seven of their 60 minutes had passed. The wizard had spoken. He spent the final three minutes outlining the legal means by which Rareterre could most quickly fight its case and enforce its rights under the agreement with RBS, and was gone.

"Oh, thank you," said Jean Cape to his departing back, leaving off the implied "my hero". Peter was pleased that, of the three points Arche had highlighted, he – "you a lawyer, are you?" Peter – had voiced two in the meeting with Videur. Peter could barely dare acknowledge the relief he felt. He could feel his shoulder muscles relaxing. He was going to enjoy the next showdown with RBS.

"We don't have the time, by which I mean the money," James said bleakly. He slid his notepad over to Peter. These steps Gandalf, I mean Arche, outlined, the "rapid legal path" he suggested we consider – they add up to four months, even if there are no hitches at all. Without the $7 million draw four months from now we are out of money, even before the legal costs are taken into account."

Cape and Peter looked deflated, differently.

"I told you, realpolitik," Peter said bitterly. "Let's send the bastards Arche's written opinion when we get it anyway. But the reality is: we're too weak for a fight. We're too weak to see justice done. And they bloody well know it."

Royal Bank of Scotland Offices, London, October 2008

Justin Arche QC's opinion, product of the most acute, experienced and highly trained mind in his field, was dismissed by RBS without even a metaphorical wave of the hand. Lofty Videur, too important to deliver such a message personally, let it be known via his minion Slight that it was in the nature of the law to produce conflicting views, and the bank had received advice of its own in conflict with Arche's. Austin Roach, ever the realist, pointed out that in London you could probably find a lawyer who was willing to express pretty much whatever opinion you told him to express, for the right fee. An increasingly disillusioned Peter did not even ask RBS for a copy of their legal opinion. If he had, Videur would have refused. It did not need to exist to have its impact.

Despite their weary lawyer's advice to the contrary, realist Austin and reasonable James conspired in persuading the board to allow the accountants Masondo to come in and do their investigation for the bank. James still thought RBS could be made to see reason, and that if the final $7 million were to be drawn the results of Masondo's work would be necessary in bringing the bank around. He was completely wrong about this; Masondo's work was at best box-ticking to validate a decision already made. At worst it was two huge service organisations conspiring to fuck over a small client.

Peter discussed it with Frits; they agreed that the fact of an ongoing accountants' investigation added weight to the story already told to Julian at NOMAD: that the position with the bank was "under review" and therefore not something about which Rareterre needed to make a stock exchange announcement.

During the course of an extremely costly process – this time the fees were not negotiated with the directors of Rareterre but rather imposed by Masondo via their friends at RBS – there were occasions where Masondo's indifference to conflicts of interest was near breathtaking. It was this rather than RBS's own breathtakingly bad behaviour that caused Peter's Explosion.

In a meeting to discuss the scope of work Masondo would undertake – a meeting Richard Videur resisted having, saying to James, via Sam Slight, words to the effect of "what the hell makes you think you have any influence over this process?" – Peter raised the possible sale of an asset, a small but profitable silver mine Rareterre owned in Peru. He mentioned it because it threw light on the value of Rareterre, value Videur missed no opportunity to disparage. Videur, flanked by Slight and Judd, looked to his right and left. James wondered if they always worked in packs, like wolves pursuing a deer. Videur's expression said "does this clown really think he's still in charge? Watch this". Slight narrowed his eyes.

"So, Peter, you're saying that you think you can sell this... 'asset'... in darkest Peru for $10 million? Might I ask, Peter, on what basis you make such a claim?"

"On the basis that we've received an offer, Richard." Actually, Peter had, over the years, occasionally received expressions of interest in the Peruvian mine – the most recent being three months earlier.

Videur sneered. "Oh, really. You've received an offer for an 'asset' we didn't even know you possessed, Peter, and now you tell us about it. Does that seem odd to anyone else present?" He looked about him, a rabble-rouser seeking crowd support. His little rabble – Swallow and Benz, the two partners from Masondo, two of their junior staff selected to work on the investigation, plus Slight and Judd – were keen to be roused but unsure where Videur was going with this. He carried on.

"That asset is *our* asset, Peter. I don't see shareholders represented here, in this room. There is no shareholder value, Peter. The value break in your company" – he paused to give Peter and James a damning look – "the value breaks well below the level of the debt, Peter." It became clear to everyone sitting there, the rabble and Peter and James, where Richard Videur was going. It was all about solvency, his claim that Rareterre was insolvent and had breached its loan agreement. *You had to admit*, James thought, *the man had consistency.*

Arthur Swallow, Masondo's sector specialist, was the only person on RBS's side of the table who knew Rareterre at all, and he knew about the Peruvian mine. It was not the fact that Swallow remained silent that pushed Peter over the edge. It was not Videur's bullying, repeated assertions of the valuelessness of Rareterre; it was what he said next.

"*If* there is an asset to be sold, Peter, then we want Masondo to take charge of selling it, subject to their normal fees of course."

Peter had been keeping a lid on a great deal of frustration and anger since the first meeting with RBS, showing a level of courtesy and forbearance to them and their henchmen that he frankly felt they did not deserve. He exploded. "Point one, Richard, there is an asset, one we are entirely capable of selling ourselves. Arthur here knows that perfectly well, and I wonder why he is so quiet. Point two, isn't it funny the way you, in the same breath, first admit you did not know the asset existed, then throw doubt on its true existence, and finally demand that Masondo lifts a fee for selling it? Point three, it is not remotely funny, however, that you repeatedly claim what you call the 'value break' falls at a point where my company's shareholders are wiped out, irrelevant to the debate, dismissed from consideration, yet you DON'T KNOW THE COMPANY at all. At RBS only Edward Bald does and he's disappeared. And Arthur Swallow from Masondo here does, but he's keeping schtum it would seem. Point four, you guys seriously don't know a conflict of interest, do you? You wouldn't recognise a conflict of interest if it came up and punched you in the face." He stopped then, savouring the pleasing image of Videur being punched in the face.

It felt good to express himself so, but ultimately it played into Videur's hands. This outburst was cited as reason for Peter to "take more of a back seat" – RBS understood that as a founder of the company he was inevitably emotional, but that meant a lack of objectivity and did not help the process. Someone less closely involved should step in and work with the bank to resolve, as far as possible, their differences. Austin Roach was well known to them – couldn't he do the job?

Everything always played into Videur's hands in the end, because might was right.

Rareterre Plc Offices, Hammersmith, London, October 2008

Peter was surprised to see Ivy's serious friend Ernest's name appear on the display of his mobile phone. He was talking to Masondo's Aaron Benz, the tall solemn Dutchman who always seemed about to declare how acutely he felt your pain, whilst conspiring to inflict it. He was a man Peter found it impossible to like, maybe because of the circumstances surrounding their acquaintanceship. Peter was glad of an excuse to interrupt the discussion to take Ernest's call. Ernest got straight to the point.

"Peter, I don't know or care about this girlfriend of yours so don't waste your breath talking about it. What I do know is that you and Ivy are behaving like kids and should get back together, and that Ivy at the moment is, would be, receptive to some sort of mature approach." He put such emphasis on the word "mature" that he might even have shouted it. Peter had never encountered this assertive side to Ernest's character before. Benz was waiting in the meeting room with his metre ticking at £10 a minute, so after a hurried conversation Peter thanked Ernest and hung up. He was touched: Ernest was always on Ivy's side.

As he left his office to cover the ten feet back to the meeting room Drew, his PA, held up what looked like a gold-coloured credit card, smiling.

"BA has upgraded your frequent flier status, Peter!" she said happily.

A thought struck him with such force that Peter forgot Benz and his ticking metre completely, and turned to Drew. "Do you remember that trip to Milan at the end of last year? Did you keep the boarding pass?

Wasn't that the time Jo made the booking and forgot to give them my membership number? You fished the boarding pass from my bin and copied it, sent it to BA to claim the miles didn't you? Was that the time?" He was yapping at her.

She did have the boarding card; he had occupied seat 23B. He possessed the means to make a "mature approach" to Ivy.

Bloom & Beck's Offices and Veroof Capital, New York, October 2008

It was lending to alchemists like Veroof, and vapourware vehicles like the Veroof Leveraged Split Strike Conversion Fund, that got RBS into trouble, not lending to little companies with real businesses like Rareterre. As it became clear to all that Veroof could not turn urine into gold, it also became clear that the highly paid, generously bonused bankers at RBS had turned their shareholders' equity capital into faeces. The bank then went about reducing its exposure with the same unintelligent indiscrimination as had gone into its accumulation. Even as it attacked little Rareterre in London, it also pulled out of its credit lines to Dick Veroof in New York.

Jay's call found Dick in a bad mood. The Leveraged Split Strike Conversion Fund was in trouble and he needed to sort it out. It was one of his favourites, the apparent complexity of its model burnished his reputation as a Wall Street alchemist, and its inexplicability – it was truly inexplicable in the literal sense – appealed to his disdain for the greedy and negligent investors who flocked to put their money, and all too often that of their trusting clients, into a fund no one understood. When amongst friends he called it the Sucker Fund. That he, Dick, should be paid a handsome fee for constructing a cleverly confusing vehicle was normal, in his opinion. That others were charging their clients for "managing their money" and then dumbly putting it into his inexplicable fund, few questions asked and none really answered, *that* really appealed to Dick's sense of superiority, sitting as he did at the head of this particular food chain.

The Split Strike Conversion Fund was a great scheme for the "wealth management" industry, as they liked to call themselves. The idea to add borrowing to the mix had actually come from one of the bastard Brit bankers. By that time, no one involved was willing or able to see the madness of leveraging up the inexplicable; it was like giving a drunken teenager a stack of banknotes and the contact details of a drug dealer. Still, so long as everyone got their fees and interest was paid on time, no one really felt like asking too many questions. And now the same bastard British bank was asking for its money back, leaving a $300 million hole Veroof was going to have to fill. Jay knew all this.

"Hey, Dick, my man!" Jay's cheery opener was already too much for Dick.

"Yeah, Jay, I'm kinda busy right now. Thanks to those cocksuckers at RBS, Retarded Bastard Slimeballs, I need to find $300 million pronto or the lid comes right off the Fucker Sund." He did not correct himself. Jay wondered if he had suffered an intracerebral haemorrhage or developed Tourette's, perhaps.

"So it's true! I'd heard, but couldn't believe it. The jerks!" Jay put on what he imagined to be a caring physician's bedside manner. "How would it be if I found buyers for your holding in White Crag? Bring you some liquidity?"

"The whole thing? I own 30 percent of that fucker, don't I? Paid $60 million. It'd certainly help."

"Oh, I don't think you'd get back a hundred cents on the dollar, Dick. Times have really changed – Lehman and Bear Stearns have both gone, we're a goddam bank holding company now, for Christ's sake! Everything's changed. But I think I could get you 50." Dick hated losing money; it made him almost physically sick. But he was in a corner, he knew it. And so did Jay.

"Fifty cents on the dollar! Thirty million bucks? Jesus Christ, Jay, is that really the best you can do?" He sounded defeated. Jay almost felt sorry for him.

"There's some of the guys here at B&B who might step in for more. But you know how tough it is – bonuses this year will be almost non-existent. Guys are being real careful." What Jay did not tell Dick Veroof was that there was only one guy at B&B – Jay Andersen – who was planning to "step in". He was the only guy Jay intended to invite.

In his years as a senior investment banker, Jay had amassed a not-so-small fortune in accumulated bonuses and investments, mostly through insider tracks such as the Bloom & Beck Principal Investment Group, which was the destination and source for most of his invested capital. The B&B Principal Investment Group was a carousel of lucrative investment opportunities plucked from the pile passing through B&B's machinery, cycling through investment to realisation and back to new investment in a leveraged upwards spiral, which amazed even Jay. He occasionally banked the winnings from one or another of the deals in which he and his privileged colleagues participated – this was how, for example, he had purchased his split-level Central Park West apartment. But mostly he was content to keep his money in the B&B money-making merry-go-round, even though the investments were illiquid, privately held company shares and limited liability partnership participations. Sure, he could not sell them easily, but he did not need the cash and where else could he hope to see annual returns of over 30 percent? 2008 had not been a good year, not even for the gilded insiders of the Principal Investment Group, but still Jay's holdings were conservatively valued at over $50 million.

At the time Jay and Lori had enjoyed a brief and mutually exploitative relationship, back when Lori was new to the investment banking game, she had once asked him why a client, universally referred to internally as "Big Al", still wanted more. Big Al was on his third everything – third leveraged buy-out deal with B&B, third wife, third billion, third chateau in France. He kept the billions and the chateaux; the deals and wives came and went. Lori was no innocent; her own career objectives were expressed in the clearest material terms: $10 million. But even she was genuinely bemused by anyone wanting to carry on, as Big Al and others like him did, accumulating. How many chateaux and billions does a man need? When she asked Jay this question, lying beside him in the Central Park West apartment, she knew from his reaction that she had failed some mysterious investment bankers' test.

"It's just a way of keeping score, Lori," Jay had explained. "Big Al can't speak French. He doesn't like French cuisine. He prefers burgers and fries. He owns three vineyards but doesn't even like wine. He's a bourbon man. I doubt he's been more than once to any of his places in France. But he had to have three because Sy Sterling has two. It's the same with the billions. Guys like that compare units; you must have heard them talk – Al's worth 30 units. Sy, at the moment, is at 25. Al's winning."

"Yes, a unit's $100 million, right?" said Lori, pathetic with her one-tenth-unit ambitions.

Even Jay did not feel he was in the same league as Big Al, but he really thought he ought to have more than a miserable half-unit. His true worth should be at least one or two units, surely? This was the reasoning behind Jay's plans for Rareterre and White Crag. The British company was struggling but was still a treasure chest of latent value, and only he, Jay, knew how to unlock it. Add that to the White Crag B&B vehicle, which he would be able to control with Dick's shares and his position in the B&B Principal Investment Group and boom! – a combo deal that got him, even after allowing for his co-owners, to two and a half units. Jay felt opportunity knocking. Times were turbulent, and he knew such times were rich with opportunity for the bold.

Using the value of his B&B portfolio and the Upper West Side apartment as collateral, Jay borrowed $30 million and bought Veroof's shareholding in White Crag. In what was, Jay thought, a delicious irony, he borrowed the money from the snobby high-net-worth individuals' private bank subsidiary of RBS, an operation consciously distant from its own proletarian parent. RBS thus both created his opportunity and funded his exploitation of it.

Veroof, who had once been a five-unit man, was not even grateful. Too bad; Jay had a plan and step one had been implemented.

James Stead's House, Chiswick, BBC Radio 4 *Today* Programme, October 2008

The woman he was interviewing sounded so out of her depth that Bill Boot had consciously to stop himself from switching to "compassionate/understanding" mode, usually reserved for the feeble-minded members of the general public, who sometimes appeared on his morning news show by virtue of having some particularly topical grievance. Despite sounding like the intimidated daughter of a Lancashire benefits cheat, this woman, however, was not an aggrieved member of the public but one of two sisters who had, through a strange dysfunction of democracy, inexplicably washed up in senior Treasury roles.

Boot pulled himself together and reminded himself that Harriet Hawk was a powerful woman, working in a key ministry at a crucial time, when billions of taxpayers' pounds were being spent in ways to which they would never have consented had their consent been sought, which of course it had not. He got back into "hectoring/bully" mode.

"Who has been advising the government on this bailout, or should I say nationalisation? You have had advice on the whole sorry affair, I take it?"

"Of course we have had advice, we went to the best available. I just want to repeat that we are only doing this reluctantly, to safeguard British savers and hard-working small businesses who rely on these banks."

She literally did repeat her timorous-obstinate assertion, word for word. James, who was listening whilst eating breakfast with his family, wondered if Hawk had it written down on a dog-eared piece of paper. His mobile phone rang. It was Peter, incandescent. James could hear Bill Boot interrupting Harriet Hawk in stereo, both through his phone and from his radio.

"Yes, yes," said Boot irritably, "so you have 'the best available advice' in safeguarding British voters' interests…"

"Are you listening to the *Today* programme on Radio Four?" asked Peter angrily. James almost felt he ought to apologise. "That woman Hawk, the one we wrote to when RBS turned on us like a rabid dog, the one who never even bothered writing back, the bloody Exchequer Secretary to the Treasury…"

Boot's questioning continued on the radio. He was definitely no longer in "compassionate/understanding" mode. "Goldman Sachs! An investment bank deeply mired in the whole banking crisis, a bank with huge financial exposure to RBS, is advising the Treasury on…"

"For God's sake, paid her salary by the British taxpayer, not even answering a letter from Rareterre, a hard-working small business if ever there was one…" James knew what Peter was going to say, similar things had already been said in the preceding weeks, but the additional bailout of RBS did make everything seem worse.

Boot had stopped hectoring and Harriet Hawk's hesitant voice was back. "… Sachs are recognised worldwide as experts in restructuring in the financial services field. They can be relied upon to act with the highest degree of…"

In James's other ear Peter was spluttering.

"… and she's on the fucking radio telling us she's investing 20 billion of taxpayers' money to bail out RB bloody S" – he put on a whining Lancastrian voice – "'to safeguard British savers and hard-working small businesses'." James had to admit the voice was an excellent caricature of Hawk, still ineptly dealing with Boot, who was now barking at her.

"Professionalism! Ms Hawk, professionalism! Expressions involving poachers and gamekeepers don't even come close, do they, Exchequer Secretary? Have you ever come across the term 'conflicts of interest'?"

The interview was over, it was straight into "Thought for the Day" with a nice inoffensive Rabbi, but Peter was still ranting into James's right ear.

"Safeguard our interests!" he was actually screaming down his phone to poor James, who agreed with him anyway. "Safeguard our interests! She's a stupid woman spending other people's money not answering their letters, bailing out banks who have no one's interests but their own in mind, and paying a fortune in advisory fees to Goldman's who helped cause the whole fucking mess in the first place. Man, they must be laughing so hard at Goldman's." He was winding down. "And at RBS. Conflicts of interest. Conflicts of fucking interest." He finished bitterly and hung up. James had not said a single word.

Government Office, Beijing, China, November 2008

In an anonymous meeting room in a grey ministry building in Beijing a group of dark-suited, white-shirted men with dull acrylic ties were arriving at a consensus decision. This was no logoed cabal planning an evil death-ray attack, doomed to be frustrated by James Bond; indeed the committee had no label at all; it was merely part of the state's capitalist machinery. Nevertheless, their consensus decision did concern a small component part of world domination.

They had considered the expert advice on the World Trade Organisation rules, and given due weight to the environmental report on the mine at Baiyun-Obo and the small-scale mining operators of south-eastern China. They had heard presentations on the five-year plans for industrial develop-ment and the desire to move up, towards the more value-added end of technology manufacturing. They had considered the demographic projections for their vast nation and analysed the data freely available in the open economies of the West on their growing rare-earths businesses. A small amount of industrial espionage was involved, mainly because it existed, not because it mattered much. The successful outcome of the maritime incident at the Senkaku Islands – which they referred to as the Diaoyutai Islands – was discussed and duly noted.

All the relevant factors had been considered unemotionally. The white-shirted men agreed their recommendations and politely left the room. All that remained to be determined was the optimal timing. Maybe the industrial espionage network could help with that.

Bloom & Beck's Offices, Wall Street, New York, November 2008

Jay had to involve Lori in his move on Rareterre; she was the obvious choice, having helped him with the White Crag deal and, as had been clear in the brief meeting with that loser Mount and his hippy friend, she had stayed abreast of developments in the rare-earths field. Besides, he still had the hots for her, she was sexier than ever and still dressed in that provocative-yet-professional way he found a huge turn on. Jay was not a man to let an old affair, even one abandoned and replaced by countless shameless dalliances, go to waste.

Even as Jay had failed to develop emotionally – and why should he? – Lori had made progress since her largely cynical involvement with him in the summer of 2006. Financially, she had advanced somewhat towards her $10 million goal, having pocketed a couple of reasonable bonuses during the good pre-crisis years – enough to feel, at the age of 25, if not financial security at least the promise of it. And then there was Montagu. Theirs was not a whirlwind romance, but one conducted against so great a challenge of time-stealing professional demands and geographical inconvenience that it might as well have been.

She had, for the first time as an adult, entered a relationship with a man that had nothing to do with her advancement. She had fallen in love at first sight with Montagu Nicodemus Montagu, a newcomer to B&B's London corporate finance department, a misfitting refugee from some smaller local outfit where his pay and bonus expectations had been, frankly, derisory by comparison with B&B. It was only after they became engaged to be married – the phrase itself giving Lori a pleasing Jane Austen feeling somehow in keeping with her fiancé's courtly style – that she had learned of MNM's family wealth, how Montagu was the only child of an unworldly professor with no use for the material accumulations piled up by generations of hyperactive colonialist ancestors. Of the many means Lori had envisioned to achieve her $10 million financial independence, playing a racially improbable American Elizabeth Bennet to some British Mr Darcy had never featured, but she loved the idea.

It was therefore a very different Lori whom Jay called into his office to outline his plans for Rareterre and the White Crag mine, the acquisition of which she had worked on two years before. Although they both played their roles to perfection – dominant, entitled, testosterone-driven senior banker and cute-but-smart junior seeking advancement – there had been a seismic shift in the power of their relationship that only Lori knew about. She no longer felt she needed him, or his approval, role playing or not.

"The way I see it, Rareterre is a busted flush." Jay could not keep his eyes from descending to Lori's cleavage, smooth breasts perfectly contained in the décolleté of a cream cashmere V-neck. "They have had serious permits issues and are dependent on RBS for their financing. RBS is a globally recognised basketcase, one of the worst, and God knows that's saying a lot."

"They came here talking refinancing, denying they needed the money but actually worried about RBS, and now you think they are getting desperate?" Lori wanted to move things along and made a mental note about wearing more conservative clothing in future.

"I *know* they are desperate." Jay did not reveal that he had bought Dick Veroof's stake in White Crag. He had acquired an entity called WC Investment 221 LLP, Dick's holding company, so there had been no evident change in White Crag's shareholder list. He should really have let his colleagues in the Principal Investment Group know, offered them the chance to participate in the cut-price deal he had struck with Veroof. What the hell.

Jay discerned something had changed about Lori. Beneath the surface a reduced deference perhaps, although sometimes chicks liked to play awkward, especially if there was some history. He could not resist the temptation to brag. "Dick had a huge problem with that scumbag bank too. I kinda helped him out. I think we can help out our English friends too. We need a financial case for the Principal Investment Group to acquire Rareterre, Lori. I know you love to write investment cases." She noted but did not question the nature of the "help" he was talking about. Lori already disliked Jay, and she was beginning to feel something deeper. She stood up.

"What about the issues with the Oregon State Assay and Mining Authority? Their permits? Surely the value of Rareterre is all about them, getting renewed permission to develop the mine and…"

Jay, still seated, was enjoying a buttock-height view of Lori's shapely, designer-clad form and wondering why he had finished with her. Again he felt a need to show off. "Oh, I think I know how we can deal with that; assume the permits are back in place, Lori."

"As an upside scenario?"

"No, as the base case. I can take care of all that stuff…" He almost winked. Lori concealed something akin to revulsion.

"Rareterre is a London-listed public company; we'll need input from the London corporate finance guys. There's one who knows the rare-earth business as well as the London takeover rules," she said, thinking of Montagu. Jay hated rules, hated detail and hated complexity. He hated the supercilious faggot-staffed London office.

"Fuck the London guy, you figure it out," he said. Lori was already doing both. In fact, Lori had things pretty well figured out before her meeting with Jay, but he had told her something she did not know. Through a friend in B&B's back office she had access to the White Crag administrative files and quickly verified what she had guessed from Jay's throw-away boast – his "helping out" Veroof was in fact through buying White Crag investment. Veroof's vehicle, WC Investment 221 LLP, was still intact, holding 30 percent of the company. Apparently, Jay had bought WC Investment, secretly increasing his personal stake in White Crag to 35 percent. *Jesus Christ*, Lori thought, *he's really gone out on a limb with this one.* She knew what Veroof had paid, and assumed that Jay must have bought it back at a healthy discount; he was not the kind of man to miss an opportunity of screwing a friend whilst "helping" him. All the same, although Lori could only guess at Jay's net worth, she correctly surmised that he had a whole lot of it riding on the rare-earths sector. And now he wanted White Crag to bid for Rareterre.

This was the final piece of a jigsaw puzzle she had been subconsciously assembling since overhearing the end of that telephone conversation in Jay's Long Island beach house. He had been talking about a "toxic blend" and was clearly uncomfortable at the thought that she might have overheard the conversation. Months later, development of the Rareterre Trillium Lake Mine in Oregon had been stopped by the authorities, after an inspection had discovered groundwater contamination. Whilst Rareterre struggled with an inflexible regulatory authority, White Crag had overtaken them and was nearing readiness to reopen full operations of its own. Then Peter Mount had visited B&B looking to raise equity financing, despite a share price bouncing off its all-time lows and despite claiming to have adequate banking lines, in the midst of the biggest banking crisis in generations.

She wrote her investment case. It was childishly easy; most merger analysis is, Lori found. Odd, then, that client corporations normally paid millions of dollars for the sort of work she now did for Jay and B&B's internal Principal Investment Group. Rare-earth prices were high and forecast to rise further; White Crag and Rareterre together would form a significant part of North American output, giving them price-fixing power; combining the operations would release synergies – bankerspeak for redundancies and cost reductions – and could be achieved with ease. Rareterre was a public company, so its value was set every minute of the trading day by the stock market; even with a standard takeover premium on the market price the whole company could be had for $20 million – about one-tenth of its value two years earlier, before the Oregon State Assay and Mining Authority unexpectedly came calling at Trillium Lake. She looked at the shareholder list and saw there were no blocking minorities; given the state of the markets and the performance of the Rareterre share price, there should be ready sellers, shareholders keen to accept hard cash for their risky stock.

Lori did a thorough job, considered all the angles, and concluded that by acquiring Rareterre the Principal Investment Group would multiply many times over the capital in an already successful investment in White Crag. Under the "risk factors" section she examined and dismissed the potential for continued or new regulatory problems, deferring to Jay's confidence on this score. Operational risks were few – both mines were opencast. She constructed a composite price index for the rare-earth ores, weighted for the relative mix of rare-earths the two mines jointly would produce – and built a financial model that showed the combined, more efficient company would be financially viable even if her index of prices fell by almost 50 percent. She analysed all the historical data available to her and found such a variation to be a four-sigma event – highly unlikely, verging on the impossible.

Conference Call New York and London, November 2008

"If it were a 'mundane detail', Mr Andersen, I very much doubt it would be positioned as Rule 1 in the City Code on Takeovers and Mergers." Julian Marian-Smythe pursed his lips in a prissy way that, were he able to see it, would have infuriated Jay even more. Man, he hated the Brits with their supercilious superiority, their use of the subjunctive voice and their wilful denial of the reality that, in the English-speaking world, they might be the old country but they were the small country too. Small, tired and rule-bound.

"Okay, maybe we screwed up, but maybe I'm making the 'Approach' now. To you, the Company's 'Advisor'. That good enough for ya?" In a successful attempt to be offensive, Jay imitated the audible capital letters that punctuated Julian's speech when he referred to elements of the Code, and made a mental note to get one of B&B's own faggot-Brits on the case ASAP so he did not have to deal with any more calls like this one. All he'd done was have B&B's trading desk buy up a bunch of loose Rareterre stock, no more than 4 or 5 percent, for about a million bucks – chickenfeed – and the next thing he knew he had some toffee-nosed, double-barrelled Brit on the line lecturing him about some arcane code.

"Well, it may be. Do you have a formal written proposal for the board of Rareterre? An 'Offer', as defined in the Code? I must make clear that you may trigger the commencement of an 'Offer Period' as def—"

"Yeah, let me guess, as defined in the Code." Jay finished Julian's sentence. He wanted to ask since when had normal people used the word "commencement" in regular speech, but thought better of it; this guy sounded like his idea of foreplay would be to switch out the lights and ask his wife whether she was "prepared for the imminent commencement of sexual congress". With a trepidation that intensified his dislike of Julian, he asked what the consequences were of an offer period commencing, as defined in the Code.

"I'm afraid we would have no option but to make an announcement to the exchange and certain clocks would start ticking, Mr Andersen. It is our quaint way of ensuring the fair and equitable treatment of all shareholders." Julian really was not trying to sound superior or threatening, it was just his fate to hit all the wrong keys with Jay, who was wishing he could squeeze down the telephone line and choke the life out of this self-satisfied bastard. "Afraid"! "Certain clocks"! Bullshit. Above all, Jay was concerned that this capitalising rule-book-maven and his Code were going to cost him money. Code! Was it the law or a bunch of clubby guidelines?

This conversation with Julian led directly to Montagu Montagu receiving a rude and somewhat panicky call from Jay, followed by a longer and far more pleasurable one from Lori. And, not long after, to the commencement of an offer period, as defined in the Code.

Restaurant in New York, November 2008

Lori met with Ed Zhang a couple of days after the bid was announced. Zhang was an earnest second-generation Chinese-American in his mid-thirties. He had graduated from law school and quickly seen the opportunities offered by a rapidly changing China to an ambitious, perfectly bilingual, perfectly westernised, business-oriented young man like him. It was only after Zhang Consulting had been in operation for three years that it became part of the Chinese State industrial intelligence service.

Zhang had been helpful to Lori at the time of the White Crag acquisition, enabling her to understand the Chinese position regarding the production and export of the rare-earths they dominated. Back then, in 2006, the unexpected state industrial espionage component of Zhang Consulting's business plan was very new – he had been approached by a nondescript man in a dark suit, white shirt and dull acrylic tie during a business trip to Beijing. His client, Jeff O'Toole, an overeager hamburger infrastructure executive from Minnesota, had been temporarily forgotten in his hotel room whilst downstairs in the bar the nondescript man in the dark suit explained how Ed Zhang could accumulate financial tokens of gratitude from the People's Republic in a secret Hong Kong bank account. All he had to do in exchange was provide a flow of commercially sensitive information, a flow Ed was uniquely well placed to access. The accumulating financial tokens were to be denominated in US dollars, and would be additional to Ed's normal income – not only could Zhang Consulting continue with its regular business, but the information flow required it to do so.

Ed could see which way the wind had started blowing, even before the West blew itself up financially with its ill-regulated, venal and incontinent banking systems and spendthrift debt-addicted governments. The money was nice, and the future: that was Chinese. All the same, for Ed Zhang, who had been brought up in New Jersey and whose views on the proper conduct of espionage were formed by James Bond and Jason Bourne, this recruitment had been a disappointing, low-key affair. Up in his room, Minnesotan Jeff hardly noticed the delay; his "Flip-o-Matic 3000" patented Teflon-coated hamburger flipping machine was anyway doomed to be quickly and cheaply reproduced in a Shenzhen factory.

Rare-earth elements were at the top of the list so far as Ed Zhang's new paymasters were concerned. It was Zhang Consulting's work for Bloom & Beck on the White Crag acquisition that first brought Zhang to their attention. This was why Ed stayed in touch with Lori in the years following the completion of the White Crag deal. He was new to the espionage business and probably somewhat inept; she was a clever and perceptive woman with an interest in international affairs. Besides, men of Ed's age who "kept in touch" were, in Lori's sceptical view, normally interested in sex at least as much if not more than business, and Ed was quite clearly gay. Lori had drawn a conclusion about Zhang Consulting's most powerful client.

This was how the nameless committee in the anonymous grey meeting room in Beijing came to know that the two most important potential sources of rare-earth elements in North America were about to merge and provide a real alternative to Chinese supply, breaking a monopoly of long duration. They also learned that as a result of this transaction the new company would be financially weak, in debt and owned by overextended shareholders whose idea of a long-term plan was tomorrow's lunch reservation.

Lori told Ed Zhang what she told him not out of sympathy for Peter Mount and the victims at Rareterre – which she felt – nor solidarity with the People's Republic of China and treasonous disloyalty to Uncle Sam – which she did not. Lori told Ed Zhang what she told him out of animosity towards Jay, who had been threatening with Montagu on the phone. His manipulation and scheming had begun to disgust her even before she became the heroine of a Jane Austen novel of sensibility.

City of London, November 2008

Like jockeys representing different owners on the racecourse, familiar to one another from frequent bouts of intense rivalry but otherwise sharing a common experience more meaningful than any relationship with their clients, Montagu Montagu, Julian Marian-Smythe and Fred Judd got to know one another rather well. In the meetings that punctuated the takeover of Rareterre – some of them seven furlongs on the flat, the going good to firm, others steeplechases with the ground soft – Montagu represented B&B, acting as advisors to the bidder, its own Principal Investment Group; Julian of NOMAD Securities acted for the target, Rareterre, and Fred represented RBS, whose position as lender bought them a place at most meetings when Rareterre was on the racecard. Of course, Montagu was under strict orders from Jay to ensure that RBS kept its loan to Rareterre in place once the company had been bought by the B&B Principal Investment Group, and been merged with White Crag. No one at B&B wanted to put in more of their own cash than they could get away with, least of all Jay, whose secretive personal exposure to the deal was huge and itself mostly borrowed.

Julian had considered telling Montagu that RBS had refused the final draw on the loan and were in dispute with the company, but thought better of it. His job was to secure the best deal he could for the Rareterre shareholders; let B&B find out for themselves, if there was anything to find out. All the circumstances were changing and it was a strange sort of dispute anyway, with the bank exercising rights due to them not in law but by virtue of their caring less about the fate of Rareterre than the company's management did. RBS was haemorrhaging money at such a rate that the British taxpayer was forcibly hooked into vein-to-vein transfusion; the bank's $33 million at risk with Rareterre was a tiny pinprick in an ocean of blood. From the start, Austin Roach, the emotionless realist, had been less keen than Peter to advance the argument that RBS was jeopardising repayment of its $33 million by putting the whole company at risk of insolvency – Peter called it the MAD, or "Mutually Assured Destruction" argument.

At the September board meeting this exchange took place:

Peter: "RBS can't credibly threaten us, fail to give the support they have to. Their security is worth squat if we go under, they'd get back maybe 5 percent of their loan. I know they're stupid, but they're not that dumb."

Austin: "But would you call their bluff, Peter? Seriously? Play chicken with the whole company?"

Peter: "You're forgetting, we have a legally binding loan agreement. They wouldn't dare."

Austin: "The trouble with your 'Mutually Assured Destruction' is that Rareterre gets destroyed. RBS does not."

Frits: "Surely Peter's right? If RBS break the agreement and we go under, imagine the publicity for them!"

Austin: "I can certainly imagine it. I just can't imagine them caring much. And we will have, as you say, gone under."

By October, after RBS had been bailed out, the insane logic of MAD was wholly in favour of the bank because, with the exception of certain discrete bonus arrangements for the bankers involved, they literally could not have cared less, whilst for Rareterre it remained a matter of life or death. At the November board meeting:

James: "Well, playing hard ball and telling them we were ready to see the company go bust rather than accept their bullying tactics, that we'd make a public stink and shame them into complying with the agreement, did not necessarily recommend itself as an option, you might recall."

Peter: "I remember the argument. But now – well, it's RBS that has gone bust… "

Austin: "Strictly speaking, no."

Frits: "But if the government had not put in, what was it, £20 billion… "

Austin: "Yes, but they did put it in. RBS is too big to fail and so it has not been allowed to."

Peter: "Let me get this straight. First, we are told that we are weak and they are strong, so we can't call their bluff on the final draw, threaten to start legal proceedings, go public about their illegal failure to perform on the loan agreement and embarrass them. So we don't. We play along. Now, here we still are and *they* are bust, but still stronger than us because taxpayers' money – your money and mine and Rareterre's – has bailed them out and kept them stronger than us? Jesus H Christ!"

Austin: "Correct. And what's more, they care even less about us, their $33 million or their reputation than they did before. They are more civil servants than commercial bankers now. Sorry, guys, them's the facts."

The race meeting at which the price B&B would bid for Rareterre was one of the short distance ones, on the flat with the going firm. Only two jockeys saddled up, Montagu and Julian. Peter, feeling a surreal sensation of exclusion, sat in a neighbouring room with James, pretending he was doing something else but actually just waiting for Julian to come in with progress reports. The best price B&B were willing to offer was 10p, a small premium above the market price on the day Jay had first spoken with Julian, and had his wrists slapped for failing to observe the Code. Julian seemed pleased with himself, although the current market price was 13.25p.

"We can't really accept an offer at a discount to the market, can we?" Peter said bleakly, when Julian left them to contemplate the proposal.

"Don't forget, only a few days ago Videur was claiming that the shares are worthless, the value break fell in the debt," James reminded him.

"God, I hate that term, 'value break'. But Videur's wrong if B&B are willing to pay 10p a share – that values the equity at £10 million, not zero." Peter inhaled nervously and remembered the time, not so long ago, when the company was worth ten times as much. He grimly thought about his mortgage. "And what the hell does Videur know about value anyway? He's never run a company. What's that Oscar Wilde thing? 'A banker is a man who knows the price of everything and the value of nothing'?"

James shared Peter's surreal feeling of being swept along, impotently observing events taking place around him. Peter was right, 10p a share was hard to swallow but the alternative – back to Videur and his value break – was equally unappealing. It was too late to go down the aggressive MAD route. Both men were tired, but James knew the inaccuracy of Peter's Wilde quotation. Rather than correcting him, he quoted back.

"'In this world there are only two tragedies. One is not getting what one wants, and the other is getting it'," he said, looking at his hands.

When, finally, they decided to recommend the B&B offer to the board and their shareholders, neither Peter nor James could have said which of these tragedies had befallen them.

Without mentioning the boarding pass, Peter asked Jerry to ask Fulki to ask Ivy if she would agree to see him. He did, she did she would – on condition that Fulki be there too.

Had it ever been in his directory, Peter would have deleted Kiara's number from his mobile phone memory, but he could not delete it from his own memory. She had called a few times since he had suddenly stopped going to her gym, but he had never answered her calls or listened to the messages. He was still raw from the injustice he felt and the anger it instilled in him, but the pictures he'd been presented with by Ivy, of Kiara embracing him and welcoming him into her home, had made him feel an understanding for Ivy – and a longing for Kiara. Recognising her number on the screen of his phone and pressing the red "reject call" button, had been an act of cowardice more than resolve. He longed for her, longed to be with her, but his desire was for something he'd never had, and probably never could.

He could not answer Kiara's call because he was afraid; afraid to find out that he could not have Kiara except as a friend, and more afraid of losing Ivy as a wife, lover, friend, partner. Afraid of failure and afraid of success, of bringing just cause to Ivy's unjust position, hence validating her anger. The longing for Kiara was, he knew, a feeling more proper to a 24-year-old. For 24 years Ivy and he had been a team, mutually supportive, confronting challenges and opportunities together, laughing and crying, sharing joy and pain.

When that first call from Kiara came he was sitting forlornly in Jerry's spare room feeling unwelcome and lost. He recognised her number and rejected the call, not only out of fear but because, forced to confront it, he knew the difference between lust and love.

All the same, Kiara's number remained in his head. When Jerry reported Ivy's acceptance of a meeting, he thumbed it in and was relieved when his call diverted to voicemail. He had rehearsed a message, and he left it.

CHAPTER 15

As Julian had pedantically and, Jay thought, rather superciliously explained, the starting gun for the offer period as defined in the Code came when B&B issued an announcement of its intention to make an offer, which took place the morning after James and Peter had tragically swapped Oscar Wilde quotations.

The City Code on Takeovers and Mergers stipulates a timetable by which certain things must happen, others are no longer permitted, and decisions have to be made. The intention is to ensure a level playing field in case others want to bid, to protect shareholders' rights and to prevent abuse of the market. In the case of B&B's bid for Rareterre none of this was really required: no one else was interested in bidding, the shareholders were only too pleased to have cash instead of their precarious equity – it might not be much in the way of cash, but at least its value would not decline every day.

According to the Code, from the moment the bid is announced the bidder has 28 days to prepare and post its formal offer document. Montagu Montagu had it done in a quarter of that time. As this was an agreed offer, with the board of Rareterre recommending acceptance, there would be a letter from Frits to shareholders explaining how the board had concluded that the offer was in their best interests. It continued to amaze Peter how little of what they fed to investors was written or said by those to whom it was attributed. A whole infrastructure of skilled and highly paid specialists – lawyers, corporate communications and public relations experts, corporate financial advisors – existed simply to put words into other people's mouths. Maybe that was why so many of the words ended up being utterly banal. No one expected Frits's chairman's letter actually to be written by Frits; some would be surprised to learn he had even read it. Montagu had the unenviable job of managing the preparation of the offer document, herding a flock of cats comprising the management of bidder and target as well as their various advisors. Luckily, Jay was only sporadically involved so Montagu and Lori had plenty of excuses for lengthy late-night phone calls. Each day, sometimes more than once, Montagu circulated drafts of the offer document to all parties.

When the first draft arrived in his mailbox, full of square brackets and black blobs for later replacement with approved text and numbers, Peter called Frits.

"Hi, Frits, I was just reading your chairman's letter. Wow, you have a boring turn of phrase!" He smiled. He normally drafted Frits's section of the annual report and both men knew how hard it was to keep it interesting, whilst at the same time satisfying the needs of the grey committee of checkers.

"Hey, I'm just an ignorant Dutchman, remember! What have I said in particular?"

"You say, 'I am delighted that with Bloom & Beck as its new owners Rareterre will be in excellent hands...'"

"I do? Well, read: 'Dear Shareholders, Bloom & Beck have lots of money and thanks to RBS we don't, so we figured we'd better follow the money and go with the Yanks'."

Peter chuckled and picked another. "'The proposed merger with White Crag is operationally rational and in the best long-term interests of Rareterre and its employees'?"

392

"I say that? Oh my. How about, 'By merging the two companies Bloom & Beck can squeeze out efficiencies and cost savings – that means you, O-soon-to-be-redundant ones – and make themselves even more money'?"

"This is the best one: 'In combination with a larger group, Rareterre will have readier access to the financial resources needed to build its business'?"

"Oh, that's easy: 'With B&B's money Rareterre can at last tell RBS to bugger off and bully someone else, then get back to the mining business.' Bloody bastards."

"I have been marking up the draft with your changes, Frits. Was that 'bloody bastards' part of it? Do you think it'll pass?"

The third draft of the offer document had a new paragraph in the chairman's letter, inserted there by B&B's New York lawyer acting on Jay's instructions. Jay was behaving like the owner of a theatre, occasionally dropping in on rehearsals, insisting on changes being made to the production, then popping back out. All the same, Montagu ought to have spotted it, the draft should never have gone out when it did, how it did. It was not even in square brackets:

```
I would like to welcome Helen Fry to the board as
CEO designate. Helen is a trained geologist and
mining engineer and has many years' experience in the
mineral extraction business, most recently as Senior
Partner at Scythia Engineering Solutions. I would
also like to thank Peter Mount for his contribution
over the years.
```

Version control, they call it. With comments coming in from many opinionated sources, people encouraged in their high self-esteem by bloated monthly pay cheques, it was hard to juggle what was included or excluded from the document. But Montagu, despite his Oxbridge degrees and overblown vice-presidential title embossed on his business card, made a simple mistake – not of editing, but of attaching the file to his email. In his defence, he had been distracted by Lori who, mid-discussion of the offer document disclosure requirements regarding RBS's revised loan, had digressed onto her very specific physical desires, and what she would be doing right then to Montagu if not separated by the breadth of Atlantic Ocean. Montagu's blood had rushed from his brain to his genitals and he had in error attached a file named: Project_BBareterre_od_1012v2SA.doc instead of Project_BBareterre_od_1012v2.doc.

For his own reasons related to the recovery of the mining permits, Jay wanted his own CEO in charge, even before the antitrust clearance process had been completed. Not that he envisaged any problems there – he knew plenty of people at the FTC. Jay had met Peter once and never would again; he was also having problems with Tim Cleary, the CEO of White Crag, and loved a quick two-birds-with-one-stone solution. He would use the takeover to get rid of both Mount and Cleary and go to Helen Fry. But no one had spoken to Peter about the intention to replace him; no one outside New York knew that such a plan existed, until Montagu accidentally sent out Project_BBareterre_od_1012v2SA. doc. And then everyone did.

Peter Mount's Studio Flat, Hammersmith, London, November 2008

On day six of the offer period, Peter sat in his underwear, elbows on his knees, at the end of his bed in his nasty little Hammersmith flat. He had made no effort to personalise it, there were no pictures on the walls, the cheap scuffed plywood furniture was exactly where it had been when he rented the place almost a year earlier. The russet acrylic curtains which, unlined, did a poor job of excluding the light, were hanging askew where the last few hooks on their plastic runners had dropped off the end of the rail. The small TV attached by a bracket to the wall was switched on, with the sound turned down. A man with big glasses and big teeth, who clearly thought himself very funny, was grinning inanely on the screen.

On the coffee-ringed table beside the bed lay the brown A4 envelope containing Peter's compromise agreement, the executive version of a termination letter, polite severance for people with service agreements, incentive plans, share ownership schemes and access to confidential information. "Compromise" – it felt like a lukewarm, shoddy, mediocre solution pleasing to no one. It felt like the triumph of realism over idealism, pragmatism over principles. They had been generous, but the compromise was all on his side: his principles, their pragmatism.

Peter compromised himself as a founder of the business, rider of the highs and survivor of the lows, denier of the naysayers, booster of team morale when his own was painfully low. He compromised himself as designer, architect, builder. He compromised himself as a leader. He had worked hard and diligently, he knew the business better than anyone, his devotion to it was uncompromising – yet to secure its financial survival he was making the necessary compromises contained in the brown A4 envelope on the cheap, stained little table in his rented, cheap, stained little flat.

A thousand petty incidents from the preceding ten years crowded his mind, to be shouldered aside by the bigger issues: the loss of the mining permits and their fruitless battle to recover them; the loss of shareholder value, money good people had invested backing him; the funding crisis caused by RBS and his failure to fight them for what was right – another compromise. His mortgage, his own unprincipled mercenary motives. His failed marriage. He had failed so many people, and now this, this new compromise, this final humiliation.

Pecking away at the fibres of his brain a flock of sharp-beaked birds filled his head, pulling at raw nerves and tearing them painfully from him like livid worms from a diseased corpse. Many more birds crowded around him, circling and cawing, fresh from a hundred cadavers across a crisis-strewn world. His mind leapt in microsecond flashes of consciousness from the inconsequential to the global: Rareterre's office lease to sub-prime mortgage defaults, to loan agreement covenants, to taxpayer bailouts, to the secretary he'd fired to Credit Default Swaps, to dead Steve Svensson to capital adequacy to rare-earth ore to interest rates to Ivy's favourite sheepskin slippers to…

He took another swig from the bottle of Highland Fling budget whisky he had bought from the 24-hour shop on his way back from the office. On the bed beside him, from the same shop, were two boxes of high-strength generic paracetamol. It was all they had.

Peter Mount cradled his head in his hands and wept.

The Mounts' House, Chelsea, London, November 2008

In her sunlit Chelsea kitchen at 8.30 in the morning, day seven of the offer period, Ivy switched on her laptop and her espresso machine, using the computer's prolonged boot-up time to grind some beans and load the little pressure vessel with coffee. Her morning routine was to read the *Guardian* online and check her emails whilst eating breakfast.

Two hours earlier, having banned Lori from calling him and after working all night, remotely accompanied by junior lawyers advising Rareterre and B&B, Montagu had finalised the offer document. Following a few sleepy approvals, at 7.30 it was electronically posted on the London Stock Exchange website and physically posted to shareholders.

When Ivy's computer finally accepted the last in her sequence of passwords and allowed her access to the internet, amongst the little surge of pent-up data released onto her laptop was an automatic email alert from the London Stock Exchange, advising her of B&B's offer for Rareterre. Since it had gone public in 2004, Ivy had followed the pronouncements of her husband's company with slightly detached interest. At first it had been exciting, like being involved with a minor celebrity, Peter's words and deeds washing around, legitimised, in the public domain. She sipped her coffee and clicked on the link to the formal offer announcement, thinking of how he had disliked this public exposure.

"I never actually said any of this stuff in quotation marks," he had told her, squinting into the screen of this very laptop in this same kitchen, when...? A lifetime ago. When they'd been happy. "So dull and pompous!"

"You mean it would have been different if you had actually written it?"

"Yes. It would have been much duller and pompouser!"

A smile had crept, unbidden, to her lips. It fell away as she scanned down to the fourth bullet point on the summary page of the offer announcement.

- **Board changes. Helen Fry to take over as CEO with effect from Completion.**

There was a quote from Peter at the foot of the announcement, pompously supporting the deal, dully declaring it to be in the best interests of the company and recommending that shareholders should accept.

Ivy had lived through all but eleven months of the ten-year Rareterre saga at Peter's side, an unacknowledged keystone in his support structure. It had been a rollercoaster of ups and downs and here it was, ending without her. Without him. As she read the words she realised that no one but she could understand how much this final insincerity must have cost him.

The sound of his Blackberry ringing woke him, but stopped before he was able to pluck up the guts to struggle upright.

On the day that the offer document was posted Peter awoke with the worst headache he had ever experienced. Somehow a small pool of corrosive fluid, concentrated acid, had collected at the rear of his skull and was eating away at the tissue surrounding it. Every movement caused it to slop and splash raw pain around his brain. On the floor beside the bed lay the empty Highland Fling bottle and, luckily, two unopened packs of paracetamol. Carefully, he reached for one.

Through the pain and a fog of half-remembered misery he tried to recall what he knew about the interaction between alcohol and para-cetamol. Fulki had explained it to them once, at one of Ivy's dinner parties. Lovely Ivy. Lovely Fulki. What was it? – trying to enhance an overdose of paracetamol using alcohol would not work, quite the opposite. Something to do with competing for the same metabolic pathways. Did that mean taking a paracetamol or two for this unbearable, Highland Fling-induced pain was also futile? What the hell. He swallowed two tablets and lay back with a groan.

The brown A4 envelope with his compromise agreement inside it was still on the table. He remembered. He did not remember. The Highland Fling taking its effect and removing both resolve and access to reason. His last coherent thought: the inconsistency of caring about being found dead in dirty underwear with the act of suicide. If things are that bad, suicidally bad, the state of your boxers is not an issue. It was an issue. Ergo, things were not that bad. Besides, he had by then completely clogged up his metabolic pathways with Highland Fling. If that was what Fulki had said. Who could tell?

The Blackberry rang again. He found it, too late, under the brown envelope. Eight missed calls. One from Ivy. In an anticipatory buzz of excitement, the Blackberry began to vibrate in his hand. He knew he was both desperately hungover and still drunk. He knew that if he answered he would talk directly to his wife, for the first time in 11 months. Lovely Ivy.

He had showered and shaved, and put on his Oswald Boateng suit along with the tie Ivy had bought for him at the San Francisco Museum of Modern Art, but Peter still looked and felt like one of the undead when he walked up the steps to Ivy's front door. The Highland Fling had mostly left his body by 11am, but traces of it remained in his bloodshot eyes, pallid complexion, gastric and overall fragility. He had taken another two of his high-strength tablets, briefly wondering if the digestion and excretion of the Highland Fling had left his metabolic channels open to paracetamol overdosing. The headache was moderated only slightly.

When they spoke on the telephone Ivy had suspected him of being drunk, but the line was not good. In fact, on the parabola of his intoxication, he was well down the right-hand side of the curve, heading back to the X-axis and a hungover sobriety; but, given that the curve had peaked at "unconscious" only 12 hours previously, he was nowhere near sober yet.

This was not how either of them had planned it. Arranged via Jerry through Fulki, they were supposed to meet at the weekend, on neutral territory and chaperoned. He had intended a "mature approach", armed with his used boarding pass and a formal introduction to Kiara, who was to be briefed. His innocence would be established beyond all doubt. He was going to tell Ivy he loved her and wanted to be back, that life without her was empty and intolerable. He was going to be conciliatory and understanding. He would accept her apologies magnanimously. It was going to require careful preparation yet, here he was, still under the influence of a massive excess of cheap alcohol, nursing a hippopotamus hangover, unprepared except for the boarding pass stub which he had stuffed into his pocket on leaving the flat.

Ivy had only jilted-lover Max's interpretation to contradict her conclusions about Peter and Kiara, but she had decided that their marriage was important enough for her to survive one suspected affair. The awkward parallelism of their efforts to address Emma's troubles, travelling emphatically together in the same direction but never intersecting, confirmed something vital to them both. The same fundamental truth underlay both their feelings: they were a life-team, parents, mutually supportive and complementary, still sharing hopes and dreams, fears and concerns; love.

By the time a couple has been married for a quarter of a century, and the hormonal chemistry has inevitably dimmed, such things define marital success. Ivy simply wanted to express this to Peter, her intentions for the planned weekend meeting were purer than his. She might or might not be the injured party, he might or might not have had an affair with a very beautiful, very young woman. Her plan, insofar as she had one, was to focus on the core truths and move on. The extent of her reaction to the Ames report establishing his freedom to operate in the field of marital infidelity, or rather the lack of such freedom, was perhaps the only achievement of their extended separation. Maybe that and a mutual appreciation of the value in what they had.

Peter, on the other hand, knew no affair had taken place and had the establishment of his innocence as an important objective. In his Cartesian male view, this was part of the equation: if he had been ejected because of an imagined affair with Kiara, proving it not to have existed was a vital step on the path to reconciliation. In Ivy's more emotional view, the apportionment of blame, guilt and innocence, were relegated to distractions from the main message.

Had their meeting gone as planned, therefore, it might well have failed. It could easily have degenerated as the couple, despite sharing a destination, took different and conflicting routes to get there. In particular, introducing Kiara, even a demure and factually on-message Kiara, into a dialogue of rapprochement, forgiveness and profound mutual feelings matured for more than a quarter of a century, would have been a spectacularly bad idea.

Lucky, therefore, that Peter had lost his job, lost his role in the company he had nurtured from birth like a child, lost most of the fortune he once possessed, unrealised, in Rareterre shares, lost the membership of most of his peer groups, got horrendously drunk and responded with an inebriated sentimental honesty to Ivy's caring call, on the morning the offer document was posted. As a consequence, their coming together in

Ivy's sunny kitchen did not involve the boarding pass, the invoking of Kiara as a risky character witness, any analysis of Peter's actions or of Ivy's. It involved an emotional pooling, a visceral sharing, a tearful embrace of their unique blessings.

Lucky for Peter that he was such a loser. It won back his marriage.

Bloom & Beck's Offices, Wall Street, New York & London, November 2008

Jay was so elated that even the experience of communicating with double-talking, double-barrelled Brit bastard Julian Marian-Smythe did not spoil his mood that much. They were on a conference call, he sitting in his New York office with its glimpse of the East River, Lori on the call from her windowless desk ten floors below, checking her emails as she listened. In London, Montagu and Julian were in their respective offices. It was a big moment; B&B had more than half the shares of Rareterre.

"So, you mean we've won?" Jay liked to think of things in simple terms, of winners and losers; he was always a winner.

"We can declare the offer unconditional as to acceptances, yes."

"Meaning we've won?"

"Meaning you have achieved over 50 percent acceptances already, so we are confident of getting to 90 percent."

"So, we've won? Right?"

Montagu messaged Lori: "OMG Monobrain! – but Julian should be clearer!"

"Well, it is unusual for acceptances to come in so quickly, institutions normally wait until day 21, to give a chance for rival bidders to come in with a higher price. Under the Code you have to keep the offer open until then in any case, as I'm sure Montagu has told you. It would seem that in this case they…"

Whilst the double-barrelled, Code-obsessed guy bleated on in London Jay suddenly had an unwelcome thought. Had he offered too much? Why was everyone falling over themselves to sell? Was he overpaying? But he, they, were only paying £10 million. Rareterre had some of the richest deposits of heavy rare-earths in North America. Lori's analysis had confirmed his own gut feel. This was a sweet, sweet deal. Combine everything with White Crag and it was fucking awesome. No need to screw the last penny out of those idiots at Rareterre, they were already selling out for a price which confirmed they had no idea of their company's true value. Still, Jay hated to leave any money on the table.

From his silence Lori sensed his mood darken. Thinking it was an Anglo-American communication thing, she stepped in as interpreter; after all, she was soon to be Mrs Montagu Montagu, she understood these Brits. She messaged back to Montagu: "Uh-oh! Jay hates this English evasiveness! Why can't Julian just answer?"

Taking her phone off "mute" she said, "What I think Jay wants, what we all want to know is, what are the effects of our 'declaring the offer unconditional as to acceptances' – why does our removing a condition serve us? Does it somehow force the non-accepting shareholders to tender their shares?"

Montagu, who also fancied he had some Anglo-American sensitivity to bring to the discussion, answered before Julian could confuse things more. He was filled with pride and affection for Lori; he loved dealing with her on business, their relationship, a secret between them, making it more special.

"It sends a message to the market that no one else will bid, so the shareholders might as well accept. Normally the 90 percent level is achieved quite quickly when you go unconditional, at 90 percent you can squeeze out the minority."[13] Jay liked this Montagu guy; he was clear. Not bad for a faggot-Brit. "I think we will be able to close the offer on day 21."

As he spoke, Montagu messaged Lori: "I would like to go unconditional with you…"

She answered: "I would squeeze out your minority…"

Montagu and Julian hung up.

"So, I win, right?" Jay asked Lori.

"Yeah, Jay. You win."

Ed Zhang had been watching the B&B bid for Rareterre closely. He had done enough research to know roughly how long the well-worn process of changing the ownership of a British public company would last. Although born and bred in short-termist New Jersey, he was genetically more inclined to a dynastic view of business; instincts reinforced by his recent dealings with his big, invisible Beijing client, the ultimate long-term planner. He was amazed at how easily the British, faced with short-term adversity, could be parted from assets of long-term and strategic importance. Zhang observed the declaration from B&B that their bid was unconditional, and knew this meant the whole thing would be pretty much over three weeks after it had started.

He sent a brief note to Beijing alerting them to the urgency in the timetable and reminding them about the dominant share of the North American rare-earths output the resulting combined company would have. They already had this confirmed from two other freelance information gatherers on their unofficial payroll, one based in London where his friends and family thought he was an unassuming bank clerk, the other a university professor in California. Zhang also repeated his intelligence on the likely financial vulnerability of the new owners of this business, information only he, through his relationship inside B&B, was placed to provide.

He wrote: "Not only are both businesses leveraged, with extensive borrowings after long periods of investment in their respective mines, but the successful bidding entity, the B&B Principal Investment Group, is owned by individuals who themselves may have borrowed their investment money. This is known to be the case of the leading investor, Jay Andersen, who plays a strategic role. In short, this is a fair-weather structure ill-suited to survive any storm."

Zhang knew his paymasters to be particularly interested in the rare-earths field and hoped they would be pleased with this latest contribution, which seemed to him a particularly valuable little analytical nugget. His secret Hong Kong account was growing nicely.

Richard Videur was keeping a tally. Nothing high tech, just an Excel tabulation with his caseload listed down the left, in a column headed "Project", and to the right columns headed "Exposure Pre", "Exposure Post", "Additional fees", "Costs", "Net reduction £m", "Net reduction percent" and "Comments". In the "Comments" column he put his bonus claim argument. Unimaginatively in line with the bank's internal name for its project, Videur had entitled the spreadsheet "DashforCash.xls". In a long career at RBS – he had started straight from school as a branch clerk in recessionary Essex, when the parent company was still called National Westminster Bank – he had never enjoyed his work so much. Cash recovery – provoke a default if necessary, additional fee generation, exposure reduction, interest rate increases. A well-defined set of tasks with easily measured endpoints, success factors he could bring into the equation at bonus time with ease and encashable simplicity.

When B&B declared their offer for Rareterre unconditional, Videur opened up DashforCash.xls and filled in the columns. It was virtually money in the bank! Not just any bank, it was money in a taxpayer-owned bank, money carrying a state guarantee against the crass incompetence of its own management. Of the many ironies swirling around RBS at this troubled time, one of Videur's personal favourites was the continued bonus expecta-tions of senior bankers such as himself; the sheer brazenness of it delighted him. Shareholders had lost nearly everything, and any prospect of renewed dividend payments was dim. Taxpayers were explicitly and implicitly subsidising the bank with billions, money they would otherwise have spent on education or the NHS, or kept for themselves. As he went about his Dash for Cash business, bullying borrowers, provoking or inventing events of default, reducing facilities, extorting accelerated repayments and additional fees, he occasionally fantasised about RBS itself being one of his projects, with its CEO Sir Fred Goodwin as one of his hapless targets.

"So, Sir Fred, this is a nice little mess, isn't it? You really went to town, didn't you? I mean, no half-measures for you! Inflate your balance sheet to a size greater than the GDP of the world's fifth largest economy, vainglorious acquisitions, squeezing every ounce from your capital ratios, keeping the best stuff off the balance sheet... what's that? You didn't do it alone? No, of course not, you had scores of millionaire acolytes helping you! Earning that much, shouldn't they be something special, your management team, you know, Fred, geniuses or something? At least the sort of person who raises the odd question as the herd rushes towards oblivion, perhaps? No? No one could have foreseen this gathering crisis? But people did though, didn't they, Fred? Some people did, just none of your highly paid, self-satisfied yes-men! Well, Fred – you don't mind me calling you Fred, do you? – well, Fred, the taxpayer has had enough and is calling the loan. Yes, I'm afraid you are in default of the 'common sense' clause of the agreement, and definitely breach the spirit of the 'greed and avarice' clause..." Shame the pay was so low at the Treasury; he could really do a good job for them.

In the case of their Rareterre exposure, RBS had agreed a reduced facility with B&B in the case that their bid for the company was successful. Videur would rather have been repaid completely, but that chap Jay had been his match. Not to the point where he resisted the "renegotiation fee" – and Videur had extracted a guarantee from the B&B Principal Investment Group itself in addition to the company's own security – but respect where it was due, Jay had impressed him in the one meeting they'd had, one hard-nosed unprincipled bastard approvingly recognising another.

Richard Videur entered $18m in the "Net reduction" column of his spreadsheet, and in the "Comments" column wrote, "Full 3 percent. Successfully denied access to balance of facility, triggering refinancing (M&A) and repayment of $10m, plus fees." $540,000 onto his performance bonus. Not too bad really, all things considered.

CHAPTER 16

Wilderness, Mount Hood, Oregon, December 2008

The bullet struck him on the back of the neck just where it joins the skull, forcing its way between the third and fourth vertebrae, penetrating the soft tissue between the bones and severing the spinal cord, killing him instantly.

Hoxie had borrowed Piet's hunting lodge – little more than a wooden shack amongst the conifers, but secluded and quiet. The forecast was for a weekend of lovely Oregon winter weather, crisp and clear, and he wanted some time to himself. As Hoxie inched his pickup as near as he could to the shack, two miles distant to the east beyond a shoulder of the mountain, Gary was crouching amongst the rocks stalking deer. Hoxie's classmate from Mr Jameson's class had spotted a large female, browsing lichen between the trees on the ridge above him.

Hoxie got out of his pickup and went back to the cargo bed.

Gary excitedly unslung his rifle from his shoulder.

Hoxie looked around him appreciatively and sniffed the cool mountain air.

Gary fumbled with his firearm.

Hoxie pulled on his gloves.

The deer, breath from flared nostrils visible in the cold afternoon sun, saw Gary and took fright, crashing off through the woods.

Hoxie leaned over the back of his pickup, reaching for a boxed pack of Bud cans.

Cursing, Gary quickly brought the rifle up to his eye, scrabbling to draw a bead on the deer.

The box of beer slipped between Hoxie's hands.

Gary lost his balance and fired off a round into the sky towards the tree tops and the descending sun. The deer was gone. The .30-06 bullet rose for 15 seconds and at a height of 2,050 metres began to fall back to earth. After ten more seconds, the bullet reached its terminal velocity of 100 metres per second.

Hoxie leaned a bit further over and grasped the box with both hands. The bullet continued to fall for a further 17 seconds.

Hoxie dragged the beers towards him.

A large grey dove with lovely black markings landed, as if called to be there, on the path to the shack: the only witness. Hoxie removed his gloves and reached across the pickup bed again. A small wet noise like a butcher's cleaver on a sinewy articulation, an abbreviated gasp. Then silence.

Gary never knew that it was his bullet that had killed his friend, unseen over the ridge. The body was found four days later when Piet, troubled by Hoxie's failure to return the key to the lodge and unable to raise him by phone or find him at home or in any of his usual haunts, had gone up to the shack and found Hoxie still slumped over his pickup. In a panic Piet fled the scene, leaping into his car and roaring back down the hairpin track, mind racing confusedly. He, Piet De Keersmaeker, was Hoxie's confidante, probably his only one, and Hoxie had foreseen this, predicted his own violent death.

Amy and Professor Palmer were together in the Hungry Possum when Piet's SUV swerved into the car park, came to a messy diagonal stop outside the door and Piet came stumbling in, eyes wild, breathing irregular. Seeing them at their usual table, he threw himself into the empty seat beside Amy.

"Dead, he's dead, shot in the back of the neck, he said something like this would happen, he said he was a marked man, he gave me a letter, a letter to release if he died. I took it, I said he could trust me, but I thought he was, y'know, I didn't think it was serious, I took the letter, I've got it. He's dead, up at my lodge. Dead." He was talking in a half-shout, everyone in his diner heard him, the room fell silent.

Amy could not conceal the sudden sting of her shock, the depth of the unanticipated pain she felt. Concern for her own safety was also present, but secondary. Hoxie was dead. Her mind sped through all they had done together, how hard he had been to like, yet how she had liked him, loved him. How stupidly constrained had been their relationship, how much better had it not been concealed. He had been so large, so alive – but she had stifled their affair, denied it oxygen, failed to enjoy it to the full. Why? Why did she let their shared misgivings about their clandestine activities, planting poisons in the ground, also infect their love? Why had he? She thought about their terrifying downhill journey in her brakeless, sabotaged car, the threatening voice on the phone. It all seemed so long ago, and the "In case of death" letters had started to feel like immature fantasist nonsense. She had not known that Piet was the custodian of Hoxie's letter. Amy was not composed, she was openly weeping, wishing for things she might have had but no longer could, wanting to curl into a ball, to escape alone and weep alone.

Professor Palmer awkwardly placed a hand on her arm and spoke to Piet.

"Tell us, Piet, tell us what has happened. Be calm. Just tell us what you know." Piet was still breathing heavily. He swallowed.

"Hoxie is up at my cabin. He borrowed it for the weekend. Said he needed to think, wanted to be alone. I gave him the keys. He and I went up there a couple of times in the summer. Now he's dead. I went up to see why he hadn't come back with the keys. He's been shot. In the back of the neck. He was lying there on his pickup when I got there. Looks like he's been dead a while. But he gave me this letter, months ago, said I was to make it public, get it published in the newspaper, if he ever died in suspicious circumstances." He was calmer now, remembering where he had hidden the ICOD letter. He would release it at once. "I guess this is exactly what he meant. He said the letter was to keep him safe. It didn't. I didn't..." he tailed off.

"Piet, are you sure Hoxie did not die in an accident – I mean, are you sure these are suspicious circumstances?" asked the professor.

"Jesus Christ, Prof! He's up at my cabin, bent over his pickup with a hole in his neck and dried blood everywhere! Hoxie didn't even have a gun. How suspicious does it have to be?"

"All the same, we should call the police, have them make a forensic investigation."

"Too right I'm calling the police! They're getting a copy of Hoxie's letter too! That's what he said to do!" Suddenly Piet did not trust Professor Palmer. He was, after all, the closest thing in Rhododendron to a member of the Establishment. He didn't know that the ICOD letter was the professor's idea. He had made a promise to Hoxie. He got abruptly to his feet and, observed by a dozen of his regular customers, headed clumsily for the stairs that led up to his living accommodation. The professor put a protective arm around Amy.

"Don't say anything. I'll drive you home, Amy."

Even the sleepy staff of the conservatively run *Mount Hood Argos* recognised that they had something special in Hoxie's ICOD letter. But it was released into a world thirsting for culprits, and no one was quite prepared for just how special, how far-reaching the effects of the letter would be, identifying as it did the arrogant bankers at Bloom & Beck as potentially involved in homicide, in addition to the less surprising wilful corruption of both local administrators and the workings of the market. This compelling mix of murder and money quickly made the story national headlines. Bloom & Beck was an investment bank universally and not unjustly reviled for three things: its greedy leading role in bringing the world's financial system to near collapse, its convenient reliance on public financial support to save its own private bacon, and its continued worshipping at the shrine of personal incentive and the bonus culture, despite these other grievances. It was easy enough to think the worst of B&B, and, like yeast in a loaf, Hoxie's ICOD letter gratifyingly added volume to the public anger towards them and, by extension, the whole banking industry.

Hoxie had been in possession of relatively few facts, but was an educated man with an imagination. His ICOD letter, tragically published after his mysterious death, was a triumph of laconic surmise which harmonised with the zeitgeist perfectly. The *Argos* ran it on the front page under the headline:

Local Native American Dies in Suspicious Circumstances
Wall Street Titan Bloom & Beck Implicated

The story spread like a virus across the local, then national, then international press. By the time the UK tabloid newspaper the *Sun* published it, a mere three days later and before the post-mortem findings were published, it had become:

Gangster Bank Accused by Murdered Native American

The report beneath this headline was a breathless account describing the extreme wealth of B&B's London-based staff, including a picture of one hapless director's "£12m Holland Park mansion". It included a reminder of previous brushes with controversy, financial killings made shorting Sterling and engineering the takeover of "national treasures", another reminder of the amount bank bailouts in general had cost the UK taxpayer, some jingoistic stuff about "feisty British-based Rareterre" having succumbed to B&B's takeover, and rounded off giving an ill-informed hagiography of Hoxie. Despite everything, the *Sun*'s angry article came closest of all the coverage to describing the overall situation that Hoxie's death brought to light.

Many of the newspapers covering the story published Hoxie's ICOD letter in full:

To Whom It May Concern

That you are reading this letter means that I have met an untimely death. You will, therefore, guess that I have reason to fear for my life and this letter, or rather a supposed desire to avoid its publication, was intended to serve as a protection of sorts. Well, it seems to have failed.

In the winter of 2006/7, I did something of which I am not proud but which achieved an end that I still believe justified the means. In order to stop the further development of the mine, and prevent the rape of my people's lands at Trillium Lake, we poisoned the groundwater locally. As a consequence, the capitalist/colonialist company exploiting the mine lost their permits and had to stop development.

We were not alone in this endeavour. We were helped by powerful Wall Street investment bank Bloom & Beck, which supplied the toxic materials we needed, and had the resources and corrupt expertise to ensure the relevant state authorities took whatever action was required to revoke the permits. Bloom & Beck

```
stood to gain from this as they owned a competitive
mine in California.
     This week an attempt was made on my life, intended
to look like an accident. I am certain that this was
orchestrated by Bloom & Beck in order to guarantee
our silence. That is why I am writing this letter. I
urge you to view my death as suspicious and inves-
tigate fully.
     Signed
     Hoxie Tomahas
```

He had not named Amy, intending to protect her, but his use of the plural would not be missed by the many who later analysed this letter closely. He did not know Jay's identity, and the identification of Bloom & Beck was more speculative than his language suggested: Amy had never confirmed that it was her old employer who had provided the critical toxic materials and the means of converting them and their actions into tangible results. But Hoxie knew about their White Crag mine and knew that B&B was where Amy had worked before escaping west; his conclusion seemed obvious to him.

The story, but not the letter, even made it into the *Wall Street Journal*, the first and most probably last time the *Mount Hood Argos* would ever get a mention there. The headline was:

Rare-earths Deal Under Spotlight
B&B May Have to Answer to FTC

The article's focus was on the business side of the story, apparently most interested in the potential involvement of haughty B&B in shabby local corruption, unfair practices aimed at reducing competition and therefore at price-fixing, and the possible consequences for the acquisition of Rareterre by Bloom & Beck's "secretive Principal Investment Group".

Bloom & Beck's Offices, Wall Street, New York, December 2008

Had any of Jay's colleagues on the B&B Partners Committee, or the board of the Principal Investment Group, by chance missed reading the *Mount Hood Argos* over their breakfast cereals, the *Wall Street Journal* article made sure everyone at the firm knew there was an issue. An issue that quickly became "Jay's Issue", as the self-preservation gene dominant in B&B's successful bankers soon resulted in a rapid distancing of the same people who so recently had been greedily attaching themselves like limpets onto Jay's deals. Jay was in charge of the Principal Investment Group and had been the most vociferous advocate of both rare-earths deals. He was the obvious person at the centre of this latest assault on their already ravaged reputation.

Laurent Tavide, successful advocate of Socialism for the Rich, whose star had been in the ascendant since he had presciently persuaded the Partners Committee to prepare for their conversion to a bank holding company, the better to suck at the teat of public subsidy, visited Jay in his office to formalise his isolation.

"You've got to deal with this, Jay. It's one thing Bloom & Beck being accused of mis-selling CDOs, or riding the sub-prime wave too aggressively, even of being responsible for bringing financial crisis down upon the world. These things we can obfuscate our way out of. But homicide, Jay…"

"That's bullshit and you know it, Laurent. Surely you don't think…"

"You know, Jay, what I think doesn't really matter. I worked for Milken back in the eighties. He was a smart guy. You know what he used to say? 'Perception *is* reality.' Perception *is* reality, Jay. We have decided to wind up the Principal Investment Group. It's a gesture. We have to make gestures these days."

Jay blinked. "It's crazy! You talk about perceptions, but that's a gesture which seems to say we have an issue, we seem to be admitting there's something in all this…"

Laurent was smiling condescendingly, holding his hands up at chest height, palms out. "Jay, Jay… look, you don't know what's been going on. We've had pressure from some very high places, Jay. Very high. People we'd rather not annoy right now. Just do what you are asked, wind up your Group, distribute its investments to the participants. Not hard, Jay, I think? Then we might be left alone to get on with business as usual. Believe me, this is a result, what I am telling you! Things could have been much worse."

The perception Jay had, in his reality, was one of being hung out to dry.

"One last thing, Jay, a tiny piece of advice, if I may?"

"Go for it, Laurent."

"In the markets, Jay, bears make money, bulls make money, pigs get slaughtered. Something else Milken taught me."

"Why, thank you, Laurent." Jay used a faux-grateful tone. He wondered what Tavide knew about the true ownership of White Crag. "I'll treasure that."

Laurent had turned to leave. "Good luck. You'll need it. You're on your own, Jay. With this dead Indian. And so much else. *Bonne merde.*"

Communist Party Committee Room, Beijing, China, February 2009

In ragged unison, rather like spectators at a football match anticipating a shot at goal, all of the dark-suited, white-shirted men with dull acrylic ties got to their feet. The door to the nondescript committee room had opened and a dark-suited man with a colourful silk tie had entered. There was something different about this newcomer, not just the quality of his clothing nor the natural authority in his demeanour, an authority derived from his elevated position in the Party. There was another authority about him, the assured authority that comes with wealth. As a Communist Party official he was not wealthy himself, of course, but somehow fortune had smiled on many members of his direct family. He had studied Marx and Engels and Mao, this silk-tied apparatchik, and knew a good bit of surplus-value-of-labour extraction when he saw it. He signalled for them all to be seated, and himself sat at one end of the long table, opposite the projection screen.

The unnamed committee had already made its recommendations. This meeting was to confirm them and get the formal blessing of the silk-tied Party official. The intelligence provided by the industrial espionage field operatives – Ed Zhang was one of many, but his advice had provided them with their decisive insight – suggested that now was the optimum time to make their move. A quick succession of recapitulatory slides projected onto the screen outlined the committee's deliberations. The final one contained five bullet points summing up months and years of People's Republic planning:

Summary

- PR dominance of rare-earth supply remains intact – for now

- Success of policy of forcing high tech manufacture to the PR via export restrictions

- Western rare-earth production imminent after intense investment
  — Leading US mines recently merged and uniquely weak financially

- Immediate implementation of Strategic Pricing Plan = maximum impact

- Capitalist short-termism is our friend!

With a curt nod the senior Party official converted the committee's recommendation into a decision. The next phase of the catchily named People's

Republic of China Rare-Earths Strategic Pricing Plan would be implemented immediately.

As he left the grey committee room and its worker-bee occupants, the senior Party official reflected that the lack of importance of catchy names somehow summed up the strengths of the state capitalist model, grimly focussed on collective long-term success. His most recent visit to the USA had officially been a "family holiday", but he had been meeting retailers and cutting out the middle-man with his daughter, whose sports-shoe empire already rivalled Nike. A bronzed Californian had explained that next year's range would carry the logo *"GFI"*, representing *"Go For It!"* distinguishing it from the current year's *"Wow!"* Most of his daughter's employees only possessed one pair of shoes, yet they would work 12-hour days to provide the Californians with their must-have *Go For It!* sneakers. He smiled. Surplus value.

Back in the committee room the instructions were issued. The People's Republic of China Rare-Earths Strategic Pricing Plan: Go for it!

B&B Offices in London and New York, Hamlyn Securities Offices, London, February 2009

"Wow!"

Stacey squinted into her computer screen. Neatly arranged in a two-by-four grid were charts showing the market prices of eight key rare-earth elements. Whilst she was out at lunch all eight had lurched dramatically downwards. Neodymium had lost 27 percent in the time it took to eat a crayfish and rocket sandwich. All the rest were down similar amounts. As she watched, the screen, refreshing every ten seconds, mapped further extensions of the downwards red lines. She clicked to the news feed.

Across the City, at his desk in B&B's London corporate finance department, Montagu's phone rang. It was Lori calling from New York.

"Have you seen the rare-earths prices?" She sounded excited.

"Good morning to you too, precious one. No. I'm on to industrial adhesives now. A Midlands company is…"

"Oh my God!" Lori was very American when she was excited; MNM had noticed this before, in more intimate circumstances. "It's incredible! That's a 40 percent…" Montagu had opened the Bloomberg news screen.

"Well, everything has its explanation, Lori. See what the Chinese Ministry of Minerals has just released?"

Ten floors up from Lori, Jay had just arrived for work, flicking on his computer before setting down his coffee cup. As the machine booted up his mobile phone rang. Helen Fry, calling from the Trillium Lake site offices out west. He glanced at his watch; it was 6am where she was. Dedication. He liked that in his CEOs.

"Jay, the Chinese have just spoiled things for us. Like, totally." Helen's voice sounded surprisingly calm to her, but Jay heard the panicky edge in it.

"Man, you're early, Helen. What do you mean 'the Chinese have spoiled things'?" Jay had spent the preceding weeks untangling the Principal Investment Group and parcelling out its investments and associated debt to his undeserving colleagues, a nightmare of tax structuring and lender negotiations, not to mention inter-partner squabbling of a most unedifying kind. What he did not need now was the CEO of his rare-earths empire, where he was not only the biggest shareholder but also personal guarantor of his large proportion of the company's debt, calling him up and sounding as if she was indulging in some sort of ham-British understatement. Jay hated understatement.

"I mean, Jay, they've just announced their national stockpile of rare-earths is equivalent to three years' projected demand. Three years! They've been accumulating quietly all the time they've been imposing those export restrictions."

Jay was fumbling with his computer passwords, his breathing quickened.

In London, Stacey was dialling a number she had never thought she would dial again. Her dislike of Carl was undiminished, and he had served his purpose as conduit of inside information on Rareterre; the company had gone, taken over for a pittance. But she was still Hamlyn Securities' minerals and mining analyst, and this was big news. She would be asked for an opinion by the traders in minutes, and Carl had foreseen this very thing. Chinese market manipulation.

Carl was at home, a victim of Helen Fry's rationalisation of Rareterre following its combination with White Crag. He had not admitted to anyone that he was unemployed, not really having come to terms with it himself. He had been alerted to the developments in the market by his iPhone. He might have foreseen the Chinese move, but he had not acted on this foresight. On their way up he had made money speculating in the shares of Rareterre and the other quoted rare-earths companies, supplementing his salary by nearly enough to pay for his more extravagant habits – the chick-magnet Italian sports car, the rented *garçonnière* in Kensington, club memberships. Greed had trumped his fear, so foresightful Carl was caught out holding more shares in C. Brown than was wise when the share price dropped over 50 percent, causing the iPhone to buzz and flash annoyingly in response to a stock-watching alarm he had set. Three taps of the screen told him why. Prices of the rare-earths C. Brown mined had fallen below the level at which they could be profitable. As he stared aghast through this miniature window onto his selected world of financial news information, the device vibrated again in his hand, announcing Stacey's call.

"Hello?" he snapped, still shocked. "Stacey?" He recovered himself. "Long time no see." Stacey felt her flesh creep but steeled herself.

"Yes, we'll have to get back together sometime soon." This sounded all wrong, what the hell was she saying? She had in mind, at most, another awkwardly defensive lunch. "But that's not what I called about."

"You called to tell me I'm right about the Chinese market fixing!" he said triumphantly. "You owe me a pound!" Stacey had forgotten about their bet.

"So I do. Is that what's going on here then? Market fixing?"

"Sure! Look, they restricted exports for years, claiming they needed the materials at home, which was just about credible, and claiming that concern for the environment meant they had to curtail certain production, which was not credible at all. It looks like they haven't curtailed anything but have been stockpiling instead."

"But everyone knows that the methods used by small-scale producers in China are horribly damaging for the environm…" She knew the feebleness of this objection before she had even finished voicing it.

"Yes, Stacey, everyone does know that, but it doesn't mean they have actually put an end to them, never mind what they say. In fact, this news today strongly suggests they didn't. Maintaining output, whilst saying they were doing the opposite, allowed them to accumulate enough rare-earths to make the announcement we've seen just now. So, what were you saying about getting back together?"

Stacey shuddered and ignored this final sentence. "Are you seriously saying that they would secretly stockpile rare-earths with the explicit intention of disrupting the market for everyone else? That sounds a bit like a crazy conspiracy theory to me, Carl. You don't suppose Prince Phillip had anything to do with it, do you, I mean in his spare time between bumping off daughters-in-law?"

"But, Stacey, just ask yourself this question: why accumulate a stockpile in the first place? And having built one, why tell the world you have it? Remember, none of their businesses are truly autonomous, there's a five-year plan for everything out there."

"So, how do they win? They have the monopoly on supply…"

"And people like Rareterre, or White Crag Rareterre as it calls itself now, were going to impinge on their monopoly. This will stop all that in its tracks. It makes no sense to finish the refurbishments or dig a single kilo of ore at these prices. You do realise how valuable the monopoly is to them, don't you? It's not just selling the rare-earth elements, but also a huge amount of additional power – strategic, industrial, political. Look at how two years ago that French company, Puissance Piles, had to relocate their high-performance battery manufacturing plant to a Shenzhen joint venture, part-owned by the cousin of some deputy minister of export affairs, just to secure a guaranteed supply of rare-earths! Not only jobs, but know-how and intellectual property were exported to China, all just to ensure access to the raw materials. If they could have bought them from us, or from C. Brown or even REM, the Chinese would never have been able to get such a high-tech foothold. Do you remember that fishing trawler captain, the Senkaku Islands incident? The Chinese got their way there too, because they threatened the supply of rare-earths to Japan – a compelling argument, as it turned out. So, Stace, when and where are you going to give me that pound?"

"So, let me get this straight." In the corner of her eye Stacey saw the head of equity trading emerge from the lift and, seeing her on the phone, impatiently look at his watch. "They push prices down to a point where the Western suppliers are no longer viable, because they observe costly environmental and labour laws which are ignored or do not exist in China, the Western suppliers exit the market, or rather fail to enter it, and the Chinese carry on exploiting all the angles being a monopolist brings them, including a good dose of cronyism?" She was thinking furiously. The equity traders would want an "elevator pitch" to summarise all this, a simple sound bite for peddling on to their investment manager clients.

"A good little summary, Stacey. Now, how's this: why don't we meet at the Royal George for you to give me my quid?"

Stacey had an idea. "Thanks, Carl," she said, and hung up, leaving him looking quizzically at his phone, the screen of which had transformed itself back into a little red window onto a world of financial pain and dire consequences for him and his former employer. Stacey turned to the head of equity trading, who by now was standing fidgeting beside her desk. "Dragon defeats St George," she said looking up at him with a smile. "China keeps its rare-earths monopoly by fair means or foul. Rare-earth extraction as an investment has a uniquely unpredictable risk profile. Avoid."

"Sounds great," said the head of equity trading. "Now come and explain it to the guys. Is it too late to go short rare-earths, do you think?"

New York, February 2009

Jay was long rare-earths. By some considerable distance, he was the longest human being on the planet. As an individual he owned over one third of the combined White Crag Rareterre business, gained through the cold-blooded bringing low of his competitors, the calculated taking of advantage, the consistent kicking of those who were down. By these means he had therefore cleverly acquired his shares at distressed prices, limiting his cost to little more than $35 million, most of which he had borrowed.

Jay's task of unbundling the Principal Investment Group, stimulated by a corporate need for distance from the accusations of Hoxie's ICOD letter, had been a thankless job with few compensations. Oregon Police's forensic unit had eventually suggested an accidental cause of death rather than murder, but B&B's need for corporate distance was undiminished – there were still the corruption accusations.

Until the Chinese intervened in the market, Jay and his colleagues in the Principal Investment Group had seemed to be the winners. In an irony that Jay would have enjoyed more had he not been so personally implicated, after a brief internal investigation and several inconsequential sackings, the Oregon State Assay and Mining Authority had reinstated the Trillium Lake Conditional Use Permits quickly after the release of Hoxie's letter. The resulting reestablishment of the mine at Trillium Lake from useless hole in the ground to attractive source of future years' production of valuable heavy rare-earth ores also reinstated the value of Rareterre, back to ten times what B&B had paid. As the new owner of the mine, the main beneficiary of Hoxie's ICOD letter was therefore B&B, the corrupting cause of the permit suspension in the first place, and the only entity named and shamed in the letter. Of the B&B group, Jay was by far the longest in White Crag Rareterre, so he was both the perpetrator and the biggest winner from this unjust stream of cause and effect.

He had thought he was well on his way to becoming a two-unit man, a cool quarter-billionaire, as befits one of the Truly Clever, and the perversion of justice through which he had achieved this would have added to the deep satisfaction he felt, but for the federal authorities. It was a big "but", even for Jay Andersen. Both the FBI and the Federal Trade Commission were investigating the events surrounding Hoxie's death, and neither seemed to be deterred by the conclusions of the forensic investigation. Jay was still alone in wrestling with his issue. Within the collegiate and supportive environment of Bloom & Beck Jay was toxic – a one-man leper colony on the 23rd floor, shunned by all.

Since the enforced winding-up of the Principal Investment Group Jay was also guarantor to $30 million of the debt contained within the White Crag Rareterre business. How they had squealed, those porcine lending bankers, lesser representatives of the species, *Untermenschen* in the banking racial hierarchy, when their beloved security was disaggregated and split between the partners in the Principal Investment Group when it was wound up! Outmanoeuvring these intellectual pigmies had been easy; relying on a foresightful bit of legal drafting in the security documentation, Bloom & Beck's guarantee was no more substantial than a holiday romance.

Apart from the lifting of the permit suspension, the one highlight during the period of winding-up the Principal Investment Group had been the satisfaction of explaining to the *Untermensch* lenders the futility of their objections at the loss of the B&B balance sheet securing their loans. Jay and RBS's Richard Videur had only met once, when Jay's B&B Principal Investment Group had taken over Rareterre, and on that occasion Videur had triumphed when he forced Jay to agree a "renegotiation fee". It was a double dip and Jay only realised it afterwards, when the finance team at White Crag discovered from their opposite numbers at Rareterre that it was RBS who had breached their loan agreement. RBS had double-dipped on fees when they understood that the new people in charge at Rareterre were unfamiliar with the history of their loan to the company, and therefore unlikely to spot the brass-necked injustice of RBS getting paid for a renegotiation they themselves had caused. Jay had spotted it, but too late, and it rankled. So when a furious Videur had called Jay in his lonely luxury leper colony, spluttering with rage at the notification of changed security arrangements regarding the Rareterre loan, he provided Jay with that rare pleasurable moment.

"You can't just do that, Jay, take away our security like this, substitute it with a bunch of individuals we don't even know."

"Oh, really, Richard. We can't? Can I refer you to paragraph 38(c) of the restated agreement, Richard?" He heard the unmistakable and rewarding sound of fires of impotent fury being stoked as Videur reread the clause. "If you like we could look at renegotiation, subject to a suitable fee of course."

"This is unacceptable. This is unprofessional. This is... unfair!" Videur shouted.

"It may be unfair, Richard, but, hey, whoopidoo, welcome to the adult world. It is certainly not unprofessional, quite the reverse, and as for acceptable – well, that hardly comes into it, does it?"

Sweet, sweet, sweet – but that had been back then, when the deal was a no-brainer, before the Chinese "spoiled things, like, totally", as Helen Fry had put it.

By chance, Jay had the same eight rare-earths price charts arranged on the left of his computer screen as Stacey who, across the Atlantic, was addressing the Hamlyn Securities equities team and explaining in easily understood George and the Dragon terms why the rare-earths mining sector was an investment best avoided. To the right of Jay's screen were the share prices of C. Brown, REM and a collection of smaller, more speculative players. Whilst he watched, the effect of Stacey's briefing kicked in and they all lurched downwards in shaky unison, little red numbers flashing briefly on the way down.

Jay had finished his conversation with Helen Fry and was sitting alone in his office looking out at his hard-won view, its scrap of the Hudson River, about 15 degrees of arc, metal-grey water between the buildings. How many backs had he stabbed, how many eyes gouged, how many rivals had he trodden into the ground for those 15 degrees of arc? It scarcely featured in his mind. What about his material wealth? The Long Island house, the split-level Central Park West apartment, the investments, the Bentley? All in hoc, except the car.

He turned to his computer screen and gazed blankly at the block of little red numbers. He knew now, with rare-earth prices as low as they had fallen, his investment in White Crag Rareterre was worthless. Both mines were nearing the end of costly investment periods, burdening themselves with debt on the basis of economics which had suddenly been rendered redundant. Debt he was on the hook to repay if the company failed to. His total exposure to White Crag Rareterre was $65 million, all debt secured on his personal assets, which on a good day might be worth $50 million. He didn't even have a wife to whom his assets could illicitly be transferred. Jay Andersen looked at his screen and knew it was all over.

That was when the door to his office burst open and in came the men with handcuffs.

There was no need for the stumbling, jacketless walk of shame that Jay was forced to take through the offices, past a shocked Betsy, down the lift, across a strangely busy reception area and out, blinking, onto a bright sunlit pavement, frozen February air megapixel sharp, through the pushy press to the police car, all the way attached by the wrist to a skinny young police officer. It did occur to Jay that he could quite easily run off dragging his puny uniformed guard with him, pulling him like a weekend bag down the stairs to the Broad Street subway. He might even have done it, but even whilst picturing a death-defying severing of his handcuff chain under the wheels of a north-bound J-line train – death defying for him, not for the puny policeman, who would rightly perish either convulsed by electrification or mutilated by the grinding train – he could not in his imagination get past the ticket barrier with the uniformed man inconveniently attached to his wrist. Nothing else was stopping him, he wanted to tell the watery youth, who was just part of the show but for Jay the personification of his humiliation.

Lori was there, in the reception area, as were several of Jay's partners, both business and sexual, in both cases "partners" only in a spun, corrupted Newspeak sense. Jay saw them, people with whom he had shared long nights of work or of pleasure, sometimes both, with whom he had been helicopter skiing and country-club lounging, sharing self-interested corporate and personal hospitality. They were not there providing support, but to be present when an "event" happened, perhaps to be glimpsed on the TV news, something to talk about in the bar, over dinner. In some cases they were there out of spite. Some even had the effrontery to cast judgemental looks, tut-tutting to their neighbours.

There was no need for this, and if asked Laurent Tavide would have claimed to be as shocked as anyone. But the FBI had enquired whether it should be done discretely or not, and the enquiry had been passed to Laurent on the same day the Oregon State Assay and Mining Authority reinstated the permits to Rareterre, the very day when Laurent had confirmed his suspicions, learning how Jay had secretly accumulated additional shares in White Crag by buying Dick Veroof's holding, without offering it to his "partners" in the Principal Investment Group. Tavide was indeed angry that Jay had implicated B&B in shady dealings, including what for a while appeared to be a homicide, and angrier still that he had been incompetent enough to let it become known. But what made him really furious was to learn that Jay had denied him the opportunity of a money-making investment; that was *unpardonable*. The FBI were given their answer and, quietly, certain people internally were recommended to secure a ringside view in the marble reception area.

Had Laurent known at the time that the People's Republic of China Rare-Earths Strategic Pricing Plan was about to be implemented, and Jay would as a consequence be ruined financially, maybe he would not have collaborated in the public humiliation of his colleague and "partner". But, hey, the guy was toast anyway, so why miss a bit of fun?

Mount Hood, Oregon, February 2009

The small community in Mount Hood was not united by Hoxie's death and subsequent events. It turned out that hard-to-like Hoxie, resentful, overweight Hoxie with his unpopular anti-capitalist views, was himself very popular. The transient unity engendered by his death, when it was believed to be murder, was only slightly diminished when the police produced a somewhat equivocal report describing the incident as "most probably a tragic accident" on account of the angle and apparent velocity of the bullet found lodged in Hoxie's neck. His funeral was well-attended and genuine tears were shed.

The impact of the ICOD letter was more divisive. Hoxie had poisoned the earth? No one liked that idea, although some were willing to concede his argument that the end justified the means. Hoxie had been behind the withdrawal of the permits at Trillium Lake, in cahoots with Bloom & Beck? Those whose employment depended on activity at the mine were not interested in arguments about means and ends, and you did not need to be a card-carrying communist to disapprove of collaboration in any form with the universally despised investment bank. The members of the Trail 26 Conservation Society were particularly disturbed to learn how close they had been to such wrong-doing.

Amy had not been named in Hoxie's ICOD letter, but she felt just as exposed as if his final act had been to write her name in his blood on the cargo bed of his pickup. From his comportment at the time they learned of Hoxie's death and since, she realised that Professor Palmer had known about their relationship. She wondered how many others had also guessed and, if they had, what conclusions they would draw from their attempts to keep it quiet. In addition, shortly after the publication of the ICOD letter, the Oregon State Assay and Mining Authority had reinstated the mine's permits, meaning that her ultimate objective of curtailing the heavy vehicle traffic on the road past her house would now not be achieved.

It had all been for nothing, she thought: The Plan, the toxic materials, the freezing expeditions up to the mine, the fear, even Hoxie's death, which she would never wholly accept as an accident. She had become established in her new home community and had, broadly, been accepted by these generous people. Now she was afraid that her true role in the affairs Hoxie's letter brought to light would be revealed, and she would be outed as a hypocritical cuckoo in their nest, bringing them poison in more ways than one, as a lover/collaborator with Hoxie, a kind of Bonnie to his Clyde.

Piet De Keersmaeker, member of the Trail 26 Conservation Society, owner of the Hungry Possum diner where many of their meetings took place, custodian and releaser of Hoxie's ICOD letter, was torn between grief at his friend's death, enjoyment of the temporary fame that his role in both finding the body and releasing the letter generated, and distaste at the revelations concerning how the society's objective of stopping the mining operations at Trillium Lake had been achieved. Piet came from a long line of dour Flemish farmers, and his practical if somewhat phlegmatic Belgian genes did not equip him to deal well with such contradictions. He had become not bipolar but, if such a thing exists, tripolar since the ICOD letter was published, cycling confusedly from grief, through pride, to condemnation.

Poor Professor Palmer, principled founder and chairman of the conservation society, felt particularly compromised with his tangential knowledge of Amy and Hoxie's Plan, their near-death car ride and the In Case of Death letters. Only he knew that Amy was the other party behind Hoxie's telling use of "we" rather than "I", but he had chosen not to confront his friend with this new information, certainly horrifying to him, regarding poisoned groundwater and common cause with corrupt investment banks. Professor Palmer decided to close down the conservation society. "After due consideration," he wrote to its members inviting them to a valedictory meeting, "that seems the most apposite course of action to pursue."

The professor was not really surprised that only the hardcore members turned up. One of the absentees had sent him a confused note saying she did not agree with pursuing the most opposite course of action, and that she for one would be doing the reverse. It was with some relief that Palmer realised there was no need to reply.

When they assembled at the Hungry Possum one evening midweek for that final meeting of the Trail 26 Conservation Society, it was a little group of men mostly in checked lumberjack shirts, Professor Palmer, Amy and Jess. They gathered at one end of the L-shaped diner, beneath a flat-screen TV silently tuned to a 24-hour news channel. At the professor's request Piet had provided food, in the shape of three platters of corn chips smothered in congealed cheese, sour cream and something green and vaguely spicy. Without Hoxie, Piet reflected sadly, this delicacy would probably go largely uneaten. The professor had also arranged for beers and sodas to be available, thus guiltily spending on beverages and high living the remaining $143 in the conservation society account – money intended for the conservation and protection of the Mount Hood environment. Such was the degenerate decline of this once high-minded organisation.

"I hear from Helen that there's a new 'Rapid Implementation Plan' for the mine," said Jess to the table at large. "They are really juiced-up, now that they belong to that investment bank and the permits have been given back. Does anyone else here find it ironic that the very people Hoxie named as guilty parties in the whole 'let's bribe the authorities' scheme are also the ones to benefit from his letter?"

Jess, Amy thought, was looking less ferocious these days, and she realised that her metallic face-piercing adornments had disappeared; she wondered when that had happened, and why. Professor Palmer was musing on how quickly everyone had become used to the rather shocking idea that Hoxie had not only taken his polluting direct action, but had done so together with the arrogant Bloom & Beck.

"The bad guys always seem to win," said Amy gloomily, thinking of Jay, thinking of the noisy road and the increased traffic to be expected as a result of Helen Fry's Rapid Implementation Plan. Only Professor Palmer knew how near to being one of the "bad guys" Amy herself actually came.

"Well, when I released Hoxie's letter it certainly identified who the bad guys are!" said Piet proudly.

"I've been meaning to congratulate you, Piet. That was a courageous thing to do, putting yourself at risk like that by agreeing to hold Hoxie's letter," said Jess, reaching for a second beer, "and releasing it," she added on reflection. Piet had not actually considered any personal risk to himself at all, and there was a short pause whilst he did.

"Yeah, well, I guess that's what friends are for," he said, a catch in his voice.

"Did Helen say just how soon they would be getting production going?" Amy asked Jess, still selfishly thinking of the road, and briefly wondering if Helen's recent elevation to CEO of the new White Crag Rareterre had anything to do with Jess's more conventional appearance.

Piet was still thinking about the risk. "I just can't believe that any member of this Society, least of all Hoxie, could do such a thing: poison the groundwater and bribe the authorities, and all that. I also don't believe he was acting alone," he said contradictorily, angrily looking around the table.

The professor pooh-poohed the idea quickly, wanting to protect Amy and also prevent the valedictory meeting (this nomenclature had resulted in a few no-shows by people who did not know what it was, but didn't much like the sound of it) from turning ugly. Palmer, who had observed Piet swinging from branch to branch like a caged chimp, oscillating between grief, pride and outrage, was keen to coax him down from the "outrage" branch and onto one of the others. Amy was picking nervously at the mound of softening corn chips.

"Surely, Piet, if it is so hard to believe he did it, it is harder still to believe he had an accomplice. No, no, no. Our friend Hoxie had quite enough weight to act alone, and besides, he was not alone, there was Bloom & Beck."

The word "friend" and mention of Hoxie's weight were intended to push Piet in the direction of the branch marked "grief", but failed. Instead, Piet became angrier. He might be a Flemish farmer but he recognised when he was being patronised. He thumped the table. Amy gasped. Piet looked at her accusingly but she was gazing, slack-jawed, at the TV screen where a shirt-sleeved Jay was being led through a throng comprising her former colleagues, handcuffed to an insubstantial officer of the law. Someone switched on the sound. The newscaster was just explaining about a letter left by some dead environmental activist, a picture of Trillium Lake briefly appeared, followed by one of Hoxie and Piet. Piet immediately swung from the "outraged" branch to the "proud" one, and preened himself. On the screen, Jay had arrived at the waiting police car, close to the camera. He was looking towards the Broad Street subway station, an expression of violent longing on his face. The scrawny policeman attached to Jay got into the vehicle and, as Jay followed, another officer's hand guiding his head through the door, Jay stared directly into the camera, providing the final still for the report. Eyes of pure poison which made Amy catch her breath. The TV commentary moved on to a dramatic fall in the price of rare-earths and someone muted the sound just as, inexplicably, the picture of a deranged-looking Chinese fishing-boat captain appeared.

The valedictory meeting of the Trail 26 Conservation Society was not proving a jolly affair at all, and even the sight of an investment banker being carted off in a modern-day tumbrel failed to cheer up proceedings.

Helen Fry came in with Rick, the site manager at the mine, both looking like they needed a stiff drink, just in time to see the tense little group of lumberjacks in the corner all focus on the TV screen. As the new CEO of the mine, Helen was Jay's directly appointed employee and knew him just well enough to dislike him intensely. In the silence immediately after the TV report finished, she spoke to Jess over the heads of the seated group.

"It looks like it's all over, honey. What they were saying there about the price of the rare-earths? It collapsed today. The Chinese saw to it. Well, we can't produce anything at a profit now, and I don't see it getting better for quite a while, if ever."

"The Rapid Implementation Plan's off?"

"The RIP's off."

Amy had to stop herself from saying "rest in peace". She had no clue what Helen was talking about regarding the Chinese, but it seemed that some beneficent power had granted what she wanted – the mine would once again fall silent, the road revert to its former quiet state. And it was nothing to do with her, Hoxie or Jay. It would have happened if none of them had ever existed.

CHAPTER 17

Victorian Wine Cellar, Hatton Garden, London, March 2009

White Crag Rareterre filed for Chapter 11 bankruptcy surprisingly quickly. It was owned by the Truly Clever, not the truly supportive, nor anyone who truly felt that any obligation flowed from all the assurances made in the course of winning ownership to employees, suppliers, customers and previous owners. The truly clever thing to do was follow Stacey's advice and avoid further investment in this unpredictable sector, so the company was abandoned to the mechanical workings of the insolvency courts. For most members of the B&B Principal Investment Group it was a small loss, even including their share of the company's indebtedness, although collectively they were of course fighting any claim that the lenders could actually call on those individual guarantees. For most of them it was something to be put down to experience and written off for tax purposes, no big deal. For Jay Andersen it was a big deal, a very big deal indeed, but he was ill-placed to do much about it.

Even if the aggregated losses to various parts of RBS from their exposure to White Crag Rareterre and its biggest shareholder, Jay, had been recognised, which they were not, and even if the bankruptcy filing had taken place before Richard Videur's bonus was agreed, which it did not, it is unlikely that Videur would have suffered much. In fact, Videur hardly needed to deploy the evidence collected in his DashforCash.xls spreadsheet, he had so manifestly achieved the objectives set for him by his superiors, intent on reducing the size of their loan book to something more in line with their crisis-struck balance sheet.

It was not just Videur and his loan-denial activities. The huge scale of RBS's casino-banking losses and their impact on the parent-bank balance sheets required drastic action. Across the bank, once-valued customers were suddenly being refused extensions to the overdrafts they had relied upon for years, trouble-free; export guarantees were no longer available, small businesses run by coping, self-reliant people were being endangered. Some proper businesses, employing people and making things, enterprises in actual engineering, not financial engineering, proved unable to survive and, with taxpayers, became the true losers from the Great Bankers' Crisis of 2008.

Richard Videur was employed by a bank which had driven itself into the ground. The bank was now 80 percent owned by the state and had taken the lion's share of nearly a trillion pounds – a thousand billions, a million millions – of explicit taxpayer support in loans and guarantees, the cost of shares the taxpayer was forced to buy, and the sector-wide support schemes where the taxpayer had assumed risk. Risk incurred by people like Richard Videur and other senior management at the bank. It was a bank that had failed horribly, the sheer scale of the incompetence breathtaking. But Richard and his peers, incredibly, still felt they were entitled to generous bonuses on top of their generous pay. Even more incredibly, they received them.

To be fair, Videur was not the extravagant party-loving, high-living, cocaine-snorting type. In fact, nobody quite knew what he spent his money on. He lived with his dowdy wife in a large house near Twickenham – but surely that was paid off long ago. He did not appear to have any of the in-your-face, money-burning interests favoured by needy rich people, desperate to prove their worth through conspicuous consumption – supercars, exotic sports, gambling, serial marriage, poseur holidaying, country

manors. Appearances were not deceptive. For Richard Videur the accumulation of money was pleasure enough in itself without troubling to spend
it, the pleasure perhaps even reduced by spending it. So, it was somewhat
out of character, a departure commented upon by others present, that he
should find himself amongst a crowd of RBS rowdies celebrating their
bonuses, in a Victorian wine cellar one Thursday evening.

It was a popular watering hole for corporate drinkers; expensive,
nostalgia-inducing shoddy, accessed through an atmospheric, brick-
built cobbled yard off Hatton Garden. Illuminated by dim electric bulbs
successfully imitating gas lights in period lantern fixtures, the cobbled yard
looked particularly Dickensian under the soft winter rain. A few tobacco
smokers, sinners segregated in a louche huddle by the door, parted briefly
to let through Carl Betts, until recently Rareterre's chief mineralogist.
Later, none of them would be able to describe him with any accuracy. Carl
was like that: nondescript, unremarkable.

As he entered the fuggy bar, Carl's glasses steamed over. The man he
had come to meet, a recruiter specialising in the mining field, saw him
take them off, pull out his shirt-tail and wipe them. He did not much
like Carl, but knew him to be an excellent mineralogist and potentially a
very valuable addition to one of his clients' teams, now that he was unemployed and Rareterre White Crag were bust. The man did not know the
details of Rareterre's story and RBS's pivotal role in it, he was just doing
his job of keeping in touch with temporarily footloose people who had
the right skills and experience. They had agreed to meet and have a drink
to discuss Carl's suitability for a well-paid but unattractive position at a
tropical Third World coal mine, a grimy sweat-soaked posting with high
tax-free pay and nowhere to spend it: ideal for an unmarried man with
pressing cash requirements and a strong liver.

Had the man known the Rareterre story, he might have suggested a
change of venue when Carl arrived, for the wine cellar was dominated by a
small crowd of happy, inebriated RBS bankers loudly bragging about their

bonuses. Carl arrived to the sound of the RBS rowdies, who, delighted to discover an enclave of Barclays Bank employees in the bar, were chanting inaccurate braggadocio at them.

Carl was perfectly aware that he had lost his job thanks to RBS's refusal to honour their loan agreement with Rareterre – he had been amongst the employees diverted to servicing the needs of the due diligence teams, first from RBS then from White Crag/Bloom & Beck. Egotistic, skirt-chasing, financially stretched, forced to contemplate a stint working in a tropical hell-hole where the only female company was likely to be of the sort only available for virus-enriched short-term hire, Carl felt he had every right to be angry and resentful. He had also spent his early post-university career in the Royal Engineers, so the unremarkable man who entered the Hatton Garden wine bar was an angry and resentful fully trained fighter.

Carl replaced the glasses on his nose and squinted around the room. He did not see the man he had come to meet, but certainly saw the crowd of suited men, ties askew or absent, two magnums of Dom Perignon on the bar in front of them. He saw Robin, a heavy young man with red braces and a red shiny face, still breathless from the rousing chorus he had just led of "RBS, is the best, RBS, is the best, RBS, R-B-S!" booming it out in the loutish bottom-of-mouth voice reserved for such chanting, the sole purpose of which is to stir tribal rivalries on the terraces or, in this case, in the small group of Barclays bankers in the corner. Carl saw Robin throw back a colourless drink in a short glass, wash it down with a swig of Dom Perignon and, with a wry comment to a colleague, turn clumsily back towards the Barclays group. He took a step forwards, stumbled, and trod heavily on Carl's foot, catching hold of his coat to break his fall. The pain was sudden and surprising. Carl cried out, but the heavy young man pushed on past him, scarcely acknowledging his presence. He was keen to continue his intellectual discussion with the little group of rival bankers.

"Oi! Barclays bums!" he began, promisingly. Behind his puffy eyes something akin to a thought process briefly made its presence known, and was gone. "How does it feel belonging to the towel-heads then?"

He was probably referring to Barclays' nationalisation-dodging Gulf bailout, billions of balance-sheet-repairing pounds hurriedly raised on expensive terms mainly from the Middle East. One of the Barclays men spoke loudly to his colleague, answering Robin without addressing him, a strained smile on his face.

"Better than having to go whining to Gordon Brown for more pocket money at bonus time," he said, annoyingly. "At least we don't need Uncle Gordon's okay for our bonuses, like those RBS losers."

Carl noticed that the lapel of his Savile Row coat was torn where Robin had used it to break his fall. His foot was throbbing. Robin, who a few minutes earlier had been informing anyone within hearing range, which was most of the bar, which model of Porsche he planned to purchase with his bonus, was busy working out a devastatingly clever response to offer the Barclays guy. The man Carl was there to see got to his feet.

"Hey you, red braces!" Carl said angrily to Robin's back, "You need to apologise, mate." Robin ignored him. He had thought out his answer for the Barclays man.

"Yeah, well, we win then, because our backer has deeper pockets than yours! The British fucking state! How much are you getting this year, net, eh? I'll bet our bonus Pool is bigger than yours. Why, just these guys here are taking home over three bars, three million quid this year!" He gestured towards his rowdy little RBS group at the bar. Richard Videur was the least drunk and the most embarrassed amongst them, and he came quickly over to Robin carrying his jacket.

"Here, Robin, take this. It's time you went home. I'll find you a cab." He half-dragged Robin out of the bar and into the wet courtyard.

"I said he needs to apologise!" shouted Carl, following them. His foot was hurting, his coat was torn, but his mind was full of the three bars, the three million quid. His salary at Rareterre had been £90,000, with a £10,000 bonus if he performed exceptionally well. The man he had come to meet sat back down inside. Videur was in the wet yard and did not stop, but he did answer Carl.

"What for? Why should he apologise?" he said aggressively over his shoulder. Robin was slow and awkward, protesting he wanted more bubbly. Videur was navigating him across the courtyard like a tug boat manoeuvring an overladen vessel in a choppy sea. They made it to the narrow alleyway leading to Hatton Garden. Carl followed them, grabbing Videur's shoulder, turning him. He did not recognise him; he did not have to.

"He should apologise because he trod on my foot. He tore my coat. He should apologise because he's a fat bloodsucking bastard who works for RBS." Carl's blood was up, he knew that Videur was with the group of drinkers from RBS and he was looking for trouble. Videur provided it.

"Oh, he should apologise for working at RBS, should he? What, we should all apologise, all 140,000 of us, eh? For what? Who are you anyway, apart from some midget Robin just trod on?"

Carl was short. Just lower-quartile short, but small enough to have been called names for it all his life. Short enough to be sensitive about it. Carl was a dapper, womanising, selfish mineralogist. He and all his colleagues at Rareterre had been metaphorically trodden upon by unapologetic people from RBS; being physically trodden on by them, even without the insults, was enough to flip him. He was a taxpayer. His last tax return, including income and capital gains tax, exceeded £40,000. Now he was unemployed and in debt, his employer vaporised because of an illegal failure from RBS, the same RBS that was now greedily guzzling taxpayers' money. The same RBS that had apparently just paid huge bonuses to Robin and this thin, insulting man who was calling him a midget. Scarcely noticed by Videur and Carl, Robin had sunk to the ground, back to the alley wall.

"I'll tell you who I am. I'm an ex-customer of RBS. You ruined my company. I am a taxpayer. I am—"

Videur had heard many whinging arguments from taxpayers and spent his days dealing with complaining customers, on their way, if he was successful, to being ex-customers. He interrupted. "Oh, diddums, did the nasty bank ruin you then, shorty? What was it, let me guess, they refused to let you carry on breaching the terms of your agreement, did they? Stopped being a charity and started behaving like a business? Was that it? And don't start moaning about being a taxpayer. No one would have chosen to be…"

That was when Carl hit him. Short Carl Betts, mineralogist, formerly of Rareterre and formerly of the Royal Engineers, broke Richard Videur's nose first. There was little space to swing punches, but Carl knew very well how to put his weight behind a close-quarters blow. Videur retaliated, moving to knee him in the groin, but Carl was too quick and cracked Videur's head against the wall with an upwards thrust to his chin. Videur sank to the ground beside his drunken colleague. Carl crouched down beside him.

"Apologise," he rasped in Videur's ear. Videur turned his head to look at him; his eyes were empty.

"Piss off."

Carl rose and, with an efficiency his army trainers would have appreciated, broke both bones in Videur's lower left leg with a sharp, well-aimed downwards chop of his right foot, the one Robin had not trodden on, and walked briskly away.

Mount Hood, Oregon, March 2009

Mount Hood was magnificent in the evening sun, a wisp of grey and orange cloud part-obscuring its luminous flank. Amy, Hoxie's favourite stick in hand, was walking with difficulty along the snow-covered track on the frozen lake's southern shore. She pulled back her mitten and looked at her watch. Quarter to five. It would be getting dark in less than half an hour, and at the rate she was going she would still be far from her car. She cursed her stupidity, out without a knapsack, no food or drink, no compass, no flashlight – Hoxie normally took care of those things. Hoxie also habitually checked the weather forecast, using a hikers' website, whereas all she had was a vague memory of the morning radio bulletin foreseeing a rising wind and cloud cover. But Hoxie was dead. She did see him occasionally, a retinal trick amongst the trees or rocks, his bulk suddenly insubstantial. And she heard him in the wind, the passage of water in a brook, even in the falling rain; she was comforted by these reminders. But he was dead and here she was, alone in the gathering twilight, the pressure mounting in her right boot, a throbbing as the blood rushed to bathe the torn ligaments in her ankle in painful, protective inflammation.

When she had trodden awkwardly at the foot of an icy, uneven rocky scree and twisted her ankle, she had called the professor on her cellphone, gasping with the pain but telling him unconvincingly that all would be well, she was sure. She regretted that call now, it had drained the last of her phone battery and failed to communicate the true situation. A gentle, undemanding walk around Trillium Lake was turning into a nightmare – the sort of thing you read about in the newspapers and can't help but feel scorn at the pathetic avoidability of the tragedy, the crass unpreparedness of the victims.

Painfully, Amy sat down on a large rock looking out over the lake and reviewed her situation. She was at least two miles from her car, but the route was normally not difficult and if she kept her head she should be able to find her way. On the other hand, the situation was not normal; she was disabled with a swollen and inflamed ankle, out alone on a moonless night. The cold from the stone penetrated her quilted trousers, reminding her of the gently deadly, vitality-sapping risk of immobility. She sensed Hoxie's bulk, insubstantial beside her. Shadow gradually crept up the slopes of the distant mountain.

The Mounts' House, Chelsea, London, March 2009

The estate agent winked again.

Ivy looked at Peter and knew at once that this winking young man, with the stripy shirt, brand-name jeans and expensive loafers, was skating on thin ice. She felt a sudden rush of well-being, a comfort derived from membership of a long-standing and successful team. Sonny and Cher, but with better songs. The sale of the house and repayment of the mortgage was the right thing to do; it would leave them solvent and provide a new beginning. But the young estate agent had just made a sweeping economic generalisation regarding the direction of property values in Chelsea. Ivy knew that Peter disliked sweeping economic generalisations, especially if they contradicted other sweeping generalisations made minutes earlier. Innocently, she asked the young man with the stripy shirt if he would mind elaborating.

"It's supply and demand, simple economics," said Gucci-loafer guy, whose knowledge of economic theory had been gained mostly from a GCSE course, soon abandoned in favour of something else where exam success was more assured. "They're not making it anymore." Peter looked at him quizzically.

"Not making what?"

"Chelsea real estate."

"You mean property, I suppose. When did they stop making it?"

"Erm, well, I guess when the borough was developed…"

"So, they've 'stopped making it' in Lewisham too? And Rochdale? So, we can expect prices to 'carry on rising nicely', as you put it, there too?"

"Oh, I don't deal with those areas," said stripy-shirt happily, as if proving beyond reasonable doubt that the laws of supply and demand therefore failed to apply in Lewisham. Ivy noticed that his cufflinks were in the shape of pound signs.

"But weren't you saying a few minutes ago that in this market sellers have to be really committed, not 'time wasters with unrealistic price expectations'?" asked Ivy.

"And that interest rates were unlikely to stay so low for long, so we ought to act quickly if we wanted to sell the house?" added Peter. "You can't seem to decide."

The young man fiddled with his signet ring. He had stupidly mixed up his "scare the sellers into selling quickly before the market crashes" and his "frighten the buyers into buying fast before prices take-off again" spiels – it was unusual for his clients to pay enough attention to what he said for it to matter. All he wanted was to sign up this— He ran through the random word selector he unconsciously used for the drafting of "particulars". Adjectives: bright/bijou/substantial/sunny/desirable/well-presented/perfectly located/Victorian? Nouns: residence/family home/town house /bijou (but only if not already used like Belinda did once, "Bijou Belgravia bijou"! How they had laughed)/pied a terre/end of terrace? Anyway, all he wanted was to sign it up, wait for someone to buy it and trouser his commission. His agency was in reality little more than a clearing-house; he didn't really care what the price was, so long as a transaction took place and his 2 percent was skimmed off. They didn't seem to get it, this middle-aged couple that kept smiling at one another as if sharing some sort of secret, kept touching one another like newlyweds.

"When you said earlier that you were not against the idea of being 'joint sole agent' with Vixen's, what did that mean, exactly?" asked Ivy, smiling at Peter. The young man, who had not given up GCSE English, could see where this might be going. Luckily for him Peter's mobile phone rang. Peter glanced at it, and was surprised to see "Julian Marian-Smythe – NOMAD Securities" on the screen. Apologising to Ivy and the contradictory young man, he answered the call, leaving the room.

"Julian, what a surprise!"

"Hello, Peter. Yes, it has been a while. I know I said we must do lunch, but it's been extremely busy here, you know how it is…" Peter did know how it was. He himself had not been extremely busy for some time now, and he rather suspected that this fact explained their failure to lunch more than Julian's diary.

"You remember that thing Warren Buffet, investor legend, said? 'When others are greedy, be fearful, when others are fearful, be greedy'?" said busy Julian, getting right to the point.

"Something like that, yes."

"Well, Peter, everyone is fearful of rare-earths right now."

"What, Julian, you want to get greedy?"

"Not to put too fine a point on it, Peter, yes. I think the time may be right to get greedy. The mines at White Crag and Trillium Lake are still for sale out of Chapter 11. This could be the ideal entry point. We have the funds and need a management team."

"But the prices…"

"The prices will come back. The Chinese can't buck the rare-earths market forever. We have some backers who can afford to be patient. The market will recover. Rare-earths are still needed. People will have to pay."

Through the window, Peter saw stripy-shirt get into a garishly customised Fiat 500, the name of his agency splatted across the side and up the windows, in fluorescent pink letters half a metre high.

"They're not making them anymore, you mean?"

"Exactly, Peter. They are not making them anymore. You interested?"

Mount Hood, Oregon, March 2009

She had made a pitiful few hundred yards' progress, each pace an agonising increment to the pain in her ankle evidenced by an asymmetrical trace in the snow on the lakeside path. Amy was wondering about death by hypothermia, whether it was a gentle way to go, a soft extinguishing of the flame, ultimately nothing more than an unconscious inadequacy of energy. She hoped so.

The chill evening air was quiet and Amy heard the sound of the snow-mobile before she saw it between the trees, coming rapidly towards her from the direction of the looping service roads where she had parked her car. Riding the snowmobile was Rick Stone, manager of the mine she had fought so hard to close, the mine that was now effectively shut down not through her dubious actions but those of a ruthlessly efficient distant government. Rick knew Amy by sight but the two had no relationship; he was out here in the gathering Mount Hood twilight in answer to a request from Professor Palmer. She awkwardly raised her hand from the elbow in a greeting that would have been more in place across a bar.

Rick brought the noisy machine to rest beside her, climbed off and helped her gingerly raise herself onto the padded seat, her feet side by side on the footrest.

"Am I glad to see you!" Amy said with feeling. "I'm not sure I would have made it back. My ankle..." She gestured to her right boot. He stooped and carefully untied the laces, releasing a new sort of pain into her swollen joint. She winced.

"The professor asked me to come out and check on you. I guess he knows I have a snowmobile. He said you'd be out here somewhere, and I saw your car on the service road."

Amy, for whom the last two hours had been an excruciating combi-nation of physical pain and the anguish of anticipated slow extinction, was overcome by gratitude to the kind-hearted community that had accepted her, still accepted her. Rick leaned against the hot, still machine beside her, looking out across the lake towards the increasingly obscure Mount Hood. A band of thicker cloud had formed above the horizon, its underside illuminated in deep orange, fading to purple. The sky was a limpid darkening mauve, its intense colour enhanced by the velvet blackness of the tree-lined shore in the foreground. They remained silent for a few moments as the light faded. It was for times like these that Amy had left New York, Bloom & Beck, the rat race, the rats, the lot.

"It was you, wasn't it, Hoxie's accomplice?" asked Rick matter-of-factly, gazing across the frozen lake. Amy stiffened. "I mean, he said 'we' in his letter several times. I figure it was you that helped him." He turned his gaze on her. She looked away, feeling caught out, ashamed. Rick was an employee of the mine, and she thought miserably of how little consideration she had given to the people whose livelihoods depended on its continued operation. How selfish she had been. "You two were lovers," he observed gently, as if it explained something.

"What's going to happen now?" she whispered, the lack of any denial confirming Rick's guess, her culpability.

"Well, they're not going anywhere, those rare-earth ores. We'll always need them, and they'll still be there when mining them makes sense again." He mounted the snowmobile and started the engine. "Hold tight."

Amy nursed her leg over the seat and unconsciously grasped Rick around the waist. The snowmobile was quickly swallowed by the dark trees, its uncalm noise and light engulfed in the surging mountain silence.

GLOSSARY

For the reader with the good taste not to be a banker or involved in the financial sector:

1. Alternative Investment Market / AIM p4 and p192
The Alternative Investment Market, the junior section of the London Stock Exchange. Smaller and supposedly more dynamic companies list their shares on AIM for trading, taking advantage of lighter regulation and lower costs. The light regulation has resulted in only a small amount of fraud – so far as we know.

2. Fractional reserve banking p34
The system, in operation worldwide and likened by some to a massive confidence trick, whereby a bank can lend out a multiple of the capital it holds in reserve. It's complicated, but in 2007 the multiple was about 12 on average. So, your £1,000 savings account was supporting some £12,000 of loans. Needless to say, only 8 percent of the loans had to be bad for the bank to be seriously embarrassed if you asked for your £1,000 back. Even without bad loans the system only works because we don't all ask for our money back at once. A so-called "run on the bank" is when we try. Nobody's happy then. Remember those queues outside Northern Rock? (see p 242)

3. Credit committee p75
Investment banks such as Bloom & Beck made most of their profits from "principal" activities – investment and trading on their own account. This might seem to you as likely to give rise to conflicts of interest with their clients. You'd be right. The other risk is that in pursuing such principal activities they fail to achieve a sensible balance between greed and fear – the two main decisive sentiments governing investment and trading. The credit committee is a senior management group within the bank tasked with judging these risks. The reader is reminded that the system as it was in 2007 – and largely still is – favours greed over fear, as the capital at risk is shareholders', not that of the members of the credit committee making the decisions.

4. SEC – the US Securities and Exchange Commission p106
The SEC is the Federal government agency responsible for regulating the securities industry – meaning everything from big investment banks such as B&B through to the exchanges where they ply their trade. The SEC states its mission as including "to protect investors; maintain fair, orderly, and efficient markets … ". They also claim to "strive to promote a market environment that is worthy of the public's trust." Surely the Financial Crisis of 2008, in which many investors lost everything including their trust and the markets were disorderly to a point of riotousness, constitutes a failure of some sort against such a mission? Now, call me old-fashioned, but in the light of this surely someone at the responsible agency was held to account? Someone felt their position was untenable and resigned? I'll leave it to you to guess how many did so …

5. Road-show p127
Sometimes also called a "Dog and Pony Show", an apt reference to early American touring circuses featuring performing domestic animals. Investor road-shows are the use of management's time to sell their company's shares (as an investment opportunity) rather than devoting themselves to selling whatever products the company actually makes. Considered a waste of time by many – particularly those cast in canine or equine roles – especially when the audience already owns the company's shares as in the case of Rareterre's road-show in Chapter 6.

6. Loan covenants p128
The biblical-sounding promises included in legal loan agreements – documents often longer if not weightier than the Old Testament. These promises, covering a variety of things such as interest cover (qv) use of funds, payment of dividends and much more – are often agreed in haste and repented of at leisure. They normally include a set of amusingly called "negative pledges", meaning promises not to do certain things – not meaning the opposite of promises, which is rather how some bankers view the entire loan agreement when under pressure.

7. Dilution p141
It is the fate of shareholders in small, growing companies to be diluted. Unless they stump up more money, the percentage they hold of the company will dwindle over time as new shares are issued – to new shareholders as the result of a fund-raise or an acquisition, or to management as options and other inducements are dished out to supplement their salaries. In theory the new shares represent capital put to good use and the shareholders should be happy – but along with the declining percent-

ages comes a diminished voice in the affairs of the company: see "minority rights" below. Shareholders do not greet dilution with undiluted pleasure.

8. Interest cover p146

Interest cover is a measure of the risk associated with a loan. As with most banking metrics, it is very simple – how many times do the borrower's earnings cover the annual interest charge? Earnings £50m, interest expense £10m, cover = 5x. What is less simple is how the earnings are calculated, which offers manifest opportunities for clever people to delude others and themselves.

9. Nominated Advisor p150

Every company listed on the AIM junior stock exchange has to have a Nominated Advisor, selected from a list of organisations approved by the Stock Exchange, to "advise and guide an AIM company on its responsibilities". Sounds thankless and in fact their main role is to avoid any sort of censure, making them holier than the Pope despite being even less infallible. Wittily, people in the City quickly dubbed them "Nomads", which is odd because they display little of the flexibility this name implies.

10. Credit Default Swaps p286

Insurance is a financial product but normally involves non-financial factors – floods, fires, icy roads. CDSs are like insurance, but a wholly financial phenomenon. The risk insured against is a financial one – the default of a borrower, normally the issuer of a bond. CDSs are therefore divorced from the tangible world, the domain of clever bankers, and therefore available for flights of pure fantasy. If you insure your house for the risk of fire, that's a prudent protection of your asset. But do you think it a good idea if your pyromaniac neighbour can buy a policy that pays out if your house burns down? Thought not. Well, something akin to that was possible with CDSs. And in 2007 there were $62 trillion of CDSs outstanding – a massive multiple of the debt risks supposedly insured. Further explanation would require much patience from you and my use of the words "synthetic" and "systemic" so let's stop here.

11. Long side / short side p286

In banker's parlance, if you own a financial asset you are "long" that asset – as in "Jay was long rare-earths" (p 422). This is probably to distinguish owning something from being "short", which does not have a normal parlance equivalent. If you are "short" an asset you don't just not own it, you do the opposite of owning it. It's like owning antimatter. If you are short an asset you profit when that asset's value goes down. Owning a CDS on a bond but not owning the bond is like owning the antimatter bond. Laurent is suggesting creating a bond that is intentionally doomed to fail, buying the CDS insurance, then offloading the doomed bond (the long side) whilst keeping the insurance policy, the CDS short side. No one would be so evil... would they?

12. Bank holding company (v investment bank) p287

Like many potentially dangerous things – nuclear power, drugs, aviation... – banking is regulated. Investment banks and merchant banks (more recently dubbed "casino banks") used to be organised as partnerships – the players were gambling their own money in the casino; unsurprisingly, risk-taking was on a much smaller scale back then. The casino banks then converted into corporations, with outside share-holders, and most went public – giving the gamblers access to much more money and, importantly, *other people's* money. Supposedly differentiated from the more mundane commercial banks, investment banks were nevertheless still afforded more operating freedom and less stringent capital requirements. *Faites vos jeux!*

The other, more pedestrian commercial banking operations are necessary for the economy to function – they provide the financial plumbing. They take deposits from the likes of you and me, are more conservatively regulated but have access to supportive taxpayer-funded emergency finance, to protect the plumbing supposedly in the last resort.

So, on the one hand you have the freewheeling, highly leveraged, law-unto-themselves investment banks, manned by Truly Clever millionaires such as Jay and his PartCo colleagues, taking "calculated" risks with other people's money and racking up mountains of counterparty exposure. On the other, the plodding plumbing bank holding companies under the supervision of the Federal Reserve (the "Fed") and protected by its emergency funding mechanisms. For the Truly Clever to align themselves with the plumbers and succumb to the Fed by converting to bank holding companies, would be a huge loss of self-esteem – by people who held themselves in the highest esteem imaginable. Yet in 2008 they did. *Rien ne va plus!* One does not need to be too hardened a cynic to suspect it had something to do with accessing those Fed emergency reserves.

13. Minority (rights) p402

One of the good things about capitalism is its racial blindness, indifference to gender or sexual orientation, unconcern for creed. Minority shareholders, as discussed by Jay and Montagu, unsurprisingly, are defined in monetary terms. Also known as small shareholders, they are not characterised by dwarfism but by the relatively small proportion of the company's shares they own. As each share normally bears one vote this translates into having a smaller say as well as a smaller investment. In the UK there are certain protections for minority shareholders but once holders of 90 percent of the shares of a company have accepted a takeover offer, the remaining 10 percent can be forced to do likewise and to sell their shares to the bidder – a process charmingly referred to as a "squeeze-out".